MW00957692

The

Fire

Reborn

The Eres Chronicles Book III

by MB Mooney

This is a work of fiction. Names, characters, places, and events are products of the author's imagination or are used fictitiously.

© 2018 MB Mooney
All rights reserved

www.mbmooney.com

This book is dedicated to those that believe in the unity and diversity only possible in the Kingdom of God.

And to Jeremiah Briggs. Wish I could have finished this with you.

The Eres Chronicles Book III

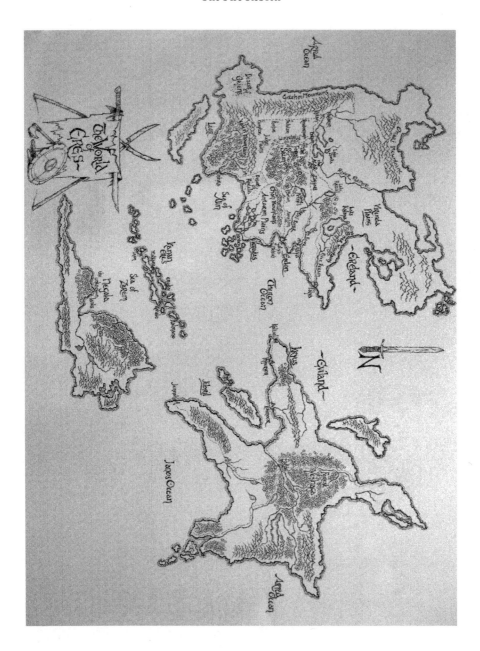

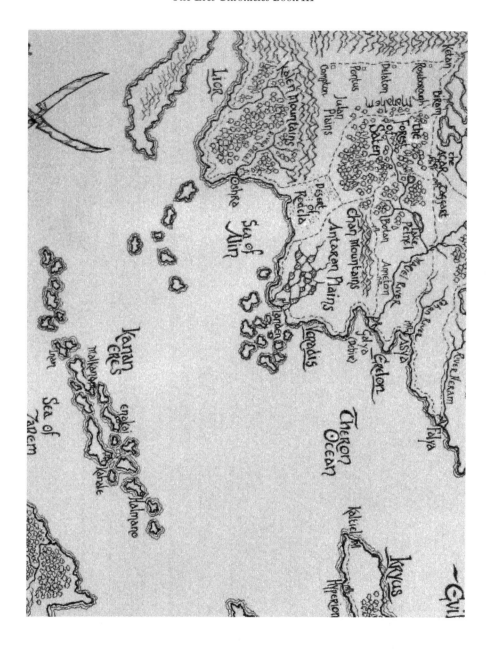

PROLOGUE

THE RIGHT THING TO DO

Macarus leaned against the bar with his elbows, took another sip of South Kyran whiskey, and bared his teeth as the cool liquid burned down his throat.

The *Mother Sun* was filled with elves, rumor and fact swimming together with ale and liquor on their lips. The low, constant rumble of conversation and the dim light should have hidden him well enough, but Macarus hunched his shoulders and allowed the hood of his cloak to fall further over his face.

Discussions, punctuated with curses, floated to his pointed ears from male and female elves around the establishment.

"I did my mandatory twenty years!" Macarus heard from one female elf. "Now our dear emperor *drafts* us back into the legions because his regulars can't handle one critty human army? It isn't right, I tell you."

Macarus glanced over his shoulder at the thirty or more tables in the tavern; elves filled the space, drinking and talking.

"Well, I'm too old for this draft," said one older male elf with a slight lisp. "But with the dwarves and Faltiel fighting to the east and this *Brendel* and his army in Ereland, I'm telling you it won't be long before the Emperor has to call us all back into service. There aren't enough militan."

The bartender sniffed. "How 'bout you, friend? You called back in?"

Macarus wanted to take the parchment missive in the pocket of his cloak and read it again, even though he had it memorized. "*Back in* doesn't really describe it. But yes."

"Well," the 'tender patted his left leg. "Got this in the last one with those men back a few hundred years ago. Can't go back. Lucky me." He grinned as he filled another mug of ale for a customer two stools away. The 'tender limped away.

Macarus returned to his drink.

Go back? I never should have left.

Over the next few hours, Macarus drank and faces came to his mind – Eshlyn, Aden, Carys, Zalman, the Rat, Chamren, and a man with so much steel in his eyes it had to come from his soul.

The *Mother Sun* emptied. One by one or two by two, the customers left, staggering or frowning or cursing. Perhaps all three. Once the night turned to more of a morning, he glanced up from the bottom of a glass to see bare tables.

The 'tender leaned over the bar in front of him. "Closing time, friend." His tone did not suggest that they were friends.

Macarus finished his last drink of South Kryan, the strongest legal liquor in the Empire, winced by habit more than anything, and stood from the stool. He wavered a bit, closing his eyes and gathering his balance. He nodded at the 'tender and made his way through the tables and chairs.

Leaving the *Mother Sun* through the front door, he staggered out to the street. He took a deep breath of the clean Kryan air, smelling the salt of the sea from the docks a few blocks to the south. The white and lifeless gas streetlights gave no warmth. Not that he needed warmth on this early summer night.

This was Kryus. His home. On the surface, it was clean and beautiful. It died inside, however, doomed to death. He had met the man that would drive a sword through the heart of the Empire. And the more Macarus thought on it, the more he wished he had stayed to help him.

By the nine gods, that's insane.

The cool air hit his face. Macarus set his shoulders and walked up the narrow street to the north, towards his home. It took effort to walk in a straight line, and after a few minutes, he only wanted to make it that last kilomitre to his bed.

Focused on the next step before him, he almost missed the movement in the dark alley to his right. *Just my imagination.* He didn't usually see things when drunk. And he was drunk. His brows creased as he paused. Squinting, he inspected his periphery. And his right hand snuck under his cloak to his side and the hilt of his sword.

A figure stepped out into the street, a long cloak and hood masking the identity. But the figure didn't move like a cutthroat or thief.

Macarus gripped the hilt.

Another figure drifted into view from an alleyway behind him.

Macarus turned to face the one across the street with the one behind now on his right. Both figures approached and drew swords. He knew the maker of those swords, had fought with her on the walls of a city a world away to the west. *Bladeguard.*

With a few quick breaths, he shook his head to clear it. He drew his sword and removed his cloak.

Both elves paused while they let their own cloaks drop to the smooth, perfect stone beneath them. The Bladeguard in front of him had dark hair in a long braid. The one to the left had shorter, blond hair that stuck straight up on his head.

The dark-haired elf smirked at him. No words needed to be said. Two Bladeguard did not visit in the dark hours of predawn to talk. They were here to kill.

He didn't need to ask why, either. Macarus had stood before Generals and the Empire and praised a human, a man, the same man tearing through the Kryan Legions in Ereland. They had relieved him of duty until further notice. Also, his mother was a powerful senator, a leader of a small but influential group of politicians attempting to curb the power of their Emperor through legislation.

And for those reasons, the Emperor could not abide First Captain Macarus to live. If they were here after him, was his mother safe? He prayed to whoever would listen that she would survive this night. He wasn't in the position to help her now.

I never should have left.

Macarus had always wanted to try his skill against a Bladeguard ... but two? He was drunk. And tired. He sighed.

The dark-haired elf attacked with an overhead strike, and the blond was behind him with a slice at his legs. Macarus rose to block the one above him and leapt over the one below. Landing, he spun away with a stab at the blond and ducked the blade coming at his head from the dark-haired elf.

Macarus jumped back as both missed him again, and he grunted with the effort. With another block and slide to his left, he found himself out of breath. The street tipped as he staggered.

But the two Bladeguard didn't give him pause. They both pressed, and he moved. Macarus felt a cut along his left arm from the blond. Gritting his teeth, he retreated back down the street to the south. He attacked the blond at a good angle, but he was a split second slow. The blond blocked, and Macarus leaned back; the dark-haired elf's blade split the air in front of his face.

He rotated, kicking at the dark-haired elf, and he deflected another swipe from the blond. His kick didn't land, and a strike from the dark-haired elf drew blood along his back. Macarus cried out, more out of frustration than anything else. Feeling the effect of the liquor on his quickness and energy, he acted out of desperation and turned his back on the dark-haired elf and attacked the blond with a myriad of quick and powerful strikes, driving him back. The blond bought a feint and Macarus struck him in the face with his palm. The blond sputtered as he fell backwards, and Macarus went in for the kill.

But he felt the other behind him, leaping in the air to cut him in two. Macarus ducked, and at the last heartbeat, spun on the one behind him, avoiding the blow and stabbing up and into the elf's heart. The dark-haired elf gurgled and blood spit from his mouth as his eyes went wide from the pain and surprise.

The blond had recovered, and Macarus slid to the side and pulled the blade from the dark-haired elf. He deflected the blade as he spun; it still drove into his side before he was able to get space between him and the remaining elf. Panting, he held his side, bowing in pain. The dark-haired elf writhed on the street as the blood left his body.

Macarus sneered at the Bladeguard and raised his bloody blade. "Come on, then," he said. "Let's finish this."

The blond wiped the trickle of blood from his nose with the back of his hand.

However ready they both were, a new shadow darted from the alleyway behind the blond Bladeguard with a whisper of wind, and the blond turned to face a whirling elf in a long, green gown. Graying hair flowed around her with perfect grace. A long, thin blade easily turned the Bladeguard's block and attacked. She struck high and then low. She spun and forced the Bladeguard to retreat, moving him toward Macarus.

Macarus straightened, measured, and stabbed to the Bladeguard's left shoulder. As the Bladeguard moved and blocked, the female elf sliced into his hamstring. He went down on his knee, and as she took the Bladeguard's sword down with her own, Macarus stumbled forward, swung, and took the Bladeguard's head from his shoulders.

With a gasp, Macarus leaned over, his left hand pressing against the wound in his side.

The female elf took a wide stance and crossed her arms. "Not bad for being drunk and stupid. Not how I trained you, but not bad."

He glowered at her. "I had that under control, you know."

"Is that any way to talk to me?" She pursed her lips at him.

Macarus blew out his cheeks. "Thank you, Mother."

First Senator Diona nodded down at him. "That's better." She grimaced. "You reek of South Kryan."

"It would be surprising if I didn't."

Diona paused a moment and extended a hand to him. "We need to go. It's not safe here."

"No crit." He let her pull him up to standing.

Diona moved his hand away and inspected the wound. "That will need to be seen. Can you walk?"

"Do I have a choice?"

"My son, there is always a choice, like not going out drinking by yourself when you know we are targets for our mad Emperor. But if you can make it a few blocks, I have a safehouse not far from here."

"A safehouse? You have a safehouse?"

Diona chuckled and looked at him sideways. "Haven't you been paying attention? The Empire is collapsing before our eyes. I have taken precautions. Stop arguing and come with me."

His mother led him down the alley to another street, and then they backtracked south towards the docks. The predawn city was quiet, and Macarus' shuffling feet seemed too loud in his ears. His only desire was to stop, sit down, lay down, even right there on the smooth stone of the street, but he willed himself to continue.

Talking might distract him. "I assume they came for you, as well."

Diona scanned the street, the alleys. Her silken, dark hair with gray streaks spilled over her shoulder as she glanced at him and spoke in whispers. "The Emperor may have closed down the Senate, but I still have my sources. I was ready. Tanicus is leading legions overseas and leaving the Empire in the hands of his yes-elves, elves more motivated by fear and power than the good of the Empire. Anyone with a brain in their head is a threat to that rule."

"You. And by extension, me."

"Normally, yes, but you have angered him all on your own. You returned from Ketan and dared tell your superiors, and others, the truth."

"I told you before," Macarus said through his teeth. "I wouldn't be his puppet, not and speak ill of a man that saved thousands of lives."

Diona took a deep breath. "And as I said, you did the right thing, and Tanicus was satisfied with dismissing you as long as you were quiet."

"And now?"

"Now he is throwing everything at your friend, the *Brendel*, and he cannot leave his back exposed."

"So he decides to kill any who could possibly threaten him."

"He did the same three hundred years ago when you left with him to Ereland. It is good strategy, for a tyrant. If it would work. Unfortunately for all tyrants, they can't kill everyone. A few always survive."

She took a right down another alley, pausing to let him move ahead for a moment as she searched the shadows to make sure they were not followed. Then she strode ahead to the other end of the alley, glancing before heading into the next street.

"What about the Fifteen?" The Fifteen were the other senators aligned with his mother. "Has he gone after them, as well?"

His mother was silent for a moment. "Yes."

If Tanicus sent Bladeguard to the others, as well ... They were not all swordmasters like his mother. "Do you know how many have survived?"

"Not yet," she said. "You left before I received news of the attacks. After I dealt with the two Bladeguard sent after me, I went searching for you. Those that survived would come to the safehouse."

Macarus stumbled. *Two Bladeguard. That's my mother.*

Diona slowed, extending a hand behind her as a signal, and they continued at a slower pace. No sound. They reached a warehouse building near the docks, two blocks away from a large pier, and Diona hesitated before opening the door that opened into the street, the sword back in her hand. Macarus drew his own.

They entered through the door, dark with thick shadows up a back stairway. The wood creaked beneath them. Macarus pushed down the pain in his side and ignored the itching cuts on his back and arm, and they stole up to a landing overlooking the vast warehouse, empty except for a few boxes, at least from what Macarus could see.

It took too long, his heart pounding, for them to move across the landing to a door. Diona glanced at him once before knocking five times, three quick, two slow. The knock came back, two slow, two quick. She opened the door, and they entered the room.

There was no light in the room, just figures made of darkness in front of them.

A voice said, low, "Diona?"

His mother tensed. "It is me," Diona said.

Someone lit a lamp, a warm, yellow light, but dim, and revealed the faces of four elves; two others were too deep in the shadow of the opposite corner.

Diona relaxed and lowered her sword. She pointed at Macarus. "I need help. He's wounded."

One of the elves stepped forward, a middle aged male elf with cropped blond hair. Macarus recognized him as Senator Woznius. "I've got a bag and bandages here." He swung a leather satchel from behind him.

Woznius pressed Macarus as if to sit, but Macarus resisted. "I'll stand." If he sat, he might pass out.

Woznius shrugged. "Very well."

Macarus sheathed his sword and removed his tunic, standing bare from the waist up and bleeding all over the floor.

"Thank you, Senator," Diona said. "Any word from the others?"

Another of the elves stepped forward, a round elf with fuzzy dark hair on his head – Qinus, the Senator from the eastern regions. "Only the four … five, of us so far."

Woznius cleaned the wounds with some sort of antiseptic and cloth. Macarus winced at the pain, somewhat glad for the numbing agent of the liquor, even though it was difficult for him to stay focused.

"We cannot stay here long," Diona said. "Others may have been taken and given to the Moonguard."

Macarus grunted. He had sent prisoners to those Moonguard, as well. Long ago. "They are very good at getting information out of people, not to mention their other talents. We're not safe."

A third elf spoke, Nizaul, a female from the south, young and tall. She nodded over at the figures. "What about them?"

Diona pursed her lips. "We have to get them over to Ereland. Somehow."

Woznius stitched the wound in his side. Macarus gritted his teeth to catch the bile in his throat. He did not want to vomit in front of a room of senators. He gathered himself and peered into the black corner. "Who are they?"

A match struck and fire bloomed before a grizzled face with a black handlebar mustache and a long black goatee. The flame floated to ignite a large, half-smoked cigar, and after a few puffs, the person stood, shoulder high to elves in the room but broad and strong.

A dwarf. He smiled as the person next to him stood, as well. Another dwarf.

The first dwarf sucked on his cigar for another heartbeat, and his head was immersed now in a thick cloud. It did not help Macarus' nausea. The dwarf showed his teeth. "My name is Sergeant Gunnar Hornswaddle, and this here is my brother Ulf." The second dwarf was the same height as his brother but with so much dark, shaggy hair that only the eyes and cheeks were visible.

Macarus' eyes narrowed. "Hornswaddle ..." He knew that name. "The mercenaries."

Gunnar bowed. "We prefer *independent contractors*, but aye, that would be our moniker."

Macarus glanced at his mother, his head clearing a little from the shock. "Why are dwarven mercenaries here? Why do they want to go to Ereland?"

"Fascinating, I agree," Gunnar said. "We have been given quite the sum by our noble King Ironsword to help the man you call the *Brendel*."

Woznius finished the stitches. Macarus moaned in pain for a moment. "Why is Ironsword trying to help Caleb?"

Gunnar raised a brow at him. "Our king says he owes your *Brendel* an enormous debt."

"What debt?" Macarus stood straight, testing the stitches at his side.

The dwarf Sergeant smirked. "Our king would not divulge such information. And with the payment, we didn't require it."

Macarus appraised him. "Your band, the Steelsides, are they with you?"

Diona answered. "We have them hidden in another location."

Macarus frowned. "You've been busy."

Diona squared her shoulders and faced him. "The Emperor has dismantled the Senate, completely piffing in the face of the will of the people and our law. His aggressive policies continue to send us into conflict after conflict with other nations, sending us further and further into debt, and he feels he must oppress the humans of Ereland to support those conflicts. But they only bring more conflict upon us, as the rebellion in Ereland makes clear." She breathed deep through her nose. "Additionally, there is even rumor that our Emperor is a Worldbreaker, those ancient wizards, which has been illegal for centuries because of the madness and the destruction that follows. He drags us into the Underland with his policies.

"So yes, I've been busy." She took in the other senators in the room. "We've been busy. Our hope is that the Steelsides will get to Ereland and help the *Brendel* defeat Tanicus."

Woznius moved to give Macarus' torn tunic back to him. Macarus gave him a bitter chuckle and shook his head. Woznius gathered the torn tunic, his materials, and moved back with the others.

Macarus raised his brow. "I've heard Tanicus is filling almost every ship in the Kryan Navy with close to thirty-five thousand elves to crush this rebellion, along with griders, trodall, and who knows what else. No offense to our friends, here, but even with their help, Caleb can't win. It's impossible."

"He has proven more than once, even by your own testimony, that he is capable of the impossible," Diona answered. "Nevertheless, that is only one part of our plan. This is an opportunity."

Macarus blinked slowly. *Of course. Here it comes.*

"While Tanicus is engaged in Ereland, and legions struggle to the east with Faltiel, then we can stage a coup here, removing the Emperor's lackeys and reestablishing the Senate. Even if Tanicus wins against the *Brendel*, it will take him time, and he will return to a very different Kryus."

The other senators glanced at her intently, the implication hanging in her words.

Three thousand years ago, one of Macarus' ancestors, Romanus, was the king of Kryus, during what some would claim the "golden age" of Kryus. Macarus considered that term somewhat romanticized, but here was Diona, the great-granddaughter of King Romanus.

"You're going to get the High Nican and the Senate to declare you Emperor."

Diona hesitated. "No. You."

"I must have had more South Kryan than I thought. You can't be serious."

She glided closer to him. "You have been loyal to Kryus while standing against the will of the Emperor. You are a hero of several battles in the War of Liberation. You helped defend a city against demics from the Underland. And you have the bloodline. We need someone the military would support, respect, someone disconnected from the Bladeguard, Moonguard, Sunguard, all of them. You could rally the veterans that are left here in Kaltiel for the coup. And you could help us achieve peace your friends in Ereland, whoever is left after this war is over. You are the best choice."

Macarus lowered his head.

He could be Emperor. Make peace with Faltiel, broker a transitional peace with the nations of Ereland, give the legions of Kryus rest, time to recover and become strong again, get out of debt …

As he looked at his mother there in the dim light of the lamp in a room over an empty warehouse, her strength, resolve, and power emanated off of her. Always had. And as much as he respected and admired his mother for her work in the Senate, he was sober enough.

He would be Emperor in name alone – a figurehead, a symbol, a puppet of his mother. He understood the battlefield, but in politics, Diona was the master, more skilled even than she was with a blade.

Macarus' heart fell.

"How are the Steelsides getting to Ereland?" he asked.

His mother stared but didn't answer.

Qinus said, "The plan was for one of us to hire a merchant ship and smuggle them into Landen. The legions have lost control in that city. Then they would meet up with the human army from there."

"The plan was for Senator Windal to do it," Nizaul said, her voice soft. "And he is not here." *He didn't make it. Probably dead.*

Macarus clenched his fist. "Very well. I will do it. I will go back with them."

Grunts and shifting around the room.

"No, Macarus," his mother said. "We need you here."

"I never should have left," Macarus said to no one in particular, simply voicing the thought that had ruled his mind for months. His heart pounded.

Diona clenched her jaw. "You will be seen as a traitor if you join that rebellion. You will never have a home in Kryus again. If you go, I can't protect you."

"I understand," he said. "You can't protect a traitor and come to power to make the changes you see necessary."

"That's what you think of me?" She sneered. "I'm the only reason you're still alive Not only tonight, with your drunken stupidity, but favors called in to generals and others to keep you safe. You can't take the life I give you and throw it away on another continent."

Macarus lifted his gaze. "I can't escape the feeling it's the right thing to do."

"Stubborn child," Diona mumbled then stabbed a finger at him. "I forbid you to do this."

Macarus gave his mother a sad smile. He reached out and touched her shoulder. "Mother, I love you, but I'm not asking your permission."

"You will raise your sword against elves?" she asked.

"Is that not what you're asking me to do here?" he responded. "I'm going back to Ereland with the Steelsides."

Sergeant Gunnar beamed and the cigar in his mouth bobbed as he spoke. "Yes. We should withdraw posthaste. I have greatly desired meeting this *Brendel* of yours. He must have testicles the size of catapult stones to believe he can destroy the Empire. I wonder if he can walk."

Mychal pointed to the elves riding by on fine horses. "They are arrogant and useless," he said to his brother, Yon. "They have no part in Yosu's army."

Yosu glanced back at the brothers as they strode into battle against Sahat the Younger. "What do you know of the First Race?"

"We know the legend of how all races were one in history past," Yon said.

"It is no legend," Yosu explained. "It is truth. Mychal, remind us of the story."

The others walked closer as Mychal spoke.

"In the beginning, El created one race, the Elinim. Over time, the Elinim grew wicked, and the Sahat brothers began to gain a following. Before the Sahat brothers could unify the Elinim, El divided them according to their weakness. For those obsessed with power, he made them elves. For those who desired great wealth, he made dwarves. And for the violent and lustful, he made human."

"Sahat the Elder and his closest followers were sent away," Yon added.

"You speak well," Yosu said. "And why do we fight, then?"

"We fight against Sahat the Younger because he is evil," Gabryel responded.

"That is not why we fight," Yosu said. "We fight for the redemption of Eres. Defeating the Sahat is only a step on that path.

"El made you one, and redemption is returning to one. Your redemption cannot happen apart from that of the elves and dwarves. See them as your enemy and you only delay the redemption. See them as brothers and sisters and hasten it."

> \-   From the Ydu, 3rd Scroll, translated from the First Tongue into common by the Prophet

Chapter 1

A True Believer

"We're here to fight in the *Brendel's* army," the young man said, a young woman at his side. A guard stood behind them.

Eshlyn stood in the central courtyard in Taggart before the couple. The busy courtyard bustled with men and women rushing to the next round of training or work, most of them eating a bread wrap on their way. The warm sun burned away the fog from the dawn just a few hours ago.

She wore her parted skirts with a white blouse, her feet comfortable in leather boots. Her dark hair fell past her shoulders.

The guard from the southern gate of Taggart, she couldn't remember his name, hovered. "Thank you," she said, dismissing him. The guard bowed and left.

Eshlyn nodded at the man and woman. "What are your names?"

The man bowed. "I'm Robben, Lady." He was Xander's age … or how old Xander had been. Robben was tall and thin but muscular with dark skin and thick hair in locks like Athelwulf's, only shorter so they stuck up on his head. Robben put his hand on the woman's back. "This is Aimi. My wife." She came up to his shoulder. She had dark skin, as well, with longer hair in two braids down her back.

They both wore long pants, moccasins, and simple tunics, their clothes worn and dirty with little holes and tears in them. Robben carried a makeshift bag, an old blanket tied together with a leather cord.

Over the past month at Taggart, people from all over the south and east had made their way to join the revolution they heard about, men and women, old and young, trickling in day by day.

People just like Robben and Aimi.

Aimi fidgeted with a braid. "You … you're Lady Eshlyn?"

Eshlyn restrained from rolling her eyes. "I am." At least they didn't call her *Bashawyn*.

They both straightened. "It is an honor to meet you," Aimi said. "Truly. We've come far to be here."

Haven't we all. "Thank you. It is an honor to meet you, as well. You're lucky. Most of the day, finding Caleb – the *Brendel* – can be a chore. We usually have to track him down. But since it is the morn, I know where he will be."

Robben and Aimi shared a glance. "And where is that?"

"The eastern wall. Come." She began walking and the couple jumped into step behind her. "Where are you from?"

They exited the courtyard onto the main street that led east past larger buildings that now housed the meeting areas and some living quarters. The buildings were made of cut gray stones with clay tiled roofs, most of them vaguely oval in shape.

"From a plantation south of Botan, Lady Eshlyn," Aimi said. "Near the foothills of the mountains."

"You're from Lior, though," Eshlyn said.

"We were bought from there, yes, Lady," Robben said. "You know Lior?"

Eshlyn held her hands behind her back. "I've been there. You were sold at a young age?"

"Very young," Robben said. "Our parents sold us into slavery to have money for food. It is bad there, in Lior, Lady Eshlyn. Bad bad."

"I understand." Eshlyn had a flash vision of Esai, bloody and dead at her feet and a city of fire, and Athelwulf and his broken body. She shook her head to be rid of the images. They didn't go away. She blinked and focused on a flying tiger. He was near. How near, she didn't know, but it calmed her. "You know each other before or did you meet at the plantation?"

"We met at the plantation," Aimi said.

"And you fell in love there," Eshlyn stated.

They both hesitated. Robb stumbled but recovered. "Yes, Lady," Aimi said.

"How did you leave the plantation?" Eshlyn asked. "Did the elven lord there let you go?"

"No," Robben's voice hardened. "He did not."

Eshlyn led them through more residential areas, more like barracks now, and the wall rose before them, beyond a few paddocks filled with animals. She looked over her shoulder. "You fought him?"

"Not the Master directly, Lady, but two of his elves, elves that worked there," Aimi said.

Eshlyn slowed for a moment. "Did you kill them?"

Robben spoke with a low voice. "We did."

Eshlyn nodded as they passed the paddocks of horses and cattle, smelling the dung and the dirt. They smelled like home, far away to the west on the plains of Manahem. "And you escaped and came here."

"We heard about the revolution, about the *Brendel*, about you, Lady Eshlyn," Aimi said. "We talked about it with others, but they were afraid. We were the only two who came."

They reached the eastern gate, and Eshlyn brought them to the left along the wall. "How long have you been married?"

Another silence. "Only a few days, Lady," Aimi said.

Eshlyn stopped before the wooden stairs that would take them up to the top of the wall. She half turned. "You didn't get married at the plantation?"

Robb shook his head. Aimi fingered a leather cord bracelet around her wrist.

"Then who married you?" Eshlyn asked.

Robben and Aimi shared a confused glance. "No one, Lady," Robben said.

Eshlyn raised a brow at them.

"We heard of a god who was everywhere and could see everything," Robben said. He reached out and took Aimi's hand. "The slaves began to speak of him more and more as we heard of this revolution. And so we asked him to be our witness. Do we need something more?"

That wasn't how it had been done in Manahem, to the sure. "Don't know. I'll ... ask."

"Pardon," Aimi said. "But who do you need to ask? Aren't you the queen here?"

"Queen?" Eshlyn exclaimed. "No. Not at all. We don't ... look, it's not like that. Break it all, I'll ask someone. But until then, don't worry about it. Just come."

"Yes, Lady," they said in unison.

Eshlyn climbed the stairs. They followed. She reached the top of the wall.

Caleb stood at the wall, leaning against the parapet on his elbows, his hair pulled back out of his face. He stared off to the east, like he attempted to understand it, or perhaps like something called to him. He wore his standard leather pants, boots, and a white shirt. The unforged sword hung at his waist. The Kingstaff was in his hand.

Was he praying? His steel eyes glistened with both fire and stone, hard and passionate.

"Caleb," she said.

He blinked, not startled, but like an awakening. He turned to her, and there was that long, ugly scar across his cheek. His beard didn't grow where the scar fell toward his jaw. As usual, she could see the weight upon him, like he carried the whole revolution upon those broad shoulders.

"Eshlyn." He said her name with both respect and familiarity. "Good morning."

"Good 'morn."

Caleb regarded the young couple. "Who have we here?"

"This is Robben and Aimi. They came to the gate this morning."

"You did, did you? Well met. Welcome to Taggart. What can I do for you, Robben and Aimi?"

Eshlyn retreated and pushed the young couple forward, an awkward move on the narrow wall walk. They shuffled forward.

"We came to join the revolution," Robben said. "We came to fight."

"Ah, yes," Caleb said. "You want to fight."

"Yes," Robben said. "With you, the great *Brendel*."

Caleb grunted. "Call me Caleb. My name is Caleb De'Ador. My father was a farmer on land owned by the elves, and when they found out he was helping people who believed in El, they killed him and my mother." Caleb brought the Kingstaff off of the wall and held it against his shoulder. "Do you understand?"

Both of them stood, frozen.

Eshlyn sniffed. *Here it comes.*

"You call it a revolution," Caleb said, "and it is. But that means war. And make no mistake, we are in a war. And in a war, you grow closer to those beside you and around you than any you have ever known. They will be closer than any brother or sister. They will be one with you in ways you cannot express."

Caleb paused and fixed them with a stare.

"We are targets of the most powerful Empire this world has ever known. Tanicus would see us all dead. I cannot guarantee your survival. I can guarantee you will see those you love cut down before you, fall to the violence and battle. Even in victory, there will be death and greater sorrow than you can imagine now. Do you understand?"

Robben and Aimi nodded slowly.

Caleb added, "If you fight and give your life for this, you will be fighting for the freedom of humanity and the redemption of all things. And one way or another, we will all see it. That is your reward."

Caleb allowed silence to reign and time to process what he said.

"I give you until tomorrow to make your decision. You will have food and a place to stay today until then. But realize, if you stay, then there is no turning back. Best to turn back now."

"We ... we can't go back," Aimi said.

"None of us can," Caleb said. "But your place may not be in the army. You have until tomorrow. Find Duglas at the service building near the courtyard. He will provide what you need."

"Yes, *Brendel*," Robben said. Caleb glared at him. "I mean, Caleb, sir. Thank you."

They turned and scurried past Eshlyn.

Eshlyn waited until they were gone. "Do you have to try and scare everyone away?"

He raised a brow at her. "What?"

"They're just a young couple, in love, married. You have to be so serious?"

"They need to understand the cost. I would think you would understand that as much as anyone."

She saw their faces again – Xander, Esai, Athelwulf. "I don't discount the need to have them know what they're committing to. But do you need to be so heavy handed? You sound like ... like that Prophet you talk about."

He frowned at her. "You like breaking my gruts or something?"

She leaned forward. "No, I only ..."

"Eshlyn! Caleb!" the voice came with rushing footsteps on the wooden stairs below them, and Aden bounced to the top of the wall.

His bushy, black hair was long enough now to be pulled back with a cord. She thought he was about to address Caleb, but his eyes met hers. "They're here."

"Wait ..." She licked her lips. "They're here?"

Aden smiled. "At the western gate."

She spun on Caleb. *Those from Ketan. Here.* "Javyn!"

Caleb grinned. Warm. "What are you waiting for? Go."

Aden hugged the parapet as she walked past him to the stairs. Eshlyn took the stairs quickly, and when she landed, she launched into a brisk walk.

My son, she thought. That ache that was both torturous and familiar, never forgotten. *He's here.*

She began to smile even as the stench of the animals of the paddock wafted to her. Tears hit her eyes. A small laugh escaped her throat. She considered taking a horse to arrive faster, but no, her own legs wanted to carry her. By the time she reached the residential barracks, she was running.

She raced past Robben and Aimi, her shoulder clipping Robben's. "Lady!"

"Sorry!" she cried over her shoulder as she kept going.

Eshlyn sprinted through the courtyard. Through her blurred vision, people gave her space, parting for her with knowing looks. Those that were with her in Taggart from Ketan and the Ghosts cried out, "Lady Eshlyn!" Those from Lior shouted, *Bashawyn!* Her hair bounced behind her and into her face.

The crowd gathered at the western gate. They noted her approach and made way. The guards at the gate – including the young man she couldn't name – stood inside the wall with Bweth, her arms crossed over her pregnant belly, a glare on her face.

Heaving breaths, Eshlyn slowed, ran a hand through her hair, and jogged over to Bweth. The scene was tense and silent. Lyam stood outside the gate. His chest expanded, but he couldn't meet her stare. Eshlyn walked towards him and gave him a mother's look, a look of disappointment, and he wilted.

Behind him, however, Eliot and Morgan Te'Lyan stood next to a wagon pulled by two horses. She smiled at her parents. In Morgan's arms was a young child, a boy, a toddler now.

In a moment, Eshlyn froze, wondering if her son might hate her for leaving, for going away without him. Her stomach clenched, and her hand went to her abdomen. She found it difficult to breathe.

Misty-eyed, Morgan whispered something into the boy's ear and set him on the ground.

"Mama!" It was a sound of joy, desperate in its purity. And it threatened to stop her heart.

Javyn, her son, waddled into a run towards her, crying her name over and over. Eshlyn heaved a sob and tried to take steps toward him, but her legs failed. People gasped as she landed on her knees, wide eyes spouting tears.

"Mama!" he cried.

Her voice cracked. "Javyn."

Eshlyn's arms extended, and Javyn leapt, his face within the crook of her neck, and her own in his.

She rocked him, kissed him, weeping, and kissed him some more. And she guffawed through the sobs, odd to the sure. She didn't know how long she held him there, but he didn't seem to mind. She didn't either.

She whispered in his ear. "My boy, I missed you, I love you so much ..."

Eventually, she pulled back. He beamed back at her. "Mama." A sound of satisfaction, contentment. It broke her heart and made it soar all at once.

"Hey, baby." She ran her hands through his dark, bushy hair, hair like hers, hair like his father's. Kenric.

He frowned. "I not a baby. I big boy."

She laughed. She couldn't help it. "So sorry. You're right. You are a big boy. So big."

Javyn smiled again.

"You want to come with me?"

He nodded.

She brushed her hair behind her ears and lifted him. She wavered a bit at his weight. "Wow. You have gotten big."

"Gramma made me eat."

Eshlyn turned, and her parents stood at her side. She embraced her mother and her father.

Xander's name, his death, went unmentioned but understood. The messengers would have told them. But together they swam in sorrow, the emptiness of his death.

"Thank you," Eshlyn told her parents.

"Of course," her father, the strongest man ever, said.

Eshlyn's only desire was to hold her son, never let him go, and grieve with her parents.

She had one thing to do first.

Eshlyn turned to Lyam, and now Aden and Caleb stood with Bweth inside the gate. Everyone watched her. She addressed Lyam.

"I'm going to visit with my parents and hold my son for the rest of the morning. Get settled. We will speak this afternoon."

He hesitated, glancing over at Caleb first, and then he nodded back.

With her parents following, she clung to her son and took him past the crowd and into the city.

───

The elf knelt before the nine gods in the small chapel of the monastery high on the cliffs east of the Kryan city of Helia. He could smell and taste the nearby ocean far below them. The chapel was dark, lit with the long golden candle of Ashinar before his statuette. The round room made of brown stone housed the shelves and the statuettes and nothing else. He wore no clothes, naked before his gods.

He was bald except for a long lock of stark, white hair he had braided. The braid fell down next to the burn scars across the right side of his face as he bowed. He kissed the dirt floor in front of the god furthest on the right and rose to face a pregnant god with the face of a skull.

"Virile Yor, god of the animals, I beseech thee, bless me with the cycle of death and life, one to the other, the cycle of all natural things. May my life and death be one with the cycle."

The elf considered his long life and how death was always near. He was thankful.

He bowed, kissed the dirt, and rose to face the next idol, the figure of a woman whose face was half joyful and the other half in agony.

"Vast Jeph, god of the sky, I beseech thee, bless me with both dreams of joy and great despair. Assist me in the balance that neither abounds nor lacks within me."

He had known both, seen such pain and terror in his life, and now he could rest, his reward of a life of service.

Another bow and kiss in the dirt. He faced a carving of a man asleep and content but with flaming swords in his hands.

"Deep Olinar, god of the oceans, I beseech thee, bless me with your fury when faced with your enemies and your constant peace within."

He did not need to touch the burn scars to feel them. He was glad of the peace.

He worked his way through the gods, one after the other – Beautiful Taghta the forest god of love and hate, Proud Lindor the mountain god of victory and defeat. Next were the three moon gods, all of them gods of darkness, Motali, Vysti, and Cynadi. He considered his life, thousands of years, and thanked the gods for their blessing as he had worshipped them with all his heart, all his life.

The elf's hand twitched at the footsteps outside of the chapel. One of the Nican monks. He bared his teeth. "You dare interrupt me now?"

The monk shuffled his feet. "My lord Julius, mercy, please, but an envoy from the Emperor is here for you. We told him you were occupied in your morning prayers. He … he cut the hand from another monk and threatened more abuse if we did not send for you immediately."

Julius took a calming breath. "That is the problem with Kryus today. We don't make the sacrifice for our worship, respect it, and so we dishonor the gods. You know the words of the ancient priests."

The monk gulped. "I do."

Julius looked at the tattoo on his forearm – a tree growing from a gray stone. "Then you will wait while I finish my prayers."

"Yes, my lord."

Julius took his time bowing, resting his lips into the dirt. He rose before Ashinar, the god of the sun, the god of all light, all power. Ashinar was a tall, beautiful elf with the sun behind his head.

"Bright and blinding Ashinar, god of the sun, I beseech thee. Show me the light. Give me your fire and your life, for you are the source of all."

The elf stood and raised his arms. "May all nature be one."

The monk spoke the blessing. "May all nature be one."

The elf turned to the monk, a slight, thin elf in a blue robe, a Nican monk of Olinar. "Where is this messenger?"

"At the archgate."

"Very well. Bring me a black robe." The robe of darkness.

"My lord." The monk scurried away.

Still naked, Julius left the small chapel and walked through the extensive garden that surrounded it – trees, bushes, vines, all types of vegetation fashioned into perfect specimens of order and beauty. The elf strode through the simple but strong brown stone buildings where he and the other monks slept and ate.

Another garden met him as he trod the pebble path to the gate, a simple arch of wood and vines at the entrance to the monastery.

Julius had come to the far northern shore, here to the cliffs, more than 150 years ago. He recruited eight other Nican, one for each god but Ashinar, and they built the monastery with simple tools. He had retired to this place because he did not want to be disturbed. And now he was disturbed.

Seven monks stood at the archgate before two elves in armor, one Captain and a Lieutenant, and both held drawn swords. The monk of

Taghta, in a green robe, knelt before the three armored elves and held the bleeding stump of his left hand, sweating from the blood loss and the pain.

Julius walked up to the Captain. "Who touched this holy one of Taughta?"

The Captain, a female with short blond hair, raised a brow at his nakedness. "Are you Julius the Bladeguard?"

The monk of Olinar brought him his black robe. Julius drew it over his head. Then he regarded the Captain again and pointed at the Lieutenant standing over the Taghta monk. "Is this the fool that touched an anointed?"

The Captain looked from the monk, to the Lieutenant, and back to the elf. "You did not answer my question. I am here on orders from the Emperor. Are you Julius the Bladeguard?"

Julius stepped to the side, and before any could react, he grabbed the Lieutenant's sword arm, pulled it down, and struck him in the throat. While the Lieutenant choked, Julius grabbed his gladus, and with a swift stroke, he severed the officer's right hand from his arm.

The Lieutenant screamed, retreated, and the Captain shouted, moving forward with her gladus raised.

Julius faced her with a bloody gladus in his hand. She froze. "I'll assume he was the one who touched the monk." He pointed to the two elves on the ground with bloody stumps where their hands should be. "Balance. The circle completes."

The other monks had never moved.

He met the Captain's eyes. "I am Julius, and I once was a Bladeguard, servant of Kryus, the greatest Empire of all ages. But I retired a century ago. Your name?"

Gripping her gladus, her knuckles went white. But after a second glance at her bleeding Lieutenant, she made the wise choice. "Captain Scalia. Of the 32nd Legion."

"I am sorry you were not patient enough to wait until my prayers were finished. But such is your generation. Faithless." He pursed his lips. "Now, what is the Emperor's message for me?"

"He leaves for Ereland, where a rebellion has formed, and he requires your assistance."

"As I said, I am retired. The monks will attend to your wounded and then you will leave. Give the Emperor my regards."

Julius turned and began to walk back to the chapel.

"The *Sohan-el* have returned," the Captain called after him.

Julius stopped.

"The Emperor says that the worshippers of El were not destroyed. They have returned, as have the warriors of their perverse one god. He needs a true believer in the gods, the killer of *Sohan-el*, Julius, his greatest Bladeguard."

Julius took a moment. "This rebellion is led by one who claims to be a *Sohan-el?*"

"Yes, a man they call the *Brendel*. Some say he is immortal and a great giant of a man, or a spirit."

Julius scoffed. "Faith in the gods has died but superstition reigns. The only giants are the old Geddai of the North, and no man, elf, dwarf, or geddai is immortal. And no man is a spirit." He spoke it as to a child.

"Even so, they have defeated a legion on the field and have taken Taggart. And the *Brendel* is not the only *Sohan-el*. Others claim that title."

Of all the rebellions over the last three hundred years, they'd been mere riots, expressions of idiocy and anger, easily ended by local violence. One going by the name of *Sohan-el* was troubling enough, but several? And they defeated a legion on the field? For Tanicus to feel he must go personally, for him to risk sending a messenger to the monastery, the Emperor must feel it was serious indeed.

"Very well." He turned to the monk of Olinar. "Pack necessities for my travel. I go to see the Emperor."

CHAPTER 2

THE COST

Aden ducked and dodged to the right to avoid Caleb's fist, but the punch was a feint, as usual, and in another heartbeat, Caleb wrenched and pulled Aden's wrist. Off balance, Aden grunted while he stumbled into a lift and throw. Weightless for a moment, his body clenched in fear, and he landed on his back.

Caleb stood over him. "You go for the feint every time."

Aden snorted and sat up. Caleb didn't offer a hand for assistance, and Aden didn't expect it. They sparred in a large room on the second floor of the main administration building. Aden didn't know its previous use, but Caleb had cleared the room and now used it to regularly kick the crit out of him.

Aden rose to his feet. "I should let you smack me in the head instead?" A breeze through the windows refreshed him in the warmth of the day.

"Or perhaps block. Or strike before I can."

"Easy for you to say. You're faster than me."

Caleb hesitated. "I wasn't always fast. At least, not as fast as I am now. You can learn speed."

"Is that what you're teaching me?" Aden brushed his hands on his pants leg.

"Hand to hand teaches many of the same principles of combat that you've been learning. Probably should have taught you this before." Caleb shrugged. "But we can start now."

"Well, I ..." Aden began but then raised his hands when Caleb spun from his standing position with a backhand strike. Aden attempted to block, which mostly deflected the blow to his shoulder instead of between his eyes, and countered with a left handed elbow.

Which Caleb gripped and used as leverage to flip and send Aden on his arse yet again.

Aden frowned up at Caleb, who smirked down at him.

"Always be ready," Caleb said.

"Looks like I'm learning how to endure pain."

Caleb nodded. The smirk died on his lips. "That's one thing to learn."

Getting to his feet, Aden groaned, and then he suddenly swept his right leg along the ground to trip Caleb up.

Caleb leapt over the sweep and kicked out with his right, connecting with Aden's rear end. Aden stumbled forward and cursed, catching himself on his knees.

"Like I said, be ready," Caleb muttered, then his voice rose. "Is it time?"

Aden was confused for a moment before he looked to the wide door of the room. Jaff, a *Sohanel* and the current voice for the Ghosts of Saten, stood in the doorway.

Jaff's long mustache fluttered as he breathed through his nose. "It is. They've gathered."

"Very well," Caleb said. He met Aden's eyes. "You ready?"

Aden got to his feet. "I guess I have to be."

Caleb nodded to Jaff. "We'll be there in a few minutes."

"Yes, *Brendel.*" Jaff left.

Without speaking, both Aden and Caleb walked to the edge of the room where cloths sat on a water basin. They cleaned their hands and face, straightened their clothes, grabbed their unforged swords and scabbard, and walked back across to the door. The Kingstaff leaned against the wall, and Caleb grabbed it as they passed.

Aden followed Caleb through the hall and down the stairs to the lower level of the administration building. As they moved, Aden could feel the strength, the tension, in Caleb.

They gathered in the large meeting room. Caleb had requested that the leaders and the surviving *Sohan-el* be at the meeting. It was a full room.

Maps hung on the wall between the wide windows that allowed a generous amount of sunlight into the room. Ornate lamps, leftover from the elves, stood in the four corners. A long, bare, wooden table stretched through the middle of the room.

On one side of the table sat the leaders of the army, the *Hamon-el.* Shecayah and Tobiah sat stone faced and calm, but Aden could see an anger simmering behind that calm. Bweth and Iletus sat next to them, Iletus with a long face and Bweth's teeth bared as if she were about to tear someone's face off. Jaff had taken his place next to them as leader of the Ghosts, his balding head gleaming in the sunlight through the window behind him.

Eshlyn's eyes were fierce in her seat towards the end of the table. Her face softened when she noticed Caleb and Aden at the door. Aden nodded at her and sat between her and Jaff.

The remaining *Sohan-el* sat across the table. Of the original twenty one who began the training in Ketan with Caleb, Nicholas and Gardo had died in the Battle of Biram. Rachelle, Chase, and Tyler had died in the Battle of the Acar. Athelwulf and Esai died while on their mission with Eshlyn, and Xander, one of Aden's best friends, died senselessly after the Battle of the Acar.

Carys was away with Zalman and the Rat.

Eshlyn, who had been trained, no longer considered herself a *Sohan-el* since she was never tested for her sword and gave back her husband's sword at the Tomb of Yosu. But she had been to the Tomb of Yosu. She never talked about it with Aden, but in his eyes she was as worthy as anyone.

Like Tamya.

Aden shook his head, trying to clear her face and skin from his mind as he looked at the remaining *Sohan-el* across from him. Eight other men and women sat at the table, people with their own stories, their own struggles and hopes and dreams, given an unforged sword by El and trained by the *Brendel*, by the sword of El himself. Aden knew some more than others, but he knew them all, fought and bled with them all ... grieved with them all – Juhl, Pynt, Xak, Ewha, Digby, Wes, Kenneth, and Yessica.

At the far end of the table, Lyam stood, his unforged sword hanging at his hip.

Another one of Aden's closest friends among the *Sohan-el*, Lyam appeared older than before. Lines had grown on his face in the past few ninedays since his betrayal at the Acar.

Caleb's eyes lowered as he moved to the end of the table. Lyam sat at the far end, opposite. He laid the Kingstaff on the wall behind him; then he raised his eyes at the man, gray eyes so full of passion and emotion that Aden flinched. Aden thought he would be used to that violent, intense stare from Caleb by now. But perhaps he never would. Perhaps it wasn't possible.

How could he not be the Brendel? It was like the anger of El stared across the table.

Caleb rested both of his hands on the unforged sword at his side. The silence held weight. Caleb broke the silence with a calm, clear voice. "Before we go forward, let us pray and ask El for his wisdom."

Heads bowed around the table, an awkward move for some. Caleb began, "Great and mighty El, we seek to follow you, to do what is right and best. Help us to find your wisdom in this matter. All say ..."

"Our hearts agree," most of the group said in unison.

Caleb addressed the young man at the other end of the table. "Lyam. Well met. Thank you for returning to speak with us today. Do you wish to say anything before we begin our discussion?"

Lyam's eyes flashed at Caleb, but he couldn't hold the gaze. He stared at his feet. "I can only say that I was wrong. I am ... ashamed of my actions at the Acar. I can only say that it was only my intention to save what I could, to save us from what I believed was certain death. I know now that El helped you do the impossible."

Lyam pulled the unforged sword from the hilt at his hip, and he cradled it in his hands. Tears fell from his eyes onto the sword. "When I climbed the mountain and went to the Stone, El spoke to me."

Many of the *Sohan-el* tensed.

Smiling, Lyam nodded. "I know. Here I am, breaking this unwritten rule again, speaking of the Living Stone when we've been so silent about it. But I need you to know." He blinked, slowly, and looked up – not at Caleb but at the *Sohan-el* that sat to his right. "He spoke to me, as he spoke to all of us." Lyam swallowed and sniffed. "He told me that I was a protector. That it was my gift, my calling, to protect others. The weak. El told me I would do the impossible. When I lost my division at the Battle of Biram, I felt a failure. I thought we should have stayed in Ketan, where it was safe."

As Lyam paused, the room remained quiet. No one moved. Aden forced himself to breathe deep.

"But like I said, I was wrong. In my grief and feelings of failure, I questioned our strategy. I questioned Caleb's leadership. I lost my faith. I was angry and afraid."

Lyam raised the unforged sword above his head, gazing at it once again. "I was so proud when El found me worthy of this sword. Now I don't deserve it." Aden watched as Lyam gritted his teeth and drove the sword blade down into the table. The action startled many, and the sound reverberated through the room. "I step down as *Sohan-el*. I'm no longer worthy. I can only hope that you forgive me, all of you."

Then Lyam sat down.

Loud breaths and movement around the table as they all turned to look at Caleb, his eyes unwavering. When he moved, he nodded and rubbed his beard. "I would hear thoughts from everyone. What are we to do?"

Eshlyn leaned into Caleb. "Should we ask Lyam to leave as we discuss?"

"No," Caleb said. "He has a right to hear what we all say about him."

Eshlyn's eyes narrowed. "Very well."

"Thank you. Now, I wish to hear what everyone has to say."

Bweth was the first to stand, her face almost as red as her hair, her pregnant belly more pronounced than ever. "He's playing you, Cal. He's still acting out of fear. With what he did, and after we won at the Acar? He knows he won't be welcome anywhere – not Ketan, not the Saten, not here with us. He's trying to save his skin again like a coward."

Lyam winced.

"So what are you suggesting?" Eshlyn pulled a strand of hair behind her ear.

Bweth stabbed a finger at Lyam. "We put him in chains, at least. You can't let betrayal and desertion go unpunished. That's no way to keep an army unified. In any other army in the world, he would be hanging with his guts splayed out for all to see."

Eshlyn raised a brow. "Is that what you're suggesting? We execute him?"

Bweth took a deep breath. "I don't know. Maybe. We're fighting a breakin' war, here. There has to be discipline."

Aden shook his head. "But we're not like every other army in the world. Our unity can't come from fear of punishment." He waved a hand at the window behind him. "We've got a few thousand people here ready to fight, but they've all volunteered. They've chosen to be here. Don't they get to choose to leave?"

Bweth hit the table with her fist. "We were left with three hundred against a breakin' Legion. He didn't only choose to leave, he took a thousand soldiers with him!"

"That is true," Shecayah spoke. Her light brown eyes measured Lyam and then swung to Eshlyn. "I do not know your ways, however, to us, he is a *foredain*, a betrayer, a curser, and worthy of death."

Eshlyn's brow furrowed. "I thought that had to do with cursing a father or parent."

"It includes that, yes," Tobiah, her husband, said. He turned on Lyam with disgust. "But it applies to a curse and betrayal of anyone in authority over us." Tobiah gestured back at Caleb. "If Caleb is truly the *Brendel* we've been waiting for, the one prophesied, then it applies."

"What about Athelwulf?" Eshlyn tilted her head. "Didn't you forgive him? Didn't you receive him back?"

Shecayah frowned. "It was not our place. Remember, my brother submitted to Kiano, his father and the chief of our tribe. As the one cursed and betrayed, it was Kiano's choice."

"So you would have allowed Athelwulf's execution?" Aden asked.

Tobiah nodded. "Athelwulf would have submitted to it, I believe."

Aden glanced at Lyam, who shifted in his seat.

Eshlyn gaped for a moment before speaking. "So you're agreeing with Bweth. You believe we should kill him?"

Shecayah pursed her lips. "No. I am saying a punishment is warranted. And Caleb, here, has the right to choose. Our thoughts do not matter. At least, that would be our way."

Aden ran a hand through his hair. "That's not our way, though ... right?" He turned to Caleb. "Right?"

"Let's hear from the others." Caleb stood still.

Jaff cleared his throat and pulled at one end of his moustache. "Lyam's actions affected everyone. He gets to leave, to make that choice, but his words swayed others."

"Exactly," Bweth said.

"So the decision is not Caleb's alone," Jaff continued. "It is really up to all of us. That's why Caleb asked us to gather."

Caleb scratched his beard. "Go on."

"Well," Jaff cringed. "Don't know if I have more than that. Only that we should decide together."

Iletus leaned onto the table with his elbows and folded his hands in front of his mouth. "I would agree that this is like no army I've ever encountered, but that does not excuse us from discipline, from doing what is necessary to show there are consequences to such things. No army, even an army of a god, can survive a lack of justice."

"What of the others?" Pynt, a *Sohan-el*, asked. "What of those that left with him? It was clear that they had a choice, as well. Do we kill them? Punish them somehow? Here Lyam stands alone, but over a thousand people went with him."

"Fair point," Jaff said. "If we hold Lyam accountable, then we should hold all of them to the same standard."

"No." Lyam sat up with his back straight. He stared at Jaff and then at Caleb. "None of them were given an unforged sword like I was. I was trained to lead, to lead them into what is right and true, lead them for the good of others." Lyam scanned Aden and the other *Sohan-el*. "I was the only *Sohan-el* to leave, and I used my leadership, what had been entrusted to me," he pointed at the unforged sword still quivering in the table, "used it to lead others astray." He met Caleb's steel stare now. "Do what you will with me, make an example of me, but do nothing to them. That is all I ask."

Caleb grunted as if struck, but he stood firm.

Eshlyn breathed in deeply through her nose. She regarded Caleb. "Well, we've heard from everyone else. What do you say?"

Aden bit his lip as he leaned back, his heart pounding in his chest.

Caleb took his hands from his sword and held them in front of him, palms up. He took a heavy breath, clenched his jaw, and pulled the sword from his side with both hands. He lifted the sword and drove it into the table as Lyam had done.

Bweth and Eshlyn sat down.

"Lyam," Caleb said. "You've heard what was said. You were wrong to leave as you did, to lead others away with you on the eve of a battle, possibly the most important battle in this war. Yes, justice could include punishment. Punishment is easy. But sometimes the justice of El, what is best, lies beyond what is easy."

Bweth groaned, "No, Caleb, don't ..."

"Lyam, I also must ask your forgiveness. Aden told me of your struggles after the Battle of Biram, but I wrestled with my own pain. I wasn't the leader I was supposed to be, either."

Lyam gulped at Caleb, his eyes wide.

"We have all made mistakes, been deceived, acted more out of fear and anger than love and sacrifice. All of us. The argument could be made that we didn't know any better, or that was a long time ago, but people were hurt by the consequences of our actions, were they not? Yes, Lyam, you should be held to a higher standard, and you will be.

"And if you had returned with a sword in your hand to kill me, then your blood would water the ground. But you did not. You realized your error and came back to submit to your brothers and sisters. And we are all your brothers and sisters.

"You sat there and bravely tried to protect others. Again. You are right. El was right, as he always is. That is your gift. You would give your life for them, just as you would give your life to save those that died in your division."

A sob escaped Lyams throat.

"Maybe I've seen too many of my brothers and sisters die. Maybe my longing for Carys' safe return clouds my judgment. Maybe I dread the battles to come and the deaths that will ultimately follow. But the Battle of the Acar was not the first battle in this war, and it will not be the last. You ache to protect the weak, to save the lost, to fight for what you believe is true and right, and now you have learned a powerful lesson. You've been humbled. We will need men and women like you in the battles to come. We will need all the help we can get.

"Maybe the greater justice is to take our sins, our deceptions, and learn from them, use them to be even more committed to what is good and right. Isn't that what Yosu taught us?"

Aden sat up straight in his chair, as did Jaff and Eshlyn beside him, as did many of the *Sohan-el* across the table.

"I cannot take your sword from you, Lyam," Caleb said. "No one can. For no one here found you worthy in the first place. I cannot find you unworthy now. It is yours to do as you wish. But for me, my opinion is that you've never been as worthy of that sword than you are at this moment."

Lyam wept, his head in his hands.

"Lyam, your heart was to stay and protect Ketan. My mistake was ever letting you to leave. I seek to rectify that mistake now." Caleb looked at the others around the table. "I say we send him back to Ketan and put him in charge of the defense of the city. Any others who feel that is what El would have them do are welcome to join him, *Sohan-el* or otherwise. We will also need leadership to stay and defend this place when we eventually leave to be the blade at the heart of Kryus.

"That is my suggestion. But it is not my decision alone. We must agree as the leadership of the *Hamon-el.*"

Caleb stood with his hands behind his back and waited.

Aden took a breath, stood, drew the sword at his side, and plunged it into the table. "I'm with Caleb."

"Shocking," Bweth mumbled.

Jaff rose. "Lyam, will you agree to address the whole of Taggart, admit your wrong, and say that Caleb is, in fact, the *Brendel*?"

Lyam sniffed. "I will."

Jaff drew his sword and stuck it in the table. "Then I'm also with Caleb."

Eshlyn stood. "I think Jaff's suggestion is a good one. I agree."

One by one, the *Sohan-el* stood with Caleb, stabbing their unforged swords into the table.

Shecayah and Tobiah shared a glance and came to their feet. "If the *Brendel* and the *Bashawyn* say it is so, then we will agree," Tobiah said. Shecayah nodded at him. "However," Tobiah added. "I must say that the tradition and evil of the *foredain* in our culture is not without wisdom. Earon, your cousin, also sits unpunished. I applaud your forgiveness and vision, *Brendel*, but I wonder when we will learn that betrayal will cost more than we can forgive. With that said, we agree."

Iletus pushed up from his chair with a sigh. "I also have my reservations, Caleb. I know what we will face in the coming weeks, whether we stay or we go, and discipline might be more important than forgiveness. But you are correct. I stand here as a Bladeguard that assisted the Empire in its machinations for centuries before I changed. I am more guilty of crimes against man and dwarf and elf than any here. Or most." Iletus eyed Bweth, and she squirmed under his scrutiny. Then he looked at Caleb again. "So I cannot condemn this man. At least, not now."

Caleb turned to Bweth. "And you?"

Bweth crossed her arms.

"Speak your mind," Caleb told her. "Don't agree simply because everyone else does. Do not decide out of your anger, either. Say what you feel is right."

"No punishment?" Bweth shook her head. "It's not right, Cal. You know it ain't. We all know it ain't. You can't have an army runnin' around doin' what they feel is right. You have to work together, and that means following orders, or else it's chaos on the battlefield. Anyone been in a battle knows it."

"So you will be the vote against?" Eshlyn asked. "If that is your conscience, then we will respect it."

Bweth glanced at Iletus once more before laying her hands on her stomach. Her belly caught Aden's eye. Did it move and shift? She stood, pushed her chair back, and stared at Lyam. "You agree, boy?"

"Yes."

"Then stand like a man, and stop blubbering like a child."

Lyam stood and wiped his face of the tears.

Bweth pulled on her tunic and harrumphed as she strode around Shecayah and Tobiah to stop half a mitre from Lyam. He turned to face her.

Baring her teeth, Bweth leapt in the air and came down with a fist right in between his eyes. Aden recoiled with the smack and crunch sound. Lyam's body flew paces back. He landed against the wall in a heap, sputtering through the blood beginning to pour from his nose. Gasps and shouts came from the group.

Bweth glowered at Caleb. "Now I agree. Long as I don't see him and don't have to fight next to him."

And she marched out of the room.

———

Watching Bweth go, Caleb shook his head. *Break me.* "Aden, will you take Lyam and get him a place to stay?"

Aden grabbed his sword, placed it into its scabbard, moved around the table behind the others in response. Pynt and Ewha hovered over Lyam, trying to help him to his feet.

Eshlyn touched Aden's elbow. "Get him a place as far away from Bweth as you can." She addressed Lyam. "You might want to avoid her until you leave."

Lyam nodded, groggy. Aden handed Lyam his sword. Lyam accepted it with a sad smile, and they left the room together, Pynt and Ewha at their heels.

"Think and pray about where your place might be," Caleb told the rest of the *Sohan-el.* "We have group training in the morning."

The *Sohan-el* made their way out of the room. "Jaff," Caleb called, and the middle aged man waited at the door. "Will you organize the Ghosts to be in the center of town tomorrow night so Lyam can address them?"

"Will do," Jaff said.

"Thank you," Caleb said as the man exited.

"We shall have the Beorgai there, as well," Shecayah said as they rounded the end of the table, stepping over the drops of blood.

Caleb thanked them. They stopped at the door and bowed to Eshlyn. "*Bashawyn,*" they both said before they left.

Caleb raised a brow at Eshlyn. She rolled her eyes back at him, but not until Shecayah and Tobiah could no longer see her.

Iletus stood and walked around to leave.

Caleb faced the elf. "Something I should know about Bweth?"

Iletus paused at the other end of the table, rubbing his chin. "Bweth was once in the legions, of that I am sure. She knows more of the Kryan military than a simple weaponsmaster would know. How did she come to be in Ketan all those years ago? As a Bladeguard, it bothers me that I do not know why she was exiled."

"Ah," Caleb said. "She could have rebelled against them, stood up to them. Could be a good reason."

"They would have executed her for rebellion in the legions. No. It's something else. We may want to know before we go much further."

Iletus was right. There were a million possible reasons why she would have been sent to the farthest reaches of the Empire, many of them troubling. She had fashioned swords for the Bladeguard, and if Iletus didn't know the secret, then that was a problem.

"I understand," Caleb said. "I must be slipping. You're right. I'll find out."

"Let me know. See you in the morning."

Caleb nodded at the elf, and soon he was alone with Eshlyn.

He sighed. "Never a dull moment, huh?"

Eshlyn scoffed. "With this motley crew? We should have expected it."

"You're right. How is Javyn?"

"Well enough. Thank you for giving me some time with him. My parents are with him now. They're deciding on whether to stay with the army and me or go back to Ketan."

"I know their leadership will be missed there, but like I said, it will be their choice."

"We'll see." She cocked her head at him, and the kindness and beauty in her face struck him again. "How are you?"

"Me?"

Eshlyn stepped closer to him. "Yes, you. Dealing with Lyam, that couldn't have been easy. How are you?"

My shoulders feel heavy. Does it ever get lighter? "Not much is easy anymore." He grabbed the sword from the table and slipped it into the scabbard at his hip. "It doesn't matter."

"What does that mean?"

"It means we're in a war. Not sure it matters how I am."

Eshlyn frowned at him and muttered. "It matters to me."

Caleb didn't know how to respond at first, and he was quiet for a moment. "You think we were right?"

"About what, Lyam?"

He nodded.

Eshlyn sighed. "I think we did the best we could with a critty situation." She walked over to the window behind her and looked out at the people, distant, walking by, busy with their roles and duties. "I tell you this, I wanted to punch the little shogger myself when I heard what he did."

I wanted to do more than that. His hand tightened over the Kingstaff. "You're not the only one."

She met his eyes. "I'm sure. But I will say that Shecayah and Tobiah might be right. Forgiveness is good, but Earon's choices killed the Prophet. Lyam almost costs us the whole revolution. And we have a group of people, a growing army, that's like a field with four different crops all mixed in. We've got the people of the towns of Manahem, from Ketan, the Ghosts, and the Beorgai. Getting them to trust each other and work with one another is difficult enough, but now we're going to add a group of people that walked out before a battle?"

Caleb peered out the window and shrugged. "I don't know. I feel like I know less than I ever did."

"I'm sorry. Don't get me wrong. I think we did the right thing. I do. I'm just wondering what the cost is going to be. There's always a cost."

"True. But the wrong thing costs even more. Far more."

Eshlyn clicked her tongue. "Speaking of the right thing, what about Earon? You decided what to do with him?"

"I should wait for Carys, if I can. But I don't know how long that will take."

"And if it takes too long? What are you thinking?"

Caleb moved to the other side of the window and leaned against the wall, facing her, the Kingstaff lying on his shoulder. "Then I will try to help him see his purpose, as I did with Lyam. I was serious when I said we were going to need all the help we could get."

"Even Earon."

"Yes, even Earon. Even unified, what Iletus said was true. Tanicus hasn't used his best against us. Not yet. We need the power of El in a way we haven't seen before, a power the world hasn't seen in over a thousand years."

"You think Earon can give us that power?"

"No. But I believe it is his purpose to help us find it. He and Carys."

"Break it all, Caleb, we don't even know where she is."

"No, we don't." Caleb gazed out the window. "But if I'm right, then we will. One way or another, we will."

CHAPTER 3

The Last Serpent

Carys scanned the misty darkness of the late evening through her peerglass. She could feel Zalman hovering over her there on the bow of *The Last Serpent*; his large form once intimidated her – he intimidated everyone – or annoyed her, but now it was a comfort.

Because he was her husband. Her breakin' husband. She was married to the big gedder.

She didn't realize how their intimacy could make her so much more comfortable around him, so safe. Had she imagined it wouldn't? Her limited experience with boys had made her think sex only made life and relationships more awkward, and she knew enough of his past to be nervous and unsure in the bed with him.

There were awkward moments, sure, but over the first few days, they found a place of comfort and fun, a place no one else could touch but the two of them. It made her more confident in herself, and she loved him more for it.

The moment she had stood over him on the deck of the ship those ninedays ago, watching his life ebb away from him, she felt the same helplessness when her uncle Reyan died in her arms in a little tavern across the world. She couldn't lose Zal. She couldn't. And so when El showed his goodness and Zal miraculously recovered, she married him as soon as she could.

She sighed, pulled the peerglass away from her face, and shook her head. Even now, he distracted her. They were on a hunt.

"You okay?" his voice rumbled behind her.

"It's nothing. And shut up." They weren't supposed to be talking. "If you're grinning behind me, I'll punch you in the gruts." She glanced over her shoulder, but his face was expressionless. Biting her lip, she faced the dim and mist and put the peerglass up to her eye again.

I should punch him in the grut anyway. Next time I won't warn him.

They hunted for an elven warship. The dove had returned from the northwest fifteen minutes ago, and based on time of flight, Aeric had calculated the ship was approximately a kilomitre away. All the lights on *The Last Serpent* had been extinguished. They approached silent and dark.

Between the darkness and the fog, however, she couldn't see more than a hundred mitres ahead of them, even with the peerglass. Once seen at that distance, would that be enough time to adjust course and attack the elves?

She wasn't a master of the sea, but she doubted it. And since the whole plan hinged on the keenness of her archer's eyes, those doubts gnawed at her.

Her body tensed at the sight of a flicker of light through the mist. She blinked, leaned forward, and gripped the peerglass with both hands now. The peerglass shook in her hand, and she forced herself to relax. She remembered the training from the Ghosts, from Athelwulf and Caleb – it was natural to her, emptying her mind of all else except the task.

There it was again. A flicker of light, like a small flame in a lamp and then joined by another at the same height. Within a moment, the glow of lamps outlined the bones of a ship, rising and falling gently on the water.

Carys stood straight, turned, and waved her arm at Aeric, the Pirate Lord and Captain of *The Last Serpent*. He leaned on the wheel with his own peerglass, watching her, and he nodded in acknowledgement. *The Last Serpent* made a slight shift towards the elven ship.

Again, Carys marveled at how the large pirate vessel moved. A minor creak of wood at random intervals was all the noise it made as Aeric pointed the ship to ram along the side of the elven ship. The expert crew moved around the deck with little to no sound, adjusting the ballista and catapults to the angle of attack.

This was the third ship *The Last Serpent* had attacked in the last ninedays, every time in the evening, silent and deadly to strike like a snake.

Carys fastened her peerglass to her belt and grabbed the bow next to her. She could see the elves without the glass now, and she pulled an arrow from the quiver at her back and set it on the string.

The elves were a hundred mitres away when the world woke with a roar.

Four stones covered in tar were lit within their catapults and launched from *The Last Serpent*, flames arcing through the dark and splitting the mists and raining upon the elves. The sounds of crackling flame, whipping of ropes, men yelling and elves screaming, all of it split the silence of the night. Balls of flame bounced and smashed into the deck of the enemy ship as the three ballista at the bow of *The Last Serpent* fired long iron spears that ripped into the side.

Fifty mitres away, an elf flailed and screamed, engulfed in flame on the deck of the Kryan ship. Carys raised her bow and shot him or her. The elf went down. She saw other figures along the deck, scrambling to put out fires or ready their own weapons, most of which were already pointed in the direction of *The Last Serpent*. Carys aimed and loosed arrows at those figures. Two more down, then another.

Two ballista from the elven ship fired and struck the side of *The Last Serpent* with wet thuds. Two elven catapults launched stones, one of which tore through the railing before hitting the water and the other missing the pirate ship completely.

The Last Serpent sailed close to the elven ship, and she felt Zalman's large hand at her waist. He grabbed the railing. Carys fired one last arrow before she leaned into Zal.

Their weapons were pointed in our direction already. How would they ...?

The ships collided, spikes from the side of *The Last Serpent* tearing through wood, her ears deafened by the thunder of the violence of wood crashing into wood. She cried out despite herself, and Zalman wrapped her in his arm against his chest, his own grunt a comfort in her ear. The *Serpent* settled; Zal released her and leapt upon the railing. He pulled both axes from his belt, and he spun them in his hands, his face an eager grimace.

The *Serpent* rocked again, down first, and then it rose. Zal used the motion to propel himself up and over to the deck of the elves. The giant man hung in the air for a moment. Carys watched the eyes of fear and awe of the elves. She took advantage of the hesitation by standing tall, her feet wide for balance, and firing arrows between frightened eyes.

Zalman descended upon the deck like a storm of muscle and axe blades. Elven bodies went flying.

Several of Aeric's men followed him over to fight the elves, long blades and short spears in their hands. As afraid as the elves were, however, they were armed, fitted with armor and ready for a fight. Either their response time was improving or ...

The *Serpent* rocked again, but not from crashing with the elven ship in front of it. Something else hit the ship. She turned at the yelling and sound behind her, and she saw another ship attacking from behind.

Elven militan poured onto a vulnerable ship. All of the *Serpent*'s weapons were pointed forward, and a large portion of her crew was engaged with the ship ahead of them. Aeric stood with only a few men against dozens of militan.

"Shoggers." Carys screamed over at her husband. "Zalman!"

Zalman backhanded an elf, crushing his skull with the flat of the axe blade, and looked over at Carys with a frown.

She caught his eye and pointed over at the other ship. "It's an ambush!"

Zalman narrowed his eyes through the mist and darkness, took a deep breath, and ran back towards her and the *Serpent*. Carys spun, set two arrows, and fired into the crowd of militan Aeric now engaged, two pirates dead around him already. Carys fired once more. The large form of her husband raced past and sprinted along the deck towards the new battle.

"Hold on, you gedder," she called, following him. They ran across the deck, and Carys swerved to his right to get some room, firing arrows as they covered the distance. The militan noticed them, and four swiveled to face Zalman.

He skidded to a halt within a pace of them, blocking their thrusts with his axes and countering with killing blows, removing a sword arm of one and the head of another before needing to block other strikes. Carys slung her bow over her shoulder and pulled her unforged sword.

The sword sung in her hand as she stood back to back with her husband, the supernatural blade blocking and striking. She and Zalman spun together, and she gutted one elf while he cut the knees from another. Between the two of them and Aeric, a great swordsman on his own, the attacking militan were dead.

Carys paused, panting, and addressed Aeric. "You go help your men." She pointed to the original elven ship. Then she grimaced at the new threat, more militan gathering on the deck, perhaps twenty more. "Zal and I will take this one."

Aeric hesitated, measuring them for a moment. He nodded and ran towards the bow of the ship.

Carys sighed at the dead pirates on the deck and unslung her bow. "They were ready for us."

Zal snorted. "Third time. Even elves not that stupid."

Carys sheathed her sword. "Our mistake. You ready?"

Zal nodded.

She nocked an arrow and jogged to the railing. Zal pushed her to the deck, however, and she landed hard. Long metal pikes from basilica speared the side of the ship and the deck. One missed her head by milimitres. Her cheek hurt, realizing it had bounced on the wooden deck, and she rose, angry, needing to nock another arrow since her original had broken. She fired across to the other ship, taking out the militan around the basilica while they attempted to reload. Two were down before Zalman could lumber the rest of the distance to the railing and leap over to the other ship.

While the militan around the basilica found cover behind the large weapons, a row of nine militan archers behind them raised bows and took aim at Zalman. Carys cursed and made her way to take position behind the railing of the *Serpent*; she fired twice more, taking out two of the archers. Two arrows flew her way and stuck into the railing near her, and three more hurtled towards Zal. Two sailed past, which meant one hit him somewhere.

Carys stood straight and took out two more archers while Zalman landed, stumbling and recovering while he fought a platoon of militan on the deck.

Out of the corner of her eye, a basilica was loaded and ready to fire. She didn't have the time to fire before they did, and so she dove to the side as an iron spear tore through the railing where she just stood. She rolled to her knees, pulled an arrow, and fired across her body to kill the remaining militan at the basilica.

Zalman had positioned himself so that the militan he fought stood between him and the archers. *Nice of the archers to stand in a row for me. Five, four, three ...*

The quiver was empty. "Shoggers!" She dropped her bow and leapt over the railing, pulling her sword as she landed.

Now that she had removed the militan, two elven archers remained, and so an arrow whirled towards her body. She split the arrow before it hit her. A splinter scraped her cheek, and she made her way to the basilica to her left for cover from another arrow that flew behind her. Carys reached down to a groaning, dying militan, grabbed his gladus, and hurled it at the archers.

Her aim with a gladus wasn't as good as an arrow, but both archers danced away from the spinning blade. She grabbed another gladus from a militan, raised it in her left hand, and she rushed the archers. They tried to recover in time, but Carys covered the five mitres too quickly, and one archer set an arrow. At this close distance, her aim with a gladus was better, and he soon fell with a blade sticking out of his chest. The other archer dropped his bow and actually got his gladus out and up in time to parry her blow. He was better than the usual militan, but as impressed as she was, he was no *Sohan-el.* Her unforged sword cut him down.

She kicked him once more to the deck as he died, and she raced to engage the militan surrounding Zalman.

A quick count of remaining militan came to eight, many of them trying to find an angle on the large man who kept moving faster than they could adjust. Zal spun and attacked, blocking and moving into offensive maneuvers. She could see the wound on his upper arm, the arrow sticking through, blood running down and dripping onto the deck from his left elbow.

She knew the loss of blood and length of time fighting would wear even on Zalman, and soon.

One of the militan surrounding Zalman noticed her approach, and he turned to engage her. Carys blocked his strike low, and she countered high; another elf peeled from the group to slice at her knees. She leapt over his blade and pushed towards him with her shoulder, moving inside his reach and kicking back at the first militan at the same time. Her foot connected with the first under his jaw, hearing the snap. She thrust her unforged sword under her arm and behind her into the chest of the second. In one motion, she pulled the blade from him and cut through the sword arm of the first.

Movement in the corner of her eye in the dim light, to the right, and an elven officer appeared out of the cabin above them, raising a small blade in his hand and throwing it at her.

She reacted out of desperation, ducking to the side. The officer's blade sliced her arm. Hearing a grunt of pain behind her – not Zal's grunt – she zagged back to her left and raised her sword to block another long knife coming at her.

Carys assumed the officer to be a captain, although unlike any she had ever seen. He wore a long blue tunic and steel armor, but across his chest and down his legs, knives had been strapped to him. His head was protected by an officer's helmet; the plume was made of streaks of different primary colors. It looked silly to Carys, but those knives he threw down at her were no joke.

She separated from the other battle around Zalman, only three of them now, and made herself a target for the Captain. Knocking another aside as the blade gleamed in the glow of the three moons overhead, she continued to move. The Captain had a knife in each hand, dancing across the upper deck, and he threw them both, one high and another low. She blocked one and leaned back to let the second soar by her.

Carys darted back and forth across the deck to the dead archers, dodging four more knives before reaching them. If she could just …

She bent down to grab a bow from the dead, and a knife buried itself into her left forearm. Screaming, she fell over onto a dead elf. Carys rolled, dropping her unforged sword as she grabbed the bow with her right. Another knife clattered along the wooden deck behind her. She tumbled again, reaching for an arrow with her injured left, the pain shooting up her arm and into her shoulder. Fumbling with one in a quiver that had been spilled on the deck, she missed and then gripped another. Rolling once more with a knife thudding into the deck near her right leg, she rose to her knees, nocked the arrow, and fired left handed.

The pain in her arm protested and caused her to miss wide left, but the Captain was still forced to adjust and hesitate. She fumbled for another arrow, finding one at her knee, nocked and fired again.

Wide right this time. She didn't know if she could do that one more time with the pain and now her hand covered in blood. She tried to switch hands, the bow back to her injured left, but her hand was weak and she dropped it. She was vulnerable and exposed.

While the Captain was focused on her, however, he did not notice that Zalman had dispatched the other militan, so he did not see the axe spinning towards him until the split second before it rent his shoulder from his neck in a fountain of blood. The Captain's body went rigid and his eyes wide and unfocused before falling stiff to the ground.

Carys breathed deeply, and she and her husband, both of them bloody and injured, shared a smile among the dead.

Zalman limped towards her. His thigh was sliced and bleeding. "Are you all right?"

Carys gasped as she pulled the knife from her forearm. Zalman ripped the tunic from his body and began ripping it to make bandages.

"Here." He began to wrap her forearm.

"You just wanted to a chance to get your shirt off."

"You know me too well."

Once he was done with her forearm, she reached up and put a hand on his shoulder. "Hold still." She glanced at the arrow.

Zalman nodded at her. She broke the shaft in front of the arm and pulled the arrow through as quickly and as cleanly as she could with her right arm, the uninjured one. He grunted one of his loudest grunts, and she took his bandages and wrapped the wound tight. "That's gonna need stitches." Carys pulled apart the rip in his trousers and saw the cut on his thigh. It bled a great deal. "Not too deep. I'll wrap it."

When done, they stood together, and she gathered her unforged sword. In the darkness and the mist, they couldn't see what happened on *The Last Serpent*, but it was quiet, which she hoped was a good sign.

Carys followed as Zalman walked to the stairs and ascended to the upper deck. He pulled his axe from the Captain and wiped the blade on the dead elf's tunic. "He the Peacock Captain or something?" she asked. Zal shrugged. Carys stared to her left into the cabin. "Come on. Let's check his things."

Zal walked behind her as they entered the Captain's cabin. He had to duck and crouch while in the small room. There was a table in the middle of the room with cabinets on the side. A sleeping room lay beyond. It was dim in the cabin from only a single lamp hanging from the ceiling, and papers had been strewn about in the collision. Carys began to pick them up and look through them.

"Tryin' to find something?" Zal reached up and brightened the lamp.

"Anything from the Empire, anything about the war. Help me."

She knew he could read, and he improved, but his ability was still elementary. Papers rattled and rustled. Most of the papers she saw had to do with rations and administrative tasks. Nothing too important.

"Car." She turned toward him. He held up a paper in front of him, and concern filled his face. "It's the Emperor's seal."

She raised a brow at him and took the paper from his hand. "You're right. Tanicus' seal." Then she began to read it.

Aeric filled the doorway, which she noticed out of her periphery, but she couldn't take her eyes off of the parchment.

Zalman spoke. "The other ship?"

The pirate captain pulled at the end of his beard. "We took it. Lost six men." Aeric regarded Carys. "What is that?"

"Orders from the Emperor," Zalman said.

Carys noted that high level of insight as she nodded. *Maybe his reading isn't so elementary after all.* "This is a communique from Tanicus himself to the captain of this boat, Captain Owil."

"Okay ... so?" Aeric prompted.

"So," she responded. "It says that the human revolution has taken the outpost at Taggart and that Captain Owil is to bring these orders to General Crokus in Galya to take a legion up and attack and engage Caleb while reinforcements are being sent to Asya."

"What reinforcements?" Zalman asked.

Carys lowered the paper and peered at her husband. "All of them. He's sending all of them."

It was silent there in the dim cabin for a moment.

Zalman broke it. "What does it mean?"

Carys lifted her eyes to her husband. They stared at one another for a moment. She grinned at him, sorrow pulling at her heart. "It means it's time to go back to Caleb. We have to help him."

Zalman grinned back at her, sadness touching his gaze. "Yeah."

Why did it make them sad?

Carys turned to Aeric. "I'm sorry."

Aeric lifted a hand to her. "We knew your time with us was short. Your brother needs you. We'll have Chronch take you back."

Carys bit her lip. "What are you going to do?" she asked the Pirate Lord.

Air hissed through Aeric's teeth. "Those reinforcements will need to arrive in Asya by ship. If we can surprise them …"

"You could stop the Empire before it ever reaches Caleb." She smiled at him. "Thank you."

"Of course. Tell your brother hello when you see him. I hope to meet him one day."

"Me too," Carys said.

Aeric nodded. "And you? Where will Chronch take you?"

Carys frowned. She squinted. Last the Empire knew, Caleb took Taggart. But her brother wouldn't stay there. He would move forward, attack. How to find him and help him?

"Galya," she said.

Zalman's brow furrowed. "The elves control that city."

"Yeah," Carys said. "What better way to find Caleb, though, than to follow the legion sent to kill him?"

"That's your plan?" Aeric said.

"It's a loose plan," Carys admitted and gestured around the cabin. "We've got Kryan coin, uniforms, and ships. We can walk right in."

Aeric pointed at Zalman. "He won't pass as an elf."

"He'll be my gedder prisoner." She turned to her husband.

Zalman's frown deepened. "Galya. I have bad memories of that place."

Carys cocked her head at him. That was where he fought and killed elves to get away from the slavery of the Qadi-bol games. "You saying you won't go?"

"Aeric is right. I don't hide well."

"True. You got a better idea?"

She could almost read his mind. These past ninedays on *The Last Serpent*, together in the small cabin, sailing and attacking Kryan ships with Aeric, it had been full of joy and purpose. Here he was a hero, a warrior respected by all. In Galya and Ereland, his past haunted him as a criminal and murderer.

For Carys, as much as she wanted to join Caleb, she had been her own woman here. She had brought the Pirates into the revolution. Back with Caleb, she would be his sister, overwhelmed by his large shadow. She loved Caleb, but he was a difficult man to follow.

Zalman could say, *Let's stay with Aeric*, and she might agree to it. Even though she knew it was time to return to Caleb's army, knew it in her heart, she wanted Zal to say it.

Zalman shook his head. "No. It is time."

Carys reached up and touched his cheek. "Together?"

Zalman's jaw tightened. "Always. Until the end."

.

.

CHAPTER 4

THE FIRE OF EL

Julius didn't pause when he entered the palace in Kaltiel. The guards didn't question him. He strode through the doors into the wide and opulent entry, all white stone and pristine glass with gold and silver lamps and fixtures.

He wore a simple white robe and leather sandals. His sword, custom made by a genius half-breed, hung from a black leather belt.

He climbed the winding stairs covered in red velvet up to the next landing, thirty mitres high. An elven underling in a decorated military uniform more for show than function greeted him at the top of stairs and led Julius through the halls and further into the palace.

Julius noticed the paintings and tapestries along the wall in the long hallway, all of them showing Tanicus defeating and killing the armies of men and elves and dwarves. The men and dwarves were depicted as animals, nothing more than barbaric brutes with crazed, zealous eyes, and the enemy elves were shown as legendary demic-type beings. One tapestry was the scene in which Julius, Galen, and Iletus fought and defeated the last elven *Sohan-el*. Elowen had been painted as a haggard and crazed elf, hideous in appearance and barely clothed while the Kryan Bladeguard appeared stately and heroic.

He paused for a moment before the tapestry. How different he remembered that day. It had taken all three of them with their considerable skills to beat and burn her to ash.

The burned side of Julius' face itched.

"Sir?" the First Lieutenant, his guide, called. The elf had walked ahead a few paces before realizing his charge no longer followed. The Lieutenant walked back to Julius and noticed the tapestry. "Ah, yes. The day you removed that evil elf that stood against our Emperor. I was taught about that day in school. I must say, it is an honor to meet you."

Julius did not look at the elf. "Take me to Tanicus, please."

The Lieutenant froze for a moment before bowing. "Yes, my Lord. This way."

They ascended stairs again, also covered in red velvet, and after several minutes came to another long hallway with more paintings and tapestries, but other objects hung on the wall – weapons and armor, all of polished steel.

Tall, arched doors made of gold waited at the end of the hall, and two Sunguard stood on either side of the doors in their golden armor and swords. Julius knew, however, that their swords were not their greatest weapon.

They bowed to him as he approached and opened the doors for him. The Lieutenant waited in the hallway. Julius did not acknowledge any of this. He walked through the doors into the cavernous sitting room.

While a sitting room was its function, it was larger than most homes in the Empire. The Emperor sat in a chair of blue silk and tassels, and he gazed out the wide and high windows that gave a view over the capital city of the Kryan Empire. The Emperor appeared as regal as ever.

"Welcome, my friend." Tanicus stood to face Julius. "Thank you for coming."

The doors closed behind Julius before he spoke. "You sent armed elves to my home. And you threatened my monks."

"That was not my intent. Those elves have been punished. Although they were zealous for their Emperor and their Empire. It was unfortunate but understandable."

"They were fortunate I did not kill them all."

Tanicus raised a brow. "Fortunate, yes. But you are here, nonetheless. At a request from your Emperor."

Julius spoke through his teeth. "I retired. I did my part for the Empire."

"There is more to do. I need my greatest Bladeguard."

Julius paused. "They said the *Sohan-el* have returned. I thought they died with King Judai."

"As did I. But like most religious idiots, they are difficult to kill."

Julius nodded. He possessed the scars to prove it. "I was told more than one."

"Several claim the title, but they are led by one man."

Julius walked over to the large window. "The one called the *Brendel*."

"Yes." Tanicus followed and stood next to him.

Julius peered out over the city. "And he has won a battle against a legion on the field."

Tanicus did not answer. He did not have to.

Kaltiel was a beautiful city, truly. Rows of homes and buildings of white stone and spires to the gods gave an inspiring vista against the rising sun.

"How has he done this?" Julius asked.

"He was trained by Galen."

Julius blinked and narrowed his eyes at the Emperor. "Galen?"

"He came to me with an idea. We needed to root out the final vestiges of rebellion against the Empire. The Prophet, among others, spoke lies against the necessary authority of the Empire. Galen suggested training a human as a Bladeguard and using him to infiltrate that network."

I retire and the world is even more filled with fools. "And you agreed." He gazed out over the city again.

"Galen had his own agenda. The man was sent to Ereland but instead raised up a revolution."

Galen? The Hero of the Liberation? If Galen trained this man, it explained how a human could do so much damage. "And now he has trained more and won on the field against a legion."

"He's used tricks and a healthy dose of luck. But his victories have led to other rebellions throughout the land of men and empowered my political enemies here. I am leading the army to Asya to defeat him, once and for all, and return the glory due to Kryus."

"The glory of Kryus is the faith in the gods. You call the *Brendel's* success a series of luck and tricks. But with the gods, luck does not exist. Kryus has forgotten the true worship of the gods, the true power of the Nine. I warned you of this three centuries ago. The people of this Empire worship in name only. They seek their own wealth in the name of the gods. Why should the gods help you?"

"Because I am the one they have chosen. You are one of the few who knows this."

Worldbreaker. "I do. But as their chosen one, you have allowed the faith in the gods to wane."

"The faith in the gods waned long before I arrived. I have extended the rule of order more than any in the history of Eres."

Julius met Tanicus' eyes. "That is true, and the gods have helped you, even as you have hidden your true self."

Tanicus scoffed at him. "You dare criticize your Emperor?"

"Did you ask me here for my assistance or to further stroke your ego?"

Tanicus chuckled. "I have missed you, my friend. I have. Do not worry. You and I are of the same mind. I go to Ereland not as an Emperor alone, not as a military leader, but I go to use the power the gods have given me and destroy this rebellion myself."

This surprised Julius. After years of hiding the magic he held? "Are you ready to reveal your power?"

"I am. The rumors have already begun. It will unify more men and elves against me, but it will also unify those of the true faith in the Nine. When they see the power of *Tebelrivyn*, it will inspire more to believe than ever before."

"I agree. All will know that El and the mythic Yosu are false gods, and the world will worship the Nine."

"Yes," Tanicus said. "They call me a Worldbreaker? I will break the earth from their feet. But I require your help."

Julius paused. If the Emperor had decided to reveal himself fully, after all this time, then why would he call for a retired Bladeguard? "You wish for me to kill the *Brendel*."

"No. That would only make him a martyr. We will be ready to fight him on the field, yes, but his strength comes from his ability to inspire with his lies. To beat him, we must breed division and doubt and strife within his followers." Tanicus stepped closer to Julius. "I need my greatest Bladeguard to foster betrayal within his army. If his own people will betray him, then we may not have to fight a battle at all."

Julius gritted his teeth at Tanicus. "You're afraid of him."

Tanicus sneered at the Bladeguard.

"You will have to face him, you know. I will do what I must, but if you are the chosen one, then it must be you who kills him."

The Emperor hesitated. "I understand."

"Very well. To cause division, I will need a person close to the *Brendel*."

Tanicus smiled at him, but the smile did not touch his blue eyes. "I already have someone close to him."

⊢——

Tamya spun on her heel and took the gladus from Aimi's hand with one of her blades and smacked her shield with the other. It drove her back, and the woman retreated; Tamya felt the rush within her – her heart beat faster, her skin tingled. Tamya hesitated to keep control over her body and mind, and had Aimi been better trained, she would have taken advantage of the opening. But she didn't.

Tamya recovered and kicked out Aimi's left knee. She cried out and went down. Tamya was on her in a second, her right blade on the woman's throat.

"Every time," Aimi said.

They sparred in a small paddock cleared for training on the north side of the city.

Tamya stepped away as she sat up. "You need a better grip."

"I was holding it as tight as I could!"

Tamya remembered when Caleb first began her training. It seemed like a lifetime ago. She had felt so weak.

"Not about strength alone," Tamya repeated Esai and Athelwulf's instruction word for word, two more men she had trusted and lost to the war and the elves. "It is a balance between strength and skill. Too tight and your grip is too rigid to adjust quickly. Too relaxed and you drop the sword on your own. Come here."

Aimi stood with a frown.

Tamya handed her the gladus. "Grip it."

She reached out and took it from her. "Like this?"

Tamya put her left blade in its scabbard and placed her hand on Aimi's. "Too tight." She relaxed. "No. Too much." She adjusted again. "There. Just like that."

Tamya swung quick and sure on her blade, and Aimi held it firm but not rigid. She gave Tamya a proud look.

She nodded at Aimi. "Like that. Practice like that."

"Yes ma'am."

Tamya shook her head. People still treated her like a leader in the division, even though she made it clear every time she was only a regular soldier in the army now. Aimi was new, and she had agreed to train her because she thought Aimi wouldn't have that notion. It frustrated her she was wrong.

I should have left when I had the chance, run with Hema before the battle. But I didn't. Especially now …

"Just call me Tamya. You're no slave, and I'm no leader."

"Yes, uh, Tamya."

"You've learned a lot in the last few days." She tried to be encouraging like Aden. It came out wooden and insincere.

She took it anyway. "Thank you." She looked at her shield and gladus. "Anything else?"

Dead men spoke in her mind unbidden. "Coordinate your shield and gladus attacks. Your shield isn't only for protection; it can be a weapon, as well. It takes concentration and practice to coordinate two weapons, to use them together, as one. If they don't act as one, it can make you more vulnerable."

She felt his presence at the fence of the paddock before she saw him. She forced herself not to turn. Her heart fought with joy and sorrow.

"Yes ma – I mean, yes, Tamya."

Aden spoke from the fence. "How's the training?"

Tamya turned to him, her lips tight.

"Good, I think," Aimi said. "I never held a sword before. Never allowed, you know."

"You'll be fine," Aden said. "Just listen to the training. You'll be ready by the time we leave, and I'll assign you to a platoon."

Tamya tilted her head. "We're leaving?"

"Don't know anything for sure, but Caleb's starting to get that look in his eye and talking about the next battle. Now that Javyn is here and Lyam is back and taken care of …" Aden shrugged. "We should be ready to go."

"How's Robben?" Aimi asked. Robben, Aimi's husband, trained with Aden.

Aden gave her a grin. "Doing great. He's waiting for you at lunch with the rest of the division."

Aimi glanced at Tamya, her eyes asking permission.

"Go already. Critness be, girl."

Aimi sheathed her gladus and jogged through the gate to the paddock, eager to be with her husband.

In the back of her mind, Tamya couldn't help wonder how long that joy would last. Then she looked at Aden, felt that spark in her heart she couldn't control anymore, and she wondered the same thing.

Aden measured her. "You okay?"

"I'm training her to go to battle. She could die in that battle."

"Hey. Come here."

When she first met Aden, he looked like a kid with a large nose and ears too big. Awkward. Now almost a year later, he had grown into a man in more ways than one. She was so drawn to him now. Had she changed, too? Yes, and she thought for the better.

Now her new secret would tear them apart.

Why had she allowed herself to get close again? She knew it would only end in pain.

Tamya sighed and walked over to him. She placed her other blade in its scabbard. Aden reached out his hands as she came towards him, and she hesitated before placing her hands in his.

Aden squeezed her hand. "We're in a war already. And she's decided to fight in that war, with or without you or me. Crit on it, she could have died from a cruel elven master just as easy, right?"

Tamya nodded, thinking of her mother.

"We don't know what the future holds," Aden continued. "But we can give each other the best chance we got to survive what is to come. And we can choose to fight for what is good and right with the time we got. That's what you're doing for Aimi, what I'm doing for Robben. Maybe we don't survive, but maybe we do. Not everything has to end in tragedy."

Tamya met his eyes. "Hema. Esai. Athelwulf. Xander. The Prophet. Berran. My son."

It was like she punched him in the gut with each name. She knew he was going to turn and leave her right then. She waited for it. A part of her wanted him to. Would make it easier.

But he didn't.

"Tamya." His voice was low and soft. "We ain't promised tomorrow. I only got one promise I can keep. I'm here now, today. And I'll love you as long as I can. And that's enough for me. Is it for you?"

That was his way of asking, *Will you marry me?* Over the last two ninedays in Taggart, he had asked once with the words and several times with implication. She had told him she wasn't ready at first, and that hadn't changed. Now she was glad she had said no before. It would make what she had to do soon easier.

She saw so much hope in his eyes, so much faith, so much love. She did love him, in a way that was more real than anything she had ever known. But they couldn't be together. Not now.

Should she tell him? Tamya peered into his dark eyes.

Not today.

She lowered her eyes. "I don't know."

Aden sighed, and she could feel his disappointment, like a wave. She winced.

"Okay," he said. "I need to go check on a few new recruits and then grab something to eat. You coming?"

Tamya shook her head. "You go ahead." She forced a smile. "I'll meet you later."

Aden's jaw tightened. He nodded, turned, and left her there.

Tears filled Tamya's eyes as she watched him go, the man she loved. As he strode into the distance and rounded a building, Tamya's head swiveled to make sure she was alone.

She was.

Tamya lifted her right hand, palm up. She could feel the water in the mud beneath her, the moisture in the air. She closed her eyes, and she moved the water from the mud. Drops lifted from the dirt underneath her and gathered in a ball of water over her palm. The sphere of clear water hovered there.

She took a breath of relief, so exhausted holding it back over the last few days.

It had started two ninedays ago, the awareness of every drop of water around her, then the desire to manipulate it. Then came the need, like her body lurched to act and use the magic within her.

Magic. She knew what Aden and the scriptures said about it. *Tebelrivyn.* It broke the world and drove the wizards and witches mad. It was a part of her. How could she deny it? How could she stop it? Change it?

She couldn't.

Their enemy, the Emperor, was a Worldbreaker. Their greatest enemy. She was like him. Tainted. Corrupted. Hopeless.

She moved the tears from her eyes and her cheeks, pulled them with her mind and gathered them with the sphere of water on her palm. The sphere grew.

Tamya thought of Aden. Caleb's right hand man. A believer. A *Sohan-el.* Her opposite.

She could never be with him.

With a remaining sob, she let the ball of water fall and splash to the dirt at her feet.

Caleb walked south through Taggart with the Kingstaff in his right hand and a wooden box in his left. He greeted men and women through the hot summer afternoon. Beads of sweat formed on his brow, and he wiped it with the back of his hand. He approached the last building on the left and the small pen of sheep next to it.

The building was a type of barn, a makeshift structure that had once been a house but was now a large storage area for feed and shearing instruments with a small room in the back. Also along the southern wall of the city were other pens for cows and pigs and even one for two oxen.

Earon stood out among the sheep. Drenched in sweat, he examined them, separated them.

Caleb hadn't spoken with Earon since arriving in Taggart. He gave Eshlyn the task of finding Earon a place to stay and a job to do. Caleb didn't know if that was the right thing or not; he only knew anger and sorrow every time he saw his cousin. Earon stayed away from everyone, and everyone stayed away from him. And Caleb had wanted it that way.

But the revolution needed Earon. He had been raised by the Prophet, and despite their conflict and Earon's betrayal, he knew the *Fyrwrit* and the testimony better than anyone alive. Earon's redemption would entail something other than caring for animals, as noble as that proved to be.

Earon would understand that redemption today.

Earon noticed him and paused, a concerned frown on his face. Caleb stopped and leaned against a post.

Earon set aside one sheep, marking it with a ribbon on the right foreleg. Then he sighed, brushed his hands on his sweat-stained pants, and walked towards Caleb.

"Those few need to be sheared soon," Earon said. "I'll do it in the morning, I think. I'll also need to take them out to graze tomorrow." He seemed both resigned and anxious.

"Will you need help?" Caleb heard the awkwardness in his own voice.

"Been doing it all by myself until now. I can handle it."

Caleb gripped the Kingstaff.

"What can I help you with, Caleb?"

Caleb met the man's light brown eyes. Even though he was a couple years older, his short dark hair and lanky appearance made him seem younger. Eshlyn had told Caleb of how they found him, strung out on ale and Sorcos, looking half dead. Breaking him of that addiction with better food and working in the sun had made a difference. He looked like Caleb's cousin again. And that gave Caleb's heart joy and pain.

Caleb stood straight. "Walk with me." He turned and moved to the east.

Earon hesitated before climbing over the fence and following. Caleb led them down the narrow dirt street with the city wall to their right.

"You spoke to me once of Athelwulf and his convictions on redemption," Caleb began.

"He had some experience with addiction to Sorcos and … problems with his father." Earon was silent for a moment. "He knew something of returning to El and trying to reconcile his rebellion, forgetting the past and moving forward."

"He never told me his story. I know Carys loved him and thought highly of him, though."

They walked past more buildings, the dust forming around their ankles in the heat.

"You heard from her?" Earon asked. "Carys?"

Caleb shook his head. They were silent for a few minutes until they reached the eastern wall.

"Athelwulf returned to El and found his place, his role, in the fight for freedom and taking care of other people." Caleb veered to his left and continued along the wall. "He even helped you overcome your addiction, correct?"

"He did."

They reached the stairs to the top of the wall, and Caleb ascended with Earon at his heels. Caleb reached the wall-walk and the battlements and looked out to the east. The sun shone behind them and threw the shadows of the city across the road and the plains to the east.

Earon stood next to him on the wall-walk.

Caleb took a breath. "You know, better than anyone, what the revolution is trying to accomplish. You were there, like I was, and more, to hear your father's words and ideas, his vision. It is good that you've returned to us to face the consequences of what you've done. You've beaten the addictions. But that isn't the redemption El has in mind for you. It is only the first step."

Caleb lifted the box in his hand and set it on the parapet. Earon frowned at the box.

"Your father gave his life for this revolution. It cost him his wife." Caleb gripped the Kingstaff tighter. "His son. It cost him his life. In this fight for freedom for all men, it has cost many of us here the same. Many have willingly given their lives for others. Athelwulf was one of those. Carys is out there, now, doing who knows what and where, giving her life."

Caleb leaned toward Earon and tapped on the wooden box with his left hand. "The question I have for you, Earon, is this. Are you ready to join the revolution? Are you ready to be truly redeemed? Are you ready to do the thing you were born and trained to do?"

Earon couldn't take his eyes off of the dark stained wooden box. "What is in the box, Caleb?"

Caleb opened it. The lid swung up on hinges. He reached inside and grabbed a long, leather cord and lifted. At the end of the cord was a golden medallion. A head of a dragon was carved into the face of the medallion.

Earon's eyes widened. "The Dracolet."

"After rescuing your father from the Pyts, we sailed to Galya. Even in his weakened state, he made us go to the hidden room underneath where the old temple had been burned and destroyed. He had hidden his translation of the testimony and the scriptures, this Kingstaff, and the Dracolet. He wanted me to have the Kingstaff. The books he gave to Aden. And this ..." Caleb extended it.

Earon reached out and took the medallion, gazing down at it in awe. "He found it. He actually found it."

"Yes. He did. When people began to lose faith and trust in their own strength, the dragons retreated from the world. The *Sohan-el* who lived during that time forged this for their return. For Johann's prophecy. It has been passed down from warrior to warrior until Uncle Reyan found it and gave it to me."

"Who ..." Earon swallowed. "Who did he say this was for?"

"He didn't. But he gave it to me to hold. I have always felt it was for you."

Earon took a deep breath. "*Unbelief will grow, and because of the great fall, the dragons will disappear from the world. But El will not forget them. Humanity will bring back the Sohan-el, and all races will unite in faith as a sign that the dragons of El will return, and the fire will be reborn.*"

"You know it well."

"I've been reading it a lot lately. After Aden gave me Xander's copy of the *Fyrwrit*."

"You have?" Caleb allowed himself a grin. "What about the prophecy, the *Isael*? Do you believe it to refer to one person or two?"

"I know what my father believed. That the words in the original were odd, like they could be man or woman or both. Were the words simply bad grammar? Or were they a reference to a pair? My father believed it was intentional, a reference to a pair."

"And you?"

"As with any prophecy, it could mean anything, really. But after studying it over the last few weeks, I think he was right."

"So do I. And I believe you and Carys were meant to fulfill the prophecy."

Earon looked up at him and furrowed his brow. "You do?"

"I do. All the pieces fall into place, one prophecy after another, and we are all connected. The way I found Carys, the way Eshlyn found you, the way you've both returned to the fight, it all makes sense."

"But Carys isn't here."

"I've been thinking about that. The dragons served the *Sohan-el*."

"Correct."

"Carys has been to the Stone. You have not. She hasn't returned yet but this gives you time to make the journey yourself, to go to the Stone and receive your own unforged sword. I could send one of the other *Sohan-el* with you. Or you could begin your training and go with Carys when she does get back. Once you are both *Sohan-el*, then you can go together."

"Sounds like you've got it all worked out."

"Like you, this has been on my mind."

Earon blew a long breath from his cheeks. "When I was young, I thought about the dragons. I dreamed about them. Were they real? Were they symbols of something? If they were real, what would it be like to find them, to ride them like the *Sohan-el* of old?"

Caleb smiled, and his heart began to fill with hope. "You can."

Earon shook his head and handed the Dracolet back to Caleb, who almost dropped it in surprise when it hit his hand.

"But it's not me. I'm not a part of the *Isael*."

Caleb closed his gaping mouth. "The war will only get worse from here. Tanicus will bring weapons and armies like we've never seen. We need the dragons. It is time."

"I'm not saying you're wrong about that." Earon shifted his feet but met Caleb's eyes. "You're right. If those dragons exist, it is time we find them and they join the fight, as well. It might save thousands of lives. And you're right about me. It is time I do more than hide on the outskirts of the city and take care of animals.

"But I'm no warrior, not like you are, not like you're training people here to be. I've seen too much violence already. That isn't my path. I don't know what it is yet, but not this."

"I don't understand. I thought ..."

"You know why I've been reading the prophecy, studying it?"

Caleb couldn't answer. His smile was gone. His heart despaired.

"Because I met him."

Caleb's eyes narrowed. "What?"

"There is someone here, now, that you don't have to train. You don't have to wait for him. He's ready. Consider what he's done. He's been the redemption and redeemed so much around him, literally. And it's not me. But I know who it is. And I think you know who it is, too."

Caleb stared at Earon for a moment, and he put his hand, holding the Dracolet, down on the hilt of his unforged sword. Caleb lowered his eyes when the name entered his mind, and his heart fell.

"Break me."

Because he knew. Maybe he'd always known.

CHAPTER 5

GALYA

Carys stood at the bow of the yacht. Chronch deftly sailed the boat in between elven warships and merchant vessels towards the docks of Galya. It was early evening, the sun setting in a clear sky to the west.

She wore a long blue tunic with tan trousers and black leather sandals. The dented steel armor over her torso and shoulders sported a captain's insignia. At her side, the unforged sword hung in the scabbard made by Bweth Ironhorn. A satchel with money and papers was slung over her shoulder, and she held a braided whip in her right hand. An officer's helmet with a plume of different colors covered her ears.

Carys had decided that drawing attention might be the best way to hide.

Zalman hovered on the deck of the yacht behind her. She glanced back at him. "You've been even more quiet than usual."

"This isn't going to work." He peered down at the eagle tattoo on his wrist, marking him as a slave. In the heat, he wore only a pair of trousers torn at the knees and a hooded gray poncho. The hood was over his eyes. A pack that included his battleaxes sat on the deck next to him.

Carys sniffed. They had this conversation several times before. He was well known with elves and humans as a Qadi-bol player in Galya. He worried he would be recognized.

"You haven't been here in years," she told him for the fifth time. "And who knows who is left from those days?" Between the war and troop movements, even among the Cityguard, many or all of the experienced and competent militan would be busy or gone. She hoped.

He had preferred to try and sneak in the city another way, to land somewhere to the south and work their way into the city. But Carys felt the gates would be even more restricted and difficult to sneak into. As a compromise, she had let him talk her out of sailing the warship to the docks. But she would have liked to try it, though.

Making their way through the warships with militan staring down at her, Carys did her best to look stately and condescending.

I'm an elf, a captain, and above them. Don't hunch your shoulders. Don't look too rigid!

The yacht bumped a short dock, and three men, shirtless and tattooed like Zalman, eyed her but caught the rope and tied them to a post. The dockmaster, an elf, walked up with a grimace and a whip in his hand.

Zalman stiffened behind her, but she didn't turn or acknowledge him at first. By now, after all they'd been through, the sight of slaves angered both of them, and with his history, she could only imagine his fury. With a slight glimpse back, rolling eyes like he annoyed her, she saw his fists clench and unclench. *Don't give us away here at the dock and try to save these slaves, please.*

She stepped off the yacht in the twilight, and he followed her, lumbering with a submissive posture, carrying the thick pack. She breathed deep and relaxed.

The dockmaster barked at the two slaves, one with dark skin from Lior and the other with lighter skin from somewhere in Erelon. "You better have that tied down like it should be for the Captain or there's a beating for you." He brandished the whip for emphasis, and Carys' hand rested on her unforged sword, wondering if she would be the one that killed the dockmaster and ruined it all.

Zalman grunted at her, a type of rebuke; she did not pull her sword, however. She stood straight and tall as she could on the dock.

The dockmaster turned to her. "Sorry for their incompetence, Captain, but they are men, after all."

She flashed a look of disgust at the men. "We cannot expect too much from them."

"Yes, of course," the dockmaster said. "Normally, I wouldn't do this, you understand, but with the war and the rebellion, I must ask you for your papers."

"I do understand, Master ..."

"Waylus, my lord. Dockmaster Waylus."

She opened the satchel at her waist and ruffled through the papers. "Your family is the Irius line, from the north, correct?" The Irius line was a major house with elves in positions all over the empire, and a large house. Lesser members of the family were often assigned to Ereland in places where bribes were common – like dockmasters. And with his obvious north Kryan accent, Carys had made a guess.

"No, my lord, don't I wish. A lesser house. One you wouldn't know." But he took the guess as a compliment.

Carys produced a parchment, written by her hand, as meticulous as she could manage. They had used the seal in the captain's cabin to make it look as official as possible. The seal stamp was also in the satchel. She handed it to the dockmaster.

He gave a slight bow as he received it. "Ah, I see you are the captain of *The Free Eagle*, a warship. Captain Fylan."

"It was a cruiser, actually," Carys sighed in frustration. "We were attacked by pirates in the southern sea."

Waylus lifted a brow at her. "I have heard that has been happening more and more." He glanced at the yacht and Chronch. "You were sunk?"

She pushed out her chest. "We gave as good as we got, Dockmaster. Three pirate ships attacked us and we sunk all three before we went down."

"Well done," Waylus said. "For Kryus!"

She raised a fist in a salute. "Yes, indeed." She lowered her hand. "I commandeered this merchant yacht and came to give a report."

"I see." The Dockmaster handed her the parchment. "Your papers seem to be in order." He eyed the pack next to Zalman. "I only need to check your pack."

She frowned at him. "If my papers are in order, then why do you need to search my things?"

"Policy, Captain. I apologize."

Carys reached down into the satchel and produced another parchment. She allowed the dockmaster to see the seal of the Emperor on the bottom of the page. No more. "As I said, my errand is urgent. We have wasted too much time already. I am to get this communique to the Steward of Galya as soon as possible. He was expecting me more than a ninedays ago."

She also put three golden suns in his hand.

Waylus' eyes bulged for a moment at the seal, and then he smiled at the gold. "I'm sorry, Captain. Please, make your way to the Steward with all haste. May I call a coach for you?"

"No thank you, Master." She placed the parchment with the Emperor's seal on it in the satchel. "I believe we are done, here."

"Yes, of course, my lord." Waylus pocketed the golden suns. He turned to the slaves. "You fools! Why are you standing there? You see the boat arriving on the next dock? Are you blind?" They bowed and ran back down the dock towards the city and another boat. Waylus followed them with the whip at their back.

Zalman grunted behind her and picked up the pack.

"I know," she said, her own heart cold and sick with anger. She turned to Chronch, who had been back on the deck but now stood against the railing of his yacht. "Chronch." She smiled at him and grabbed a handful of coin from the satchel and placed it in his hand, discreetly. "Thank you."

Chronch frowned at her. "Look, I didn't do this for money."

"Yes, I know. And I don't mean to offend you, but please take it. Go back to the pirates with our blessing or to Landen. We have more than we need here, and it would help me to know you had it if you needed it."

After a long moment, he nodded and put the money in his pocket. He regarded her with tears in his eyes. "Thank you, Carys. If you see your brother ..."

"I will tell him the truth." Tears threatened her own. "That the man who tried to kill him a year ago is now a man of honor and integrity, that without him we would have surely died and the pirates would not be a part of the revolution now." She wanted to reach out and touch him, embrace him goodbye, but she could not here, not in the open. Not dressed like an elven peacock. "We owe you our lives. If you ever need of anything, you only need to ask."

"Anything," Zalman agreed, and she thought she heard a catch in his throat. *Big gedder, if I look at you and you're gonna cry, I can't keep it together.*

"Your friendship is all I require," Chronch said. "Thank you."

Carys sniffed. "Come," she said to Zalman. "We gotta go."

Zalman nodded and moved down the dock, his head lowered. With a last look at Chronch, she closed her satchel and walked down the dock towards the city.

Carys clenched her teeth and moved to lead Zalman, and he shuffled behind her. They reached the end of the dock and joined the bustle of people moving to the gate. The guard at the gate were not Cityguard, they were militan with long spears, searching the crowd for any who didn't belong. The guard narrowed their eyes at her and her colorful plume, but they allowed them to pass without incident.

Once through the gate, the streets of Galya opened up to them. Lamps were being lit along the main road through the city. It had been years since Carys had been in Galya – she had been in her early teens – but she remembered the way to the Steward's palace, which was to the northeastern part of the city, the wealthy region.

When the crowd cleared on the street after a few blocks, Carys whispered, "I told you it would work."

"Fine. It worked. Let's find an inn in the tenements."

"An elf wouldn't go there," she hissed over her shoulder at him.

"But more chance people will recognize me near the palace."

His fans. "Keep your hood up and don't worry about it." They took a right on the next major thoroughfare. She could see the palace up ahead of them, towering over the other buildings.

The city of Galya did not have one central square, as Asya did, but five spread around the city in a circular pattern. Each square had a large fountain and statue at its center and were generally dedicated to serve one of the major economies – the Food Square, the Animal Square, the Garment Square, the Banking Square, and the Lumber Square. The main streets of Galya led to these squares and between them. The current street they walked led to the Garment Square, where Carys knew Ezmelda, Reyan's contact, would be … if she were still alive.

She tried to scan the men and women and elves along the way without being obvious.

Up ahead under a streetlamp a few militan officers sat at a small table drinking ale. One of them, while laughing, caught sight of her and froze. He was a male and his uniform was neat and his armor shone. The insignia declared him a major.

She kept walking, her eyes darting away and watching him from her periphery.

He followed her with his stare. She could feel Zal tense behind her, his breathing quickening. The major held a hand to stay the conversation at his small table with the two other officers.

Carys kept walking.

As they passed the officers, the Major stood, his eyes narrowing. The other elves – junior officers, it seemed – rose with him. Now three officers looked at them.

The Major moved around the table. "Captain? Captain Fylan?"

"We have to run," Zalman whispered.

"No," she said. "Keep going."

They were past the Major now. "Captain Fylan!" It sounded like an order. "You! Halt!"

She ignored it. If she reacted, they would be in trouble. Well, they were already in trouble.

The Major jogged towards them. She heard his feet slap against the dirt of the street. He darted in front of them, the two lieutenants with him, and stood in their way.

Carys brought up short.

The Major frowned at them. "I know one elf who wears that helmet. Captain Fylan of *The Free Eagle*. And you're not him."

His hand lashed out and grabbed the helmet off of her head. She tried to dodge it, but he was fast. The helmet fell off her head to the ground, and even through her long blond hair they could tell she did not have elf ears.

They gasped, angry. Zalman stood to his full height, a shadow over them all in the twilight. The elves froze.

Carys kicked out at the Major's knee. The snap of broken bone echoed in the street. He cried out, and as the other lieutenants started to react, Zalman slung the pack from his shoulder and knocked one of the lieutenants three mitres across the dirt of the street. The other lieutenant cried out as Zalman's elbow connected with his face. After the crunch, the elf collapsed.

Carys kicked the Major again in the face, putting him down.

Screaming in the street, voices yelling at them, and figures began to move towards them, many of them militan.

Zalman sneered at the bodies around them. "Now we run?"

"Now we run," she said through her teeth. "But where?"

"Follow me. I know one place. But you're not going to like it."

And he ran off to their left, away from the wealthy quarter of the city. *No. No, I probably won't.*

CHAPTER 6

DREAMS OF FIRE

Caleb sat at the desk in his small room. He didn't feel as if it were his own; the small room had belonged to the General he had beaten on the field at the Acar.

I'm not enough for the path in front of me. I'm no general. I can't inspire.

But somehow the army continued to grow in spite of his deficiencies. His only comfort was that he did not work alone. However, he kept watching those people, the people he loved the most, leave him for their role in the revolution.

It might happen again today.

While small and simple, it was a nice room on the third floor. The bed was comfortable, and the desk sat next to a wide window that allowed sun in through most of the day. Even now, the early afternoon sun shone across his desk, papers strewn about with numbers all over them. He didn't know why he tried to keep up with how many people were part of his army. The numbers kept changing.

In the middle of his desk, a leather bound notebook rested, open, and his pen was in his hand. On the corner of the desk was a stack of heavy and thick books. A stained, wooden box waited on the other corner.

The knock came at his door. He dried the pen on a cloth and closed the ink bottle. "Come."

Aden opened the door and walked inside. "You said you wanted to see me?"

"I did. Close the door. Come and sit."

Aden pulled a wooden chair from near the bed and placed it across from Caleb at the desk. He pointed at the notebook, the drying ink, as he sat. "What are you writing?"

Leaving the notebook open, Caleb set it aside, behind one of the large stacks of books. "Something I'm working on, for later."

"Ah." He eyed the books. The young man loved books. "Where did you find these?"

"Belonged to General Pyram, part of his personal library."

Aden perused the bindings. "*Kryan Legion Strategy. History of the War of Liberation. A Discussion on Troop Movement and Resources.* Wow. Light and fun, huh?"

Caleb chuckled. "Yeah. Interesting and important, as long as I remember they come from an elven perspective." He stared at Aden. "But that's not why I asked you to come in."

Aden noted the serious tone in his voice, and his brow furrowed. "Okay."

Caleb pointed at the wooden box. "You remember that?"

"To the sure. Reyan gave it to you when we were near Galya."

"Yes, he did. The Dracolet. You know what this is?"

Aden steepled his fingers. "From what I've read, Yosu gave the first *Sohan-el* charge of a race of dragons. They fought with the *Sohan-el* against evil and kept the peace. But faith waned, and since faith is the power of the dragon, they left the world, somewhere to the north beyond the Geddai. The Dracolet was forged then. Maybe to give access to the dragons or control them."

"Very good."

"Some say the Dracolet had supernatural power. Others that it was just a myth."

"Until it was found by Reyan. And there is a prophecy ..."

Aden grinned. "There's always a prophecy, right? When the faith of humanity returned, the dragons would come back with the *Sohan-el*." His face grew serious. "Wait. You think they are real?"

"Wasn't the Underworld real? The demics? The Stone? We saw dead water come to life again. Are dragons that much of a stretch? After all we've seen?"

Aden shook his head and looked at the box. "I guess not. So you think that it is time we went to find these dragons?"

"I believe we're going to need them. We beat a legion on the field, and El helped us with that, but Tanicus is about to send everything he's got against us. He has to. And he's a Worldbreaker. I'm going to run this army all the way to Asya before he can muster his resources, but I don't know if it will be enough."

"The dragons were supposed to help the faithful at a moment of greatest need. I get it. But who? Who is going to go find these dragons?"

"I talked to Earon already."

Aden's face fell. "Yeah. That makes sense. I mean, if Reyan was the *Arendel*, and you're the *Brendel*, and the *Sohan-el* are back, then Earon makes sense. All in the family and everything. You always thought it would be Earon and Carys."

"I did. But Earon refused."

"What?"

"He disagreed that he was the one."

"Yeah, but almost all the scholars agree that first comes the *Arendel*, then the *Brendel*, then the *Isael*, and finally the *Dae'Grael*. The messenger, the sword, the fire, and the dawn. And if the dragons are real and not some myth, then it makes sense that the *Isael* would be next."

"It does, but Earon thought it should go to someone else. And I think he's right."

Aden froze, and his face went blank. "Who?" he whispered.

Caleb opened the box. The hinge creaked. He stood and pulled the medallion from the box by the leather cord. He extended it to Aden.

Aden's jaw tightened and his eyes grew misty. He reached out and gently took the Dracolet from Caleb.

"Unbelief will grow, and because of the great fall, the dragons will disappear from the world. But El will not forget them. Humanity will bring back the Sohan-el, and all races will unite in faith as a sign that the dragons of El will return, and the fire will be reborn."

He knows it by heart. "Reyan told me, several times, that you had your own destiny, your own path apart from mine."

Aden peered at the Dracolet.

"You are the story of human redemption. You were an orphan but found your father in El. You showed me that it was not the training and skill El was looking for but the heart. You changed the dead water at the Acar to living water, water that brought life. Aden, you are the *Isael.*"

"I've been having dreams. Dreams of fire and ice, death and life. It's different every night, but they seem so real."

Caleb leaned against the desk. "I'm sorry I didn't see it earlier."

Aden wiped his face and placed a hand on his unforged sword. "It is true. I didn't know how true it was until this moment, until I held it in my hand. But it is."

"I know."

Aden met Caleb's eyes. "This scares the crit out of me. I feel like I'm supposed to do this, but I don't know if I can."

Caleb gave him a sad grin. "I know."

"Wait a minute," Aden said and gripped the Dracolet. "You and Reyan thought it was supposed to be two, and a lot of the scholars agree. You thought it was supposed to be Earon and Carys. Two."

"Yes," Caleb agreed.

"But what about me? If I'm supposed to go, then who goes with me?" He lowered his gaze to the Dracolet.

"I don't know. Maybe we are wrong about the interpretation. Maybe it is only supposed to be one person. Maybe you should wait for Carys, but now that we know, can we afford to wait anymore? I can't tell you for sure. Prophecy is funny. But if it's supposed to be two, then maybe ..."

Aden groaned. "But she's not a *Sohan-el.*"

Caleb shrugged. "And you weren't trained before you went to the Stone with me. Maybe you can take her anyway."

Aden ran a hand through his hair. "I don't want to leave her. But does that mean she's supposed to go? Just because I ...?"

Love her, he didn't finish. "I'm sorry. But it's your decision. Let me know what you decide."

Aden gazed at the Dracolet for a moment. He lifted it and placed the leather cord around his neck, and the golden amulet hung over his heart. Like it was made for him.

"I will."

—

"Where are we going?" They didn't need any more attention.

They made another right turn through a narrow alley – Zal had to turn sideways – and then wove left at the next street.

The streets were dark here in the southeast corner of the city, a poorer area, and Carys winced as they passed an unpleasant scent – a combination of death and rot and crit. She had been young the last time in Galya, the main ghetto was further to the east and the River Docks to the south.

Avoiding the major squares, they had lost the militan two or three alleys ago, and now Zalman headed south towards the River Docks.

The River Docks were an odd place. The elves controlled the Ocean Docks, as they had experienced earlier in the day, and security was strict and the trade vigorous. The River Docks were a place for humans; many were poor but free and contracted their labor out to the elves along the river. With a more lax security, many humans smuggled and haggled with each other on the river, and that meant violence and gangs. Uncle Reyan brought them in through the River Docks years ago, but they did not stay there. He had considered it too dangerous.

"Are you trying to get us out of the city already?" Her wary stare focused on the shadows and figures around them.

"No." His heavy feet plodded on the dirt street. "Too many who would turn us in for money or kill us ... as soon as word gets out."

Carys spoke through her panting. "Then where?"

He did not answer right away. "... a friend's."

That doesn't tell me crit.

Four blocks away from the River Docks, Zalman led her to the right at the intersection, his head on a swivel. The street now cobbled, he moved to the right, in the shadows under the awnings and doorways of the buildings there. He slowed, continuing on the balls of his feet, and while Carys felt relief at the change of pace, she was skeptical.

He paused and looked up at the sign above him, sighing. *The Beauty and the Bed*, the sign read in faded red paint over a depiction of a feminine form with a miniscule waist and mountainous bosom laying over a long bed or couch.

"A shoghouse! You brought us to a shoghouse?"

Zalman spun on her with his brow furrowed. "You have a better idea?"

She snarled at him. "We need to find Ezzy, Reyan's contact here."

"Fine. You know where she is? If she's still alive?"

She didn't answer.

"Look. This is the safest place. The ladies here will hide us, help us."

"Ladies?" she scoffed. "And they'll help us, all right, for money."

"Wasn't that long ago I wasn't any different."

"Yeah, and I hated you then, too."

"You want to know about the city? They know better than anyone."

She raised a brow at him. "They know you here?"

He pursed his lips and nodded.

"I don't want to go in there."

"Me neither. Not what I want you to see." He scanned the dark street for effect. "But we need off the street."

Her eyes bored into his. She despised his logic and their immediate need. He was right. Those militan were still out there, looking for them. Carys waved him forward in surrender. He turned and walked the few paces toward the main door under the sign.

Fool man doesn't even look happy he won.

Zalman paused at a tall wooden door painted with flowers entwined with female naked bodies. A rectangular panel was cut about eye level, which came to Zalman's chest. He rolled his shoulders and gripped his pack to his chest. He knocked on the door.

A faint shuffling sound came from the other side of the door, and the panel swung away. A dark skinned woman with heavy paint around her eyes peered from behind the door. "How may we please you tonight?"

Zalman crouched and showed his face. "Trayci."

Trayci cursed and slammed the panel shut.

Carys chuckled. "They do know you ..."

Zalman frowned at her and then leaned closer to the door. "Trayci. Let us in. Please. We need your help."

The panel slowly swung open again. "Help you? Like you helped me?"

"I'm sorry. Please. Militan are looking for us."

Her painted eyes narrowed. "A familiar position for you to be in, I assume."

Carys pushed her way in front of Zalman and stood on her tiptoes. "We have money. And we just need a place to stay tonight."

"We are not an inn," Trayci said.

Zalman leaned on the door. "Trayci."

Carys did not like the way he said that woman's name.

Trayci cursed and closed the panel. Then the door opened to a tall and beautiful woman standing in a long, silken green dress. Carys almost cowered before her, like the woman was a queen. But Carys made sure her back stayed straight.

"Hurry," Trayci said. "Before I change my mind."

Zalman grunted and went through the door, Carys on his heels. The door closed behind them, and Carys followed Zalman into a large lobby with couches and pillows of different colors and patterns. Large drapes and tapestries covered the walls. Carys saw the scenes depicted on the tapestries, men and women in naked and passionate embraces; she blushed and gritted her teeth. Women sat or lounged on the chairs, five women in all from different parts of the world of humans – another dark skinned Liorian, two Veraden with light brown skin, and two lighter skinned women from Erelon.

The whole room stared at Zalman with tension, a mixture of anger and fear. Zalman rested his heavy pack at his feet as he stood in the middle of them. He nodded to the room. "Ladies."

Carys stood next to him.

Trayci stood at the transition from the hallway to the lobby. "Tell me what you're doing here before I send for the Cityguard."

Zalman faced her. "We had a run-in with militan near Ocean. We need off the street."

"And this was the only place you could think of?"

"The only place that might not turn us in," he admitted.

Trayci snorted, her eyes intent on them both. "So you just need a place to stay?"

He gave her a curt nod. "For the night."

She raised a brow at them. "And that is all?"

Zalman scanned the room, at all the eyes peering at them. "No."

"I thought not. I've been reading men's desires for a decade."

Carys clenched her fists.

"Need information," Zalman said. "There's a contact in the city we need to reach … and anything about the militan."

Trayci chuckled but glared. "A tall order, as usual."

Carys had enough. She stepped in between Trayci and Zalman. "You going to help us or not? Or just make breakin' eyes at us?"

Trayci turned her smirk on Carys. "And who are you?"

"I'm his wife."

Zalman grunted like he was in pain.

A couple of the women laughed, but Trayci's smirk disappeared. Trayci recovered quickly, her face blank and then a smile more painted on than the thick makeup on her face. Carys thought she could see the calculation within the woman. It made her nervous.

"The infamous Zalman has been tamed. Well, congratulations are in order, then." Another pause. "You have money?"

"We do," Carys said.

"Very well." Trayci waved at one of the women. "Rosa, they will stay in your room, and you will pay Rosa for a full night."

Zalman nodded. "Fair."

"Do not speak to me of fair, Zalman," Trayci spat. "Rosa will show you to your room. We will meet in my room later. Stay in your room and quiet. I have a business to run here."

Rosa, one of the Veraden women, short and petite, nodded and rose from her seat to lead them back to her room. Carys and Zalman followed her through the dark hallway and past rooms to the right and the left, all closed doors. Carys could hear moaning and creaking from a couple of the rooms. She knew how to gut a man with a sword but not how to keep her face from feeling hot.

Rosa stopped at the last door on the left, opened the door and showed them inside. The room was small but big enough for a high bed and two chairs and a dresser. Rosa eyed the two of them. "Stay here until Trayci sends for you." She closed the door behind her.

Zalman hunched his shoulders and went to the bed. He placed his pack next to the bed.

Carys frowned at him. "How well did you know that woman?"

He pulled his axes from his pack. "Well enough."

"You want to tell me exactly *why* she's so piffed at you?"

Zalman ran a hand over his bald head and didn't answer. He only shook his head.

"Shoggers," Carys said as she walked around to the other side of the bed with her own pack and away from him.

Chapter 7

Promises

The knock came to Tamya's door, and her heart sunk.

She sat on the edge of her bed, waiting, dreading this moment. She closed her eyes and wished it didn't need to come.

Then he knocked again. She felt him there, impossible but true.

"Tamya?"

She tried to deepen her shallow breaths, the ones that threatened to become sobs. She found the strength to say, "Come."

Aden opened the door. He stepped into the dim room, lit only by a candle next to the bed. A bowl of water for washing sat next to it. The wooden door creaked as he closed it behind him. His brow creased as he looked at her, and she met his eyes for a split second. Then she tore her gaze away.

His voice carried caution. "Hey."

"Hey."

Aden took another step toward her. "I ... have something to tell you."

"I heard. You're leaving."

Aden chuckled, a nervous sound. It reminded her of the unsure boy she met a year ago. "News travels fast, I guess."

He took another step toward her. He reached under his tunic and drew out a golden amulet with a dragon carved into it. "Caleb gave this to me. It's supposed to help find the dragons." He shrugged. "Help me find the dragons." He was next to her all of a sudden, and she groaned. "Help us find the dragons."

"Aden ..."

He sat next to her on the bed. "I need you, Tamya. I need you to come with me, help me find these dragons and bring them into the revolution."

"You don't need me, Aden. You never have."

Aden blinked. "What?"

"You don't need me. You've got all you need. And anyway, I'm not a leader anymore. I'm not a *Sohan-el*."

Aden scooted closer to her. "But that's the thing. It doesn't matter. Caleb reminded me that I wasn't supposed to go along to the Living Stone with him, but I did anyway. And it's the same with you. El looks at the heart." He put his hand on her arm. She closed her eyes at his touch, how much she wanted it. "And I'm telling you, you have the heart of a warrior, of a *Sohan-el*."

Tamya pulled her arm away from him. "You don't know what you're saying."

"Of course I do. I was there. I went to the Stone with Caleb. Just like you can go with me."

"There's a difference."

"What's that?"

She turned and stared into his eyes. Her own began to mist. "You chose to go. You wanted to go. I'm saying no."

Aden scowled and leaned away from her, like he tried to get a better angle, to see her better. "What?"

"I'm telling you that I won't go with you. I can't."

"What do you mean you can't?"

Tamya sighed. "You don't want me to come with you. Just trust me."

"But that's maddy. I do want you."

"No you don't."

Aden stood, moved away. "I don't understand. Are you afraid? I thought we ..."

"I'm not afraid. But you don't want someone like me with you. Not on a mission like this."

"What are you saying?"

"I'm ... tainted."

He lifted his hands in a question. "Tainted?"

Tamya sat up straight. She lifted her hand, palm up, and she focused on the washbowl of water next to her bed.

The water stirred. Aden froze.

A column of liquid rose from the bowl, and Aden's breath caught. The water from the bowl curved over to her hand, and it hovered there as she formed it into a large sphere.

"Holy El," Aden whispered.

"I started to feel it a few ninedays ago, before we came to Taggart and after you healed the Acar." She played with the sphere of water, spinning it, rolling it. "I didn't know what it was at first." She cleared her throat. "But then I did."

He opened his mouth but closed it again.

"I am part elf, you know," she continued. "And my ... father ... he was one of the high families. Centuries ago, those who could work magic used it to gain power, become those high families. So ... it makes sense."

Aden looked at her for a long time. His dark eyes searched her, made her feel vulnerable and uncomfortable. He placed his hand on his unforged sword.

He shook his head. "I don't care. I don't know how, but we're going to figure this out. I still want you to come with me."

"But I don't know how to stop this." She glanced at the hovering sphere of water. "I can't have you worried about me while we go search for breakin' dragons."

And that part of him that she loved and frustrated the crit out of her surfaced. His face hardened. His eyes steeled. That part of him that always believed against hope. "Tamya. El will help us. Come with me."

Tamya lowered her gaze. "No, Aden."

Aden growled. "But you have to. I need you."

"No, you don't. And are you going to make me? Force me to go with you?"

Disgust covered his face. "No. I would never …"

"Then go. Get ready and go."

"Tamya, please …"

Tamya stood and threw the ball of water against the wall with her magic. It splashed, and Aden flinched.

"Go," she said. "Get out."

Now tears fell from his eyes and ran down his face.

She wanted to manipulate those tears. "Go! Leave!"

Aden shifted his weight, like a fighter, like a warrior, and he set his jaw. He reached out to her.

She swatted his hand away. "Get out of my room, Aden."

Aden sniffed and backed away. With a last glance, he opened the door and left, slamming it behind him.

Tamya walked over and placed both of her hands on the door. She set her forehead against the wood.

———

Caleb stood on the wall of Taggart, looking to the east, leaning on the ramparts with the unforged sword at his hip and the Kingstaff at his side. The late evening sky hid the three moons of Eres with dark clouds.

Creaks on the stairs up to the wall-walk. The walk, gait, the way her feet sounded on the wooden steps. *Eshlyn.*

All of her haunted him, and he thought of her often when he closed his eyes, those precious moments when the blood and violence and death did not wait for him there in the night.

"He's leaving tomorow," Eshlyn said.

He didn't turn to face her. "He is."

"And Tamya is going with him, right?"

Caleb shook his head.

Eshlyn stood next to him now and leaned in close. "Wait. You're not letting her go with him?"

His brow creased. "That's not it. I told Aden it was his decision and he asked her."

"Then why?" She squinted at him. "She said no."

"She did."

"But why? I thought she …"

Loved him. "She probably does. But there's another problem." He faced her. "She's developed *tebelrivyn*."

Eshlyn cocked her head at him. "Magic."

"Yes."

"Oh, Tamya."

"So she said no. She couldn't go with him. Not while she dealt with that."

Her face grew pained. She turned and stared out to the east, as well.

"It's probably for the best," Caleb said.

"What?"

"I know they want to be together, but he's going north into dangerous ground to look for dragons. Might be best if he goes alone, not get close. Less sorrow that way."

She scowled. "Do you really believe that? Do you?" Her nostrils flared. "Do you really believe that we should keep from getting close to people … to avoid some sorrow that *might* happen in the future?"

"I don't know. Maybe." He stood straight. "And *might* happen? We are in a war. When Tanicus arrives, we'll face armies of trodall and flocks of griders and more. I know what I'm running towards, Eshlyn. I know what it will cost me. There will be enough pain without adding to it."

"How can you live with that fatalistic attitude?"

Because I'm tired, and I know that at the end, I'll be able to rest. When this revolution finally takes my life. "El helps me."

She scoffed at him, looking into his eyes and reading him like a prop poster that he hid deeper truths. And he saw the love in her eyes, the judgment and the longing within them, as well. He tore his eyes away.

It took her a few moments to speak. "If I find a way for Tamya to go, will you allow it?"

"Like I said, it's not my decision. But no, I won't stand in the way."

"Good," she grunted at him.

She turned and marched away.

CHAPTER 8

THE BATTLE OF THERON OCEAN

Three hours before dawn, Zalman sat awake when the door opened and Rosa stood there. This was her room, and she frowned at them. "We are closed for the night. Trayci will now see you in the lobby." She stood aside.

Zalman sat in a wooden chair in the corner as Carys – quiet and brooding – sat across the room. Zalman should have spoken to her, but he didn't know what to say. Not here with memories in every corner.

Zalman rose and exited the room, Carys behind him. They made their way down the corridor to the lobby.

How did he get back here? He had left this city years ago in a whirlwind of violence and blood. Many never understood his convictions; he had fame and women, more than anyone could want. Yet he had been just as much a slave of the elves and their power as the workers in that hell of the mines. Other humans would have killed for his position, but he killed to be rid of it.

His solution hadn't been to confront the corrupt system around him. He never wanted to be a revolutionary. So he had run. He ran as far as he could to Ketan, a place where he could forget his past and his past could forget him.

Somehow, his choices had led him right back here, even back to *The Beauty and the Bed* and to Trayci. Had he really thought that working with Caleb, traveling and loving Carys, he would escape his past? He should have known better. His sins followed him, as they do. Given his options, should he have kept running after the Battle of Ketan?

He could have gone anywhere. He could have gone south into Manahem and helped rebuild one of those small and obscure towns destroyed by the demics, become some sort of hermit. Why didn't he?

Zalman peered over at Carys and sighed. *Shoggit.* He had been inspired by Caleb and an idea of freedom that sought the freedom of others instead of for one's own pleasure. And in the process, his heart had been bound to this strong young woman unlike any he had ever known. And he had known more than a few.

Along the path, people changed and understood the reality of El and the faith Caleb taught. How could he not be inspired?

The greatest miracle? Carys had learned to love him.

But all of that had brought him back here, to his shame, to the disappointment on her face, and a part of him wished for that ignorance once again. An ignorance where he could live with himself if he ran away.

Two lamps shone near Trayci as she sat on one of the couches. She gestured to another couch. "Sit. Please."

Zalman nodded at her and sat. Resting on the far end of the couch, Carys didn't speak or look at him.

Trayci regarded Zalman. "It has been a long time, Zalman. You remember the last time you were here, I assume."

Carys shot him a look. He preferred when she looked away.

"I do, and I am sorry."

"Are you? I wonder."

Carys glanced at the both of them. "Sorry for what?"

"Oh, your husband has not told you what happened here in Galya the night he left us?"

Carys glared at her. "He told me he escaped from the elven guard, killed them."

"Did he tell you how?"

Carys shook her head, slow.

Zalman wanted to stop Trayci. As big and strong as he was, he never felt more helpless.

"Allow me to tell the story, will you?" Trayci's voice dripped with bitterness. She leaned forward on her couch.

"Zalman was the star of the city, the great Qadi-bol player, the greatest there ever was, some said. As the star player he was, he made a lot of money for the elves who owned the team. They did all they could to satisfy his every desire, which primarily included ale and women."

Trayci stared at him. Zalman's jaw tightened.

"Galya is known for many things," Trayci continued. "It is a city of art and peace. We never even fought the elves, you know. After the fall of Asya, we opened our gates to them, proclaiming them the liberators they said they were. Galya, rich in trade and diversity, is also known for one other thing," she waved at the lobby, "the women of pleasure. Zalman took full advantage of all the pleasure houses in the city. But he always came back to this one."

Trayci paused. Carys clasped her hands in her lap.

"He always came back to me," Trayci said. "He talked to me of his thoughts, his feelings, and as he grew more disenchanted with the sport that gave him every pleasure, we spoke of escaping. Together.

"One of the advantages of being a woman of pleasure is that our guild deals in something far more valuable than sex. We deal in secrets. It is a dangerous business, but we must survive using the weapons we possess. I knew Zal's secret, that he was going to leave. I told him I woud help him if he took me with him.

"I arranged it all. I knew the least guarded gate that night. I drugged the guard, both of them, after they were served by my ladies. He killed them, doing his part. I waited here for him. But he never came."

Zalman shook his head. "I was wrong. Confused. I'm sorry."

Her eyes narrowed at him. "They questioned me for days, for a month. They have ways of hurting you that don't show on your skin, you know."

How many different times could he say he was sorry? How could it mean anything now? "No excuses. I only ask your forgiveness."

"But you are here for more than forgiveness, are you not?" Trayci said. "You are here for my help, to use me once again."

Carys cleared her throat. "We do need you. That is true. My question, though, is this …" Carys shot Zalman another look, hesitating, then addressed Trayci. "Why did you take us in, help us? For that matter, why haven't you called for the Cityguard or the militan? Zal did you wrong, I get it. Why aren't we in the prisons?"

It took a moment before Trayci responded. "She's a strong one, isn't she?"

Zal grunted assent.

Trayci took a breath. "As I said before, we deal in secrets and information. We hear rumors, but we do not believe all we hear. We must confirm it, have more than a simple word spoken in the throes. Men," she glowered at Zalman, "do not always say what is true.

"Over the past month, we have heard things. We have paid close attention to any rumors of the revolution from the west, anything about this *Brendel* character, and information about what is happening in other cities like Landen and the land of Lior. One rumor caught my attention – a large man who took out a crime lord in Landen. As the Pirates of the south have been more active, even more reports of a man fighting with two axes and defeating the Seahawk.

"I had the thought, perhaps, that this was our Zalman. But I was not sure. The Zalman I knew was no revolutionary." She met his eyes. "Are you? Now? Are you connected with this *Brendel* and the revolution out of the west?"

He wanted to look away but didn't. "I am."

"You went west when you left to Ketan, didn't you?"

Zalman nodded.

"And you've met him."

Carys scowled at her. "He breakin' married his sister."

Trayci's eyes bulged for a second. "By the nine gods, Zalman. You have joined a cause bigger than you."

Carys leaned forward. "You still haven't answered my question. You're dealing in secrets instead. Why are you helping us instead of turning us in? Especially since the gedder wronged you."

Trayci turned to Carys. "Because it is time the revolution came to Galya," Trayci said. "Now that I know who you are, it is we who need your help."

"Shoggers." Carys rolled her eyes.

"I hate the elves, which Zalman knows. That's why he brought you here, despite his betrayal."

Carys raised a brow. "You're part of some sort of resistance here?"

"More than that." Her voice lowered. "I am the resistance here."

"Since when?" Zalman asked.

"When word came of a free Ketan, free of the elves, I began to reach out to those I knew were already part of the underground resistance here."

Carys bit her lip. "My uncle Reyan had a contact here. Ezmelda."

Trayci hesitated. "The haberdasher."

"Yes," Carys said. "You know where she is?"

Trayci's shoulders slumped. "Ezmy is dead."

Carys bent over, and she groaned. Zalman placed his hand on her shoulder for comfort, and she pushed his hand away.

"I'm sorry to tell you," Trayci said. "The Empire rooted out who they could over the winter. They brought in a Moonguard and people began to disappear. Ezmelda was one of the first."

Zalman's gaze lingered on Carys. "Have many disappeared?"

Tracy sniffed. "Many, some of whom were not a part of the resistance at all. But the Empire takes no chances. One of the people who have disappeared … was one of my girls. Last week. Janny. They may suspect me, suspect us all."

Zalman ran a hand over his head. "And you want us to protect you?"

"I want you to find Janny, if she is still alive. We've found the building where the Moonguard are operating. But we are not warriors. It is well guarded."

Carys sat up and squinted at Trayci. "You say you deal in secrets. What do you know about a legion that arrived here recently and is about to move north?"

Trayci held her hands before her. "A legion did arrive here, two days ago. They rested, but from last I heard, they have not been used as reinforcements with the militan and Cityguard. They could leave at any time."

"Then we don't have time for this," Carys said. "I'm sorry, but we need to help Caleb. That legion could leave at any time. We need to find a way out of the city."

"The gates and docks are watched, closely. It will be difficult for you to get out."

Carys squinted at her. "Let me guess. You can get us out."

"I could."

"But for a price," Carys muttered through a clenched jaw. She turned to Zalman. "See? All for a cost."

Trayci's composure slipped, just for a split second. "I don't need money. The only thing I ask is that you save my Jeany."

"*Your* Janny." Zalman shifted his weight on the couch. "Who is she to you?"

Trayci lowered her eyes. "Janny ... is my daughter."

Zalman's breath caught. "A daughter?"

Trayci glared up at him. "You think you knew everything about me?"

Carys snorted. "Your daughter? And she's one of your *girls*?"

Trayci whirled on Carys. "Don't you dare judge me. What do you know of my life here? We do what we do to survive, to find some advantage in a world designed to oppress us. I protected her as much as I could, but she went to meet with a contact and got taken."

Zalman's heart sank. "And that night, when you wanted me to take you with me ..."

"Yes," Trayci admitted. "My daughter was waiting near the western gate for us."

Zalman cursed and rubbed the top of his bald head.

"How old is she?" Carys asked.

"She is seventeen."

"They will come for you if she talks," Zalman said.

"Which is yet another reason to save her." Trayci's glare faded. "Please."

Carys growled. "We don't have time for this."

"Maybe not," Zalman agreed. "But ... what was the vow of the *Sohan-el*?"

"Don't you do that." Carys snarled. "You shoggin' gedder!"

He didn't say it. He knew it as well as her.

Before Light of El, the hand of Yosu, and the witness of the Living, I dedicate my soul, my heart, and my life to defend the innocent, free the oppressed, and spread light in dark places.

"You decide, then." Zalman kept his voice calm. "Whether we help."

Carys closed her eyes and put her hand on the sword at her side. Her face fell, and she looked away from him.

"Fine." She turned to Trayci. "You know where she is?"

"I do."

Carys sighed. "You'll show us this building tomorrow."

"Yes." Trayci stood and straightened her skirt. "Get some rest. You are safe here for now."

Carys rose. "One more thing." She pulled a golden sun out of her pouch and handed it to Trayci. "I want a room by myself. This may not be an inn, but I'm not staying with that gedder."

Trayci stuttered. "Very well … you may have the room across the hall from Rosa's room. It belongs to Maris."

Carys left the lobby.

Zalman rolled his shoulders, the tension running through his whole body as he watched her go. "Are you happy now?"

"Happy? Me? Oh, dear Zalman, I haven't been happy since before the day my parents sold me into the slavery of this life. I made the best of it, but I haven't been happy for twenty years."

—+—

Tamya stood on the road outside the gate to the west of the city. The guards watched her, but she didn't pay them any attention. Unable to sleep, she gazed out to the west, a few hours before dawn.

I should leave. I can't help what I am. I can't stop the madness that will come the more I give myself over to the power that seduces me all the time. Draws me. I should leave.

The Forest of Saten rustled far to the south. She had spent time there with Athelwulf, found Hema there. She could live there again. But no. The Ghosts wouldn't want someone like her around.

Tamya gazed to the north. She could go beyond what used to be the Acar, the Living Water, and live in the bush and forests there. No one lived there. No one for miles. She would be all alone. No one would find her there. She couldn't hurt anyone there.

So why haven't I left?

I'm a coward.

"There you are."

Startled, she spun to see Eshlyn standing ten paces behind.

"Lady?"

Eshlyn approached her. "Been looking all over for you. For hours now."

"Y-you need me for something? Something happen?" Something with Aden?

"No." Eshlyn stood next to her. "But I think you need me."

Tamya frowned at her. "Lady?"

Eshlyn nodded to the west. "You going somewhere?"

Tamya glanced over her shoulder. "I think it's for the best."

"Your choice, but I think you should go."

Tamya's stomach tightened. "You heard, then. You know."

"News does travel fast. At least with friends who care, it does."

"Then you're right. I know. I should go."

"You should go, I agree. You should go pack so you can go with Aden."

Tamya scoffed. "You, too? I thought you said you knew. I'm tainted. Corrupted. I can do magic, Lady Eshlyn. I can't go with Aden. Or stay here."

"I understand. But I think I may have a solution. If you'll humor me."

Tamya stood stiff. "A solution?"

"To the sure." She took another step. They stood close. Eshlyn pulled the sword from the sheath at her hip. Then she handed it to Tamya, hilt first.

"A sword?"

"Not just any sword. Xander's unforged sword."

Her brother. Tamya stared down at the blade. It seemed to glow in the light of the moons.

"This sword is connected to the Everworld, to El. I don't pretend to understand it all, but I know it speaks. It leads. It guides. It directs. And it can do amazing things."

Tamya reached out but didn't touch it.

"El is about redemption, right? He helped Athelwulf with power over addiction. Why couldn't El help with this, too?" Eshlyn shrugged. "You don't have to believe me, but when I couldn't find you, I asked the sword to help and it brought me here." Eshlyn leaned down and caught Tamya's eyes. "Take it. Don't be limited by what your father or mother gave you. Maybe El wants to make you more than that."

Tamya looked down to the sword then back at Eshlyn. The woman waited.

Tamya reached out and took the sword in her hands.

And she was transported to another place.

From dark to light, bright light, warm sun all around her. She stood in the midst of a garden with trees and vines. In front of her, she could see a large gray stone with steel veins all through it, and a tree grew out of the stone. Branches spread out over a pond.

The Living Stone.

A man walked from the far side of the Stone. His face shone so she couldn't make out the features, but he wore a simple, common gray robe.

"Tamya." He spoke her name as if he had waited for her, longed for her. "Come closer."

He stood on the other side of the pond.

"Are you …?" She couldn't say the name, but it appeared in her mind.

Yosu.

"Is this … a dream?" she asked.

"You are in a place more real than any place you have ever been before. And yet not as real as what lies beyond."

"But how did I get here?"

"You took the sword."

"The sword?"

"Each unforged sword was born here, made of the material of this place but its power comes from the place beyond."

"The place beyond ... the Everworld?"

"When you took the sword, you took the first step."

"To what?"

"To why I chose you."

"You chose me?"

"Of course." His smile was warm. "You must take one more step."

"More?"

The walked into the pond. "Come closer."

Tamya swallowed, hesitated. But what could she do? She had to see, had to know. She waded into the pond. The cool water came up to her knees. The braches above swayed like a lullaby.

The man reached out his hand. She took it. Comfort filled her. The light from his face almost blinded her.

"You must go with Aden." His voice came to her ears, her heart, her mind. "He will need you. But you must not be afraid. If you hold on to me, there is no power that can overcome you. Not your fear or pain. Not any magic of your world. Hold on to the sword and to me and you will be part of the redemption of this world."

And he was right. In this place, she didn't even have the desire to use magic. She hadn't thought about it at all. She felt peace. Joy.

His other hand touched her cheek, like a husband and father and brother all at once. "Do you trust me?"

She didn't trust herself to speak. She could only nod.

His smile widened.

Then he grabbed her shoulders and plunged her into the water.

The ships sailed silent and dark before sunrise under the cover of a thin, rolling fog. Aeric knew even a sunrise could have a mind of its own, but he relied upon it for the element of surprise.

Aeric surveyed the ocean to the northeast. Bade stood next to him on the deck of *The Last Serpent*. "We are close."

Bade only nodded, as nervous as Aeric was this far north of the Theron Ocean.

Since seeing the missive on the elven ship a ninedays ago, Aeric had been busy. His doves had been sent to every pirate lord, all of them operating in the south. They, in answer to Aeric's summons, sent doves to their own ships. They had gathered and sailed north as one, hoping to intercept the fleet sailing with tens of thousands of militan and weapons and creatures to the land of humanity to crush Caleb's rebellion.

Aeric lowered the peerglass from his eye and glanced to his right through the dark to the shadow of *The Titan Song*, Mikayla's ship. He prayed to Carys' god for her as they prepared for battle.

His crew knelt or stood at the ready for his command. They held bows with arrows ready to be lit for flame; they quietly tightened the winches on the ballista and the catapults, loaded and also waiting for a spark to bring their destruction.

Aeric did not know the size of the Kryan fleet they were about to encounter. The doves could give approximate position – a coordinating calculation based on distance and time for the doves and their return – but they could not give numbers.

The pirate archers had shot down Kryan pigeons over the last few days; the Empire checked for other ships in the area, as well. Some of Aeric's doves had not returned, and how many of the Kryan pigeons did they miss that returned to warn the Empire? He didn't know.

"Aeric," Bade mumbled to him.

Aeric turned his attention to his second, and the man gestured towards the front of *The Last Serpent*. The man there held the position Carys did just a few days ago. To be true, he missed the young woman and the large man. He knew he would miss them even more in the coming battle. Their presence would have given him some comfort. But the man there now, Neidal, also possessed a hawk's vision; he had been trained by Carys and was a more than competent archer.

Neidal gave the signal. He had seen the fleet.

Aeric took a deep breath and looked up at the sky. Dawn was close. Nodding back at Neidal, he raised his own peerglass in the direction Neidal pointed. First, he saw shadows. Really, one long shadow like a dragon with ridges riding the waves. As they neared, he saw more distinct shadows, ship after ship after ship. The caravan of ships did not seem to end. He could see distinct flickering lights, only a few, and drawing another hundred mitres closer, he got a better idea of the number of ships.

More than a hundred, easily, perhaps 150 large cargo vessels, well armed. And Aeric's pirate fleet? Forty-seven ships, only sixteen of them as large and imposing as the ones he saw before him.

Aeric gripped the peerglass. "Well, we've found a mouthful of crit now, haven't we?"

Bade noted the Kryan fleet and also cursed.

Aeric's heart sank. A part of him wondered if they could turn around now, retreat before they engaged. He didn't think it was cowardice, but it didn't matter. They wouldn't be able to turn in time. They were sailing at top speed. Surprise with a full attack was their only strategy, the only way they would be able to survive.

With a glance at Mikayla's ship, he drew his sword and raised it above his head. He didn't have to look at his crew to know they were ready. He narrowed his eyes at the Kryan fleet. He sucked in a breath, lowered his arm, and roared his command.

"Fire!"

———

Julius woke from his bunk on the ship to a sound of screaming and yelling. It was pitch dark in his room. He rolled to his feet, the boat rocking underneath him, adjusting course. In a second, he blinked, fully awake, and reached out in the dark for his robe. He pulled it on and strapped his sword to his waist. Barefooted, he opened the door to his small room on the ship and darted into the narrow corridor that led to a ladder leading up onto the deck.

As he crested the top of the ladder to the deck of *The Crown of Gods*, he paused. It was like they had sailed into the myths of the Underland.

Balls of fire arced through the dark sky. Long spears from ballista tore into ships. Arrows rained down upon them. They were under attack from the south.

He leapt up onto the deck, elves running past him, hurrying to their posts. To his left, he could see several ships already on fire, dozens of them, sinking, among them the large battle cruisers *The Ocean Throne* and *The God of Death*.

Julius placed his hand on his sword, and looked up at the quarterdeck. Tanicus, the High Lord of Kryus, stood and gripped the railing in a long white robe with High General Felix behind him. Felix, to his credit, shouted orders while the Admiral of *The Crown of Gods* relayed them. Tanicus stood with bulging, angry eyes as he stared at his fleet being destroyed. Two Sunguard dressed in their golden armor stood next to him.

Julius bared his teeth and pushed his way through desperate elves to the quarterdeck. He ran up the stairs, two at a time, and ignored the commanding voices of Felix and the Admiral to stand next to Tanicus.

"Julius." Tanicus scanned the dozens of ships to the south, a ragtag group, several of them large ships, but others of different sizes, even a few no more than a yacht.

Julius bowed to his Emperor. "My Lord."

"We are turning to engage," Tanicus said. "The General is moving us to surround and kill them all. But we will lose too many ships that way."

Julius glanced again at the battle before him. All the Kryan ships were caught unawares, this early, this dark; all their weapons needed to be turned and adjusted to even have a chance. Thirty ships burned with fire and a few of them sinking.

"Yes, my Lord." Julius worked the strategy in his mind. We will win but at great cost, perhaps half the fleet.

Tanicus scowled at him. "You were correct in Kaltiel. I see that now. Rebellion in every city. And the pirates join the fight. Now is the time to show them all they do not deal with an elf. They deal with a god."

"Yes, my Lord."

The Emperor's ice blue eyes blazed with desire. Tanicus stared at him for a few more moments; their eyes locked. Fire bloomed against the hull of *The Crown of Gods*, and Tanicus blinked.

The eastern horizon grew lighter with the coming of the sun. The contrast between the darkness of the sky one moment to the orange glow was breathtaking. It looked like the eastern ocean was suddenly aflame.

Tanicus grinned at him, but his eyes were wild. "The world will worship the nine gods again, Julius."

Looking like the Emperor he was, Tanicus stood taller somehow, and walked to the edge of the quarterdeck to his left. Julius followed. Tanicus raised his arms. His long blond hair flowed in the ocean breeze. The Emperor's eyes slowly turned black like onyx.

The wind grew stronger around them and contained a foul odor. It smelled like death.

—+—

"Holy depths," Bade said to Aeric on the quarterdeck of *The Last Serpent*. "We're winning this breakin' battle."

The tip of the sun peeked over the eastern horizon and bathed the battle in new light.

Aeric agreed. The Kryan ships were large, all of them, and in a direct conflict, the pirates wouldn't have had a chance. But they were so big, they could not turn well. The ships attempted the turn, though, which ruined their ability to adjust their own weapons. Ballista missiles and arrows and balls from catapults went far wide or beyond or short of the pirate ships.

The pirates had sunk eleven ships so far while others were aflame or severely damaged, perhaps thirty more. Within minutes, Aeric had taken almost a third of the Kryan fleet from the battle without a scratch to his own vessel.

The wind began to pick up, the sails of *The Last Serpent* snapping in the new force. Aeric turned to Bade and saw the same twisted face he possessed. "What is that stench?"

Bade shook his head with a further grimace.

The explosion to his left was unlike anything Aeric had ever seen or heard, like the air itself was a drum. In shock, he covered his ears and crouched, and he spun to look in that direction. A column of water a hundred mitres thick launched from the ocean and ripped *The Island*

Maiden, one of the pirate lord ships, in half. Screams of men and the sound of ripping wood followed the sight a second later.

Aeric's jaw dropped. He had no way to understand what had just happened, and before his mind could be forced to react, another column of water, even larger this time, shot into the air and consumed another three smaller ships.

Shaking free from his shock, he put his peerglass to his eye. In the newborn light of the dawn, a tall and beautiful elf with long blond hair wirling around him stood on the deck of the lead ship. The elf had crazed eyes. Smiling. The elf struck the air with his right hand, and another column of water emerged and capsized *The Angra* and *The Godshark,* two large pirate ships. They sank under the enormous wave and were gone in a bevy of froth and violence.

"What in the name of El." He lowered the peerglass. "Turn around! Retreat!"

That woke Bade from his own daze, and he moved, shouting orders, and other of the crew responded, although a handful stood agape at the terror before them.

Chaos and confusion reigned around him, but he turned to his right. *Mikayla.*

Aeric's breathing was quick and his heart pounded in his chest as he raced to the side of the quarterdeck. More waves lifted high into the orange sky to smash down onto ships. The distant screams of dying men were silenced almost as soon as they begun. He ignored it all, his heart heavy within him now, and he peered over at *The Titan Song.*

He was thankful for the dawn light as he saw his wife – her dark skin and long, wild dark hair, the tattoos on her face and arms – gazing back at him. Their eyes met over the distance. She smiled at him, but it was a sad, resigned smile. Aeric gasped a sob as he reached out for her.

Dark and sinister, a mountain of a wave rose from the ocean and loomed over *The Titan Song* and consumed his beautiful and strong Mikayla in shadow.

"No," he said once more, but it was the most helpless word he could have afforded.

The wall of water crashed down and broke *The Titan Song* into a dozen pieces, dragging his wife down into the cold depths.

Tears rolling down his cheeks, Aeric bent over the side of his ship and roared.

In the churning water below, he saw thousands of fish and men floating, dead.

The foul wind whipped around him, and *The Last Serpent* began to spin, slowly at first. The ocean foamed as a current formed around the ship. Aeric gripped the railing, and he looked up as men fell and rolled across the deck, searching for some purchase. Hopeless. The water around *The Last Serpent* lifted and the ship sunk as the whirlpool gained strength and speed.

Aeric hooked his elbow around the railing, his abdomen aching from the effort. Wind and water roared, and he knew his men had open mouths in screams, but they could not be heard above the maelstrom. The water around them, dirty and black, caused the sky to grow dim as it hovered over the ship.

Aeric looked up in awe as the ocean he loved, which was his life, came slamming down upon him and his ship.

———

The water to the south heaved and groaned as it recovered from the violence.

Julius coughed at the thick stench around them. He watched birds fall from the sky, dead, upon the surface and the decks of the ships that remained. Thousands of fish dead in the water – and hundreds of men. The ocean was the color of mud and blood.

He looked over to Tanicus, and the Emperor panted from the effort. His eyes were blue again, but they were wild, mad eyes. Tanicus lowered his arms and leaned against the railing of the ship.

Julius glanced behind him. The Admiral, High General Felix, the officers and the militan, they all stood frozen and in awe. Terror bathed their faces.

Tanicus took a deep breath and gathered himself. He moved, slowly, and turned to face the elves around him.

"The men who rebel against the Empire claim their single god deigns to help them. They know nothing about gods."

The air began to clear as a breeze blew through. The yellow sun was now half visible above the oceans horizon.

Tanicus' voice rose. "We elves, we are the masters of the gods. And they have given me their power to go and fight the deception and lies of this *Brendel* and his so-called god. You have seen that power today."

The elves did not move.

Tanicus eyed Julius for a moment before surveying the elves gathering on the deck of *The God Throne*.

"The faith of Kryus has been weak." His words boomed across the deck and the sea. "The gods have allowed this rebellion, to test us, to show us how we must worship the gods again. Will you serve the gods with me and crush this rebellion in the land of Eres? Will you fight to show the true power of the Nine Gods?"

Elves nodded. And then a militan sank to his knees. Others quickly followed. Once the Admiral and the High General dropped to their knees, every elf was on the deck, bowing before their Emperor in the name of the gods.

Julius was last. He bowed at the waist and found himself on one knee next to the Emperor.

Tanicus smiled. "Thank you. In the name of the gods, I accept your service. Obey me and you shall see what great miracles the gods will show you … and the world!"

And the elves cheered.

CHAPTER 9

BEYOND THE HORIZON

The sky was a bright color for the dawn. Aden led his horse, Petraus, through the quiet streets of Taggart, as Caleb walked beside him.

Caleb held out the map in front of him. "There is a road that leads north and then northeast past Lake Razael. It once went to the Gedai cities but they were long gone by the time the elves came. Road hasn't been used in centuries, probably. Follow it if you can."

Aden didn't answer. He gazed off to the north.

"Once you get to Lake Razael, though, there isn't a road. You may find a path here and there, but as you see, you'll head northeast to Lake Kalaya and then straight north up through the Virenda Plains. At that point, you'll be on your own."

I'm on my own anyway. He gazed at the large and leather map, the best they could find, and it only led them beyond the tundra. Into the northern nothing.

Caleb folded the map and handed it over. Aden placed it in the satchel at his side.

They walked along the main road that led to the north gate. Within mitres of it now, a crowd had gathered outside the walls, waiting for him.

Caleb cleared his throat. "They all want to say goodbye."

Aden knew it to be true, and he should have been comforted. But all he felt was empty.

"Before we go out there," Caleb said as they continued to walk. "I wanted to tell you that ... well, I'm proud of you. Proud to call you friend."

Aden raised a brow at him.

"Even though I don't want you to go ... to be honest, I can't think of anyone better for this job. You've become the very definition of a *Sohan-el*. El is with you."

He's right. I'm not alone. El is with me.

Aden wiped his sleeve across his nose and stopped ten mitres from the gate. "Caleb, you changed my life. I owe you everything." He turned to the *Brendel*.

Caleb chuckled. "I couldn't stop you. I don't know that I did much. You would have found your way to El one way or another. But thank you."

The two men embraced.

They parted, and Caleb said, "Come. They're waiting."

Caleb and Aden walked through the gate; thousands of people, a large portion of the population of Taggart, stood and stared at them. Aden forced a smile at them, feeling a very real burden on his shoulders, the weight of need of a whole revolution. Without El, he would have felt hopeless.

Then the crowd parted. Aden frowned at their movements, but after they cleared the way, there on the road stood Tamya.

She held the reins of a horse and a bulging pack behind the saddle. Eshlyn stood to her right, and Bweth stood to her left. Eshlyn wore a satisfied look.

Caleb scoffed and continued to walk forward. Aden followed. They came within a few paces and stopped.

Caleb looked at Eshlyn. "You did this?"

Eshlyn smirked at him.

Aden locked gazes with Tamya. "I don't understand ..."

"Not sure I do, either." Tamya glanced at Eshlyn. Then she put her hand on the sword at her hip.

One sword. Not two. Wait, that is a ...

Tamya stepped closer. "It's Xander's sword. Lady Eshlyn gave it to me." Her face brightened and beamed. "When I wear it, when I touch it, well, I still feel the magic but it's like an echo, like it has no power."

Aden barked a laugh that he couldn't contain, and he moved to hold her hands.

Tamya leaned up, and their foreheads touched. "So I'm coming with you ... if you'll have me."

Then she kissed him. It was almost painful as she pressed her mouth to his. He moaned in surprise but threw his arms around her and lifted her. Her arms went around his neck, his shoulders, and she pulled him in tight.

His heart laughed.

Aden set her down.

Eshlyn and Bweth stood nearby now.

Bweth snorted. "Okay. Ain't got all day, you know. I got something for you, too."

Aden and Tamya stood and regarded Bweth.

Bweth reached into the pouch at her side and pulled out a golden marriage bracelet. "Your lady here had me make this for her. She and Eshlyn came to me in the middle of the night and woke me up. Not even a sorry or nothin', just a hurry up and get it done." She handed it to Aden. "Put it on her wrist 'lready so I can go catch up on me sleep."

He looked from the bracelet to Tamya. "Are you sure about this?"

"Yes. I am."

Aden undid the clasp and then placed it on her wrist. He looked around at Eshlyn, Caleb, Bweth, the crowd around them. "That's it?"

Eshlyn beamed. "Kiss her, young man, and yes, that's it."

"Yes, ma'am." He gladly obliged.

—+—

With his hands behind his back, Caleb stood next to Eshlyn. "You were busy last night." Aden and Tamya rode horses more than a kilomitre to the north.

The goodbyes had taken a couple hours – the Beorgai wanted to sing a few of their traditional songs about marriage. The people from Manahem and Ketan circled and did a wedding dance. Caleb couldn't keep his eyes from Eshlyn through the ceremony. Bweth finally began to push people away from Aden and Tamya, forced the newlyweds on their horses and whipped them down the road north herself.

The men and women of the *Hamon-el* walked back through the gate into the city with full hearts. Only Caleb and Eshlyn remained. Aden and Tamya shrinking on the horizon.

"To the sure." She yawned. "I'll get some good sleep tonight."

Caleb gestured at the diminishing newlyweds. "Don't think they will."

"You stop." But she smiled.

"You're pleased with yourself."

Eshlyn huffed at him. "Don't pretend you didn't enjoy that. I saw you tap your foot during that Beorgai wedding song."

"Can't deny it. Especially liked that dirge about the death of a single man."

She groaned at him. "Always the pessimist."

His grin faded. "No. I actually think that maybe their end will be happy after all."

"Aren't we all promised a joyful end if we follow El?"

He thought about Reyan and Galen and others. "In the next life, yes. But in this life? No promises." He sniffed at the air. "Those two will have to cross leagues of frozen tundra to climb mountains of ice to get to a land no one thinks really exists. And yet, I think our road is about to be the dangerous one."

She gave him a blank look. "What do you mean?"

"Lyam and others leave tomorrow. After that, we will organize and move the army further east."

"Asya."

"Yes." He gripped his hands tight behind his back. "The end of our story will be in Asya. No use waiting any longer."

—+—

"She's going to betray us," Carys whispered to Zalman.

They made their way across the city, moving through side streets wide of the Lumber Square. They followed a few paces behind Trayci, and while she whispered, Carys didn't really care if the woman heard her.

All three of them wore cloaks and hoods, which was ridiculous to Carys. Either way, Zalman was large enough to get noticed. Their only advantage was the through back alleys and poorer streets where others hid from the Cityguard, as well.

They moved toward the middle of the city, where the five main roads met ... and the location of the Steward's palace and the Temple of the Nine. Trayci led them directly into the elven stronghold of the city. And it made Carys nervous.

Zalman grunted. "She has no love for the elves. Never has."

"I'm not saying she loves the elves. I'd be surprised if the elves love themselves. But she might love money enough."

Zalman shook his head at her.

"Shoggers, Zal. She shogs people for money."

Zal's heavy feet echoed in the alley. "You trusted Pirates."

"This is different."

"How?"

Because you had a history with her. A close, intimate one. Was he a different man now? Yes. But for some reason, she couldn't trust his mind on Trayci. And with the look of guilt and shame upon her husband's face, he knew.

Trayci stopped at an intersection up ahead, and they slowed. Zalman loomed over Trayci's shoulder, and Carys snorted at having to look around the side of her.

An enormous square sat where the five main roads intersected, and a fountain roared in the middle of the square. Statues of elves in heroic poses loomed in the fountain and water shot from their hands high into the air.

"There." Trayci pointed past the fountain. "That's the place."

Carys gazed over at the building. It was on the north side of the central intersection with towers that reached into the sky made of white stone and pure glass.

"The breakin' Temple of the Nine Gods," Carys said. "You want us to attack the Temple of the Nine Gods?"

Zalman lowered his head.

Trayci stepped back into the alley. "My sources tell me that is where they have taken the people who have disappeared. The Moonguard operate in a subterranean room."

"There are, like," Carys did a quick count, "twenty Cityguard at the entrance to the Temple compound. And a wall. There's a wall around the compound. Who knows how many we'll have to deal with once we get inside or how to get to this crittin' basement."

"I can get you some of those details," Trayci said. "But you are correct, we do not know for sure what is inside."

Carys stepped back, as well. "Shoggers. Once we get inside, then we have to deal with a Moonguard. From what I've heard, those elves are maddy as you can get. They made the trodoll and trained the griders."

Trayci remained quiet and still, gazing at the Temple.

Carys took a breath. "And they perverted their own kind by making the Deathguard. You ever heard of them? I heard stories of those like to make you scream just thinking about them, like the dragonmen come to life."

"That is true." A tear escaped Trayci's painted eye.

Carys squinted and cursed. *Not much comfort to a mother. Even if she does shog people for money.*

Zalman gave her a sharp look.

"I know, I know. The vow. But don't we have a responsibility to warn Caleb about this legion coming to flank him?"

"Caleb can take care of himself."

She couldn't argue with that. She laid her hand upon her sword. ... *defend the innocent, free the oppressed, and spread light in dark places.*

"I guess there isn't a darker place than some substructure with a Moonguard ..."

"What did you say?" Trayci asked.

"Nothing." Carys looked up at Zalman. "I guess we have to figure out how to get either through that gate or over that wall without bringing the whole city down on us."

Zalman gestured at her sword. "That sword should be able to cut through the wall."

"Not bad." Carys clicked her tongue. "But cutting through that white stone will be loud. Even if we could find a part of the wall no one saw us, we'd still bring the militan right to us."

Zalman crossed his arms over his broad chest. "A diversion?"

He's getting good at this. But she shouldn't be surprised. He knew something of strategy from that stupid Qadi-bol. "Something big and loud enough to cover us breaking through a wall?" Carys said.

"The fountains," Trayci said.

Zalman scowled. "What about them?"

She leaned around the corner and pointed beyond the fountain to the south. "The water comes from the river, the pressure from an underground aqueduct."

Zalman hummed. "The aqueduct control at the Docks?"

"You know someone who could give us access?" Carys regretted the question as soon as she asked it.

Trayci grinned at both of them. "Oh, I have my ways."

Shoggers.

CHAPTER 10

THE MORIEL RIVER

Dark fell in Galya. The warm summer air hung thick with the scent of salt from the ocean nearby.

The day had been spent in silence and boredom as Trayci and her ladies worked to gain access to the acqueduct valves. Trayci claimed that the men only wanted coin, of which she had plenty, but Zalman noted Carys squinting as she did every time Trayci spoke.

Trayci's contacts told her they would open the valves to full two hours after dark. It would take time for the pressure to build, and they questioned the ancient pipes, whether or not they would hold. Zalman prayed it was enough to cover their entrance into the Temple compound.

Zalman, Carys, and Trayci had watched and scanned the wall for hours through the afternoon. They found a part of the wall with little or no activity on both sides, both the street and the compound. The three of them hovered in the alley across from their target in the dark.

Carys was a shadow as she turned to them. Under her cloak, she wore her usual green and brown pants and tunic with deerskin boots. Her unforged sword hung at her side. "You know one part of this plan that could go to crit?"

"All of it could." His cloak hid his face and the axes at his belt. "A mark of our plans."

He couldn't see the scowl he knew she wore. "Shut up. Yes, all of it could, but here's the thing. We're going to bust the fountains and maybe flood the city?"

"Right." Trayci didn't wear a cloak. Her tight blouse and ballooning pants were made of silk, dark blue, and she wore soft slippers.

"But we're also going to some underground room, right?" Carys turned to Trayci. "Won't those places flood first?"

"Don't know," Trayci said. "Could be, but I don't think so. The city won't really flood, not for long. It will slow down movement, especially in lower parts of the city, but the men of old that built the fountains also built an extensive draining system in case the river flooded. And some of the buildings were contructed to be sealed from flooding."

Carys sniffed. "Such a wealth of information. But did the elves think of that when they built the compound?"

Trayci hesitated. "We'll see."

Zalman scowled at Trayci. "You know you don't have to come."

"I'm going," she answered in a firm voice.

Zalman grunted but didn't argue further. He was nervous already about entering the compound. Too many things he didn't know – were there Cityguard or militan in the compound? If so, how many? And while he knew he and Carys could handle themselves in a fight, anything could happen once a battle begun, and he didn't want to be distracted protecting Trayci while it all went down.

The tension with Carys had continued through the day, and while she worked with him to come up with the best plan, she didn't stand close to him or touch him unless necessary. He could feel her simmering anger.

And yet, what was he supposed to do? He had never hidden his past from her. She knew it well enough to hate him for it before. Was that supposed to exclude them from helping Trayci and the resistance in Galya? She didn't believe that, but somehow he was still at fault.

He glanced over at Trayci in the dark. The guilt of his betrayal pressed down on him. Not only had he left her behind to deal with the elves and the consequences, his abandonment meant Janny had been brought into the undignified life of a shoghouse. Was he only helping out of guilt? It wasn't the primary reason, but the shame did drive him. He felt he owed Trayci.

Perhaps Carys was right to be angry at him, after all.

Zalman looked up at the moons over the city, bright and glowing. "It's been three hours or so since sunset."

Carys tapped her foot. "It's taking too long."

"The men said that it might take a while for the pressure to build ..."

The ground shuddered beneath them, and Carys reached out to grab his arm. All three of them crouched to keep their feet as a deep groan rose from the concrete of the street.

Zalman stood straight and dropped his cloak. He stepped out into the street as the groan became a roar. Looking up into the central intersection of the city, the statues of those mythic elves began to shake back and forth. He felt and heard a deep groan. Cracks formed on the statues. In the next second, they broke in large pieces, down the middle, as a tower of water shot upwards and out, a hundred or more mitres in the air. Zalman flinched and then turned to Carys and gestured towards the wall.

Carys jogged out with Trayci at her heels, and they leaned together against the wall. Made of white stone, the wall was five mitres high.

The women dropped their cloaks, and Carys pulled her unforged sword from its sheath and handed it to Zalman.

Grabbing the hilt, he felt calmer, stronger. It felt small in his hand. He raised a brow, took a step back from the wall, and he lifted the stone above his head with two hands. He plunged the unforged sword into the white stone. With a clapping sound, the wall cracked vertically. He removed the blade easily and repeated the motion. Each time the sword split the wall further with a reverberating sound drowned out by the screaming pipes and the noise of rushing water.

Shouts came from within the compound and cries down the street.

Zalman paused after a minute of hacking at the white stone, and the wall now possessed a thin crack, a pace wide. It might be wide enough for Carys. He gritted his teeth and moved to the right. He continued striking the stone, and within another minute, the space might be big enough for him.

He moved aside for a moment; his feet splashed in water flowing down the street from the fountain. He handed Carys her sword, and he pulled the axes from his belt. Before Carys or Trayci could make their way through, he darted in the opening and entered the compound, eyes scanning the dark for any signs. When he was satisfied, he waved Carys and Trayci through.

They stood in a small courtyard with benches and bushes and a tree at its center. A path that led between two buildings toward the main Temple beckoned.

Zalman gestured at Trayci. She was supposed to know where to go.

Trayci set her shoulders and slid forward, her feet not making a sound as she crept.

Carys sheathed her sword and held her bow, a quiver of arrows nestled behind her shoulder.

Trayci led them between the buildings. Zalman's face turned back and forth. The noises of croaking pipes beneath the city distracted him. Trayci held out a hand at the corner of one of the smaller buildings, some sort of residence, and they stopped, leaning into the shadows to their left.

A five elf squad of Cityguard passed by, their armor winking in the moonlight. Unseen, Trayci led them right to a corridor up ahead. The corridor was long and lit by lamps with the main Temple doors at the other end. The three of them walked along the side, Carys now with an arrow nocked in her short bow.

Footfalls behind them. Zalman turned to two figures.

"Hey!" one said. "You ..."

Carys spun in a crouch, aimed, and fired once, then again, and both figures dropped. Zalman thought he saw long robes flapping – elven priests, Nican.

"Come," Trayci whispered, and she jogged towards the massive wooden double doors that were the entrance into the Temple. "Zalman."

He stepped forward and gripped the thick golden handle of the door on the right and pulled. He grunted with the effort, and the door swung a mitre or more open with a hiss.

Trayci went first this time, without a weapon. Following her inside the Temple, the main worship area was dimly lit but lighter than the corridor outside. Hundreds of kneeling cushions dotted the marble floor. Statues representing the Nine Gods stood on the far wall, Ashinar the Sun God higher and more impressive than all of them. Thick white stone columns held the arched ceiling in place. Carvings and paintings covered the ceiling. They depicted different scenes of the mythos of the Nine Gods.

"This way." Trayci led them to the right of the nearest column, and as she moved, she encountered two Nican, within two paces of her. Their eyes bulged.

Zalman was closer, so he moved to take care of the Nican, but he wasn't fast enough. Trayci leapt and twisted in the air, and before she completed her turn, she had kicked one Nican in the head and the other in the chest. When she landed, she kicked them both again for good measure.

Standing there, she pulled a strand of hair back behind her ear.

"More I don't know about you?" he asked.

Without answering, she continued on her path to the right side of the Temple. He saw the scowl on Carys' face this time before she followed. He cursed and ran after.

Areas for individual meditation and worship were spaced along the sides of the Temple. Each area had a fine, low seat. Vines or other vegetation surrounded the seat. There were nine on each side, and Trayci headed to the last one at the back, the individual chapel dedicated to the animal god. It had a particularly odd statue – a golden eagle in flames, spreading its wings.

Trayci approached the golden eagle, and she grabbed the wings and twisted the eagle on its base.

The wall behind the eagle split and opened a large door into a dark entry.

"That's as far as I know," Trayci said.

Zalman took a deep breath and rolled his shoulders. "Behind me. Carys, the rear."

Carys followed his instruction.

Zalman moved into the opening, his hands gripping the axes tight. A wide stairway wound down into greater darkness. "Light." Carys pulled a lamp from a hook on the wall and handed it to him.

He descended the staircase, taking them slowly but two at a time. The lamp threw yellow light down the stairs but also created eerie shadows on the walls and further below. As they descended, scents of chemicals and filth reached him. He forced himself to breathe in his mouth and out his nose. It helped a little.

And then the noises, sounds of something alive, groaning in anger or pain or both, wet sounds.

Zalman tensed each step down the stairs, waiting for something to come at them in the dark. Minutes felt like hours as they reached the bottom of the stairs. A simple doorway opened to a cavernous room with rectangular slabs down the middle, the one in the center with bottles of various liquids and different colors. Cells with iron bars had been cut into the wall of black stone to the left. Torches burned on the right.

Zalman coughed and only kept himself from gagging by sheer force of will. Trayci fell to her knees and vomited.

Carys leaned over with her hands on her thighs. "Great and mighty El."

Closed doors waited at the other end of the room.

The noises came from the cells – labored breathing, low growls, shuffling of chains.

Zalman's jaw and stomach tightened. He walked forward. He lifted the lamp and shone it into the first cell. He cried out as a creature threw itself against the iron bars, rattling them. Recovering, he crouched and squinted to get a better look.

It had the arms and legs of a human, but the skin and hair were red. The face elongated in a snout with sharp fangs. "Moonguard," Carys spat from next to him. "Perversions. Crossed a bloodwolf with a human."

There were ten cells overall. Zalman gathered himself and continued to walk to peer in the other cells.

Carys followed. "We have to be quick. They're gonna find the Nican we killed." He heard her swallow. "We don't want to be stuck down here."

Understatement of the century.

The next cell was empty, but the lamp showed chains on a floor stained with blood and other filth.

Trayci remained at the first cell, peering into it. "Janny?"

"I think that was a man, once," Carys said.

From further down the room came a soft moan. "Momma?"

All three of them froze, and Trayci moved first. She rose from her crouch and passed the other cells, three other creatures snarling or squealing at her as she sprinted and slid to a kneeling stop in front of the next to last cell.

"Janny?"

A muffled whisper of fear and awe. "Momma? Momma?"

"Zal," Trayci called. "Please, the light!"

Zalman jogged over to her, trying to ignore the creatures in those cells, shadows with either too many limbs or not enough, sounds that were both animal and human at once. Carys paced him. He reached Trayci and knelt with her. He held out the lamp.

And his heart broke with sorrow and horror. It lay against the iron bars. It had once been a woman, a young woman if Janny, but her legs and arms were long and thin with claws at the end. Her torso was stocky, and she had four wings growing from her back. Her skin was white and leathery.

The skin had grown over her eyes, making her blind, and her nostrils stretched wide over her face. Flapping membranes were set on each side of her head, like ears. Long, sharp teeth filled her mouth.

Carys lay a hand on his shoulder. "El help us. They made her a grider."

When Janny spoke, it appeared difficult for her to form words with the large teeth in her mouth. "Momma, is that you?"

"I'm here, baby." Trayci reached through the bars to touch her daughter's face. Tears flowed from Trayci's eyes. She turned to Zalman. "Get her out! Please!"

Zalman noted the iron bars and the chains on Janny's spindly limbs, and he waved at Carys' hip. She threw the bow around her shoulder and pulled her unforged sword. Her voice was soft as she spoke. "Trayci. I need to ..."

Trayci sobbed and shuffled to her right. With one swing, Carys tore through the lock on the cell. Zalman opened the cell door and Trayci reached into the darkness and lifted Janny into the dim light and into her arms. Carys cut the chains from Janny with deft moves and the chains fell to the ground.

Trayci swept in and embraced the grider girl. "I've got you now. I'm here."

Janny wept, as well, but there were no tears.

Zalman turned at the noise on the stairs, footfalls, more than one. "Need to go."

Carys cocked her head to the stairs. "Can't go that way."

"Where does that go?" Zalman pointed to the doors three mitres away at the end of the room.

"No!" Janny screamed, a shrill, non-human sound, and Zalman winced. "Not there!"

Sound of footfalls grew louder.

"Don't know we got a choice." He rose with the lamp in his hand and went to the doors. They swung towards him, and he flung them open. He lifted the lamp and shed light beyond. And he heard Carys gasp beside him.

It was another room filled with human and animal parts, a gruesome collection of flesh and bone and blood. Some of the bodies seemed more intact than others. A flesh garbage heap.

Janny curled up into a ball, more flexible than a human should be, and she squealed.

"We have visitors," a voice said from the other end of the room.

Zalman spun on his heel; three elves had descended the stairs. The two elves on either end were militan but specialists of some kind. Each held two long, thin swords.

The elf in the middle wore a long red robe and red leather sandals. The robe was embroidered with an ancient, flowing script that Zalman guessed went with the Nican of Yor, the animal god. He had long, black hair that was slicked with some sort of oil and plastered to his head. His eyes were too wide and large for his head, as if they had once belonged to someone else. When he smiled, each tooth had been filed to a point.

A tattoo of the three moons covered his right forearm.

The Moonguard.

Carys, to her credit, did not hesitate. She sheathed her sword, threw the bow into her left hand and grabbed an arrow with her right. She drew, and when she stopped moving, she fired an arrow at the Moonguard.

The militan to the Moonguard's left moved in front of his master and split the arrow in half with his swords.

"Shog a goat," Carys muttered.

"I'll handle them," Zalman growled. He met her eyes. "Get them out of here."

He didn't wait for her agreement. He threw the lamp at the table of chemicals in the middle of the room.

Carys reached for his arm. "Zal, no!" But it was too late. They watched the lamp sail near the ceiling and then fall onto the table. The Moonguard's eyes widened, which seemed impossible.

A wave of flame blossomed from the table and rolled across the ceiling, filling the top half of the room. Zalman cursed and threw himself over Carys, both of them hitting the floor. He raised his left arm and felt the flame over his skin. He roared in pain but ignored it.

The flame disappeared the next moment; the room filled with a noxious smoke. Zalman rose into the smoke, his hands gripping the axes. He could move his black arm, although it hurt like crit. The elves on the other end of the room still recovered, and so he held his breath and ran towards them.

He hurdled the first slab. The elves coughed and searched around them, confused and disoriented. Leaping over the next slab, he took only one more step before jumping through the flame simmering on the table in the middle. Singed, he spun the axes to his side as he hurdled another. One of the militan noticed him and lifted his sword.

An arrow flew past his ear and sank into the militan's chest. Zalman smiled.

Zalman bounded over the last slab, his axes over his head and ready to split the Moonguard in two.

The Moonguard stood, grinned at him, and lifted a hand in his direction.

Something invisible hit Zalman in the chest. His whole body was wracked in pain, a pain from within. He cried out and dropped his axes as he stumbled and fell. The Moonguard rose and hovered over him, laughing, now with both hands out like claws.

Zalman writhed on the floor in agony, like the Moonguard sucked the very life from his body.

—+—

Carys shouted Zalman's name as she ran around the slabs and table towards the elves on the other end. She continued to fire at the remaining militan, but he had recovered and swatted her arrows down with both of his swords. She was running out of arrows, and the militan began to move towards her, as well, all with her husband dying on the floor.

The Moonguard stood over Zalman and caused him severe pain without touching him – some form of the magic of *Tebelrivyn*. *Thought that magic was outlawed. Obviously not.*

She slid under the militan's strike, and she swung her bow at his knees. He jumped over it, but it enabled her to turn and face him. Before she could attempt another swing or shot, a form flew past her in silken clothes and kicked at the militan. He blocked the kick but couldn't stop the punch at his jaw that sent him reeling, and Carys watched for a moment while Trayci disarmed him by grabbing his wrist and twisting.

"Get Zalman!" Trayci said.

Carys whirled, nocked an arrow, and pointed it at the Moonguard. The Moonguard moved one of his hands in her direction. The pain she immediately felt threw her shot wide as she fell to her knees. Her breath caught at the sudden pain. It felt as if every organ within her body was about to burst.

She fell to her hands and knees.

"Fools," the Moonguard said. "Humans have always been fools."

Was he talking to me? She didn't know and didn't care. All she wanted was the pain to stop.

The sword.

The message like a whisper in her mind. It was difficult to focus on it. Every muscle in her body clenched at the effort.

The sword.

The unforged sword. Wasn't there some legend about the unforged sword protecting against *Tebelrivyn*? It was near impossible to follow the train of thought. But she fell to her side and forced her right hand to move down and touch the hilt of the *barabrend* from the Living Stone.

When she did, the pain ended.

She breathed in like she had been drowning, sputtering and heaving. Her body ached, sore, but the pain was gone. Quickly, she jumped to her feet and drew her sword.

The Moonguard's face flooded with fear. His hand shook with his effort, but it had no effect on her. The Moonguard bared his filed teeth at her and shifted his attention to Trayci, who wrestled with the remaining militan. Trayci screamed and fell to the floor in pain.

The militan winced at the sound but retrieved his swords from the floor, readying them to stab down.

Carys turned and engaged the militan. He deflected her blow, maneuvering his position to get both his swords in play.

Trayci continued screaming in pain on the floor as Zalman thrashed nearby.

A high-pitched squeal filled the room. "Momma!" Carys took a step back and lifted her sword in defense.

Janny lifted through the smoke as the squeal continued, wings flapping, and she flew close to the ceiling towards the Moonguard. He cowered underneath her cries, the sound echoing off the stone of the room. He moved both arms now in her direction, but not fast enough. Janny descended upon him with claws and teeth.

Carys turned and swung at the militan again, who had also gathered himself. She pressed him and moved to his right and around so he wouldn't see Zalman, who picked up his axes and stood. Zalman took a lumbering step and with a snarl, he removed the militan's head from his body.

Janny continued her torturous screams, but they were now screams of pain. Even as she tore into the Moonguard, red satin and blood and flesh flying about him, his hands grabbed her head and a white mist moved from her body into his hands, sucking life from her.

"Zalman!" Trayci yelled. Zalman ran over to the pair, lifted the axe in his right hand, and dropped it on the Moonguard's skull, splitting it in two.

The Moonguard twitched and stopped moving. Janny shuddered once and fell to the side, still. Trayci ran to her, cradling her head. Drool and spittle fell from her gaping mouth.

"Janny," Trayci called in desperation.

Janny moved her head slowly to face her mother. She mumbled something incoherent.

"Oh, Janny, Janny," Trayci said. "I'm so sorry."

Carys was tired, more tired than she had ever been. "We need to get out of here."

Trayci did not move, shaking her head at the horror that was now her daughter. Zalman hooked his axes on his belt and limped over to her. "I'll take her." *I don't know if I can keep going much longer, and he was under the Moonguard's magic longer than any of us. How does he have the strength?* He bent down. "Come." He reached out and took Janny and lifted her easily.

Now the battle calmed, the noises from the other cells returned. She turned her head and pursed her lips at the horrors there.

"Carys?" Zalman said.

She took a deep breath and gripped her forged sword. "We can't leave them."

Zalman didn't answer at first. He lowered his head. "They dead already."

"No." Trayci pointed to the first cell. "Not that one."

Carys looked into the dark of the cell. Trayci was right. The other cells, the shapes didn't move. Not a sound from them in the silence. But the first one …

"Please," came a squeaking growl from the shadow.

She just fought a breaking Moonguard, but she froze at the fear of that shadow.

Carys squeezed the hilt of her sword with all her might. *El, help me.* She glanced at Trayci. "Gather up as many arrows as you can." She obeyed.

Janny lifted her head from Zalman's arms. The membranes on her face twitched in the toxic smoke. "Help him. He's my friend."

With another breath, Carys forced the few steps to the cell, to the iron bars. She knelt down. She peered in and could see the huddled form, the red fur. "What's your name?"

"Sh-shannon."

He's just a boy. What have they done to him? "Okay, Shannon. We'll get you out."

Carys cut through the lock with the sword. The bars creaked when she opened them. Shannon held out his arms … muscular and covered with red fur, bloodwolf fur, and they ended in five fingered claws. She cut the chains that held him.

"Carys." Zal's voice dripped with urgency.

Carys looked at the face that emerged from the shadow, a cross between human and wolf. The eyes were human. "Can you walk?"

Shannon bared his teeth. Almost like a smile. "Yes."

Carys nodded. "Then come on." She stood, took the arrows from Trayci, and placed them in her quiver. "I'll take point." She sheathed her sword, nocked an arrow, and headed up the stairs. Zalman followed with Janny in his arms.

Shannon, the wolf boy, crawled on all fours behind Zalman.

Trayci wiped her face and took two swords from one of the dead militan and brought up the rear.

Carys climbed the stairs, each step an effort, but the fear kept her focused as she ascended. They reached the main Temple area without incident. With a hesitation and quick scan, she led them into the main worship area. Feet ran on the stone outside. She took a breath and raced to the main doors, her nocked arrow swinging back and forth at the ready.

When they were fifteen mitres away from the main doors, a squad of Cityguard entered. The elves noticed them, and they slid to a stop. Carys fired twice and dropped two of them before running to her left to round a thick pillar.

Behind her, Zalman shifted Janny's limp form to his left shoulder – she appeared so small with him – and pulled an axe with his right hand. He did not shift to the pillar; he ran towards the Cityguard with Trayci behind him.

Shannon the bloodwolf boy raced to Zalman's right, and it surprised Carys how fast he moved.

The five remaining Cityguard saw the wolf boy, and they shouted and scattered.

Zalman ran one down. He blocked a gladus with his axe and kicked out the knee. Once the elf was down, Zalman followed with his axe to the chest.

Trayci spun and whirled, her silk trousers whispering with her movement and her hair down in her eyes, but she deflected a gladus and ripped her other sword through the elf's throat.

Shannon leapt and landed on the back of a third, ripping into cloth and flesh with claws and teeth. The elf squealed and then fell silent.

Coming around the pillar and to the door, Carys shot and killed the last two. She pulled her arrows out of the dead elves and continued to run to the door. Zalman, Trayci, and Shannon met her there, and they entered the long corridor together.

Panting, she looked down the dark corridor. "Back the way we came or another way?"

Zalman shrugged. "Maybe they found how we came in." He was pale and slick with sweat. "Main gate too open, though, too many eyes."

"Back the way we came, then." Trayci coughed a breath and jogged forward. Shannon, red blood on his red fur, growled and followed her.

Carys ran and moved beside them with Zalman behind her as they went down the corridor, an arrow nocked and ready. The four of them kept to the left side as they ran.

Nican and Cityguard argued and shouted somewhere in the complex, but Carys and the group with her didn't encounter anyone else. They came to the small courtyard where they had fashioned a hole, another squad of five Cityguard stood there, inspecting the hole, water flowing into the courtyard from the street ankle deep.

Before they could notice newcomers, Shannon growled and raced forward on all fours, Trayci right behind him. He ran through the courtyard toward the guard, and their eyes bulged, turning to flee. But Shannon clawed at one while Trayci sliced another in the back.

Carys shot two more while the first two died, and the last one escaped. She didn't bother chasing and shooting him. The city would be on alert already, and if not, it would be once the Moonguard was discovered.

They needed to move.

Zalman had stayed back, holding Janny, but now that the way cleared, he moved through the hole in the wall. Trayci and Shannon followed, and Carys came last to stand in the quiet, dark street, the water halfway up to her shin. The three of them splashed over to the alley they waited in before.

Zalman and Carys leaned against the wall in the alley and Trayci hunched over with her hands on her knees.

Shannon leaned against the wall, panting, watching them.

"The city will lock down tonight," Carys said. "We have to get out of the city. Now."

"We need to get Janny to a safe place." Trayci eyed the wolf boy. "And Shannon."

"Is there a safe place?" Carys said. "You can't go back to the *Bed and Beauty*."

"No," Trayci said. "The other ladies packed it up today and moved to another location."

"Gates will be watched, guarded," Zalman said. "Can you get us out of the city?"

Trayci frowned at both of them. "I know a way. But you have to help me get Janny to our safe house first."

Carys shared a glance with Zal. "We will." She took a deep breath. "But the streets are a mess."

Trayci lifted her gaze. "We go up. But we have to move north a little, first."

Checking the flooded street, Trayci led them out again and then northeast, their tired feet dragging through the murk, the wolf boy crawling along. Once past the Temple Complex, the buildings were smaller, shorter, and without walls for protection. Trayci found one with stairs up to the roof, and they climbed. Carys wondered how Shannon would fare, but his claws allowed him to shimmy up with the rest of them.

On the roof, they paused. The three moons shone overhead through the clear sky and lit the city. Most of the buildings were of a similar height, and with narrow streets and narrower alleys …

"You want us to move across the rooftops?" Carys balked.

"It is the fastest, most direct path to where we are going. And it will hide us from the elves." Trayci turned to Zalman, frowning. "Can you do it?"

Zalman grunted in annoyance. Carys could tell he wasn't so sure. But he said, "Lead the way."

Trayci hesitated but then ran towards the edge and took a flying leap over the alley to the next roof over. Zalman ran and followed, easily making the jump. Shannon was next, bounding on all fours and jumping across.

Carys shook her head. "Shoggers." She shouldered the bow and followed.

They had to take breaks, periodically, and wait at times for platoons or squads of militan or Cityguard to pass. After more than an hour of exhausting travel, Trayci stopped at one roof.

Panting, she gestured to a trap door. "Wait here. I'll be back."

Zalman watched her go down the trapdoor with heavy eyes and then sat down on the roof when she was gone.

Carys sighed and sat next to him, on his right. She leaned on his mountain of a shoulder and pointed to his blackened arm. "You're hurt."

"Nothing." His eyes were closed.

"My pack is back at the *Bed and Beauty*. I have supplies in there that could …"

"I'll live," he interrupted.

"You'd better live. Or I'll kill you myself."

The white form in Zalman's arms giggled. Janny lifted her head from the big man's shoulders.

"Looks like you're feeling better." Carys smirked over at her.

"You can let me down," Janny said. Zalman cradled her and let her back legs down first. She was shaky, but then Janny crouched there next to Shannon. He nuzzled her face.

Zalman caught Carys' eyes. He gave her a tired smile.

They both started when the trap door opened with a snap, echoing across the rooftops. Rose and a young man, both weeping, climbed up and out. They took notice of the bloodwolf boy and backed away from him. They recovered and then embraced Janny.

Trayci rose to the roof a few seconds later, dragging up their packs. Carys cried out in surprise and lunged for hers. "Thank you." She opened her pack and rummaged for strips of cloth and her water bag. She poured the water over Zalman's arm. He twitched while she cleaned the arm as gently as she could.

"The militan will be guarding the gates," Trayci said. "But I know another way. Come."

Carys poured ointment over his forearm, a general healing oil. Zalman's muscles tensed.

"Thank you, but …" Carys faced Trayci. "Why don't you come with us? You can't stay here. It's too dangerous now."

Trayci gave them a sad smile. "I appreciate that. I do. But this is my home. I can't run now, not when I could help the most."

"Trayci," Zalman rumbled. "Come with us."

Trayci looked at him in a way that got Carys' blood rushing through her veins. "No, old friend. We will stay. But first I will take you out of the city."

Shannon growled and nodded. "Thank you. We owe you our lives."

Carys reached down and ruffled the fur on the top of the boy's head. "Remember to thank El and help others. That's all you owe."

Janny reached out a long arm and put a bony hand on Zalman's cheek. "Thank you."

Zalman touched her face, as well. "Take care of your mother."

"I will."

Carys finished wrapping Zal's arm in the cloth. The burn would leave an ugly scar. Carys placed her supplies back in her pack and tied the top. Zalman clenched his left fist and nodded.

"Let's go," Carys said.

Gathering their packs, it was only another few minutes of moving over the rooftops until they reached the city wall. Trayci made one final leap onto the balcony of a tall building that rested near the wall. They followed as she climbed up the side of fine apartments using trellises and balconies.

The top of the wall was only a few mitres from the roof of the top apartment, and a ladder and a full canvas bag was there. Zalman and Carys extended the ladder to the top of the wall. Trayci grabbed the bag. Zalman led the way up the ladder to the wall-walk, and Carys and Trayci followed.

When they all reached the wall-walk, Trayci opened the canvas bag and pulled out ropes and hooks. "There are only a few hours left before dawn. Get as far away from the city as you can. I'll hide these things after you leave, but they'll be searching the city. Once it is light, they'll be searching everywhere."

Carys and Zalman each took a hook and tied a rope to it. They set the hooks on the parapet and let the ropes fall down to the ground.

Before they climbed down, Zalman stared at Trayci. "I'm sorry."

Trayci cocked her head at him. "For what?"

He rolled his shoulders and shifted his weight. "For what I did years ago. For not being able to save ..."

"Ah." Trayci nodded and touched his arm. "You are more than forgiven. In fact, I give you thanks. You are a different man than the one I knew so long ago. You've become the man I wished you'd be. I will be forever grateful. I only wish I could do more. Luck to you."

Zalman's eyes burned at Trayci for a moment, and then he nodded. "El be with you." He climbed over the parapet, holding onto the rope, and began to slide down the wall.

Carys stayed for a moment, biting her lip.

Trayci smiled at her. "You take care of him."

"I plan to. When I reach Caleb, I'll tell him about the resistance here. He will be glad to hear it. Maybe others will come to help."

"We will survive. We've learned that well enough. And if we can, however we can, we will fight. But tell your brother one thing for me."

"Anything."

"Tell him to win. It's all for nothing if he doesn't win."

CHAPTER 11

NEW AND OLD ALLIES

Caleb rode at the front of the *Hamon-el* on the road east to Vicksburg, the next major town. The army stretched for kilomitres behind him, five thousand strong.

The morning before, Lyam and Eshlyn's parents took almost a thousand people back with them to Ketan to reinforce and support the defense of that city. It was unlikely Kryus would go through the trouble of avoiding the *Brendel* to travel all the way west to Ketan, but a strong Ketan was the foundation of the revolution. So the city needed a good defense, just in case.

While he knew it pained Eshlyn to see them leave, Caleb was glad for her parents' leadership in Ketan. The more he considered it, he was also glad Lyam, a *Sohan-el*, would be among them.

The grasses moved like waves along the low hills on either side of them. Caleb leaned over in his saddle and looked to his right at Iletus, the Bladeguard and elf.

With the inclusion of the Beorgai and the Ghosts, and the continued addition and subtraction to the army moving forward, Iletus had been tasked with organizing the *Hamon-el* into new divisions, companies, and platoons. It was a nightmare of a job. To make it easier for organization, cohesion, and leadership, Iletus allowed people from similar backgrounds to remain together – the Ghosts of Saten, the Beorgai, the people of Manahem – when possible.

Caleb looked to his left, to Eshlyn. For someone who balked at being called a queen – and he understood why, probably more than anyone – she appeared more regal in that moment than she ever did. He sat up a little straighter simply looking at her.

She had been in charge of resourcing the *Hamon-el*, even setting up a system of communication with pigeons to report back to Taggart if reinforcements or provisions were needed. Another thousand trained warriors had remained at Taggart with another *Sohan-el* in charge, Pynt. He was young but had proven himself from the Battle of Ketan to Biram and the Acar as a capable warrior and leader. Aden, Eshlyn, and Iletus spoke highly of him, as well.

Other leaders rode behind Caleb, Iletus, and Eshlyn. Shecayah, Jaff, and Bweth rode together. Next were the bosaur, over a hundred, ridden by Beorgai and led by Tobiah. Other divisions led by Ghosts and *Sohan-el* marched behind them. At the end of the column were the siege engines – the catapults and ballista – and wagons of provisions. Another division, Xak's, brought up the rear to defend against any attack from behind and to protect the provisions.

Iletus sniffed and inclined his head to the east. "The scouts return."

They were three hours away from Vicksburg at the current pace. Caleb squinted, and two scouts trotted toward them along the road. As usual, they were Ghosts of Saten, people who could move silent and quick.

It took a few minutes for the scouts to arrive, a man and a woman, Bron and Kaz. Caleb glanced at Iletus and Eshlyn. "With me." He rode forward with them.

They stopped and assembled two hundred mitres from the traveling *Hamon-el*.

Kaz, a pale skinned young woman with black hair, greeted them each individually, and they returned the "well met" to her and Bron, a young man with tussled blond hair and tan skin.

Kaz began their report. "Vicksburg is preparing for defense."

"What type of defenses?" Iletus asked.

"They're digging ditches around the town," Bron said. "And building a wall behind the ditches with fresh cut trees."

"They're also using cut trees as pikes in front of the ditches." Kaz leaned forward in her saddle.

Eshlyn shifted in her seat. "Who is building them? Human? Elves?"

"Both," Kaz said. "Looks like the elves are making the men and women work on the defenses."

Iletus frowned. "Who knows what the Steward is thinking … or what he's been told."

"Maybe we should tell him something different, then," Eshlyn said.

Caleb scratched his beard. "Wait here." He turned his horse and rode it back to the *Hamon-el*.

"What's the word, Cal?" Bweth said as he reached them.

He pulled up his horse to face them. "We're going to try and talk to the elves there, decide what our options are. Bweth, you and Jaff are in charge. Keep them moving until we return, but don't get within a kilomitre of the town before you stop. But we should be back by then."

Shecayah moved her horse forward. "As leader of the Beorgai, I would like to go with you."

"Very well." With a glance at Bweth and Jaff, Caleb spun his horse and rode back to the others with Shecayah at his side.

He didn't slow as he passed the others – Eshlyn, Iletus, and the scouts – but he urged them to join him.

At a trot on the horses, it took them an hour to reach Vicksburg.

Vicksburg was an ancient town that rested on a slight hill, not as large as Taggart but larger than Biram. It sprawled with buildings and homes, more than a few several stories tall, and over the hasty fortifications, Caleb could see the Kryan administration building and steward's mansion. The River Moriel lay on the eastern side.

The scouts spoke true about the defenses, the ditches and the log wall.

"They've been busy," Eshlyn said. "That should have taken them a while."

"A couple ninedays, at least," Iletus said. "Digging ditches is hard work."

"It's like this all the way around, too," Bron said.

Humans and elves worked together. Caleb rolled his shoulders. "How close can we get?"

Iletus knew what he asked. "They shouldn't have any siegeworks. Vicksburg wouldn't have any, and we didn't give the elves any when they left Taggart. A few hundred mitres would be safe from arrows."

"They could have been supplied or reinforced by the legions from Asya," Eshlyn said.

Caleb pulled his peerglass from his belt and lifted it to his eye. "There would be more militan. We would see them. And they'd have the humans working, not working with them."

"Could be a trap," Iletus said. "Get us to commit to an easy target." He scanned the countryside around them, noting the forest to the south and the trees to the north. "Then ambush us."

"And give us the high ground and the advantage?" He lowered the peerglass. "No, this is the elves trying to survive. They've been at this since we took Taggart."

"Let's get closer, talk to them directly," Eshlyn said.

Shecayah shifted on her horse. "And allow them to lie to us? How can we trust anything an elf says?"

Caleb glanced at Iletus and rubbed his beard. "They might lie. They might not. But either way, we'll know more than we do now."

Caleb kicked his horse and moved forward, the rest of them following. About three hundred mitres away, in plain sight of several humans and elves, Caleb stopped. He waited for the people in the city to notice the contingent. The people saw him and scrambled from their work, and humans and elves rushed to the inside of the log wall.

Minutes passed, and Caleb waited patiently, the Kingstaff across his saddle.

A makeshift wooden gate opened, a series of logs with leather lashes as hinges, and an elf in uniform rode out on a horse from Vicksburg towards them. He rode alone. As he neared, Caleb recognized him.

"It's Andos," Iletus said.

Andos jogged his horse and halted five mitres away.

"I thought I told you to go back to Asya," Caleb growled.

Andos tensed. "You did. But things have changed."

Shecayah scoffed and muttered something under her breath that Caleb didn't catch.

Eshlyn's eyes narrowed. "What's changed?"

"I received orders from Asya," Andos said. "From the Emperor."

Iletus gripped his pommel tight. "What orders?"

Andos reached into a pouch on his saddle and produced a slip of paper. He handed it out. "We stopped here on our way east and the Steward here got this for me by pigeon."

Caleb hesitated then urged his horse forward, closing the distance. He took the paper, unfolded it, and read it.

Scorch Vksbg + Gnns. Kill humans. Legion on route from Asya. A small seal was at the edge of the paper.

Caleb gave Andos a sharp look before returning to the others. He gave the paper to Iletus first, and Iletus nodded back at him after perusing it. *It was real.* Iletus handed it to Eshlyn.

"As you can see, we have not obeyed this order," Andos said.

Eshlyn looked up from the paper. "Why not?"

Andos' brow rose. "Do I have to tell you what will happen if I did this? Let's say I burn Vicksburg and Giannis to the ground and kill all the humans, as the Emperor orders. What then?"

"Reward?" Shecayah said.

"No," Iletus said. "The Emperor can't allow the failure at the Acar and Taggart to stand. Since Pyram is dead and unavailable to punish, Andos would be the example. Once the legion from Asya arrived, Andos would be placed into custody or executed, likely by a Bladeguard."

"I would be guilty of mass murder and then blamed for the defeat at the Acar." Andos scanned the group. "And losing Taggart. Not an attractive proposition, so I made a decision."

Caleb lifted his chin at the town of Vicksburg. "So you decided to defend the humans?"

"*We* decided," Andos corrected. "Once I arrived and read the orders, I spoke with the Steward. We then spoke to the Cityguard and militan in our midst, they all agreed – then the Steward and the Cityguard of Giannis, as well."

"You spoke to the Steward of Giannis?" Iletus said.

"The town of Giannis is in a valley. This is high ground and a larger town. We suggested joining forces here and work together. Giannis is empty. They heard our argument and unanimously decided to stay, work on field fortifications."

Caleb peered at Andos in the silence that extended. "How did you convince them all, Steward, Cityguard, militan, to stand against their Emperor?"

"Some did not," Andos admitted. "We allowed them to return to Asya. But my argument was simple."

"Which was?" Eshlyn said.

"Survival?" Andos barked a sarcastic chuckle. "My Emperor is a Worldbreaker and probably going mad. The Emperor has sent a Bladeguard and a Legion here to kill all the humans and burn the towns to the ground so you can't use them for your army, and probably kill the stewards, too, like he did in Biram." Andos met Caleb's eyes. "You, however, allowed us to leave in peace if we would go in peace. You cared for our prisoners and gave them back to us, and those prisoners have given further testimony that you are different. You have an elf as an advisor, a Bladeguard. What would you choose?"

"Wait," Eshlyn said, her brow furrowed. "What are you saying?"

"You fight for freedom, right? To save humanity? Well, we have more than fifty thousand humans in Vicksburg. With your army and the catapults and ballista, it is an easily defended position. I give the town of Vicksburg to you, the *Brendel*. But I give it to you on one condition."

Caleb's stomach tightened. "What condition?"

Andos squared his shoulders. "You make us a part of your army."

Shecayah cursed, and Eshlyn gasped. Iletus' eyes bulged and the scouts exchanged a glance.

It took a moment for Caleb to respond. "Who do you mean by *us?*"

"The militan, the Cityguard, and any humans of the towns that wish to be," Andos said.

Caleb stared into Andos' eyes, measured him. "You're not joking."

"I am as serious as I can be, sir."

Caleb scowled at him. "We will discuss and give you an answer. Go back to Vicksburg and tell them to wait for us. The whole army should be here by the afternoon."

Andos pursed his lips, bowed, turned and rode his horse back to Vicksburg.

Once out of earshot, Caleb moved his horse into position so he could see the whole group. "Kaz, Bron, do you have supplies for the next day or so?"

After sharing another glance, Kaz said, "Yes, *Brendel*."

"Good." Caleb lowered his voice. "I want you to scout ahead to the west and find this other legion, if it exists. Giannis is another day and a half east. See if Andos is telling the truth."

"Will do," Bron agreed.

"And be careful," Caleb said.

They grinned at him knowingly. They rode away to circle wide around the town.

Ghosts. He shook his head.

After they were gone, Shecayah spoke first. "You cannot do this, *Brendel*. We cannot accept elves into the *Hamon-el*."

Caleb grunted at her and pointed to Iletus. "We have elves in our army, now."

Shecayah took a deep breath. "These elves were our enemy not two ninedays ago. How can we trust their change of heart?"

"They believe their Emperor is going mad," Iletus said. "He is a Worldbreaker, which has been illegal for more than a thousand years because of the danger. Those prisoners saw our compassion after the battle, even after Pyram killed Xander, and how Aden healed the Acar. It is a compelling argument."

"What does it matter?" Eshlyn lifted her chin at the town on the hill. "There are thousands of humans there that need our protection, our help. That's what is important."

"Precisely," Shecayah said. "We have the superior numbers. Those soft walls would be destroyed by our bosaur alone. We do not need him to give the town to us. We can take it and set up a defense without having to stand with militan and Cityguard."

"And do what with the elves?" Iletus asked through clenched teeth.

Shecayah paused for a moment. "You already warned them, *Brendel*. This Andos did not keep his word before; what makes us think he will now? They did not obey, at a forfeit of their lives."

"Kill them?" Eshlyn breathed.

"If they do not surrender willingly, if they choose to fight us, then yes," Shecayah answered. "We have no obligation to their conditions. This is no negotiation. This is a war."

Eshlyn lowered her eyes and shook her head. Iletus' nostrils flared. Shecayah bore into him with his eyes.

Caleb's voice was calm. "Shecayah. What is the purpose of this revolution?"

Shecayah blinked at him. "The revolution?"

"You are correct, this is a war," Caleb said. "But it is so much more than that. We fight for a purpose, and it is important we remember that purpose. You know the prophecies, the heart of El, do you not? So I ask again, what is the purpose of this revolution? What are we fighting for?"

It was silent and heavy. "For freedom and redemption."

"Yes," Caleb said. "For freedom and redemption. For whose freedom and redemption?"

"All of Eres," Shecayah said.

"For humans alone? Or for every race?"

Her voice was barely audible. "For all races."

Caleb nodded. "Eshlyn and I fought beside Cityguard and elves before. We stood with them on the wall of Ketan and protected humans and elves. We even had a dwarf up there with us. Well, half a dwarf."

Eshlyn looked up at him and grinned.

"And she's still among us, pregnant with the child of a human father," Caleb said. "You stand with her, as well."

Iletus relaxed.

Caleb waved to the town of Vicksburg. "There are over fifteen hundred trained guard and militan over there in that town that want to stand against the oppression of the Kryan Empire with us. They want to fight for life and what is right. They want to be free to make their own decisions. Isn't this what we fight for? If we fight for freedom and redemption for all, then this will not be last time we will have to embrace people who were once our enemy.

"The best way to defeat an emeny is to make them your friend. I heard that somewhere." Caleb gripped the Kingstaff tight. "I can't deny them the choice to fight with us. Just as we did not deny your desire to join in the revolution, I will not deny theirs."

Shecayah stared at him and she sighed. "I believe in the revolution, *Brendel.* But these elves do not seek the redemption of Eres."

"We will teach them, then," Eshlyn said. "As we taught the people of Lior and the slaves we rescued from the mines."

"This Andos seeks survival, that is all," Shecayah said.

"That is a place to start," Eshlyn said.

"They protect humans, as we speak," Iletus argued.

Shecayah growled. "They hold them hostage against us. And in the Battle of Ketan, you fought creatures from the Underland. Noble, yes. But now you will ask these elves to fight officers and militan of their own kind, from their own country. When it comes to it, I do not trust them to do that."

Iletus clasped his hands in his lap. His eyes glistened. "Do you not trust me to do the same?"

Shecayah made a point of ignoring him. She faced Caleb. "We Beorgai will not stand with the elves to wait for them to betray us."

"Shecayah ..." Eshlyn pleaded.

"I am sorry, *Bashawyn.* I will not."

Caleb lowered his gaze. "I understand." He met Shecayah's gaze. "And after listening, I respect your perspective, but I do not agree. I have made my decision. Given that the scouts do not expose any lies, we will do our best to work with these elves, teaching them what it means to fight for freedom, as Lady Eshlyn said. If you cannot abide that decision, then you and the Beorgai are free to return to your home in the mountains of Lior."

Eshlyn's face fell.

Shecayah's breath shuddered. She bit her lip and rode back to the *Hamon-el* without a word.

"Break it all," Eshlyn said. But her gaze at him spoke pride and love. "I'll speak with her."

"Thank you." Caleb forced a smile at her.

She nodded and rode away after Shecayah.

Iletus watched her go. "Do you believe what you said?"

"What do you mean?"

"About the freedom and redemption of all races."

Caleb looked up at the sun, just past noon.

"I do. With all my heart. With all my life." He leaned over and faced the elf. "Do you?"

Iletus didn't respond for a few seconds, and his eyes glazed. "I don't know. Depose a despot, yes. I believe in that. But I've seen dark things in this life, Caleb. I've done dark things. Often, I did them believing I was doing the world a favor, that someone had to. I'd not seen anything that gave testimony to a greater good, a greater power, to hope … or a god who cared."

Iletus also looked up into the sky. "Until recently. I've seen things I never thought I would see, joining your revolution. I would not believe had I not seen." Iletus blinked and turned his gaze over to Caleb. "Shecayah is right, you know."

Caleb lifted a brow at him. "How is that?"

"Asking those elves to fight their own kind for some greater purpose, it is a difficult proposition, near impossible."

Caleb frowned.

"But I've seen you do the impossible before, with the help of this El you talk about. It seems insanity to continue to rely upon doing the impossible, and yet you do. Something tells me you will again."

Iletus backed his horse to face west and rode to return to the *Hamon-el*, leaving Caleb alone.

——

Zalman woke to her quiet voice, her touch on his shoulder.

"Zal. Wake up. Come on."

He barely opened his eyes, and the bright sun through the trees overhead met him. Groaning, he rolled away from her and covered his face with his arm. Every muscle in his body was stiff and ached. The burn on his left arm stung. The oil helped, but it hurt to move it.

They had traveled only another hour from Galya before finding a place far from the road hidden by brush and trees. They both collapsed in exhaustion, her folded in his arms.

"The legion," she whispered. "It's moving."

He forced his eyes fully open and sat up.

Carys knelt over him. "'Morn, sunshine."

Where was the road? Over to his left, to the west, dozens of mitres away. Noises echoed up the hill to him – feet marching, distant shouting orders. Zalman's eyes adjusted to the light. Noting the sun, it was late in the afternoon.

They had slept a while, or he had, at least. Rubbing his face, he coughed and turned to face the road.

Now in the light of day, they had chosen a good spot. The thick brush hid them well. The long road from Galya was covered with an army of elves.

"A full legion," he mumbled.

"Yep."

"Moving slow."

Carys pointed to the back of the column. "Siege engines."

"Big ones." Large figures lumbered in front of the catapults. "Wait. Are those ...?"

"Trodall."

"There's fifty of them or more."

She stood and brushed dirt and grass from the back of her pants. "If we get moving, we can reach Caleb before they do. We can move faster."

"Move?" He stretched his neck. "Don't know."

"Sorry. How are you feeling?"

He sat back on the ground. "Give me a minute, I'll be okay." But he wasn't so sure. He was tired, even after sleeping for hours.

Carys dropped next to him. "We can wait a few minutes."

Zalman grunted. The summer heat of the day simmered around them. He enjoyed how close she felt. Another battle in another city, and they came through alive and together. He wondered if this would be their life. One battle after another. He didn't care, as long as they were together.

But at some point, he'd be too old to swing those axes. Wouldn't he?

"I'm just waiting, you know," she said.

His brow furrowed. "What?"

"For you to be gone." Her voice caught. "I don't know. It's not good, but I'm waiting for you to be gone like everyone else."

He cocked his head at her.

"I trusted Cal, you know, and then he was gone. Of course, I don't even remember my parents. Not really. Images in my mind, and I don't know if those are my memories or something I was told so many times I made it real." She shook her head and stared at the legion. "I loved and trusted my aunt and Earon, and then she was dead and he was gone ... so I left. You know."

Zalman reached out and took her hand. "I know."

"Then I found Reyan, or he found me. Whatever. He died. In my arms, Zal. I thought I had gotten over it, but when I saw you on the deck of that ship, dying ..."

He pulled her closer to him.

"I didn't know what to do. You lived, though. A miracle. So wanted to make the best of what time we had left, and we got married. After that, we get to Galya where you have all this history with this woman."

"I'm sorry. Please believe …"

Carys chuckled as she looked him in the eye. "I don't blame you or her. I blame me. I let it distract me from who I am, what I am. When I saw what the Moonguard was doing down there in that horrendous place, I knew you were right to remind me."

She reached up and touched his face. "I'm rambling, I know. But I wanted to say thank you. Thank you for reminding me."

"What would I know of purpose if not for you? The least I could do."

She smiled at him and moved closer. He could taste her breath. "I love you."

He smiled back at her. "I love you."

Zalman swallowed her in his embrace and kissed her. She threw her arms around his neck. He lifted her and pulled her down with him to the leaves and the grass.

Carys pulled away from him with a smirk. "What are you doing?"

He smirked back.

"We have to get going, warn Caleb."

"Just doing like you said." He ran a hand through her hair. "Legion's moving slow. We've got time. Make the best of it."

She laughed as he kissed her neck.

In another moment, his mind was lost in her, and he began to pull on her tunic. She wiggled, helping him.

Then she tensed and froze.

He retreated, panting – he didn't feel as tired anymore. "What? What is it?"

She shushed him and sat up. He watched as her eyes scanned the trees around them.

He started to speak, but she bared her teeth at him and mouthed. *Shut. Up.*

Carys escaped his arms and rose to a crouch without a sound, her head swiveling. Since she had trained with the Ghosts of Saten, he trusted her ability to hear things he may not understand. She could distinguish between natural sounds and the unnatural.

Still crouching, she stepped over to her pack and picked up her sword, tying the belt around her after straightening her tunic back to function. She grabbed her bow and clipped the quiver to her belt.

Zalman grunted and rose, the leaves underneath him rustling. Her bulging eyes at him were a clear rebuke, but he didn't have her training. He did his best to move quiet. He gathered his axes, not bothering with a belt.

Carys signed for him to be silent and follow her. She pointed further east and used her fingers to mimic someone walking. He nodded he understood. She heard someone walking and moving to the west.

He rolled his shoulders and gripped his axes tight. She nocked an arrow and began to walk to the west. He did all he could to copy her, to step where she did. He forced his breathing to calm.

They wove through trees to the west for another fifty mitres or so. She paused, and he waited while she closed her eyes and turned her head in a slow circle. Nodding, she pointed to the southeast. He followed her for another thirty mitres where they rounded a large tree. Beyond another copse of trees, there was a clearing, and he could hear them now. A group. Were they elves? Scouts for the legion? Militan or Cityguard chasing them from Galya, trying to track them? Had they gotten to Trayci, despite her assurances, and made her talk?

Carys practically sat on the ground as she waddled forward in silence, and he did the same, the aching muscles in his legs screaming at him. He came through a copse of trees, and through branches and leaves, figures appeared.

Dwarves. Twenty or more of them in thick, steel armor, resting in the grass or on trees and rocks. One of them stood and looked at them through the trees.

Carys cursed.

The dwarf laughed. "Come out, will you? Your man there made more noise than a bosaur trampling a room of broken glass."

Carys sighed and glared at him before pushing beyond the branches and the brush. She aimed her arrow at his face. "Who are you?"

The dwarf turned to another nearby. "I like this one, Ulf. She is outnumbered yet advances."

"Talk, dwarf," Carys prompted.

"Aye. My name is Gunnar Hornswaddle. This is my brother, Ulf, and we are the Steelsides."

Zalman hovered behind Carys, his axes ready.

"Never heard of you," Carys said.

Gunnar frowned. "Well, that can be troubling. Our reputation would help us raise our price, would it not?" The dwarf broke from his musing and smiled at her. "Our king sent us to help your little rebellion."

Carys lowered her arrow. "You're ... you're here to help Caleb?"

"Is that the *Brendel*? Then yes."

Zalman swept them with a gaze. "A King sent you?"

"Did I not say it?" Gunnar gestured at the other elves. "King Ironsword remembers a kindness from this Caleb and wishes to help." Gunnar shrugged, his armor clanking. "In his own way. As he cannot send an army, officially, he sent us."

Carys shared a look with Zalman over her shoulder. She stood straight and removed the arrow from the bow. "How did you get here?"

"I might have helped," came a familiar voice to their left.

Zalman watched as a tall elf emerged from behind a tree, his steps as silent as a Ghost. He wore a long green tunic and dark trousers with elven military boots. He had long, dark hair and an annoyingly handsome smile. Zalman remembered well the fine sword that hung at his side. It had cut through a thousand or more demics on the wall of Ketan.

"Macarus!" Carys dropped her bow and ran across the clearing to throw her arms around him.

Macarus laughed and lifted her in an embrace before setting her down. The elf looked up and raised a brow. "Zalman."

Zalman walked over to him and spoke through tight lips. "Captain."

"What are you doing here?" Carys asked him. "I thought you went back to Kryus."

"I did," Macarus said. "Then Tanicus tried to kill me with a couple Bladeguard, so I decided to join the fight against him."

A couple Bladeguard? Zalman shook his head.

"I could ask you the same question, though," Macarus said. "What are you doing here?"

"We're going back to Caleb to warn him about that legion." Carys thumbed to her left.

"Aye," Gunnar said with excitement. "A whole drunken legion."

"Well, we could go together," Macarus said. "Safety in numbers."

"We could." Carys glanced back at Zalman, who stood a pace behind her now. "Or we could do something maddy."

Zalman frowned at her. "Carys ..."

"What do you mean?" Macarus joined Zal's frown.

Carys' eyes brightened. "Well, they'll be looking for Caleb and the army, trying to flank him, surprise him. They won't be expecting, say, a small force to sabotage them or attack them ..."

"Attack a legion?" Gunnar said. He and his brother walked towards them. "I told you I liked this one, Ulf! Maddy like that *Brendel*."

She scowled at the dwarf. "He's my brother."

Gunnar grabbed his gut and threw his head back in laughter. "Of course. That makes perfect sense."

Carys turned to Zalman. "What do you think?"

Zalman grunted. "A plan sure to go to crit? Sounds like something we would do."

She grinned at him.

CHAPTER 12

THE BATTLE AT VICKSBURG

"Kaz and Bron returned." Iletus approached, and Eshlyn tensed.

Eshlyn, Caleb, and Andos stood on the hill in the middle of the town of Vicksburg, on the second floor balcony of the elven administration building. From their vantage point, they could see the entire countryside for kilomitres.

It was morning the day after arriving at Vicksburg, and for the evening, the *Hamon-el* had camped five hundred mitres to the west of the town. Eshlyn, Caleb, and Andos had been discussing where they would be able to put another five thousand people in a town that was already accommodating the added humans from Giannis.

Caleb turned as Iletus joined them on the balcony. "And?"

Iletus glanced at Andos. "The town of Giannis is empty. And a legion is on its way. It will be here tonight."

Eshlyn relaxed. She had not been looking forward to the conversation if the scouts had returned with word that Andos and the elves had been lying.

Many in the *Hamon-el* did not appreciate the idea of Eshlyn and Caleb coming into the town full of Cityguard and militan without a contingent of soldiers. Caleb risked it, she knew, meaning to show his support of the elves joining their army.

Eshlyn looked to the west. She had convinced Shecayah to stay, at least until the scouts returned, but the Beorgai camped to the north, separate from the rest of the army. They were not the only ones separate, however. The veterans who had remained for the Battle of the Acar camped to the west, even though they were parts of other divisions. The Ghosts of Saten congregated to the south. On the east side of the camp, the people that had deserted at the Acar made their own group.

The division between them grew, and she didn't know how to stop it. They were about to make it worse and invite another group even more separate from the rest. Elven militan and Cityguard, the very symbols of Kryan oppression to most of the men and women of the *Hamon-el*. How could they incorporate the elves into the army if they weren't unified already?

Should they? Ideally, yes. But after the acceptance of Earon, Lyam, and now the elves, the mood of the army was skeptical and anxious. No one spoke to her or Caleb, but she had lived in a divided Delaton long enough to see the warning signs. The marriage of Aden and Tamya had been a welcome distraction, a celebration, but the army returned to its somber tone quick enough.

And now they entered into battle with another legion.

"If they remain consistent with Kryan strategy, they will attack in the morning," Caleb stated.

Iletus inclined his head. "If they remain consistent."

Andos looked from Iletus to Caleb. "Which gives us today to organize and get ready."

Caleb turned his attention back to the fields and forests around the town. "What does the legion have?"

"Scouts say the full five thousand militan, five hundred cavalry, and catapults," Iletus said.

Caleb's brow furrowed. "No grider or trodall?"

Iletus shook his head.

"That's good, right?" Eshlyn asked.

"Good, yes," Andos said. "But curious. Your army defeated a legion with a full cavalry before. Generally, Kryus believes in overkill, which is why they rarely lose on the field. The fact that they didn't bring those other resources isn't, as we said before, consistent."

Caleb held his hands behind his back. "Which means they have something else planned, something we don't see yet."

"Or they think our former victory a simple fluke," Iletus said. "Given the flammable nature of the Acar."

Eshlyn remembered the long swath of black ground when she arrived after the battle, the piles of dead, charred bodies. She suppressed a shudder.

Caleb lifted a brow at the *Hamon-el*, separated in five different camps. "Or perhaps they have information about how divided we were before the battle." He faced Eshlyn. "You think the Beorgai will leave or stay and fight?"

Eshlyn sniffed. "I don't know." She tried not to look at Andos. "I hope so, but ..."

"While we have the high ground," Caleb said. "Losing their numbers and the bosaur will hurt."

"I'll try and talk to Shecayah again," she said.

He grinned at her. "Thank you."

"They will attack from the east," Andos said. "It is the best option with the most cover."

"They'll get across the river?" Eshlyn asked. "There's just the one bridge."

"They will have makeshift bridges ready," Andos answered. "They know the terrain."

"Agreed," Iletus said. "However, we will still have the range with our catapults and ballista."

Caleb took a step, gripping that wooden staff, and leaned on the railing of the balcony. He gazed to the east. He nodded. "We have a lot to do before tomorrow morning. Let's break the news to everyone and shore up our defenses. We will fight in the morning and show them the last victory was no fluke at all."

Running footsteps sounded from the room behind them, and as they turned, Eshlyn saw one of the *Sohan-el*, Yessica, stop a few paces away. She leaned over, panting.

"What is it?" Iletus asked.

"A dwarf," Yessica said through breaths.

Caleb scowled at her. "A dwarf?"

Yessica stood straight. "A dwarf just arrived to our camp. Says there's another legion approaching from the south. With a hundred or more trodall."

Eshlyn stepped closer to the woman. "A dwarf?"

"Yes, Lady." She met Caleb's eyes. "Says he's part of the Steelsides, a gift from King Ironsword."

Caleb looked struck.

Eshlyn cocked her head at Caleb. "What does that mean?"

Caleb didn't answer.

"One more thing." Yessica addressed Caleb.

Caleb's grin disappeared. "What is it?"

Yessica beamed. "He says Carys is with them, Cal. Your sister."

Eshlyn saw Caleb's eyes tighten. "Carys? What is she doing with them? And why didn't she come?"

"Not sure. But he says they're going to attack the legion."

"They're going to take on an entire legion?" Iletus said.

Caleb leaned on the Kingstaff and closed his eyes. "Break me."

—⁍—

The legion from Galya camped under the cover of trees two kilomitres south of Vicksburg. The camp had quieted and settled three hours past sunset.

"They are trying to surprise Caleb." Macarus crouched in the brush fifty mitres away to the east of the camp.

"Hopefully your dwarf got word to him." Carys gave Sergeant Gunnar a sideways glance.

"He did," Gunnar mumbled. "Question is, are we all clear on the plan?"

The tents of the camp spread through the forest south of Vicksburg. While not a thick forest like the Saten, Carys had to give the elves credit, they hid well behind trees and brush. No campfires. The horses and cavalry huddled at the rear with the command tent, to the south, and militan tents to the north; the trodall lounged against chains connected to heavy spikes in the ground. Last the siege engines were arranged at the front.

Carys and the others had developed the plan over the last day and a half while they followed and observed the legion. After several discussions and a few maddy ideas – maddy in comparison, at least – they had agreed.

"We're good with the plan." Carys faced Macarus. "Get moving. And keep those tin cans quiet, if you can."

Gunnar scoffed at her. "We are professionals, lassie."

"No promises." Macarus rose and adusted his belt and sword. "And you keep that bosaur of a man from waking the whole camp."

Carys smiled as Zalman grunted. "No promises." She stood and faced Macarus, Gunnar, and the Steelsides huddled a few paces away. "The strength of El with you."

Sergeant Gunnar nodded. "Luck o' the iron to you."

Macarus and Gunnar moved through the brush to the north, and the Steelsides followed with surprising ease, considering the amount of armor and weaponry they carried.

Leaving Carys and Zalman alone.

Zalman stood and towered over her. "You ready?"

She checked the quiver of arrows – many newly made over the last day or borrowed from the Steelsides – the bow over her shoulder, and her unforged sword at her belt. "Ready enough."

The plan had two parts. First, Macarus and the Steelsides would capture and use the siege engines to cause confusion and fear in the camp. Second, Zalman and Carys would infiltrate the camp and free the trodall. Angry and terrified trodall could cause a lot of damage.

Looking up at him, her face flushed. Would she ever feel differently, next to him? "What are we going to do when there isn't a maddy plan to follow?"

Zalman shrugged. "I'll get cattle, start a ranch."

"What will I do?"

He smirked at her. "Tend a garden like an old lady. Make baskets."

She frowned at him. "No I won't. You tend the garden like an old lady. I'll run the ranch."

Zalman chuckled and his large muscles heaved. "Either way."

"Let's go" She started her way through the brush. "Try not to step on every branch and leaf on the way."

He followed her, his eyes intent on the shadows of the forest under the three moons. "Ground is covered in leaves and twigs."

"Exactly. Maybe take off your shirt."

"How will that help?"

"Dunno. You seem to like an excuse to take off your shirt."

He grunted. "Not true. But it is more comfortable."

"Try to keep it on this time, though." *Not that I mind.* "Remember, don't look directly at the guard." Something she had learned from Athelwulf. Looking directly at a person somehow caused them to tense and feel watched. She had thought Ath was insane and stupid, but the more she practiced it, the more she found it to be true.

"I remember."

Carys removed the bow from her shoulder and pulled an arrow from the quiver. She moved forward. The three moons shone through the branches overhead.

Since the camp was more spread out, more militan guarded the legion by twos. Carys kept to the shadows and made her way north before beginning to weave her way to the west and towards the trodall, praying that Zalman would keep his noise to a minimum. For the most part, he did, but a few twigs snapped and she would wince.

El help us.

The elven strategy of attempting to surprise Caleb worked in their favor; no fire or lamps meant less light to expose them to guard.

Moving past a guardpost, she kept them in her periphery, nocking an arrow. Another tent waited to her right, a gray shadow. She crawled along, confirming that there were no elves guarding the other side before stepping lightly through an open space, her head on a swivel, wincing as Zalman's boot shuffled a whisper. A group of tents passed on their left as they moved, two guard there. Carys tiptoed to the shadows to their right.

The trodall slept up ahead with heavy breahing and an occasional groan. She crept closer and made out black figures in the night, like large stones arrayed in rows in the forest.

A gap opened between the tents of the elves and the chained trodall, guard to her right and left. She didn't want to walk across that open space, not with the big gedder behind her. Carys raised a hand, stopping them both. She cursed under her breath and retreated. They would have to go backtrack and go around the tents to the left to gain the cover of the bush. Zalman saw her eyes and nodded his agreement.

They walked back to the south side of the group of tents, and her husband impressed her as he moved silent. However, he broke from her and approached the guard from behind.

She wanted to yell at him, scream at him, break his tree trunk legs if she could, but she could only watch helplessly as he took long, slow steps to reach their backs. And as much as her heart was beating out of her chest, the man was a step away from reaching them.

The elven guard rocked, bored and comfortable. A mistake on their part.

The moons above peeked out from a cloud and threw light from behind her husband. Zalman rose up behind the guard, and his shadow fell across them.

With a gasp, their boredom ended. They turned to see Zalman. He moved fast, grabbing their heads and bashing them against each other with a sickening, wet slap, but not fast enough. One of the guard exclaimed, "Hey!"

"Shog a goat," Carys hissed and pulled the arrow she had nocked, aiming it at the nearest guardpost. The elves there lifted their heads and gazed in the dark.

Zalman rushed over to her, his footsteps sounded like a herd of bosaur, and the elves heard it. But it was fifteen mitres in the dark, and while her eyes had accustomed to the forest dark, the elves hadn't that advantage. They moved anxious, pulling their gladi.

"Sword," Zalman whispered. She unsheathed her unforged sword and handed it to him. She rolled her eyes. *It almost worked*, his shrug told her. He took the sword from her and jogged over to the nearest trodall. Zalman lifted the unforged sword and cut through the chain that restrained it with a clinking sound that echoed in the night.

That hurried the elves, and they strode towards the trodall. She waited until they were ten mitres away before she shot the one on the right in the throat. He fell with a gurgle. The other guard cried out before she put him down with a shaft between the eyes.

The tents rustled behind her to the sound of the elf's cry and Zal freeing the trodall. The trodall also shifted in their slumber. She had heard that it took the shaking of the world to move a trodall, but if you could …

One militan stepped from his tent, followed by another, scanning the dark for the sound of iron chains being broken. She nocked another arrow.

Clank. Clink. Shunk.

Hurry, Zal. She should have been counting. The noises got further and further away.

One elf, a sergeant or squad leader, peered toward the trodall. "What's going on?"

The other group of tents far to her right began to stir, as well. Her body itched to move. *Patience. Wait until you have to give away your position.*

The sergeant stepped from the group of tents, now ten militan with him. Five had risen from their tents to her right. *Wait. Once he finds the …*

Then he saw the dead elves on the ground. He noticed the arrows. The sergeant stood, crouched low, and raised the gladus over his shoulder. "Squad! To me!"

The clinking sound stopped.

That gave her an easy target. She placed an arrow in his chest. The militan around their sergeant now held their gladi and shouted, pointing towards Carys. She stepped from the brush around her and fired. She continued to shoot, and they scattered and ducked for cover; three were down and dead before she lost the majority of her targets.

Elves emerged from tents, wiping their eyes, shaking their heads. She walked towards the trodall, shooting as she went. Her main goal was to keep them watching for her arrows.

Where was Macarus?

A figure appeared next to her. She started as her husband handed her the sword and spoke to her. "Switch."

"No." But she took the sword. "How many did you free?" She shot another elf she thought was a sergeant fifteen mitres away. He stumbled and grabbed his gut.

Zalman held his axes, now. "Fifty two of them. Let me hold them here. There's still twenty or so left."

The trodall began to rouse, standing. They dwarfed even Zalman.

"You big gedder." Another of her arrows stuck through the temple of a militan to her right. "Until Macarus gets his arse in gear and helps us, we'll have to deal with all the trodall, too!" Two militan down with her arrows.

"So we can take militan and fifty trodall but not a hundred? Stop shooting so many. Leave a few for me."

"I have a feeling there will be enough here in a second." One, then two more dead. "You know, when I run out of arrows."

"Fine," Zalman growled and ran forward to their right into the thick of the scrambling militan.

Idiot man. She watched as he cut down confused militan. He spun, blocking a gladus and slicing two of them near in half, blood spraying. She fired around him; once, she even fired an arrow under his arm, missing him by centimitres, and hit a militan in the chest. Zalman scowled at her over her shoulder, and she grinned.

An elf in a longer green tunic raced up to the clearing between the tents and the trodall. He raised a silver horn to his mouth. With a few breaths, he sounded out a pattern.

The trodall all growled and roared.

"Carys!" Zalman cried out. "Shoot him!"

She rolled her eyes at him. *Of course I'm going to shoot him.* She reached into her quiver.

No more arrows.

The elf sputtered another pattern with the horn then pointed at her. The trodall swiveled and trudged toward her.

Carys shouldered her bow and pulled her unforged sword. "Crit on a stick!" She ran to her left and towards the brush, but a trodall lumbered too fast and cut off her escape. She ducked a swipe of one of his arms – one of his four arms – and the claws as big as swords that swept past her. Changing her position, she came around to strike at his arm, cutting deep into the flesh of the arm. The trodall bellowed in pain and stumbled backwards.

More trodall hurried towards her. All fifty two of them. One approached her from behind.

And did not see Zalman attack. Her husband leapt and led with his knees to the back of the trodall, his axes high over his head. The trodall changed direction from the blow, and it fell forward. Zalman brought the axes down on the back of the trodall's skull with his full force and roared like an animal himself. The trodall twitched as it died.

Carys woke from her hesitation and ran forward toward the first trodall, which had recovered. She sliced through the joints of its legs. It fell to its knees and struck at her with its three remaining arms. She dove into a roll and came up cutting into one arm then a second one. The trodall reared back in pain, and she pressed forward. She jumped as high as she could, raising the sword, and she stabbed the trodall in what she hoped was the heart. The trodall fell backwards; she held onto the sword and rode it down. The trodall fell on its back, black blood spurting from its mouth.

In a second, she scanned and saw both trodall and a hundred militan surrounding her. Zalman rolled off of the trodall he just killed to stand between her and elves and creatures.

She looked up as a ball of flame appeared in the sky in a high arc. The trodall and the elves beyond Zalman followed her eyes. The whole scene was quiet. The fireball hovered in the air for a moment before falling onto the tents far to her right. Elves, tents, and dirt erupted in flame.

Nice shot, Macarus.

Then more flaming missiles arced down upon the legion and the forest around them, a dozen or more, both near and far. She flinched as she saw a trodall skewered by a ballista spear.

The noise became immediately deafening – the screeching of trodall, the shouts of elves, the falling stones of flame that shook the ground and destroyed trees and bodies.

The trodall flailed. They could not hear the elf's trumpet anymore, however desperately he tried. They raised claws to the sides of their heads, bellowing, growling, whimpering.

Carys vaulted off of the dying trodall's chest to the ground and ran towards the dead militan ten or more mitres away. Bodies were scattered around her, and she bent to grab the shaft of an arrow sticking from a bloody militan. Tugging hard, it came free, and she slid to a stop, aimed and fired.

The arrow sailed twenty mitres away and went through the silver horn, into the elf's mouth, and out the back of his head.

At first, the trodall paused, appearing confused, maybe afraid. Their fear turned to rage, mindless. They pushed and struck one another, breaking formation and attacking anything in sight of their black eyes. One grabbed two militan with its four arms and ripped both of them in half.

Militan screamed and ran.

Zalman ran toward her. A trodall caught sight of him and followed. Zalman wove and spun to face the creature. He ducked one arm, then another, blocking a third and cutting at the beast, but his axes weren't made by the Living Stone. They cut but not deep.

Well, crit. She darted to her right and grabbed another arrow from a dead militan. She fired at the trodall, but the arrow had been bent and flew wide.

Balls of flame continued to rain down upon them and spears of the ballista whizzed by them.

Zalman retreated, avoiding the claws and arms of the trodall.

She ran to another dead body and lifted an arrow, praying it would fly straight, and she fired. The arrow bounced off of the trodall's thick hide.

Zalman continued to hack at the trodall, hurting the creature with cuts that bled black but not bad enough to put it down.

Shaking her head, she grabbed another arrow from a dead elf, pulled, and fired into the trodall's right eye. The trodall stopped, leaning back and crying in pain. Zalman took the advantage to go on the offensive, striking the trodall's stomach, five times.

By then, flames spitting around her, she pulled a last arrow from a dead militan. A stone of flame fell five mitres away and knocked her to her knees.

The trodall lurched toward Zalman again, blood pouring down its red and scaly face from the wounded eye, and he split the creature's skin with both axes before jumping back to avoid the long arms.

Carys recovered, felt a pain in her side, drew and fired into the left eye. The trodall was blind and struck at the air. Zalman took the opportunity to dive forward and drive both axes into the trodall's chest. It fell backwards, and Zalman gave no quarter. He climbed up the trodall's torso as it fell, and he chopped at its neck. Black blood spewed upwards. Zalman took another step on the body of the gurgling creature and sunk both axes into the trodall's forehead. The creature went still.

Carys jogged toward Zalman as chaos continued around them. She touched her side, and it was wet and sticky with blood. Zalman saw her approach.

"You're welcome," she called to him.

He eyed her side. "You're hurt."

"No crit." She collapsed into him. "You think we can go, now?"

Zalman didn't respond except to lift her in his arms and run through the anarchy and confusion and death towards the west to the rendezvous point. She buried her face in his neck and held tight.

—+—

Zalman reached the rendezvous fifteen minutes later, two hundred mitres or more from the legion camp on a short hill with good vantage of the camp.

He did not survey the camp, however.

Macarus and the others hadn't arrived yet, but the catapults stopped firing five minutes ago. Shouts of fighting reached his ears, however.

Zalman removed the branches from over their packs and set his aside to get into Carys'.

"I'm fine," she said.

"Tell me what to do." He dug and found the pouch that held her medical supplies.

"It's too dark to see how bad."

He grunted at her. "Then we make a fire."

"They'll see." It lacked conviction so he didn't waste time arguing.

He built the fire from the branches that hid their packs, using her flint to light it. Within thirty seconds, a nice flame blossomed. He shifted her tunic out of the way and adjusted her position to better see by the fire.

"Stone in your skin. Not deep but bleeding."

She gave him a weak grin. "See. Told you."

"This is going to hurt."

"What is going to ... ah!"

He pulled the stone from her stomach. He removed his tunic and pressed it to the bleeding wound.

"Always with the breakin' shirt," she said. "I have bandages in the bag!"

He met her gaze. "Tell me what to do."

"Fine. Since I don't trust you to stitch it, you'll have to cauterize."

"With?"

"There's a knife in there. Put it in the fire."

After more screaming and cursing and her fingernails that drew blood on his shoulder, he held her down and cauterized the wound. She screamed. He rubbed the healing oil on it and then bandaged her side.

She took deep breaths. "Now help me up. I want to see."

She stood, leaning on him and drew the peerglass. She scanned the camp.

"Great and mighty El," she whispered.

"What?"

She lowered the glass from her eye. "They're killing each other."

He frowned at her. "What does that mean?"

"I mean, part of our plan was to get the trodall to kill as many as possible, but the whole legion is killing each other, attacking anything they see. Like they're all maddy. For the real."

He held out his hand, and she put the peerglass within it. She was right. Elves attacked anything that moved, horses, militan, officers, trodall. The forest around the camp burned, and the fire spread. Pandemonium.

It took him a moment to realize the growing light was not from flame but the coming dawn. He lowered the peerglass.

"We just took out a whole legion," he said.

"No." She pointed over at the camp of death. "They did."

+——

The legion attacked from the east at dawn. Caleb leaned forward, gripping the Kingstaff.

The Kryan divisions moved into place systematically; long wooden platforms pulled by large horses led the way to the River Moriel with siege engines behind them. It took them an hour to get into position. Each division was shaped like a rectangle and used their shields to protect them, spreading like a crescent moon around the town.

Where was their cavalry?

Bweth had command of the *Hamon-el* to the east. She had half of them arrayed behind the pikes with the siege engines spaced between the divisions. The other half waited in the city as reinforcements.

To the south, smoke rose from the trees. *Carys?* That dwarf had said Macarus was with the Steelsides. Caleb prayed they all were well.

Caleb stood on the roof of a three story building on the eastern side of the town. Eshlyn, Iletus, and Andos stood with him. As expected, they had the high ground, so Caleb gave the order to fire their own catapults over the river at the legion. The humans trained in the longbow – two thousand of them – arrayed behind the makeshift log wall stayed ready to fire when the militan came in range.

Caleb laid a hand upon his sword. He wanted to be down there, fighting. He was no general, no king. He was a weapon, and he itched to be using the sword, even if it was him alone against the legion.

Now that the militan came into range, the longbows fired. Together with the catapults, they rained missiles down upon the center of the Kryan line, attempting to cut the legion in half. The divisions split into smaller units, squads, creating smaller targets as they continued to use the shields for protection. It worked. More of them survived the barrage.

Caleb gave the order to fire in a less concentrated pattern, and the arrows and stones spread wide. Squads were decimated and militan dropped with arrows protruding from their bodies. But the legion jogged forward.

"They are testing our placement." Iletus pointed beyond the line, and the cavalry shifted to the south.

Most of the veterans and Ghosts took position on the eastern side of the town. The members of the *Hamon-el* that had recently returned defended the west. The 1,500 elves – militan and Cityguard – were all to the south. Shecayah had been hesitant, but Eshlyn convinced her and Tobiah to stay. Her word as the prophetic *Bashawyn* pulled a great deal of weight, and the Beorgai with the bosaur defended the north.

Andos had his peerglass to his eye, following the shifting cavalry. "They have hooks, chains."

"They're going to pull down the wall on the south side to enter the town," Eshlyn said.

Caleb called down to the street where a runner on a horse waited. "Send word to Tobiah and Shecayah. Move the bosaur around the west and engage the cavalry." Thimis, a young man from Giannis, nodded his understanding and rode to the north.

"They are expecting reinforcements," Iletus said. "But with that fire and smoke to the south, it looks like they may not be able to expect much."

Caleb scowled. "Surely their general sees that, too."

The 500 Kryan cavalry rode to the south and out of range of arrows and stone. Three of the elven riders broke away and rode even further south as the rest swung to the west and back towards the city.

"What are they doing?" Caleb asked. No one responded. One of the three led the way and drew a silver horn from his saddle. Lifting it to his lips, he blew a pattern upon the horn.

"Calling for reinforcements," Eshlyn said. "We'll see how many answer."

"Reinforcements, yes," Andos said. "But not elves."

Eshlyn breathed through her nose.

The trees to the south moved, like something large moved through the forest. A herd of something big. He shared a glance with Iletus, and they both said the word together. "Trodall."

Through his peerglass, red and black shapes, hulking figures, lumbered in the trees. He didn't know how many, but several trodall walked towards the town.

The cavalry approached at a dead sprint from the southwest, dozens of them with hooks on chains at the front and bows. The militan and Cityguard positioned to protect Vicksburg began to fire arrows as a deterrent, but the cavalry was well trained, weaving and dodging as they ran. The cavalry also fired back, the ones without the chains and hooks.

Trodall began to emerge from the trees, 250 mitres from the log wall. Ten at first, then a score more.

Caleb counted thirty eight trodall, growling and snarling.

He cursed as he spun on his heel on the roof and tried to catch the progress of the bosaur. He scanned for a moment. "What in the name of El? The Beorgai haven't moved."

"What?" Eshlyn peered over to the north, as well. "Break it all! What are they doing?"

Caleb lowered his peerglass and gritted his teeth. "They are about to cost us the battle."

Eshlyn gaped at him. "I'm sorry, Cal. I talked to her. I thought they understood."

"Don't take the blame for the decision of others," Caleb said. "Go to them, now. We need them."

Eshlyn nodded and moved to the ladder that led to the street.

She left, and Caleb turned to Iletus. "Go to the *Sohan-el*, as many as you can find." Shouldn't be difficult, most were leading their divisions to the east and west. "Have them meet me on the south."

Iletus nodded and walked with Caleb towards the ladder.

"Wait," Andos said.

Caleb paused and gazed at the elf over his shoulder.

Andos lifted his hands in question. "What are you going to do?"

"I'm going to make sure we don't lose this battle," Caleb answered. "Even if I have to kill all the trodall myself."

Andos gulped at him as he looked around the roof. Alone. "And what about me? What do you want me to do?"

Caleb climbed down the ladder. "Come with me."

The babe turned within her while the Kryan legion marched closer to the city. The wooden platforms – Bweth counted thirty of them – rose like towers, looming forward across the field to the river. She measured the distance with her eye. Another few minutes and the towers would be in range. But looking at the siege engines next to the towers, the threat would break both ways.

She wasn't looking forward to that.

Caleb had tried to get her to ride a horse. She hated riding horses and a wagon among the pikes wouldn't work, so she used her feet and short legs to pace back and forth in front of the line. She checked with the division heads, even accusing one of intimate acts with his mother, which she regretted but moved on.

The land sloped downhill from the defenses to the river; slight but it might give them a few mitres advantage.

Bweth gazed at the one bridge over the river, an ancient and large structure. She and Caleb had discussed destroying the bridge, but they might need it at some point. And then she had an idea of how to use it. If it would only breakin' work.

She jogged her way to the catapults and the ballista, one by one. "Get ready! Aim for the platforms! But wait for my shoggin' signal!"

Without waiting for their response – she would break their arse if they didn't do it right – Bweth climbed up on a catapult at the center.

Thousands of militan slid as one organism behind the towers and siege engines. Large supply wagons waited at the rear with the command structure – the General and his officers. Any student of war had to be impressed with the organization, the monolithic nature of the Kryan war machine. Unfortunately, it also made them predictable.

Bweth raised her spiked steel mace high in the air. "Wait for it!"

The Kryan militan loaded their own machines, tightening the wheels and pulleys. Ready.

Bweth cursed under her breath. *Here we go.*

"Shog those towers!" She lowered her mace in a long arc.

Ropes snapped and wood groaned as dozens of stones sailed in the air over the river and smashed down on the field on the other side. Two of the platforms were hit, both damaged and broken, but most of the stones missed.

She was going to have to break their arses in half.

"We're not going to get a better shot at this! Adjust and fire!" She had trained and taught the humans as best she could. She requested elven consultants from Andos, but some of the *Hamon-el* didn't fully trust them. It weakened their defenses, but she could tell the elves wanted to stay with their own, as well.

The catapults slung more stones, and the aim improved. Twelve more were hit, eight of those broken and dead on the field.

Bweth squinted as she noticed thirteen of the supply wagons moving between the divisions toward the front line of the battle.

What the shog are they doing?

The Kryan catapults were almost within range.

"We've got one more shot before the Underland breaks all over us," she yelled. "Take them all out!"

They needed to bottleneck the Legion on the bridge. It was their best chance to stop five thousand elves before they got to the city and the weak defenses. One more volley from the catapults destroyed ten more of the platforms. Only ten functional ones left. Not bad.

The babe kicked her belly. *We might make this yet.*

Seeing movement, she raised her peerglass and saw the calvary move to the south. "They're making their way to attack from the south," she muttered to herself. Turning, she saw smoke rising to the south. *Another legion there?*

She focused on the legion across the river. She had enough to deal with here.

Her brow furrowed. Those supply wagons kept moving forward, large wooden boxes usually used for perishable goods. Why would they ...?

The Kryans fired at them; Bweth cursed as large stones hung in the sky before raining down at them. "Take cover!"

The three thousand of the *Hamon-el* behind her raised shields and huddled in their assigned platoons and behind pikes. Stones tore through the grass and dirt and pikes. Men screamed while stones crushed them.

"Aim for the engines." The din drowned her out. "The engines!"

Those wagons, however, kept moving forward. Something in her gruts didn't feel right.

The platforms also kept moving forward. Ten of them crawling toward them. They came within twenty five mitres of the bank of the Moriel River. *Now.*

The front wheels of the trailers that held the platforms sunk deep into a ditch a mitre wide and two mitres deep. The good people of Vicksburg and Giannis had spent most of the previous evening digging that ditch and then covering it with sod to deceive the legions. Ten or twenty thousand people might not be trained enough to fight but they could dig.

The wheels of the trailers sunk into the ditch; the platforms lurched forward with screaming wood, per their design. The platforms slammed into grass and the riverbank and only reached halfway across the river. Water splashed up into the air as the front edge of the platforms sunk into the water. The militan around the platforms scattered and ran back to the main force. Which simply waited while the catapults and trebuchets moved forward. Along with those supply wagons.

They traded catapult volleys with the Kryans again. Scores of her men crushed. More injured. They took out three of the Kryan catapults.

Those breakin' wagons.

Bweth shook her head. "Ballista! Fire on those wagons!"

To their credit, her men turned and fired on those thirteen wagons within a few seconds. Most of the long spears missed, however. But two impaled one of the wagons, creating large holes.

Something within that wagon moved. Something yellow and green through the holes. And it made a noise. Something animal.

The damaged wagon splintered as the creature thrashed. It had a large, round head and a long segmented body with dozens of legs on each side. Thin antennae and red pinchers extended from the head.

The ballista spears still stuck in it, and it fell to the field near the bank of the river. The horses pulling the wagon reared and screamed. Militan ran.

Big crittin' centipedes. That's new.

The militan at the other wagons knew the trick was up, so they unhitched their own horses, releasing them. They opened the large door at the front of the wagon before they ran.

Another traded volley between her men and the Kryans, men dying, screaming.

Twelve enormous green and yellow centipedes, twenty mitres long, came rushing across the field to the river. Their red pinchers open while the antennae twisted and searched in front of them, they entered the river water and began to swim across toward them.

And the Legion followed.

———

Zalman winced as Carys grabbed his shoulder even tighter.

"Those cavalry," she said. "They're going to pull down the defenses."

He didn't have a peerglass, but squinting his eyes, she was right. Those log walls wouldn't hold for long.

"And the left side of the Kryan line is shifting to support," Macarus added.

A thousand elves in a rectanglar shape moved like a shadow underneath their shields in the morning light.

After Macarus and the Steelsides had arrived at the rendezvous, they traveled to a different hill with a better vantage point of the battle.

Macarus and the Steelsides had returned without losing a member since they were able to take the guard around the siege engines without much of a fight. And with Macarus' expertise in the engines, they easily turned them around to successfully fire back at the legion. They had fifteen horses, as well, large ones meant for pulling the catapults and ballista, perfect size for Zalman.

Carys shook his shoulder. "That one, he's calling the trodall like the other one did."

Caleb can handle it. But his throat tightened with the rustling trees to his right.

He turned to look at the enormous creatures, now crazed and enraged from the chaos that began an hour ago. They moved through the branches and trees.

"Big shoggin' beasts," Sergeant Gunnar said with awe.

"We have to help," Carys said.

He shook his head. "You're hurt. There's no *we* doing anything."

They sat still while thirty or more of the cavalry shot hooks from their bows. Missles arced over the wall; the elves tied the chains to their saddles and ran, away from the wall. Twenty hooks found purchase, and the elves pulled. The wall strained, groaned, and then snapped, and a piece of the wall thirty mitres wide fell with a crash.

Carys lowered her peerglass and wheeled on Macarus. He flinched at the look in her eye. So did Zalman. *That's Caleb's look.*

"Did you use all the ammunition for those catapults and ballista?" she asked the elf captain.

"No. Most, but not all."

Carys squinted at him. "Get the horses."

Macarus sighed. "By the time we move those engines into position, the battle could be over."

Gunnar humphed. "Are those *elves* behind the wall, defending the town?"

"We have to try." Carys pulled away from him and walked down through the trees to the horses.

"Aye!" Gunnar said. "Can't stand sitting and watching a battle." He joined Carys.

Macarus shared a glance with Zal. "I guess we're going back down there."

Zalman glared at him.

"What? You married her."

"You coming?" Carys yelled back at him.

Exhausted, he shook his head, checked the axes at his belt, and he followed.

—

Caleb saw a piece of the wall fall to the south. He and Andos rode up together.

The elves were organized by platoons, a mixture of militan and Cityguard, behind the wall in a gap before homes now empty. Hundreds fired arrows, volley after volley, from ten mitres back and the rest huddled in front. The elves who had been in position at the now-vacant wall began to scatter.

A captain turned with fear in his eyes. "General Andos. They are pulling down the wall."

Caleb raised a brow. "General?"

Andos averted his gaze, then addressed the Captain. "We see." Andos dismounted and handed the reins to a sergeant.

Caleb jumped from his horse with the Kingstaff in his hand, landing on his feet a few paces away. "Captain, we have to keep elves on that position."

"We need reinforcements," the Captain said with desperation.

Caleb unsheathed his unforged sword. "Sorry. I'm all the help you've got for now." He strode past the Captain. "*General* Andos, with me."

Andos stumbled forward. "Y-yes sir."

Caleb pushed through elves toward the hole in the wall. "If we make it through this, you get to call me *Caleb*."

"Yes, *Brendel*."

Caleb rolled his eyes and began shouting orders at the elves around him. "Do not leave your posts!" He pointed to a sergeant. "You. Take your platoon, go back into those homes and find whatever furniture or anything that we can use for cover. Move."

The sergeant ordered his platoon to follow as he obeyed.

Caleb gestured at the rest of the elves. "I need shields where the wall used to be. Two rows of shields. Archers behind."

The pounding hooves of the Kryan cavalry announced their arrival, swinging around for another attack.

Elves raced to form a shield wall, two rows deep. Andos and another captain organized them. Archers nocked arrows behind the assembling elves.

Caleb stood in front of the forming shield wall. "Remember, we have the high ground." He raised his unforged sword over his head. "Archers, on my mark." He measured the distance as the mounted elves sprinted towards them. Not longbows. Shortbows of the elves. The cavalry nocked their own arrows as another twenty of them readied hooks and chains.

He lowered his sword. "Fire." Two hundred arrows sailed towards the cavalry and thirty went down. "Again, again!"

The elves behind him fired more volleys as the cavalry drew closer. This time they attacked a piece of the wall far to Caleb's left, shooting the hooks over the wall.

Caleb shouted over his shoulder. "Make sure those hooks don't grab hold."

Andos ran towards the wall, giving orders, even calling names.

The cavalry attempted to give cover to their fellows by shooting at Caleb's position. Arrows darted at him, and as the elves behind him ducked behind their shields, he batted arrows aside with the Kingstaff and his sword.

The ground shook. Beyond the cavalry attack, Caleb could see the trodall approaching. As could the elves around him. The trodall were seventy mitres away.

"Nine gods!" he heard from behind him.

"Hold!" Caleb said.

Glancing to his left, elves removed the hooks from the wall with their gladi, but three dug into the top of the wall and strained. The wall groaned but held. Those three elves were pulled from their horses to the ground, and Caleb directed the next volley in that direction. All three died under a flood of arrows.

The cavalry also saw the trodall loping toward them, and they peeled away.

"Archers, target the trodall," Caleb ordered.

To their credit, the line held and they fired at the trodall. The arrows bounced right off of them.

"Break me," Caleb said. The trodall were fifty mitres away now. Were there forty of them? "The eyes. Aim for the eyes!"

Another volley launched, and he watched as seven of the trodall were hit in one eye, but not both. They all still drove forward, more enraged than ever.

Caleb sighed. How he missed Carys. Where was she now? To the south?

He shook his head to clear it.

"Again!"

———

Eshlyn stepped closer to Shecayah. "We need those bosaur on the south side."

The Beorgai were spread through the north behind the wall with their corran and bows at the ready. The bosaur stood to her left near the makeshift gate, a hundred of them.

Shecayah shook her head. "We were given the task of protecting the north. We will not leave our people here without the bosaur."

Eshlyn waved her hand over the empty fields to the north. "There's no one here! We're fighting to the east and south. They need reinforcements."

"It could be a trap." Tobiah stood next to his wife. "They could be drawing us to the south while a force attacks here."

Eshlyn ran a hand through her dark hair and took a deep breath. "Caleb is down there, fighting. Cavalry, trodall, maybe more. Get on those beasts and support him."

Tobiah and Shecayah eyed each other. Shecayah faced Eshlyn. "We will hold our position here."

"Break it all," Eshlyn hissed and laid a hand upon the sword at her waist.

Shecayah's brow rose. "Would you raise a sword to me, *Bashawyn*?"

Eshlyn's nostrils flared. "You want a message from your *Bashawyn*, from your messenger queen?" She moved within centimitres of Shecayah, their noses almost touching. "You're a coward, and your brother would be ashamed of you."

Tobiah bared his teeth at her. "And what happens if we leave and the elves attack here and take the town? We are blamed for losing the battle, for not doing our part. Don't you see? You ask this of us, and we look bad no matter what we do."

"Based on assumptions, possibilities," Eshlyn said. "Caleb is in trouble. Now. He's asked for your help."

Shecayah blinked and stepped back. "Sorry, *Bashawyn*, we believe we help him best by defending this position. We hold."

Eshlyn groaned and shouldered past both of them and toward the line of bosaur.

"*B-bashawn ...*" Shecayah called. "Where are you going?"

Eshlyn didn't answer as she walked down the line of bosaur and reached the animal closest to the gate. She hesitated, looking up at the enormous beast. Her heart thundered in her chest. One of these things almost trampled her in the forest of Lior.

She closed her eyes and felt for the Mahakar. She did this often, knowing he was far away in Lior, but a part of her wished to ride him once more. But she felt nothing.

Opening her eyes, her jaw tightened as she reached up and climbed to the top of the bosaur using the lashes for that purpose on the strap of the saddle. She threw her leg over the shoulder of the animal. The saddle was a thick and formed piece of leather with a high pommel behind the bony frill. A leather cord looped around the pommel, the reins.

How do you get this thing moving? She gripped the leather cord and shook it. She kicked the bosar, gently. It raised its head but didn't move.

"*Bashawyn.*" Shecayah stood below and next to the bosar. "Don't do this. You don't know how ..."

Eshlyn set her jaw. "You better open that gate, 'cause one way or another, I'm going through it." *Once I get this breaking thing to walk.*

Shecayah continued to try and talk her down, but Eshlyn ignored her. She prayed to El. *Please. I need to help Caleb and the elves to the south.*

She leaned over and spoke low to the animal. "Come on, girl. Work with me here."

Eshlyn hunched her shoulders and gripped the reins tighter, pulling the head up more. The animal groaned, and she kicked once more, with more force, and squeezed the shoulders with her thighs.

The bosaur moved.

Suppressing a gasp, she guided the moving bosaur toward the gate. She shouted down at the Beorgai men at the gate. "Open it!"

Thankfully, the men obeyed. The log door swung open just as she and the bosaur walked through. She kicked the bosaur twice more, and she sped up. Eshlyn yanked the reins to the left, and the bosaur moved with a snort. With another double kick, the bosaur was at a run, feet pounding loud in her ears and her hair whipping in the wind.

I should have asked how you stop this thing ... But she would worry about that later.

+———

Bweth ducked a stone a couple mitres over her head. It sailed by and crashed into the log wall, and she rose to see twelve green and yellow centipedes skittering across the space between the river and the *Hamon-el.*

Where had they found these things? Centipedes that swim? She briefly wondered how Kryus had trained these things to come straight at them. Had Moonguard been involved?

And the Legion moved toward the bridge, the only way across the river. They could march ten across if they get there. And if they take the bridge ...

"Archers, ballista, on the shoggin' bugs!" Bweth pointed to a man to her right. "Miller and Spring's divisions, to the bridge! You have to hold!"

Miller and Spring yelled orders at their own divisions, and they ran forward to the bridge, more than a thousand men and women following them.

Shouting at each other, her men on the ballista turned and focused on the centipedes. Their aim was clumsy, and only two centipedes were hit. And even they kept going.

Well, crit. They're going to get to us.

Bweth began running to intercept the closest centipede, her pregnant belly bouncing painfully, but she wouldn't make it. She watched arrows from behind the log wall bounce off of the carapaces. The ballista fired once more and skewered three, killing them, including one of the original wounded.

Her men engaged the militan on the bridge.

While stones rained upon them, nine monstrous centipedes tore the platoons left behind the pikes. The pikes made it difficult for the creatures to maneuver. But the creatures still grabbed men with their pincers. Bweth gritted her teeth at the screams.

Bweth reached the nearest centipede, a dozen men stabbing at it. Two men were crushed in its pincers, blood pouring from their mouths. They writhed to get free.

Roaring in anger, she leapt as high as she could, raising the spiked mace above her head. She landed and struck the left pincer of the 'pede, and it snapped off with a spray of yellow blood.

The wounded men fell from the mouth. The 'pede made a screeching sound and came around to attack Bweth with its remaining pincer. Bweth got her shield up in time, but it struck her with enough force to knock her to her knees. Grunting with the effort, she pushed up and smashed her mace onto its head with a sick crunch. The mace stuck, and when the creature flailed to retreat, it pulled her along with it.

Bweth held on for her life as it lifted her in the air. When she came down, she dug her feet into the dirt and yanked the mace free. Ten men stabbed the thing with their gladi, and it fell still.

Panting, she came to her feet and saw four of the 'pedes still alive. Men had pulled the thinner pikes from the ground and used them to impale the creatures.

She ran toward the nearest one. Two platoons surrounded it with gladi and spears and the makeshift pikes. Broken bodies lay on the grass before the 'pede. A stone slammed into the ground next to her, a couple mitres away, the Kryans still firing catapults at them. Dirt sprayed over her and caused her to stumble. She stayed on her feet somehow and turned to approach the creature from behind.

Bweth jumped on the tail end and ran the length of the creature. It twisted and bucked, so she had to ram the sharp end of her shield into one segment to keep from falling. Once she got her feet again, she raced the remaining five meters, her boots slipping on the hard surface. She allowed herself to fall the remaining few steps, lifting her mace and shield at the end and striking down on the back of its head.

The creature twitched and went still.

Bweth stood on the creature and scanned the battlefield. All the 'pedes were dead, but at a great cost. Between the volleys from the Kryans and the centipedes, they had taken a lot of casualties. Turning to the bridge, she saw Miller and Spring's divisions being pushed back.

The Kyran militan linked their shields to push forward across the bridge, one step at a time.

Bweth also saw a division peel off from the main legion to move south along the river. Where were they going? She cursed but didn't have the resources to do anything about it.

"The bridge," Bweth cried to the ballista operators since the catapults still engaged the Kryan siege engines. "Target the other side of the bridge, the militan there!"

They turned the ballista and began firing. Long spears ripped through the shields and armor of the militan on the far riverbank.

Bweth noticed that their exchange with the Kryan catapults and trebuchets was going in her favor. Several of the elven engines lay smashed on the field. The elven commander had made a mistake. While he or she focused on her soldiers, the *Hamon-el* had targeted their engines, and Bweth's army still had some defense with the pikes.

But it would all be for nothing if the Kryans took the bridge. The ballista fire helped. But she wished she could be there on the front line, fighting. With two divisions in the way, it would take forever for her to get to the front line. She needed to get there now.

Well, there is one way …

Bweth headed over to the nearest catapult. She yelled over the log wall. "Reinforcements! We're gonna need you! We need archers on the rest of the legion."

She could hear the movement behind the wall, but she ignored it. The bridge was the priority.

She approached the operator of the catapult, Walsh. "Turn this one to the elves on the bridge."

Walsh frowned at her, but he ordered the men to point the catapult more to the south. He started adjusting and aiming.

Bweth inspected him. "No. You need to make the rope two degrees tighter."

Walsh's frown deepened. "But that will take the stone over the target."

Bweth climbed into the bucket.

"What are you doing?" Walsh squealed. "The fall will kill you!"

"Against dirt or the stone of the bridge, you'd be right." Bweth sat in the bucket. "But I'll be landing on elves. Elves are much softer than stone."

"But still …"

"Dwarves are known for their ability to take punishment. Between that and my armor, I'll be fine. Now adjust the two degrees. Don't shog it up."

"But you're …"

"If you try to use the babe as an excuse, I'll come down there, stick my mace up your arse! The babe'll probably enjoy the flight."

Bweth crossed her arms, the shield out in front of her. And waited.

"Ready," Walsh grumbled.

"Then fire!"

Wood creaked and the rope snapped and suddenly Bweth was in the air. She would've cussed but she couldn't talk. *This was a breakin' stupid idea.* And she prayed that Walsh hadn't shogged it up. At the apex before she started to fall, she stole a glance past her shield and through her legs.

Critters, this is high.

But she would land right at the front line onto elves and their shields. She quickly drew into a ball.

The impact shook every part of her, but she landed shield first, which absorbed some of the impact. For a moment, she didn't know if she was badly injured or not … but she didn't have time to guess. Elves scattered, shouting, and she kicked out as the elves slowed her momentum and she hit the stone of the bridge.

In desperation, Bweth jumped to her feet, surprised nothing was broken – although her shield arm tingled and a little numb. And her right side spoke a sharp pain. Probably a broken rib. She gathered all this information in a split second.

She was alive and able to fight.

She raised her mace and shield and looked to see the elves around her struggling to recover.

Bweth Ironhorn smiled and attacked.

———

The horses were hooked to the catapults and ballista and a wagon of ammo. They only had enough horses for six of the catapults and two of the ballista. Carys rode one of two horses pulling a catapult.

On the eastern side of the town, the long Kryan platforms had failed, and the *Hamon-el* fought the Kryans on the bridge. *Wait, was that a person flying in the air?* An armored figure slammed into the militan on the bridge. *Was that Bweth?*

She turned her attention back to the south – the trodall closed in on the town and the cavalry peeled away to the south. A thousand elves with shields and spears moved from the east along the river to support the attack to the south. One division carried a long platform to get across the river.

They were going to overwhelm the southern position. She kicked her horse, hard. She'd apologize to it later.

"Can we load these things as we move?" Carys asked.

"Never done it before." Macarus led a horse to her right. "But I don't see why not."

"How strong are your Steelsides?" she called to Sergeant Gunnar.

Walking ahead of them, Gunnar shared a glance with his brother Ulf. "Stronger than you know."

"Wind and load these shoggers, then," Carys spat. "Zal!"

Her sword was sheathed, and the bow lay across her lap. Three quivers full of elven arrows hung from the harness of the horse. She wouldn't run out this time.

Zalman moved to the wagon and hefted a large stone; Macarus hopped down from his horse and ran to the moving catapult behind. He began to work the winch and the arm of the catapult stretched back. Gunnar and Ulf and seven of the Steelsides worked the other engines, as well. Another ten of the Steelsides ran to the wagon, taking stones and long spears from the wagon.

Macarus finished setting the catapult. Zalman threw the stone up in the bucket.

"Macarus," Carys called. "Are we in range?"

"For who? What's our target?"

That was a good question. Cavalry? Militan? They weren't close enough for the trodall yet. "Cavalry. Take out the horses."

"Then you need to adjust to your right, two degrees," Macarus answered. "And I'll adjust the range."

How do I know what two degrees are? "Can we fire on the move?"

"I wouldn't suggest it," Macarus said. "It would throw off accuracy."

"But we can do it."

"Yes."

"Gunnar, I need seven of your dwarves to ride the horses and help aim these breaking things," Carys said.

"We ain't horsedwarves, lassie," Gunnar shouted back at her.

"Then grab their harnesses and lead them. Just do it."

Gunnar assigned seven of his dwarves to horses, and the rest of them to help work the machines.

Carys pulled on the harness in front of her and moved the catapult's aim to the right. "Now?"

"Now," Macarus said, and she maneuvered straight.

"Steelsides, adjust to this direction, as well as you can." Her side hurt when she yelled.

The catapult behind her fired, the whole machine rocking on its wheels. The stone made its way through the air and fell at the edge of the cavalry, since they were moving, but still bowled through ten horses. The rest of the cavalry tried to stop but halted directly into their line of fire.

"Everyone, release," Macarus ordered.

They did. Two spears went through horses and elves before digging into the ground. Six more stones fell in and around the cavalry. Half of their number was gone in an instant.

Carys grinned as she pulled an arrow from a quiver and nocked it. "Again. Load and fire again."

———

The trodall were within fifteen mitres when six of the other *Sohan-el* arrived. They were going to have to deal with the trodall hand to hand. Caleb turned to the elven Captain. "I need your fourteen best marksmen … markselves, whatever. Now."

The captain moved and pointed to fourteen of the archers. Those archers looked at Caleb, their eyes wide. "The unforged swords can cut the trodall. Two of you with every *Sohan-el*." Caleb began to assign them. "The rest of you, fire over the heads of the trodall and keep the cavalry away."

Caleb and six other *Sohan-el* – Jaff, Juhl, Xak, Ewha, Digby and Yessica – moved forward.

"Spread out, engage the trodall," Caleb instructed. "Archers, behind the *Sohan-el*. Aim for their eyes. Blind as many as you can. We will take care of the rest."

Three *Sohan-el* spread to the right and three to the left, and Caleb moved forward down the middle.

The ground beyond the trodall began to quake as stones and ballista spears tore up the field. Someone fired at the legion and the cavalry from the south. Caleb looked up and smiled. *Carys.*

With the other volleys, twelve trodall were blinded and writhing in pain twenty mitres away. That left another twenty five or so to deal with.

Caleb pointed to the trodall nearest him with the Kingstaff. Two arrows flew, and one hit the trodall's right eye. Another moment and two arrows blossomed in the left eye. The trodall stopped moving, two arms reaching up to the eyes bleeding black, yowling in pain. Caleb moved forward, swatted an arm away with the Kingstaff and made three cuts, one to each knee and through the gut. Black and smoldering entrails spilled out, and the stench overpowered. Caleb moved back to let the trodall fall.

Two came at him now. One trodall ripped a large sharpened tree from the ground and swung it at him. Caleb ducked and rolled under the pike as the elves behind him continued to fire. They blinded one and then focused on the one with the tree. Arrows bounced off the cheek of the trodall. Caleb blocked one arm with the Kingstaff, which almost knocked him off his feet, and he spun around to cut through the elbow of another arm. The unforged sword sliced clean and the limb fell to the ground.

The elves had blinded the trodall by now, and so the trodall cried out in agony. Caleb leapt up and drove his knee into the chest of the trodall, dropping the sharpened tree in its fall backward. Caleb brought the Kingstaff down on arrows in the creatures left eye, slamming the shafts deeper into the thing's brain. He followed with a stab into the forehead with the unforged sword.

He launched himself from the crouch toward the other blinded trodall. Dodging the flailing arms, he snuck in to stab the beast through the chest and then gut him.

"Brendel!" he heard from the two elves with him, and he turned to see three more lumbering toward them. The elves were a step away from panic, but they held it together long enough to blind one of the trodall and then the other as he ran in their direction. Their aim was getting better.

The third trodall, however, reached out and grabbed one of his archers, the claws piercing the elf's chest. The archer screamed while the other dropped to the ground and rolled away.

Caleb swung with the Kingstaff, breaking the bones of one arm, and the unforged sword struck the arm holding the dying archer. The trodall arm separated at the wrist, and the archer plummeted back to the dirt and grass, blood everywhere. Caleb moved behind the trodall, jumped and stabbed the monster in the back of the head. The trodall twitched as it died.

Caleb didn't have time to check on the archer; he sprinted to the other two blinded trodall. Passing one, he cut through a knee, and reaching the second, he planted the Kingstaff in the ground and vaulted in the air. Leading with his feet, he slammed into the trodall's face, hearing a sick crunch. The blow carried him over the falling trodall's shoulder. He landed, spun, and cut through the neck, black blood spouting mitres high.

He looked up from his knees, panting, and three more came toward him, growling, snarling. His archers were down and bloody – the second also wounded in the arm – out of the fight.

Scowling, he stood and raised both his Kingstaff and the unforged sword. "Come on!"

Harder, louder pounding on the ground to his right. That wasn't a trodall. It sounded like a ...

He turned, and a bosaur barreled forward and targeted the three trodall in front of him. Caleb took a few steps back and watched the bosaur lower its head and skewer one trodall with the long horn. Then it used the dying trodall as a battering ram to knock a second trodall ten mitres back. The third trodall swiped at the bosar with its claws. The rider ducked but the claws dug into the tough bosaur hide and red blood spouted.

Eshlyn.

While the trodall swiped at the passing bosaur, Caleb took the opportunity and darted forward, cutting at the hamstring and the back of the neck. The trodall's head hung limp to the right and the body fell to the left.

The bosaur continued to run, throwing the dead one off of its horn so it could target more.

Taking the moment to survey the battlefield, he counted only eight more trodall standing. Further to the south, the few cavalry that had survived the barrage were scattered and riding to the east. The stones and ballista were focused on the legion militan now.

We might make this yet.

—

"What do you mean, we're out of ammunition?" Carys snapped at him.

Zalman sighed. "Sorry. We're out."

Carys grunted in pain as she looked up at the battle to the north of them. While they had decimated the cavalry, to the point the remaining twenty retreated, five hundred or more militan moved to the hole in the wall.

She swallowed. "Then let's go. It's not over yet."

"No." Zalman's voice was firm. "You're pale. You need to rest."

Carys shook her head. Using the sword, she cut the straps and the harness off of her horse. She grabbed the mane. "Are you coming or not?"

He frowned at her. "You keep asking me that. You know the answer."

"Then why do you make me say it?" But her voice was weaker than she liked.

Zalman hopped up onto the horse – the animal groaned in protest at the new load – and sat behind her.

Macarus and the Steelsides also mounted horses. There were fourteen horses, so some of the Steelsides also had to ride double. The dwarves tottered awkwardly on the horses.

"I told you we're not horsedwarves!" Gunnar growled.

"Stop your complaining," Carys said. "And let's see what more we can do."

———

Caleb saw the bosaur stumble and fall, throwing Eshlyn to the side. She landed and rolled twenty mitres away from him.

The stones and spears from the catapults to south had stopped, so the militan regrouped with shields and spears to their position.

Eshlyn rolled to her back and groaned. Only a handful of the trodall were left, and Caleb raced toward her. He passed Ewha dodging the arms of one of the trodall, and he ducked and hamstrung the beast as he ran to Eshlyn.

He saw Digby to the west, dead among four slaughtered trodall.

Caleb reached Eshlyn and slid to a stop. He knelt down. "You okay?"

She had killed or maimed six of the trodall before the bosaur succumbed to the wounds, deep cuts from claws and teeth.

"Just … breath knocked out of me." Eshlyn sat up, holding her elbow. "And maybe broke my arm."

Caleb set his weapons down to feel her arm around the elbow. "Doesn't feel broken. But we'll have the physicians check to make sure."

Eshlyn scowled at him. "Well, it hurts like a shogger."

"What were you thinking? You rode a bosaur into battle?"

"Me?" She gaped at him. "You waded in to fight a hundred trodall by yourself."

"Not true. It was more like forty, and I had plenty of help"

"The legends will say it was a hundred." She smirked at him.

"No, the legends will say I fought a thousand of them alone and tore them apart one handed."

"Probably."

Caleb's smile faltered as he looked past her to the approaching militan, fifty mitres away. "Can you move?"

Her head swiveled to follow his eyes. "You're not going to fight all of them by yourself?"

"I will if you insist on sitting on your arse."

"Help me up."

Caleb took her uninjured hand and pulled them both up to their feet, and then the noise of the thunder of boots rose behind him.

He looked over his shoulder; a thousand elves with shields and gladi ran forward, led by Andos and that elven captain. As they ran past him and Eshlyn at the legion, Andos paused. "Take a break, *Brendel*, sir. We've got it from here."

With a war shout, those thousand elves sprinted towards the battle and engaged the remaining militan to the south.

With Eshlyn's arm around his shoulder, he snorted. "He gets to call me Caleb now."

———+———

Once Carys and Zalman reached the battle before the town, there wasn't anything more to do.

Carys led Macarus and the mercenaries through dead trodall and elves and deep holes in the dirt and grass. Carys saw elves fighting one another. She looked closer, and one group had red armbands to distinguish them from the others. It took her a moment to register the sight, militan and Cityguard fighting a Kryan legion, but she could not deny it. *Where did Caleb find elves to fight with him?*

Elves without armbands began to surrender. Ewha and Xak directed the ones with armbands not to kill the ones that were surrendering, and when the enemy elves heard this, more laid down their spears and gladi.

Ewha looked up and noticed Carys and Zal, and her eyes bulged. "Carys!" She and Xak came running over.

They reached the horse and eyed the group behind her with some curiosity. "We heard you were close," Ewha said and grabbed Carys' knee with affection. She inclined her head to the man behind her on the horse. "Zalman."

Xak beamed through his thick, dark beard. "Welcome back. El has shown his goodness."

"Yes. Thank you." Carys laid her hand on Ewha's. "Where is Caleb?"

Ewha's eyes softened and pointed to the north. "He and Lady Eshlyn are back there."

Zalman grunted thanks from behind Carys and kicked the horse forward, and Ewha stepped back out of the way.

The field was littered with dead horses, elves, and trodall, red and black blood covering the ground. And there, next to a dead bosaur, Caleb sat with Eshlyn, using straps and cloth to make a sling for Eshlyn's arm. Eshlyn noticed them first, and her face lit with joy. Caleb turned and looked over his shoulder.

His face was covered in dirt and dried trodall blood, and there was an ugly scar across his cheek.

But he might have been the most beautiful thing she ever saw.

Her eyes erupted with tears. "Caleb."

Caleb finished tying a strap of leather, touched Eshlyn's shoulder, stood, and ran towards her as they walked his direction. He met them. She fell into her brother's arms.

She buried her face into his neck and sobbed. She heard him laugh in her ear.

"Thank El," he said. "I prayed and now you're here."

Sniffling, she pulled away from him. "We came to warn you about a legion coming to attack you."

He raised a brow. "But you decided to take care of them by yourself?"

She glanced over her shoulder at Zalman, Macarus, Gunnar, Ulf, and the Steelsides. "Well, I had help."

Caleb's steel eyes brightened when he saw the elven Captain. "I'd say. Macarus, I can't tell you how glad I am to see you."

"I never should have left," Macarus said. "Correcting my error."

Caleb shook his head. "No reason to question. It is as El willed. You're here now. That's what is important." With his arms still around Carys, he faced the dwarves. "And you're the infamous Steelsides, I assume."

"We are." Gunnar bowed and almost fell off his horse. "A gift from our king, returning a favor."

"He honors me," Caleb said.

"Wouldn't tell me what that was about," Carys said. "Said you had to tell the story."

"He'll have to tell us all." Eshlyn reached them, then, and Carys stepped from Caleb's embrace to Eshlyn's. "Welcome back, sister."

"So glad to see you," Carys said as she stepped back, holding Eshlyn's hands. "You returned from Lior."

Eshlyn's face fell into sorrow as she nodded. Carys frowned. Caleb's arm was around her shoulders, and the three of them stood together.

"We have a lot to talk about," Caleb said.

With a final and pointed glance at Zalman, she met her brother's steel eyes and said, "You're right; we do."

Caleb scowled up at Zalman, and the big gedder blushed.

"Break me," Caleb said.

Those few warriors faithful to the memory of El huddled on the cliff as the horde of Sahat the Younger's army moved to surround them. The great ocean churned beyond.

"We did what we could," Gabryel said. "But we could do nothing without him."

Yon wiped a tear from his eye. "We will die for truth and freedom as he did."

The Sohan-el gathered their unforged swords to fight their final battle.

"You believe it is over?" said a voice behind them.

They turned to see a figure.

Matheo cried out. "Yosu!"

Yosu stood at the edge of the cliff, dressed in simple clothes. He had no sword.

The Sohan-el gathered around him, weeping, touching him.

"How are you still alive?" Yon asked. "We saw you die. We buried you."

Yosu said, "Did I not say I would bring the next world to this one? You cannot kill what is of the next world. Remember that. Always."

"Sahat comes," Gabryel said. "Will you fight with us?"

"I will," Yosu said.

"But you have no sword," Tamas said.

Yosu smiled. "I bring more than a sword. I bring the fire." Yosu raised his arms, and the Sohan-el heard the roar of something greater than thunder from below the cliff.

Twelve tremendous beasts with leather wings and flames for breath appeared behind Yosu and soared into the sky.

Dragons.

- From the Ydu, 6th Scroll, translated from the First Tongue to the common by the Prophet

Unbelief will grow, and because of the great fall, the dragons will disappear from the world. But El will not forget them. Humanity will bring back the Sohan-el, and all races will unite in faith as a sign that the dragons of El will return, and the fire will be reborn.

- From the Fyrwrit, 2nd Scroll of Johann, translated from the First Tongue to the common by the Prophet

CHAPTER 13

The First Time

Despite not leaving until noon, Aden and Tamya covered a great distance the first day. They continued to ride until almost sunset before finding a nice clearing to the west of the path.

The *path* was once a road, well-traveled according to Iletus and Caleb, which went around the lakes to approach Falya from the west. The northern peoples, large humans called the Geddai, lived in tribes in the north and had used the road, to trade with Taggart and the cities and towns of Ereland. The Geddai had disappeared centuries before Kryus conquered the land of humanity.

The journey began well enough. They spoke easily, laughing at the celebration from earlier in the day, but as they drew closer to evening, they both fell quiet.

Aden felt the tension, the expectation, as if it hung over them while he tied the horses to a nearby bush and removed the saddles. Tamya started a fire and arranged their blakets together next to the growing flame.

He first met her in the travels across the continent with Caleb – Anneton, the bloodwolves, the Forest of Saten. He had tried to reach out to her even then. But he didn't speak of this now. He didn't want to say the wrong thing, do the wrong thing.

After setting the packs over with the saddles, Aden stepped through the grass and sat next to her on the blankets. They sat together for a moment, silent. Aden took the map from his belt and opened it.

"We should reach the lake by tomorrow," he said.

Tamya nodded and laid her head on his shoulder, looking at the map with him. "Uh-huh."

"Then we'll have to use the compass to make our way north through the old Geddai territory and then the tundra."

"Mmm."

He cleared his throat. "But that's not for a few days, so ..."

Tamya reached between his arms and took the map from him. She folded it gently and set it aside.

Aden sat there with empty hands. He didn't know what to do with his hands.

Tamya took his left arm, the one closest to her, and pulled it over her shoulder. He turned to her, feeling and tasting her breath, and he leaned in and kissed her. She drew even closer, the fire crackling and popping in the dead silence of the night, a breeze rustling the brush.

He found some things to do with his hands.

She pulled back; he gasped. She wiggled, reached down, and dragged her tunic off over her head.

He fumbled at his belt, removing it and his tunic in one awkward motion. He pressed to her again, his mouth finding hers. Her hands were on his skin, and he felt suddenly cold even though the night was warm. She had to adjust her position to get her trousers off, and he wondered how she was so adept at such things while they broke so he could do the same.

Aden sniffed. "Look, I just want you to know …"

"Again with the talking?"

"Sorry. I am. It's only, I want you to know … I think you know … that this is, well, that I haven't exactly …"

She frowned at him. "Your first time?"

He nodded, looking away.

"You mean, living on the street in Asya, you never got with a girl?"

He shook his head. "I mean, I know what to do. I watched the shogshows every now and then."

She smirked at him and leaned in close. "This is no shogshow."

His heart beat like to break his ribs. "I – I know."

"Well, let me give you the first secret."

"Yeah?"

"You shouldn't interrupt it with the talking."

He smiled at her.

"Don't worry." She reached up and touched his face. "I won't expect too much, if that makes you feel better."

He chuckled, nervous, but it didn't, in fact, make him feel better.

Aden rolled his shoulders, and his hands darted around her waist. He tugged her close, and she groaned. He kissed her, and her fingers were in his hair. They fell to the blankets together.

He broke away for a moment, gazed into her dark eyes lit by the three moons, and he said, "Expect too much, okay?"

He pressed his mouth and body to hers with purpose, and she giggled.

—✝—

The Kryan fleet arrived in Asya with 87 ships, nineteen of them towed by others from the damage in the attack from the Pirates. Fifteen had sunk, hundreds of elves dead at the bottom of the ocean.

The fleet had sailed the final few days of the voyage with a mixture of tension and awe. Conversations were brief, words chosen carefully.

Emperor Tanicus is a Worldbreaker.

Julius, who had supported Tanicus from the time the elf was a simple regional political and military hero, had known. For over five hundred years, Tanicus had used his significant powers in secret. He had found others with abilities in *Tebelrivyn* and promoted them, used them to gain more political clout and military resources. The Sunguard were weapons, swordmasters with magic. The Moonguard had used *Tebelrivyn* to create creatures like the trodoll, adapt animals like the grider and cyanou, and manufacture the destructive Deathguard.

The Bladeguard had been initiated and developed by Julius, Galen, and Iletus. While they did not possess the powers of the other guard, they had been the Empire's greatest weapon since they could operate both in the light and the dark.

However, the Bladeguard had failed. Julius retired and left Galen in charge. Galen had been swayed by the very ideas they conquered. How had those ridiculous fantasies seduced him?

Tanicus no longer felt he needed to hide his true powers, and as Julius walked behind the Emperor, Tanicus moved with even more purpose, an even greater regal air. Power exuded from him.

They walked together from *The Crown of Gods* down the platform to the dock below. High General Felix strode behind them.

A host of elves waited at the dock, officers and militan and the wealthy of Asya, all on their knees with their heads bowed. Tanicus stopped at the space left for him at the bottom of the platform. The retinue from *The Crown of Gods* waited behind him. Other than the sound of other ships docking, Julius could hear no sound on the docks or the city from the thousands of prostrate elves and human slaves.

"Steward Rinai," Tanicus said.

The elf at the forefront of the crowd spoke. She did not move. "Yes, my Lord."

"Rise."

The elf rose, but she did not allow herself to look up.

"You have done as I instructed?" the Emperor asked.

"The city is ready for you, my Lord. The legion was sent west a ninedays ago to wipe out the illegal human rebellion."

"Any word?"

"None as yet, my Lord," Steward Rinai responded. "Although our last pigeon from General Hiasen reported that Giannis was empty and they drew close to Vicksburg."

"Giannis was empty?" Tanicus spoke in a tight voice. "Any sign of the *Brendel*'s army?"

"None. It appears the Steward of Giannis and the Cityguard ..." The Steward took a breath. "My Lord, it appears they took the humans with them to Vicksburg."

Tanicus let a silent moment pass. "Very well. We shall wait until we hear a final report. Our legions will give their all for the Empire, for the good of all. We will pray to the Nine for their success. In the meantime, we shall prepare this city's defenses. You are ready for us?"

"We have made room for the legions, the security for the Deathguard, and the pen for the Vualta."

Tanicus nodded at her. "Lead on, Steward."

The Steward bowed once and turned. The crowd shifted and parted for her to pass.

"Julius, we have work to do," Tanicus said.

Julius took a breath through his nose, knowing that the greatest weapon they possessed stood before him. "Yes, my Lord."

Carys couldn't sleep.

She needed it. Desperately. After the army physicians looked at her wound and dressed it, Caleb had given her and Zalman his room, despite the murder in his eyes when he looked at her husband. They were both too tired for anything else but sleep, and they lay in each other's arms with blinds over the window. Zalman breathed easy in a few minutes, and even though Carys was as exhausted as she had ever been, she could not sleep.

The names ran through her mind, their faces and her love for them stabs in her heart – Athelwulf, Esai, Xander, and others. Dead. Gone.

Uncle Reyan.

Earon was somewhere in the town. Alive. And waiting for her. Caleb had forgiven him. How, she couldn't imagine. But he had. The betrayal was more agonizing than the grief. She expected the enemy to kill her friends, her family. That was common to her. But betrayal …

Hours or minutes passed as she stared up at the ceiling. She wasn't sure. She grew more frustrated as she attempted to still and calm her mind and fall asleep. And failed.

Cursing under her breath, she gently moved Zalman's arm off of her stomach. He snorted once but did not wake. She rose from the bed and dressed in new, fresh clothes given to her by Eshlyn. She walked without a sound to the door. Her eyes were drawn to the unforged sword in the corner near the door. It was a shadow in the dim room, but it called to her.

She froze as she stared the sword down. She did not want to pick it up and put it on. The weapon that made her a hero also made her afraid. She shuddered at the thought that El would use the sword to speak to her and tell her to forgive Earon. Is that what had happened with Caleb? Had the sword stopped him?

But without the sword, how would she kill him?

She decided that if she came to it, she could kill her cousin with her bare hands. She opened the door, and it made a soft creak as she walked through the door and closed it, leaving the unforged sword behind her.

The early evening light painted the sky a light orange color, and she traveled through the town of Vicksburg underneath it. Many of the *Hamon-el* greeted her, those she had known from Ketan, but she responded to each with a brief nod or smile or word, nothing more.

She reached the building at the north side of the town within a half hour. She did not see Caleb, and she was glad. She didn't need him now.

Caleb made the mistake of telling her where their cousin stayed. She made her way down the hall and paused at the third door, laying her hand on the handle. Her heart raced.

With a curse under her breath, she pushed the door open and stepped inside.

He sat there at a small desk to the right, a cot on the other side of the room. When he saw her, his eyes bulged, and he gripped the book in his hands tight.

"Earon." She closed the door behind her, and it echoed in the room.

His neck moved as he swallowed. He whispered her name. "Carys."

The book in his hands was the *Fyrwrit*. She refused to look at it. He set it down and placed his hands in his lap.

She didn't know what to say. She wanted to curse him, rail at him, but most of all, she wanted to hurt him.

Earon stood, his eyes misting. "Carys."

Stop saying my name. She didn't know if she could speak.

He took a step towards her. Then another. Her vision blurred. When she blinked, something wet journeyed down her face.

He was in front of her now, his face a grimace. Then he dropped to his knees in front of her.

"Don't," she said through her teeth.

"Carys, I'm so sorry." He gazed at the floor.

"All those years, you were a brother to me." Her face twisted in pain. "More than that. You were my best friend. I could tell you anything."

"I know."

"Shut up. Don't talk. You don't have the right to say anything. You left. When I needed you the most, you left."

He nodded.

"I held him in my hands, Earon. In my hands. His blood, all over me." A sob escaped her then, a hateful sound. "And it was you that brought that Bladeguard to us. You."

No answer. He didn't move.

"We had to bury him and move on, just run because we knew they'd be after us. Because of you. You betrayed us, betrayed the whole shogging family."

She closed her eyes – Earon's face, the horror, how he ran from the inn, the *Crying Eagle.*

She opened her eyes and leaned over him. "Not to mention the revolution. You turned against all you were taught, all you knew. You were part of the hope and you turned your back on it. We've been fighting and dying while you sold us out and drank and sorced your way through life."

Her jaw was sore from gritting her teeth. All of her exhaustion, her pain, her grief both familiar and fresh, all of it broke from her. She lashed out, grabbed the collar of his shirt, and lifted him off of his feet. Her side screamed at her. She didn't care.

She had loved him so much it hurt. She realized her hate hurt even more.

She threw him over and onto the cot. Tears streamed from her eyes. From his eyes, too. She was on top of him now, and her hands were around his throat.

He didn't fight her. He didn't resist.

A hoarse roar escaped her.

Then the voice came to her. *Forgive.*

Breathing in sharply, she shook her head, trying to silence the voice in her heart, in her head, in her gut. She shook him, but he hadn't said it.

Forgive.

She gasped. It was the same voice she heard when she held the sword. And yet, she didn't have it on her or anywhere near her.

Was El bound by a sword? She had worn the supernatural weapon for the last six months, trained with it, lived with it. It was a part of her now. She couldn't leave it behind or escape it.

Shoggers.

With a cry, she released his throat, and he panted for air. She stood up and away from him.

The door opened behind her. She glanced over her shoulder. Zalman stood there, leaning against the doorway, his arms crossed. He was dressed in trousers and a new tunic.

She didn't speak for a moment, her fists clenched at her thighs, glaring down at Earon. "What the break are you doing here?"

"Surprised he's still alive," Zalman answered in his deep voice.

Earon sat up on the cot.

"He deserves it, you know," she said.

"He does," Zalman said.

Her whole body shook in a sob. "But I can't."

Zalman grunted his assent. He knew her too well. That was why she didn't want him here.

"Want me to do it for you?" Zalman asked.

Earon's brow shot up on his forehead.

Carys scoffed at him. "What are you talking about?"

"Well, we're married now, help each other out and things," he said like it made perfect sense.

"Stupid gedder."

"Yeah, well, you married me. So tell me, what do you want?"

As frightening as it was, she didn't think he was joking. The man would kill Earon for her. After all they'd seen and been together, it shouldn't surprise her.

Earon looked from her to Zalman as he sat up further. He wiped his eyes with the back of his sleeve.

"I'm supposed to forgive him," she said. "Does it matter what I want?"

Earon caught her eyes. "Yes. It matters. To me."

Her shoulders slumped, and her face pleaded with him. "I don't know how. Can you tell me how?"

"I can't bring him back." Earon shrugged. "I can't undo what I've done. But I would do anything to make it right. Anything. That's what Athelwulf taught me. If I knew what to do, I'd do it."

Her heart broke when he said Ath's name, and she groaned. Zalman placed his arm on her shoulder. She could feel Athelwulf's presence in her heart, his wisdom. The last time she spoke with Ath, the night they said goodbye ...

You know the man I am now, but you did not know the man I was twenty years ago.

Oh, and what type of man were you?

Worse than those men, I guarantee you. Much. I was so lost, Carys. So lost.

Yes, Athelwulf would have taught Earon a great deal about redemption.

She thought of Uncle Reyan, all the teachings through all the years. What would the Prophet say here, now, in this moment? Would he want her to kill Earon or would he seek his redemption? She knew what the man who preached the redemption of the entire world would say.

And a father greater than Reyan spoke to her.

"There's nothing," she said. "You deserve death. You don't deserve to be forgiven. You can't earn it."

Earon bit his lip and nodded.

"Because that's now how it works. It's not forgiveness if you can earn it or deserve it. You know the teachings better than me. Here's my question for you, though."

His whole body waited for her.

She leaned in, close. "Now that you've been redeemed, now that you're here and breathing, what are you going to do now?"

Earon opened his mouth as if to speak, but he hesitated and stammered. "I ... I don't know."

Carys stood straight and placed her fists on her hips. "You want to do something for me? Figure that out. And then do it."

He licked his lips. "What if I know ... and it scares the crit out of me?"

Carys frowned down at him. "Then you might be one of us after all."

She turned and left, leaving him with his own thoughts, passing a scowling Zalman on the way out. He grunted as he followed her.

They exited the building together. As they walked back to their room, she heard Zalman say from next to her, "I'm proud of you."

"Well, I'm not." Then she leaned into him as they walked, and his arm became a blanket of warmth and love around her shoulders. "Thank you."

CHAPTER 14

THE MISSION

Aden and Tamya continued to travel on the road northeast as it reached Lake Raziel. Raziel spread out before them as far as they could see, the cooler winds whipping across the water, and they pulled their tunics tighter despite the warmth of the day.

Upon reaching the lake, a group of buildings appeared in the distance. They rode closer, and the buildings took the shape of a town. Now it was deserted.

Tamya looked, but nothing existed to tell her its name. When Aden checked the map, there was only a dot.

They passed dilapidated houses without roofs. The main part of the town consisted of twenty larger buildings, several of them like inns, all of them surrounded by long grass and overgrown vegetation.

The sun hung low in the west, late afternoon. Tamya surveyed the abandoned town. "Might as well stay here tonight."

"Good a place as any." He glanced at the sun. "Should be time to look around a bit before dark, too."

They entered the town and found an old inn that didn't have a roof, but since it was several stories tall, the floors above gave them cover. The tavern room of the inn was devoid of furniture, and after they moved a few random items and trash, they had a nice bare, clean corner for the night. They unsaddled the horses, found buckets for water, and brought the animals into the tavern room, tying them to the bar.

After arranging their blankets and packs for the night in the corner, they explored the town.

There were more than twenty buildings, now that they were able to weave through the wide streets of the town, and two large warehouses sat near the shore of the lake by long docks.

Walking to the end of the dock, the breeze from the lake blew his hair in his face. He pulled it back. "Looks like it was a halfway point between Taggart and Falya."

Tamya hummed an acknowledgement. Aden always had those two parts of him, the reckless hope and confidence mixed with his insecurity. But without Caleb around, Aden spoke his thoughts to her alone. Made her love him more.

Earon had given Aden pages of notes on the prophecy of dragons and the Dracolet, what were popular theories, and what the Prophet had thought and taught about it. Every night, before or after their times of physical intimacy, Aden would pull out those pages, and he would discuss with her what it might mean and ask her thoughts.

It was fascinating, enormous creatures that flew on massive wings and breathed fire that could level cities, how their bones were stronger than steel and their blood could heal injury or sickness, how they were wise with the knowledge of El and their scales were thick and stronger than any armor. One story told of an army of dragons with Yosu and the first *Sohan-el* that fought a horde of demics and twisted creatures as Bana Sahat and his followers were banished to the Underland.

Tamya had seen amazing things, she and Aden both, but they both agreed much of what was written was surely legend and exaggeration. Surely. But if they weren't? The revolution could use them.

The magic within her continued to be a lingering echo in her heart and mind. As long as she stayed close to the unforged sword, the desire didn't overwhelm her.

And while she gave him crit about how much he talked, she found it intimate to be the one he came to for everything, even things she wasn't interested in. He had always talked through things with her before, or tried to, but she possessed him now in a way that she had never known with another person.

Her marriage to Berran had been love, but not a love of equals. She felt indebted to him for saving her from her life of abuse and violence and prostitution she knew in Lior. Berran never tried to, but she felt it. Aden was different. He did not ever make her feel inferior. Never. Even though, as Caleb's unofficial right-hand man, he could have.

Perhaps she was different, after all that had happened.

So while she may have had more experience in areas of physical intimacy, the last few days with Aden had been a first for her – the first time she loved freely, from her will without obligation. She was his partner and equal.

She stared at him, lost in her thoughts, and she shook her head to clear it. She stood next to him and looked out over the vast lake.

Aden started thinking aloud. He often did. "Ships here at the docks and trading with the people of the town and travelers from the north."

Tamya didn't tell him her perspective, the elves coming and taking over businesses and farms in the name of progress, pushing people out as the slow decline of the town was expedited by the oppression of a new rule. She saw men leaving to find work in the bigger cities or the plantations to the south, and she imagined women and children starving as they were left behind or sold into slavery. Had the elves run the last remnants of the town out as they had so often in other places? It had become a town without a name.

She grunted an assent.

Aden turned around and gazed back at the town and the setting sun. "You know, after all this is over, we could tell people about this place. These docks are sturdy, still, and some of those buildings, they could rebuild them. Some plains could be farms. This could be a town again."

Tamya chuckled at him. "*After this is all over*? We're headed north to hunt for dragons in mountains where we'll probably freeze to death. And we don't know even where to start looking."

Aden grinned at her and reached up to grab the amulet that hung from his neck. "Oh, I'm aware."

"But you're making plans for after that." Her tone mocked him.

"Yep."

"Well, if I had known marrying you would have made you even more maddy, I would have reconsidered."

Aden moved to stand in front of her, and he drew her in his arms. "Okay. One thing at a time. Finding dragons that might not exist, that has to come first."

"And getting them to help us."

"Definitely."

"And surviving. Don't forget surviving."

"Yeah. That's a lot. That's probably enough."

"You think?"

He laughed at her before he leaned down and kissed her. She went to break the kiss, but he held her tight. She sniffed in annoyance, but her hands reached up, pulled his long, thick hair from the leather cord, and ran her hand through it.

That feeling of intimacy with Aden surged within her, the feeling that they were the only two people in the world and nothing else mattered. She knew it was rare to appreciate the good she possessed in the moment. How many ever did? She wanted to hold onto it, never wanted it to end. But that fear hovered at the back of her mind with the magic … this would come to an end soon.

It always did. They stood in a dead town as proof.

—+—

Julius rode with Tanicus in a carriage made of silver, gold, and glass through the streets of Asya on the short ride from the Steward's palace to the Pyts. Five hundred militan surrounded the carriage.

The past day had been full of details, most of them handled by the High General, but Tanicus received continuous reports of the progress. The massive scale of organization amazed Julius, the amount of resources spent on housing the militan and the weapons and the supplies.

Word had spread through Asya, confirming the rumors. Tanicus was a Worldbreaker. Another riot had broken out in the square and vandalism on the golden statue of the Emperor. Many of the rioters had been human, but some had been elves. While it was tragic that elves would side with the humans and against their own government and Emperor, the truth was bound to have consequences, and it surprised Julius more had not turned.

The legions in Asya had reacted violently and ended the riots with more than five hundred dead.

Word from the west was that an officer, Andos, and the stewards and Cityguard of Giannis and Vicksburg had betrayed the Empire and fought with the *Brendel* at Vicksburg. Both Kryan legions had been defeated.

Tanicus had been quiet through the afternoon after hearing that report.

As the western sky darkened, the carriage reached the Pyts, the infamous prison of Asya, and stopped. Two militan captains opened the carriage doors and Julius stepped out with his hand on his sword, and his eyes scanned every shadow. Tanicus followed, unconcerned, deep in thought.

Two Sunguard rode in a second carriage, and they exited the vehicle to follow Tanicus and Julius.

The militan separated for them to approach the Pyts.

The Pyts had been constructed centuries ago by a human king, a massive dome shape on the skyline of Asya that could be seen from many parts of the city. An iron gate functioned as the entry. It lay open, waiting for the Emperor, and a Captain stood at the gate. He bowed as the Emperor drew near.

"Rise, Captain," Tanicus said.

"My Lord," the Captain said. "You honor us by your presence."

Tanicus paused to consider the Captain. "We must use all our resources to fight the human evil that comes from the west."

"Yes, my Lord."

"Are you the Captain that was in charge when the Prophet was broken free?"

The Captain shook his head with force. "No, my Lord. He … is no longer at this position."

"As it should be." Tanicus peered into the darkness inside where hundreds of cells formed into the stone floor were spread in even rows with grates over the entrances. "What is the inmate population at this time?"

"It varies, my Lord," the Captain said. "But at this time, we have two thousand inmates."

"Why does it vary?" Julius asked.

"With recent events, we are overpopulated, so we must reduce numbers from time to time."

"You execute some inmates," Julius interpreted.

"Only the sick and old, my Lord Bladeguard. We simply don't have the space."

"Do not apologize, Captain," Tanicus said. "You do what you must. We all do what we must."

"Thank you, my Emperor."

Tanicus took a deep breath. "I want you to check that all the locks are secured, Captain, and then I require you and your elves to leave and wait for me outside."

"W-what, my Lord?"

Tanicus glared at the Captain, and Julius narrowed his eyes as it seemed Tanicus grew taller, larger.

"Forgive me, Lord." The Captain bowed low. "I will obey." He turned and went inside the prison.

Tanicus spoke low to Julius. "Elves have joined the *Brendel's* army."

Julius nodded as he heard shuffling feet and iron clattering within the prison.

"If that is true, then your mission is even more urgent," the Emperor said. "You must use our contact within his army to foster division, to ensure his failure."

"I understand."

"You leave tonight," Tanicus said. "After I am done here."

"And what are we doing here?"

The Emperor's jaw tightened. "What must be done."

The Captain and 100 guard left the Pyts in a double line.

"Close and lock the entrance behind me," Tanicus said. "Allow no one in. No matter what you hear, or what you think you hear, do not open this gate until I return."

"You're going in alone?"

Tanicus glanced over his shoulder. "The Sunguard will be with me, my friend. Do not worry."

Tanicus entered through the gate and into the darkness beyond, and the two Sunguard were silent as they followed. The darkness enveloped them. With a look of stark fear, the Captain helped Julius place the locks back on the gate after they closed it.

The chorus of horrific screams began minutes later. Every elf in the street covered their ears and grimaced from the deafening din of pain. Julius would forget that sound. No one could.

———

Caleb walked across the bridge over the river Moriel, and Earon stood at the end, staring over the field of battle.

They had taken over six hundred prisoner after the battle's end. But there was no room in the town, so the prisoners were bound and placed in tents guarded by men and women of the *Hamon-el* on the other side of the river. Caleb supposed another few hundred elves had escaped and fled to the east. Towards Asya. Where Caleb needed to go to face the Worldbreaker.

Caleb reached the end of the wide bridge, and he stopped next to Earon. Even though the sun was dim and orange in the west, Caleb could follow Earon's eyes that sought the field beyond the prisoners, a field destroyed by weapons of destruction, stone and spear and arrow, and soaked in the blood of elves and men. At the south end of the field, three mounds rose above the ground, mass graves of elven militan. To the north, individual graves of men, women, and elves were spread along the river, those that had given their lives in defense of Vicksburg.

While the victory was a day in the past, the horrid stench of death filled Caleb's nostrils.

"So many dead," Earon said.

The scars on Caleb's back itched. *More blood on my hands.* "This is war. We had to protect those in the town."

Earon scoffed. "Yes. War."

Caleb frowned. "What is it?"

Earon cleared his throat. "Do you believe, Caleb? Do you believe that all come from the First Race? Do you believe the redemption is for all people?"

"The scriptures say it's true, so yes, I do."

"I know what the scriptures say. But do you really believe it?"

Caleb's frown deepened. "I do. Now more than ever. We have elves as part of our army. Even dwarves."

"Do you hear what you're saying? How you're saying it? The army. Our army."

Caleb crossed his arms. "They've all chosen it. I haven't forced anyone be a part of this."

"I know. You're not making people kill each other, and yet they still choose it."

"Look, this is what the revolution is all about, what the prophecies are all about. This is what your father talked about."

"You're right. And it was one of the reasons I left."

Caleb cocked his head at his cousin.

Earon waved a hand at the blood red field and the mounds of graves. "Is the revolution for them, too?"

"Not if they stand against it, no."

"So the revolution that is supposed to bring redemption for all is so important that we have to kill the ones that fight against it?"

"To protect those that choose freedom, yes."

Earon took a deep breath. "What if that isn't what El wants? Is war really the way to peace?"

"Wait, you think I want this? You think I want war? Kryus is doing this. The Emperor, a Worldbreaker, he's sending these legions to kill us."

"Yes, he sent those legions, or the Empire did. But here's my question – what choice did you give him?"

Caleb couldn't answer.

"Have you talked with him? Have you given him another option?"

Caleb spoke through his teeth. As he blinked, he couldn't stop the images of flayed men, women, and children on pikes around a town and ravens consuming their flesh. "You didn't see what he did at Biram."

"No, I didn't." He turned to Caleb. "I'm not defending what he did or what he's doing, but I am looking at the thousands dead, the thousands we've killed by the sword, and I'm wondering, what is El's greatest weapon? What is the weapon that truly frees all?"

I am. But he knew the answer Earon sought. "Truth."

"Yes. Exactly. Truth. Who has spoken the truth to the Emperor? Who has given him that choice?"

"So, you want me to go and talk with Tanicus? Give him the truth of El, give him that choice?"

Earon lowered his gaze. "It's not what I *want*. And I'm not asking you. I'm saying I should go."

Caleb's brow rose.

"Carys asked me yesterday, she asked me about my part in this revolution. And I knew. I sat there with that giant of a man about to kill me, and I knew what I was supposed to do. I'm not a warrior. I'm not going to fight and kill. I've seen enough death. I don't want to see any more."

Earon raised his eyes to peer into Caleb.

"But what I can do is tell Tanicus that no matter what he's done, he can change. I can tell him to stop before thousands more die. I can tell him there are other choices to make than what he's doing. Just as I'm telling you. Because if you go and fight him, I don't know that anyone really wins. Death isn't peace."

Death sounds like peace to me. "No, Earon. He'll kill you."

"You attack an army of trodall, and you're telling me I can't do something because I might die?"

"Not *might*," Caleb corrected. "You will."

"You believe, in your heart, that Tanicus is beyond redemption?"

Caleb looked into his cousin's eyes. "Yes. As bad as that sounds, he's a Worldbreaker. He's mad. I've seen what he's done. No one can come back from that."

Earon groaned. "That's it, Caleb. I don't believe he is that far gone. I know what it means to be hopeless, to think you have no choice, and it took someone telling me different. With El, no one is that far gone."

"I find it ironic that you're done with death, but you're asking to commit suicide."

Earon shrugged. "But there's more hope for life this way."

"No, Earon. I won't allow it."

"What if I'm right? What if me telling him the truth is the one weapon that saves thousands of lives and brings us to peace and freedom? What then?"

Caleb laid a hand on the unforged sword. "I remember when we were younger, there was a dog we had on the farm. I loved that dog. Carys loved that dog. He was great with her. She would lay on him and pull his hair, and he would just take it. He came back from the woods with a bad bite. My dad watched the dog, said it could be bad news."

"Caleb …"

"The dog turned rabid. Snapped at Carys, tried to rip her face off." He stepped closer to Earon. "My father took a rope, tied it around the dog's neck, and choked it to death. He wept while he did it. We loved that dog. But he did what he had to do for the good of us all."

Earon was quiet a long time before he spoke again.

"You let people make choices based on their convictions all the time. Whether they join the army or not, fight or not. You tell everyone they should find their place based on their convictions. That is freedom. Are you telling me I can't go and try to talk to Tanicus?"

"Yes. I'm not letting you dive in the pen with the rabid dog to convert him. It's not noble, it's suicide."

Earon dropped his head. "Caleb, this could work."

"You'll never find out." Caleb spun on his heel and strode back to the town.

CHAPTER 15

GEDDAI

The morning sun broke through the clouds, and Eshlyn squinted at the light. She walked through the town towards the meeting, bumping and pushing through bodies. There were too many people in the town. Combined with the summer heat, the number of humans and elves suffocated her. And to make the morning even more wonderful, Robben and Aimi followed her.

"No," Eshlyn told them. "I don't know when we're moving to Giannis. That's not my decision."

"Okay," Aimi said. "Is it Caleb's?"

The leadership isn't united right now, but she shouldn't say that to anyone, much less a young couple that recently joined them. But there were rumors. People knew the Beorgai refused orders during the battle. And they talked among their own groups.

"Sorry, Lady Eshlyn," Robben said. "We know the plan is to go to Asya, but well, we were on the western side of the battle the other day, and we didn't get to see much of the fighting."

"You're fortunate," she told them.

"We'd like to be in the fight, you know," Robben said. "That's why we came."

"And to make sure we're not near the Beorgai," Aimi added.

Eshlyn slid to a stop in the dirt of the street. "Why do you say that?"

The young couple shared a glance. "You know, they're just out for themselves, and we want to make sure we're alongside those who are really a part of the revolution."

Eshlyn's brow furrowed. "Like the elves?"

"Oh, well, no, not them, Lady," Robben said. "They're elves, after all."

A crowd paused around them, listening. The crowd grew as they waited for Eshlyn's answer. She looked around at the humans gathered.

"You don't like it," she addressed Robb and Aimi. "Then go back."

Robb flinched. "Lady?"

Eshlyn raised her voice. "If that's the way you think, then it's best if you go back to the slavery you came from. Because coming here has been for nothing."

She changed direction and walked back towards the administration building at the center of town, leaving many with their mouths open.

Eshlyn still fumed when she pushed past hundreds more people to get to the main doors. She stomped through the corridor and came to the big room Caleb had commandeered for the new meeting of leadership of the *Hamon-el*.

The people considered part of leadership had evolved once again. The *Sohan-el* were there, minus the tragic loss of Digby with the trodall, six of them along one side of the room in chairs. Other *Sohan-el* were there, too, Jaff and Carys. Zalman sat next to his wife. Carys and Zalman were married! She continued to adjust to that revelation. They were all on one side of the room.

On the other side of the room were Shecayah and Tobiah of the Beorgai, Gunnar and Ulf of the Steelsides, and those representing the elves – Andos, Steward Roers of Vicksburg, Steward Halus of Giannis, and Macarus. Also on that side of the room was Iletus and Bweth.

At the far end of the room, Caleb stood. Alone.

Eshlyn took a deep breath, and many nodded at her as she walked toward the end of the room and stood with Caleb.

"Sorry I'm late," she whispered to Caleb. "Javyn ... well, he might have emptied his pack all over the room this morning. And mine."

Caleb straightened a little. "It's all right. Glad you're here."

Eshlyn caught Carys staring at them, and Caleb's sister gave her a wry look. Eshlyn frowned back at her.

Bweth rocked, gained momentum with her belly, and stood. "Well, now that we're all here. I'll breakin' start this meeting. Before we talk about anything else, we need to talk about how the Beorgai betrayed us during the battle."

Shecayah and Tobiah both stood, their hands in fists, and they shouted back at Bweth. "We betrayed no one!" Tobiah said.

More shouts from across the room and from the Stewards next to them.

Eshlyn stepped forward. "Bweth did not mean betrayed. She does not understand the idea of the *foredain* in your culture. She meant ..."

"I know what I meant," Bweth said. "And they know what I meant. A part of our army was being attacked by trodall and militan, and they did nothing. You call it what you will, but I say they betrayed the elves."

"We betrayed no one!" Shecayah said. "We did as the *Brendel* instructed. We defended the northern position."

"You did not do as Caleb instructed," Iletus said. "He sent new instructions through your *Bashawyn*, and you denied her."

"We did what we felt best," Tobiah answered. "There was already one legion attacking us from the south. How were we to be sure there would not be one from the north that we did not know about?"

"In a battle, you cannot do what you feel is best," Macarus said. "Not when you've been given orders."

176

"And if he was wrong?" Shecayah asked. "What if he had been wrong?"

"But he wasn't," Iletus said. "And that's not why you didn't obey the orders. You made it clear you did not want to fight with the elves."

The room fell still and silent. "It is true, we do not trust the elves," Tobiah said. "Who could blame us? We've seen them rape our land for centuries for wealth while many of our people starve. We would have been between the legion to the south and elves that could turn on us, catching us unawares."

"But they didn't," Carys said. "And we took care of most of that legion anyway."

"We are getting away from the point." Jaff stood and addressed Shecayah and Tobiah. "You chose not to act out of fear. And as a result, people fighting in this army died when they did not need to, and one of the *Sohan-el* gave his life to fight trodall and militan you could have easily handled."

Shecayah's eyes blazed as she looked at them. "Men and women died fighting the legion to the east. Are we to blame for their deaths, as well? We cannot be responsible for all the consequences during a battle."

"We're not asking you to be responsible for all of them." Jaff sat down. "Only for what you refused to do. You are responsible for that."

Eshlyn faced Shecayah. "You were given a choice. Before the battle, you could have decided to go back to the mountains of Lior. You knew the way. But you decided to stay. Why?"

Tobiah pursed his lips. "Prophecies have been fulfilled. You rode the Mahakar. It is time to join the fight. We have joined."

Eshlyn shook her head. "But you didn't. You've only joined halfway. Elves are a part of this army now, a part of this revolution, and dwarves, for the sake of El. If you can't fight with them, can't fight to save them, then you haven't joined the revolution."

Shecayah and Tobiah scowled and sat.

Eshlyn lowered her head. *It's all falling apart, right here.*

Steward Roers stood and looked at Caleb. "*Brendel*, sir. What say you? For us and the elves under our command, we took the word of Andos when he said we would be treated fairly. We are elves and not demics or dragonmen. How can we stay and fight with you if we are not trusted? If many in your army would rather see us die than fight with us?"

Caleb rubbed his beard, listening, and leaned on the wall. The room waited for his reply. He stood straight, the Kingstaff in his hand. "The greatest weapon is truth."

Macarus caught Eshlyn's eye and raised a brow. She lifted a shoulder back at him.

"Cal?" Carys said.

"Something someone said to me," Caleb said. "Jaff, send a runner for Earon. Bring him here."

Jaff stood and left the room.

"You're inviting that traitor to this meeting?" Bweth asked.

"Why not?" Caleb said. "Can't be any more misled than some other people in this room."

Eshlyn saw many stiffen, primarily Shecayah and Tobiah. Caleb was quiet until Jaff returned.

"Thank you," he told Jaff. Jaff nodded back.

Caleb walked to the center of the room, the Kingstaff clicking on the stone floor.

"Truth doesn't change. That's what makes it the greatest weapon. It is unbreakable. Governments change, rise, fall. Kings and emperors come and go. Heroes clamor for fame and are forgotten within another generation. But truth doesn't change. It endures. It has endured since before this world was created, and it shall endure beyond the day it is reborn again in fire. That is the greatest weapon we've been given, and more than anything else, that is the weapon we need to learn to wield."

Caleb kept walking in a slow, tight circle, meeting the eyes of everyone in the room.

"Almost a year ago, I landed in Asya. Aden and I broke the Prophet out of prison and then made our way west to the Living Stone."

Caleb paused. Eshlyn squared her shoulders.

"El gave us our unforged swords through that Stone, and some of you in this room. We trained and set out to fight those that would oppress us, and we did. And we won. But our true mission is spreading the truth that does not change, that will never change. For only that makes us free. Reyan tried to tell me that one time. Maybe I'm finally ready to hear it, old man."

Caleb's eyes misted.

"Others left us to fight and spread truth in other lands, some as far away as the islands to the south, the end of the world before the unknown. A few returned. Some did not."

Eshlyn swallowed. Ath and Esai …

"Many have given their lives for this revolution," Caleb said. "And I believe many more will in the future. But one thing has not changed. And that is truth.

"The truth is this. El seeks the redemption of all. No matter what you've done in the past, he can redeem a life if it is willing to know the truth. There is nothing more powerful than that. Even I can't fight that."

Caleb walked back towards Eshlyn at the end of the room. He met her gaze, and she saw those steel eyes soften at her. He turned and spoke to the group.

"Tomorrow, the *Hamon-el* will leave and travel to Giannis. As we travel, we will train in the greatest weapon of all. If you are willing to learn, you are welcome. If not, go your own way. That is your choice." Caleb faced Shecayah and Tobiah. "The *Bashawyn* is correct. For what is coming, half-way isn't good enough. You fight with us all, or none."

Footsteps in the hall, and a young woman came to the door, panting. Jaff stood. The runner he sent. "Marsa?"

"Is Earon with you?" Eshlyn asked.

Marsa swallowed at the faces in the room. She shook her head. "No, my Lady."

Caleb frowned at her. "Then where is he?"

"That's just it, *Brendel*," Marsa said. "I went to look for him … but he was gone."

"Gone?" Carys stood.

Marsa nodded. "All of his things are gone, too. Just the cot and a desk are there. No clothes. Nothing."

Eshlyn's brow furrowed. "He left?" She turned to Caleb. "Where would he go?"

"Traitor left us again," Bweth snarled.

Caleb lowered his head and closed his eyes.

"No. He left to try and save us all. Even from ourselves."

The city rose from the plains like a beacon to the north as they walked the horses through the plains.

They had left the town on Lake Raziel the morning before. Since the road turned to the east from the town without a name, they set out across the high grasses where there was no path, only a compass Bweth had made for them. Later that evening, the city appeared like a speck an hour before they made camp. That night had been cold, and they used the small tent to keep them from the wind.

The next morning, as they traveled towards the city, remnants of what could have been homes or barns creaked in the wind on either side. They passed a small stream with frigid, clear water, and from his time in Ketan and the plains of Manahem, Aden imagined crops as far as the eye could see. Would there have been roads or paths through the plains from the city? None now.

At the same time, the sky, which seemed further away and bigger all at once, grew darker with black clouds. Thunder rumbled to the north from the midst of those clouds.

He thought they would reach the city by the afternoon, hoping to beat the storm, but distance was difficult to measure on the plains. After increasing their pace, they drew close by evening.

The architecture of the city appeared similar to Ketan. The walls were high and smooth and gray. Large portions of the wall were gone, rubble in piles where it had worn over time or been broken down by battle. The buildings that still stood intact had sharp edges.

And statues of dragons. Large and small, fierce dynamic images of dragons watched them everywhere.

They rode through a gate thirty mitres tall and another thirty wide. The moat around the city was dry and caked, thankfully, or they could not have entered. The buildings were built for people twice as tall as Aden, maybe more. Even Zalman would have been dwarfed by the doorways and the height of ceilings in the buildings.

Aden and Tamya discussed how planned the city seemed. Every street paved and straight, every structure perfectly positioned.

He looked over at Tamya, and she shivered. "Is it colder here?" she whispered.

His brow furrowed. She was right, it did feel colder, but it shouldn't have since they were now out of the wind. Perhaps because the sun set.

It was almost dark, and they paused to gather wood and brush and fashion a couple torches. They led the horses through the city, their hooves echoing throughout the night. The orange light of the torches gave an eerie glow to the large buildings missing walls and roofs.

Images of dragons surrounded them. They were carved into walls; small and large statues remained on what was left of the city. And where the broad street came to the center of the city, a massive stone image of a dragon stood there. Several streets converged at the dragon. The dragon appeared to be attacking, jaw open with long teeth, claws clamoring forward, one wing missing and laying on the ground while the other spread wide.

"They worshipped them," Aden said.

Tamya stood next to him and gazed up at the enormous statue. "Looks like it."

Aden scanned the dark around them, the buildings were shadows nearby. His skin tingled. "A whole civilization, gone."

"Were they human?"

"I believe so," he answered. "Just bigger."

"What happened to them?"

"The Geddai are mentioned in the scriptures as a strong people, a faithful people, but that's all I know. There may be books somewhere that recorded what happened, maybe even back in Taggart. I know the general there had a great library. But I didn't get a chance to read much." He frowned at having to leave so many behind when they left Taggart.

Tamya was silent for a moment, her face glowing from the torch in her hand. "You think they're real? You think we'll find them?"

"The dragons?" He surveyed the rubble and the statue. "Well, the Geddai seemed to believe in them. I do believe they are real. But will we find them?" He reached into his shirt and grabbed the Dracolet. "El will have to help us. That's really all I know."

Tamya scoffed at him. "How is that different from everything else?"

"True." He smiled at her. Thunder boomed a warning overhead. "Let's find some shelter. Make a fire. Going to be a rough night."

—+—

Caleb sat on his horse and watched the *Hamon-el* organize and settle for the night halfway to Giannis. Eshlyn sat next to him on her own horse, Javyn nodding off in her lap in the saddle.

The different groups within the *Hamon-el* camped in separate areas, gaps between them – Beorgai, Ghosts, veterans of Ketan, elves, and those that had left at the Acar. He felt tired and leaned forward, his forearm on the pommel.

Eshlyn took a deep, sad breath. "You think it will work?"

Before they turned in for the night, each of the *Sohan-el* were assigned to a different group, to read scriptures to them, to talk about the redemption El sought for them all.

"Maybe. We have some time before we reach Asya. I have hope."

And he did. What more could he do? Each group had to move beyond their own assumptions and injuries, whether perceived or real, and in the end, if the people who fought for the redemption didn't truly believe in it, then it was all for nothing.

Was Earon right? The army fell apart around him. Was there a better way? Where less people died? A part of him held hope that Earon might succeed. And what would that mean? If they won their freedom without his death? Was that even possible? What would his life be then?

He stole a glance at Eshlyn and foolishly allowed his mind to wander. He tore his eyes away and shook his head.

No. He could not trust in Earon to succeed. He would be ready to end it one way or another.

"We could have sent someone after him," Eshlyn said. "A couple Ghosts would have caught up to him in a day."

He turned to her and narrowed his eyes. "How do you know what I'm thinking?"

She smirked at him. But she didn't answer.

A rider approached from the camp, and Caleb turned his head back to watch her approach. It was Ewha, one of the *Sohan-el*. She arrived, pulling up her horse within a few mitres, a look of fear in her eyes.

"What is it?" Eshlyn asked.

Ewha gulped and faced Caleb. "It's Shecayah. She …"

Caleb scowled at her. "What did she do now?"

Ewha shook her head with force. "Not what she did. Caleb … she was attacked. She might be dying."

Caleb lowered his head.

"Attacked?" Eshlyn cried. "By who?"

"She's in and out of it," Ewha replied. "But she says it was an elf."

CHAPTER 16

SERPENTS

Something woke her in the middle of the night.

Tamya's eyes popped open. The fire had burned to embers next to them, and the dark surrounded her.

They had been inside when it began to rain, the city fully lit for a split second with lightning, the sky breaking in rolls of deafening thunder. They had settled in for the night with the pounding of water overhead in the corner of a vast space, the first floor of some building they didn't know the purpose of. The horses stood off to the side.

Lying there awake all of a sudden, she could hear the rain continuing to pour, a dull roar around them. Thunder sounded, distant. She supposed any of those sounds could have been what woke her, but she didn't think so.

After living on the streets in the city of Oshra, she trusted certain instincts, one of those being the sense of danger, no matter how easy it was to dismiss. It had saved her life several times, kept her from the predators that crept in the alleys, men and women looking for the smallest amount of money to keep them alive another day. Or from those men seeking an abusive thrill.

But Aden had been raised on the streets, too. Why was he snoring away like the storm had traveled up his nostrils? She doubted that instinct, despite how familiar, for a brief moment.

Until she heard it again.

Something scraping. Or sliding.

The horses woke, too, shifting their weight on their hooves, snorting.

Aden stirred, and she slipped from his arms and sat up, her eyes adjusting a little to the dark. But there were only dark shapes, and shadows could play tricks on you when your heart pounded.

The scraping sound, like a large hand over rough stone, trying to find purchase, returned. Something was in the room with them. It came from her left, towards the giant door. Whatever it was, it moved to block their exit.

"What's that?" Aden whispered next to her, and she wanted to scream at him, *shut up!* But she laid a hand on his shoulder instead.

More thunder. Then lightning flashed, and with the scant light that flickered in the room, something long and black, a shuddering shadow, writhed towards the horses.

Without a sound, she hopped up to her feet. With the storm and the rain around her, her first desire was to use her magic and manipulate the water. But instead, she reached for Xander's unforged sword a pace away, and the desire subsided and became the echo once again.

She was in her underclothes, and their blankets were spread around the glowing embers. They would need those. And if they moved any further north, they would need the heavier clothes and coats in the packs; they would need those, as well.

She stepped off her blanket, keeping her eye on the shape moving to the horses. Critters. They were going to need the horses! She began to roll the blanket and her clothes together with one hand towards the pack nearby.

Aden, for once, did not speak and appeared to realize her plan, because he rose and gathered things in his pack, quiet.

A skittering noise came as a warning from deeper into the room; then a long and immense shape shot towards them.

She grunted and dove, but Aden reacted with blinding speed, raising his unforged sword and spinning under the shape, slicing into it. The shape screeched above her; Aden had wounded it. But she also heard the horses screaming.

Tamya rolled to her feet and looked over at the horses. The long, black shape wrapped around one of the horses, two shadows wrestling together in the dim light. The other horse ran away from the attack, towards the center of the room.

"The horse, get him!" Aden yelled at her.

She shouldered her pack and raced to the horse. The horse reared and kicked while the other screamed and died. Tamya spoke to the surviving horse, her horse, and waited until he landed on all fours before darting in. Grabbing the mane with one hand, she leapt onto the back.

More sounds from Aden, and when she was able to glance his way, the embers gave enough light to show her husband jumping to the side, turning and stabbing his sword into the head of some great serpent, the body and tail flailing until falling still.

Without hesitation, Aden threw his pack over his own shoulder and ran towards where the horses had been. While the other serpent crushed Aden's horse, he hacked at the serpent body twice, cutting right through it.

There were more sounds from the far corner.

Tamya kicked the horse towards Aden. She held out a hand as she passed, he grabbed it, and he swung up behind her.

"Go!"

She was already kicking the horse forward and towards the giant door out into the night. Smoke snorted and shook his head as they raced out to the street, a snarling hiss coming from behind them.

The horse, Smoke, stumbled out into the street, and she thought they were going to go down on the wet cobblestone. But the horse recovered, and she pulled him to the left, back to the city gate. As they turned a corner, the rain pelting them, another flash of lightning showed two more serpents hanging from the dragon statue.

Tamya had seen snakes before, but these were different. They did have long, cylindrical shapes, thirty mitres in length or more, but they possessed heads more like a dog with pointed ears and horns from the middle of their forehead. Two pair of stubby legs with claws protruded from their bodies.

Both creatures roared at them in the storm.

"Right, go right!" Aden said in her ear, and Smoke screeched as she yanked him hard to the right down another street and away from the serpents.

"What the shog!" she yelled as the horse sprinted.

"Just go."

Up ahead, shapes emerged on both sides of the street, serpents uncoiling from above on walls and roofs. One sprung towards them, and she turned Smoke away to the right.

"No," Aden said. "Back to the gate!"

"Shut up," she said, but he was right. She had turned away from the gate, and if these creatures were all over the city, they needed to get out.

The next corner she made a left, the next another left, and she thought she was going in the general direction of the gate, but at the next turn, two more of the serpents – or perhaps the same two – waited in the street, snarling and hissing at them. Tamya didn't have to pull at the horse to get it to stop. Smoke neighed and slid on the stones, trying to retreat, and Tamya threw herself forward and her arms around his neck, Aden's arms around her waist.

"Those creatures," Aden spat through the pouring rain. "They're herding us, trying to keep us from the gate."

Tamya sat straight, groaned, and spun the horse around, running the way they came. "So what do we do?" She made another left and away from their goal.

"Go to the wall. North. With the holes in the wall, we might be able to find a way out."

These serpents seemed intelligent. They had tried to distract and corner them in the room and keep them from the gate. "They might know all the exits."

"Maybe. But they're going to keep us from the gate."

"Fine." She got turned around in the city, a place she didn't know, so she came to a stop. Her head swiveled. "Which way am I going?"

Aden slung the pack to his side and dug within it. He retrieved the compass. "Crit on a frog, it's spinning like an elven dancer. Something maddy is going on here."

"Shoggit." When they entered the city hours before, they noted the order, the structure. The streets converged ...

She kicked the horse, chose a direction, and they ran.

"That's back to the dragon." Aden struggled to shoulder his pack as they bounded.

"I know." In another minute, they came to the center of the city. She didn't think the creatures would still be there, and they weren't. Tamya slowed the horse to a jog and scanned the area. Wiping the rain from her face, her teeth chattered. Aden shivered behind her.

There, that was the way they came in. So if that was the south, then the opposite should be north, right?

She heard noises to her right. Aden had guessed it; they herded them from the gate. Tamya cried out and urged the horse to the north.

Aden gasped over her shoulder. "Smart."

She grinned as her teeth clattered together in the wet and cold. The horse raced past buildings, farther into the city. One building loomed so far above them, she couldn't see the top of it. She heard screeching and hissing behind them. She didn't want to look and see, but as they neared the wall, she did. Six serpents followed at impossible speeds, their long bodies hurtling and leaping forward in a disturbing display. Something was maddy here.

They reached the towering wall, and Aden pointed to their right. A large opening in the wall gaped at them. They trotted towards the gap, and once they reached it, she stopped Smoke.

"Crittit," Aden said, and she had to agree.

The serpents were intelligent. There was a reason they were only concerned with the gate. The moat around the city, which had been dry on their way in, now filled with water and mud. The moat bubbled; water rushed into it.

Sputtering in the rain, she turned and saw now seven creatures coming towards them. She gritted her teeth to the cold. Were they smiling?

Aden slid from the horse and ran to the gap, standing on the rubble.

The serpents slowed and organized, surrounding them as they approached.

She watched as Aden surveyed the rubble and the deepening water. The horse could not get across. Even frigid and terrified, she loved watching his mind work as he looked from the gap to the high piece of wall next to it. The piece was twenty mitres wide until another gap.

The serpents were ten mitres away.

Soaked, the water rising in the moat before her, Tamya felt the temptation rise within her. Could she make a bridge out of water that would hold them? Could she use the water as a weapon against the serpents? Tamya held out her right hand, and it trembled.

No. Not like this. Not now.

Tamya took her right hand and gripped the hilt of the unforged sword. She breathed easier as the temptation subsided.

Aden adjusted his pack and raised his unforged sword. He struck the piece of wall vertically, and the crack split the air. She cringed. The stone shuddered before her, and he hit the wall once more with the sword. Even the serpents shuddered and hesitated five mitres from them.

Smoke reared at the serpents, snorting.

He struck the wall, this time with the flat of the sword, and it tottered. Aden turned to her, panting. "Tamya," he said and pointed at the wall.

She understood his meaning, and she urged Smoke forward. The horse kicked the wall with its forelegs, and Aden hit the stone with the flat of his sword one last time.

The piece of wall broke at the base. It leaned towards them for a moment, and Tamya prayed, *El, no. The other way!*

And she watched it teeter back and fall away from the city and over the moat. The stone crashed across the moat and threw mud and water and dirt up and out. Tamya threw her arm over her face, and she was splattered hard enough to almost knock her off the horse.

When she raised her head again, the piece of wall now made a type of platform that the horse could navigate. And Aden stood between her and the serpents in a battle stance with the unforged sword ready to defend her. Wearing only his undershorts and the pack on his back, he was covered with mud and water, his hair slicked back on his head. He didn't turn as he said with a calm voice, "Go."

Her heart tightened within her. She thought to argue, but something in his voice reminded her of the voice of El from the sword and that vision from the Living Stone, and she cursed as she drove the horse forward over the stone, dodging jagged areas where it split.

She looked over her shoulder to see Aden step forward, toward the serpents, seven of them closing in on him, and he raised the sword over his head. Lightning flashed and the sky wept and groaned like it was alive. Aden lowered the sword, point down, and buried it into the stone of the city at his feet.

The whole city shook as Smoke leapt from the stone platform onto the wet ground and grass beyond. After running a few lengths, she twisted the horse back around. She gaped, transfixed, as the street Aden stood upon cracked and ruptured, booming and echoing with a deafening sound. The serpents screamed like they were in pain, coiling and uncoiling and even snapping at one another. They retreated back into the city.

Aden waited a moment, and then he lifted the unforged sword from the remains of the street. With a deep breath, he turned and jogged over the former piece of wall that now allowed escape. In the new quiet, his bare feet slapped on the stone and then squished in the grass.

Tamya helped him back on the horse. She wanted to say something sarcastic, but she couldn't think of anything.

"Holy crit," she said.

The compass worked now that they were out of the city, and Aden used it to point to the north. "Let's get out of here."

She didn't have a problem with that.

—————

"My wife is dead," Tobiah said, glaring at the leaders of the *Hamon-el*. His burning, red eyes rested on the elves. "And we know who did it."

Shecayah had died before dawn. She had been stabbed several times through the chest and torso with a gladus. It took her a long time to die.

Macarus took a breath. "We grieve with you. But we do not know it was an elf."

Tobiah bared his teeth at Macarus. "We do. She said so. With her dying breath, she said so."

Eshlyn's heart broke as she watched Tobiah, in agony. She knew what it was like to lose your lover, to have it feel senseless and unjust. Eshlyn stood next to Tobiah. His whole body was tight, compressed like a spring.

While they had experienced conflict over the past couple days, Eshlyn considered the woman a friend, a sister even. She thought of Athelwulf, her brother. She thought of Shecayah's father back in the mountains of Lior. Both of his children were now dead. Her heart grieved, but she couldn't allow it the space. The whole revolution could be lost right here.

Macarus inclined his head. "That is true. She said that she saw someone in militan armor. But if he or she was wearing a helmet, who knows? It was dark. We don't have all the facts, yet. It could have been anyone."

"Unbelievable," Tobiah growled, shaking his head.

"There is more," Andos said. "We found an elf in our camp, also dead last night, stripped naked of his armor."

The room, silent before, erupted. "What?" Carys stood and cried.

Caleb gripped the Kingstaff with white knuckles. "Why are we only hearing about it now?"

"I apologize, *Brendel*," Andos said. "We found him only a couple hours ago."

"Lies," Tobiah hissed. "This was revenge for our perceived betrayal. And now you're covering it up."

"Why would we do that?" Steward Roers said, getting angry. "You think we would kill our own? If we didn't want to support this revolution, if we wanted to fight you, we wouldn't be here."

"Not true," Gunnar said. "What better way to defeat an army than from within?"

"This from a mercenary?" Steward Roers said. "Did the Emperor pay you to come and cause division?"

Sergeant Gunnar raised a brow at the steward.

"What has happened is tragic." Caleb's eyes were cold and piercing. "We will all grieve with you, Tobiah. Do not doubt that. We do not know who is responsible, yet, and we can't move forward until we do. I will do everything in my power to bring that person to justice, I swear to you."

Caleb scanned the room and then faced Tobiah. "For now, you and your people will decide how you wish to proceed with any funeral arrangements. You have my full support. We will meet this afternoon. Thank you all. Bweth, Lady Eshlyn, I need a word."

The meeting was short, and a few blinked surprise. But they knew when they were being dismissed. The humans, elves, and dwarves all left, one by one.

Eshlyn waited with Bweth, both of them sharing a glance of ignorance, and Iletus was the last to leave. He leaned into Caleb. "The dwarf was right. This was calculated. We have an operative in our midst. This is how the Emperor works. It could be anyone."

Caleb closed his eyes while he sighed. He looked up at Iletus, a Bladeguard who had been second only to Galen. "Find who it is."

Iletus nodded. With a final and pointed look at Bweth, he left the room.

"Why do I feel like I've been called to the breakin' foreman's office?" Bweth frowned.

Eshlyn's brow furrowed at Caleb.

"With all that's going on," Caleb began, "I thought it was time to tell us."

Bweth was silent a moment. "Tell you what?"

"A half-dwarf exiled to Ketan to make swords for Bladeguard?" Caleb said. "You've been quiet about your past, and what brought you there. I respected that. But now I need to know."

Bweth stood and her fists clenched. "You think I did this?"

Caleb shook his head. "No. But you obviously trained with the legions, with the elves, and you have connections with the Bladeguard. Iletus knew about a half-dwarf who had some business with the Moonguard and then disappeared. Even he didn't know the name."

Bweth stared hard at Caleb. "How long have you known?"

"Within a few days of Iletus' arrival, months ago. Like I said, I respected your silence. But Iletus is right. We're being manipulated as we approach Asya. The Emperor is there waiting on us with who knows how many militan. Earon ran off, and we're fracturing, Bweth. I need you to be honest with me. You might have information that could help us."

"I don't know anything that could help," Bweth said.

"I'm sorry," Caleb said. "But I need to make that decision."

Eshlyn crossed her arms while they waited. Bweth turned to Eshlyn, her red curls falling over her shoulder. Her eyes pleaded. Eshlyn stepped to her and put a hand on her shoulder. "Cal is right. Trust us. Please."

Bweth sighed and walked over to the window. "My father was an ambassador from Kryus to King Ironsword. He had been part of the royal family from before Tanicus. He was sent as far away as possible, to the dwarves. There, he met my mother, King Ironsword's sister." She shrugged. "As it happens with people, they start shoggin'. That's where I come from."

Eshlyn cocked her head at Bweth. "Macarus is of the royal family."

"Yeah, but not close. His mother's a senator," Bweth said. "Related, but distant."

"Does he know?" Eshlyn asked.

"Doubt it," Bweth said.

Caleb narrowed his eyes at her. "Wait. Are you saying King Ironsword is your uncle?"

"The first one, yes," Bweth said.

"The first one?" Eshlyn asked.

Caleb sniffed. "Long story. Another time." He gestured for Bweth to continue. "So you were raised at Ironsword's court?"

"Learned weapons and smithin' from the best in the world," Bweth said.

"But you left," Eshlyn said.

"My mother died when I was young," Bweth said. "And being of royal blood but a half-breed, well, people can be shoggers, you know. So I left."

Caleb shifted the Kingstaff from one hand to the other. "Where did you go?"

"Tried to find my da. Went to Kryus. But he wouldn't see me. Wouldn't talk to me. I joined the legions."

Caleb scoffed. "They let a half-breed in the legions?"

Bweth scowled at him. "Remember, boy, this was two hundred years ago, and Tanicus wasn't as much a shogger about such things as he is now." She gazed out the window. "I made my way through the legions, made a name for myself, as it was, making weapons and such. That's when the Moonguard came to see me."

Bweth leaned on the wall next to her, lowering her bright green eyes, her long, curly red hair fluttering in a slight breeze.

"In Ironsword's court, my mother said I had a gift with metal, like I was born to shape it, to bring it to life. Didn't make me any more popular with the dwarves, I tell ya, a half-breed better than all of 'em. So when an elf in power come to me, he say I got a gift and he could use me to do something great, something never done before, I say yes. I thought of my mother and how I could make her proud."

Eshlyn lowered her voice. "What did he have you make?"

"He had an idea. Since elves healed at a faster rate than humans or dwarves and lived a long time, he thought we could fuse metal to their bones and skin, make 'em living weapons."

Eshlyn swallowed, her mouth dry. Her skin crawled at the thought.

"But it went wrong," Caleb said. "As it always does."

"At first, the work excited me," Bweth said. "Bein' in secret and all, seeing if it would work. I met the elves. They were volunteers, so they told me. But when I started melting down the metal, attaching it to their bones, into the bones, really, they would die." Bweth looked over at Caleb and Eshlyn with wet eyes. "The screaming. I had killed in battle before, but I never seen anything like that. But the Moonguard would tell me it's okay and then took them into another room. And the next day, they'd be alive."

"Carys told us about the Moonguard from Galya." Eshlyn rubbed her arms. "How they found that lab." Half-human creatures …

"Moonguard are wizards," Caleb said. "They use magic."

"I didn't know what he did," Bweth said. "Their bodies came back alive, to the sure, but their minds came back … broken. Every time, more and more maddy."

Caleb's steel eyes hardened. "The Deathguard. You helped them make the Deathguard."

"I saw them in battle, the first time," Bweth said. "The destruction, the madness. I couldn't do that again. They never used them again. It was a failure. The Moonguard gave me a choice of remote assignments. I chose Ketan."

"Making swords for the Bladeguard," Eshlyn said.

"Bastardizing the ancient quest of the *Sohan-el*," Caleb said. "And keeping an eye on your cousin?"

Bweth shrugged. "Didn't hurt, did it?"

Eshlyn grinned at her. "And Hunter, did he know?"

"He knew my secrets, yes," Bweth said. "As I knew his."

Caleb looked from Eshlyn to Bweth. "Hunter had secrets?"

Bweth smirked at them both but faced Eshlyn. "Hunter's family were exiles, too. From Lior. When the Empire took over Lior, placed their own Steward and killed the last King, the survivors of the royal family fled to Ketan. King Judai gave them asylum. Once King Judai and Ketan fell to Tanicus, the secret died. Until, well, me."

Eshlyn gaped at the half-dwarf.

Bweth uncrossed her arms and laid her hands on her pregnant belly. "It's even more important I keep this secret, you see. If there be a Kryan agent at work, then the babe could be in danger if anyone knew. This wee one, he or she be royalty in all three races."

Eshlyn and Caleb spoke at once.

"Break me." "Break it all."

Chapter 17

The Message

"Maybe we should head back," Tamya said to him.

They couldn't get warm. The storm had soaked everything – the clothes in their pack, their provisions. They couldn't find enough vegetation to make a fire, and it was all wet anyway. While the rain had stopped mid-morning, Aden spent energy he couldn't afford on trying to start a fire on the next night after the Geddai city, and it hadn't worked. Cold water, jerky, it sustained them but did not touch the cold that was at his core. That night, they slept in each other's arms, trying to use what little body heat they possessed with damp blankets around them under the tent.

When they awoke from fitful sleep, it had snowed.

On a horse with no saddle or bridle, shivering in layers of clothes, they packed their damp possessions in their packs and made their way north.

They broke for lunch under the noon sun, bright but cold somehow, the snow falling. Smoke dug through the snow with his nose to find the grass beneath. The white, vast tundra waited ahead as they sat on the frigid ground. The gray shadows of mountains towered beyond.

He didn't want to agree with her, but she made a valid point. He didn't know if he had the energy to climb back on the horse, much less make it through the snow and mountains to a place he didn't know how to find. He'd been thinking the same thing, only he hadn't wanted to say it.

"Maybe." He looked at her. "You want to turn back?"

Tamya stared to the north. She felt the same fear and concern he did. She was pale, her skin lighter, and her lips had a touch of blue. She gnawed at a piece of jerky with her arms around her knees. She wore a coat, the hood up over her head. "I don't know. Can we?"

"We could. Well, if we make sure we go around that city this time."

Tamya frowned at him.

"We have enough provisions to make it back," he said. "If we stretch it."

She finished her jerky and hugged her knees tighter. "You're saying we should?"

"I'm saying it makes sense. If we go back now, we know what we're facing. We'll live. Forward? I don't know. Doesn't look good."

Tamya was silent a long time. "You'd be okay with that? Turning back?"

"Living? Sure."

Her brown eyes glistened. "But we'd have to go back, tell Caleb and the others we failed. We gave up."

"But then we'd get to keep fighting with the army." He shrugged and grabbed the Dracolet on the inside of his coat.

Tamya and Aden both gazed at the north, the snow, the mountains.

After a long minute, Tamya stood. She gathered her coat tight around her. "All those statues in that city. Those serpents, they were ... wrong. The whole city was broken, even the air. Something had been lost, Aden."

"Yeah, but what?"

"Don't know. But I think it has to do with the dragons. They were like dragons but different."

"So what are you saying?"

She shrugged. "I don't know. But I think the only way we find the answer is to keep going."

Aden squinted at her and the cold as he stood. He faced her.

Tamya shook her head at him. "You know you want to find out."

He smirked. "You know me too well."

"That's my job."

"Could be a short marriage."

Her eyes held his. "Those dragons are real. I know they are. All we have to do is stay alive until we find them. And you and I? We're survivors. Whatever else we are, I know that."

Aden leaned in and kissed her. They held each other for a moment.

She reached up and moved his hair out of his face with a gloved hand. "Besides," she said. "*There is no victory in retreat.*"

His mouth hung open and he chuckled. "That's from the *Fyrwrit*. You've been reading it."

She climbed up on Smoke's back. "Don't tell anyone."

Aden sniffed and climbed up behind her. "You're secret's safe with me."

Using the compass, they faced north and rode forward.

—†—

The towers of the palace of Asya pierced the sky like spears. A hundred militan escorted Earon to the front gate of the palace made of white stone and thick glass. He walked with the Captain at the front, his hands bound behind him. The Captain of the militan raised a fist and the rows of militan behind him stopped, as did Earon.

They had taken his horse and pack at the city gate. The Lieutenant and then the Captain had not believed him when he told them who he was and that he wanted to see Tanicus with a message from the *Brendel*.

That was a lie. Caleb had been clear he did not want Earon to come. But Earon didn't know another way to leverage a meeting with the Emperor. Earon figured if he had argued with Caleb long enough, he could have convinced his cousin. Perhaps. But he had not been willing to waste the time and snuck away in the middle of the night. The fact that a few Ghosts – or Caleb himself – had not chased him down told him that maybe Caleb had agreed in the end.

Now a General stood at the entry to the palace with two Sunguard standing behind him. The Sunguard wore golden armor with helmets that covered their eyes. A wall separated the palace area from the rest of the city. The General looked Earon up and down with disgust.

"They say you are from the *Brendel*," he said.

Earon bowed. "It is an honor, General. My name is Earon. And yes, I bring a message from the *Brendel*. What is your name?"

The General scowled and stepped closer to him. "I am the First General of the greatest army on Eres."

"I understand. I humbly ask that you tell the great Emperor that I have a message from the *Brendel*."

"You believe I would let a humie close to the Emperor?"

"I do not know," Earon said. "That is why I asked. I am no assassin, I can assure you. Your militan have searched me. All too well. I am only a messenger. And anyway, what threat could I be to someone as powerful as a Worldbreaker?"

Militan sniffed and flinched as he spoke.

The First General stood straight, trying to rise to a height to look down at Earon. He was not successful. "You should be thanking all the nine gods the Emperor wants to meet you before you die."

Earon did not answer. His throat tightened.

"Thank you, Captain," the General said. "I will take the humie from here."

The General turned and walked through the arched entry into the courtyard. After Earon passed them, The Sunguard spun on their heels to follow behind. The hair on the back of Earon's neck rose as he thought of the Sunguard watching him, waiting for any excuse to kill him.

He drove the thought from his mind and focused on the First General's back as they entered the palace. The General led them to a long corridor. At the end of the corridor, an elevator sat, open. The four of them stood in the elevator, and the General rang a bell for the number of floors they were to rise.

Earon knew that below them, in some basement or dungeon, human slaves pulled on chains, and the elevator rose into the palace and ascended the main tower. Gears and chains groaned. After several minutes of slow ascent, they stopped at another corridor with a lofty ceiling. The General led them to the end of the corridor to double doors.

Without any announcement or signal, two Sunguard opened those doors. Earon walked with the General into a spacious sitting room with widows that looked over the city. The Emperor stood at the window.

Earon didn't know if the powers of magic had any influence – would he know if they did? – but Tanicus was a beautiful elf. Tall with long, silken blond hair and eyes the color of a clear blue stream, he wore a white robe and a golden crown. All of a sudden, Earon was aware of his own trousers and tunic, worn and dirty, and the mud on his boots.

Tanicus shifted to face them. "Unbind his hands, General, and leave us. I will speak to him alone."

The General bowed and obeyed, taking the dagger from his belt and cutting Earon free. Earon rubbed his wrists as the General and the Sunguard all left the room, closing the doors behind them, leaving Earon alone with a Worldbreaker.

Maybe this wasn't so smart after all.

The Emperor met his eyes, and it took all of Earon's will to hold the gaze.

"They say you are his cousin," Tanicus said. "Is that true?"

"It is. He and I grew up together. We are more like brothers."

"I see. And are you the same young man that Zarek turned to get to the Prophet?"

Earon, what have you done? His father stabbed through the heart, bleeding, dying on the floor of the inn so far away. The look of murder in Caleb's eyes.

"I am."

"And now you are with the *Brendel* again?"

"That is one way to say it."

Tanicus took a step in front of the window. "How would you say it?"

"That I returned to the truth of El. That I am with the one true god. And so Caleb and I are both with him."

The edge of the Emperor's mouth twitched. "You dare come to me and speak of your god? When you know your life is in my hands?"

"Whether I live or die today, my life is in the hands of the great and mighty El. You may kill my body, but he has my heart and soul."

"Ah, yes, so you are here to be a martyr?"

"No," Earon said. "I am here to give you a message."

"That is what they told me. You have a message from the *Brendel.*"

"I do. Well, to be precise, I have a message from El."

Tanicus chuckled. He clasped his hands behind him. "You truly believe you can speak for your god?"

Earon cocked his head at the Emperor. "Do you not believe you speak for yours?"

Tanicus frowned. "I have power. I could kill you with but a thought. I have built an empire. All evidence points to the fact they have chosen me. What do you have?"

Earon spread his hands. "Nothing but the truth."

"You have your truth, you mean," Tanicus said. "A truth that has only led to corruption, to death, throughout the history of humanity. A truth that has made you a traitor to your Emperor. A truth that has delivered you to me, powerless."

"Powerless?" Earon repeated. "The great kingdoms of men and elves that followed the teachings of El and enjoyed prosperity and freedom would not agree with you. It was only when they ceased believing in the freedom and power of El, and began to rest in their own power instead, that they began to fall."

"Legend and propaganda from a false religion."

"Then I will tell you what is not legend," Earon said. "Was the truth of El powerless to unite a city, human and elven, to battle demics from the Underland? Was it powerless to cleanse the legendary Deadwater at the Acar? The Deadwater, which your power created, made alive again. Is it powerless now as men and dwarves and elves from your own legion join a revolution, out of choice, one that promises freedom for all?"

"A lie," Tanicus said. "They have freedom now, under my rule, and they refuse to acknowledge it."

Earon lowered his eyes. "What better proof do you need in the power of El than the fact I would come, unarmed and alone, to bring a message to the most powerful person on Eres?"

"Suicide is not an argument. What, then, is your message?"

Earon licked his lips and sighed. He raised his eyes and spoke.

"I come to you, Tanicus, and I plead with you. Find a way to make peace with the *Brendel*. All races were born to be free, and this revolution will bring more death to humans and elves. Find a resolution between those who cry for freedom and the Kryan Empire. Do not deny the freedom that El desires for all. I come to you with no weapon but truth. The *Brendel*? He will come to you with a sword you cannot break and a power that you cannot withstand. And if you try, the whole of Kryus will fall."

Tanicus stared at him. The Emperor blinked and took a deep breath. "You expect me to treat with traitors? To negotiate with a man who seeks my death?"

"Don't you seek his? You both seek the death of the other, and you both may get what you seek. But neither will win. And many more will lose in the process. So yes, I plead with you for that. For your sake and the sake of this world and the lives of thousands of humans and elves, I ask you. Meet with the *Brendel*. Make peace."

Tanicus raised a brow at Earon. "He is willing to sit and treat with me, an elf he believes is evil?"

"Yes." *Or I hope ...*

"He will require I leave these shores and return to Kryus, give him control over the land."

"Most assuredly."

Tanicus gave a short laugh of derision. "And you think I would agree to anything other than his complete surrender?"

"For your own survival and those you lead, I would hope so."

Tanicus gazed out the window for a moment, the skyline of Asya, a mixture of both human and elven structures, a beautiful city.

"I will tell you what is true," Tanicus said and faced Earon. "The revolution will fail, and the freedom the *Brendel* promises will only lead to pain and death. His army is divided. He can't hold what he has gained. You know this. He knows this. That is why you are here. The *Brendel* knows, in the end, that his weapons and armies and rhetoric will not be enough. He hopes that words will bring peace. And so he sent you as a pig ready to be gutted. You have been manipulated and used, my young human."

Earon shook his head. "He did not send me. I came, freely, of my own will and choice."

"I am sure you believe that is true."

Earon breathed in through his nose. "Have you met him?"

"Who? The *Brendel*? I saw him once or twice at the Citadel. Galen did well to keep him away from me."

"Perhaps. I have looked into his eyes. He will not stop, not until he completes his mission. All I ask is you meet with him once. Look in his eyes. You will see what I know."

"Are you saying I should be afraid of him? Of a man?"

"I am."

Tanicus frowned and walked from the window to stand before him. For a moment that stretched too far, Tanicus glared. Earon tried not to shift uncomfortably. He did not succeed.

"You fascinate me," Tanicus said. "The level of deception you've endured, first from your father, the Prophet, and now the *Brendel*. I ... pity you." Tanicus sniffed. "Yes. You will not die today, human. I will think on these things and speak with you again."

The doors opened behind Earon without a signal or word. *How did they do that?* Two Sunguard strode forward and waited.

"Take him to a guest room and place a guard upon him," Tanicus said to the Sunguard; then he addressed Earon one last time. "Even now, one of my agents is close to your cousin, ready to strike and spread division at my command. I have had the ability to kill him for months now. But I have other plans. Instead, you will wait and watch with me as all you hope for is proven false. And then you will believe what is true. You will know what I am."

—+—

Julius waited in the room, alone and in the dark.

The rebellion had remained camped since the murder the night before. Tensions boiled over. A fight broke out between the elves and the men from Lior earlier in the evening. Several were injured but none were killed. Another group of humans – called the Ghosts, a ridiculous name – had broken up the fighting but another had begun between all three groups. Once it all settled, and the *Brendel* restored order with several that appeared to be his personal disciples of some sort, the camp had quieted.

Guards had been posted, and with the added division and distrust in the camp, movement was difficult for Julius but not impossible. His Captain militan uniform hid him well among the elves. Getting into the center of the camp without being seen took effort and time, but he had made it to the command tent before his target.

The handle of the flap rustled, and Julius remained seated in the chair towards the back, his legs crossed, a sword over his lap. The flap opened, and a shadow moved inside and reached for the lamp but did not find it.

The lamp sat on a small folding desk next to Julius. He lit the lamp and the tiny flame blossomed in the room.

The shadow crouched and laid a hand on his sword, bared teeth in the dim light.

"You," Iletus said. "You did this. You killed the woman."

"Peace, Iletus. I have come from the Emperor. It is time to put the plan into place."

CHAPTER 18

DEATH AND COLD

Tamya wondered if her clothes ever truly dried. They found more brush and wood to make fires each night along the tundra, improving on their skill at digging in snow and finding what they needed, so they had opportunity to heat and dry their clothes. But the second day into the tundra, the cold was a real thing.

Tamya realized she never knew cold. Born and raised in Lior, she never experienced cold until the winter in Ketan, which was bad enough. In Ketan, there had been rooms with fires and heat to protect you. Here on the tundra, nothing could shield you from the cold.

She didn't know that cold could be alive, and the more time she spent in the tundra, the more the truth of it became real. She couldn't escape it. By a fire in a tent with blankets surrounding them and dug into a snowbank, huddled next to each other, the cold was distant but there. It never left. She was never warm, and the cold hovered over her, around her, seeking its way in every moment, every second. Tamya had been through battles before, fought bloodwolves and elves and Bladeguard, but she thought the cold might be the greatest enemy she ever faced.

Aden grew quiet, which concerned her. For the first day and a half, he had talked with her about the prophecy, about the dragons. He spoke with her about El and how he sent his son, Yosu. Yosu had other names – the Lord of the Redemption, the King of Eres, and the Master of War. One sect of worship to El had called Yosu the Peace, which in the First Tongue was spoken as *Dryshalom*.

The mountains grew closer, the tundra turning to hills and large black stones that broke from the snow.

But the evening of the second day into the tundra, with the mountains close and looming over them, Aden stopped his talking, and his skin grew even paler. Since his silence concerned her, once they set up the tent and fire for the evening, Tamya tried to get him talking as they snuggled in together.

"You think we'll reach the mountains tomorrow?"

Aden grunted and shrugged.

Her teeth clattered as she spoke. "We'll have to look for food. Provisions almost out."

He closed his eyes and nodded.

"Once we get to the mountains, where do you think we should look?"

"Dragons are big," he said. But that was it. He lay still, falling asleep.

Tamya sighed and held him close.

Perhaps they should have turned back after all.

They woke in the morning and packed. She saw that Aden moved slowly, but she found she didn't have the energy to do much more than notice. Smoke groaned as they sat upon him, a worrisome noise. Tamya patted the beast and encouraged him, but he had eaten less than they the past few days. They dug up as much vegetation as they could find for him, but she doubted it was enough. She was no expert at horses, though. What else could she do? They barely had any food for themselves, only a few crackers and a piece of jerky.

Smoke navigated the narrow passes through hills that reached higher and higher, weaving through stones that grew larger and sharper. His breathing became labored and shallow. By the afternoon, they crawled forward. Finally, the horse stopped and wouldn't move. They slipped off with their packs.

"Maybe he needs a rest," Tamya said.

With a snort, Smoke toppled over like a stiff tree and landed on his side in the snow. Her heart sunk with him. She knelt next to the horse and stroked his neck.

"It's okay," she whispered to him. "We'll rest. We'll just rest here tonight, find you some food."

Aden stood over the horse and pulled his sword. She could not see his face from the shadow of his hood.

"No," she said, but when she looked at the horse, Smoke felt great pain. He had given them all he could. Without glancing up at Aden, she nodded.

He moved to Smoke's shoulder, lifted the sword, and he stabbed down into the heart. She threw her arms around the horse's neck, and she said through tears, "Thank you." The horse moaned and died.

Aden knelt next to her, and he held her hand as she wept.

After a few minutes, Aden said, "Find as much wood as you can."

Sniffling, her tears were ice on her cheek. She rose, her body sore and tingling, and she scrummaged for brush and anything dry they could burn. Aden set to skinning the horse.

It took the rest of the day to skin the horse, build the fire, and cook the meat. The three moons hung high and to the south by the time they could eat any. Sorrow filled her heart at the loss of Smoke. Guilt nagged her at the pleasure she felt in eating her friend.

Tamya sang a song she remembered from the Prophet, a year ago.

"When I am afraid, when I am alone
There is one thing I know

The Creator loves the world
Even when we fall
He will return us again
To a land without sin
If we only believe
The blind will see
While we are surrounded by the dark of night
The Creator will give me light."

Aden reached out and took her hand.

Their packs and bellies full for the first time in days, they set out the next morning into the mountains.

"If there are dragons, they are deep in the mountains," Aden said. "They won't be easy to find."

Despite his words, his voice held a little more hope than the day before, and that brightened her heart.

They clambered through passes. The second day through the mountains, waist deep in snow, Aden pointed up at the highest mountain they could see.

"There. That's where we are going."

But it's so far. "How do you know?"

"Dragons fly, don't they?" He grunted as the snow parted before him. "That's the high ground." Like that explained anything.

Having a goal, even a vague and distant one, seemed to help them. They camped under a large stone where the snow wasn't deep. Cutting down a tree for some firewood, they ate well and spent a needed night happy in each other's arms.

The third day into the mountains, they slipped on rocks, and they had to climb more than hike. She missed the deep snows.

They ascended; it got colder, which she didn't think was possible, but it was a cold so hard it burned her skin, even through her several layers. They covered their faces, everything but their eyes. They traveled with their heads down and away from the wind.

She felt them before she saw them.

Narrowing her eyes, she raised her head into the torture of the frigid wind. She and Aden struggled over rocks, her hands and fingers numb, but there were cliffs above them. She didn't see or hear anything, but she felt something was there. Or someone.

"Don't look," Aden muttered. So he felt them, too.

"What is it? Dragons?"

He kept his voice low. "No. Dragons are bigger. We would see them."

They kept moving forward, and after an hour or more, they reached a small, flat place filled with snow with crags of black stone above them contrasting with the pure, white powder. Trudging through snow to their thighs, they made it to the middle of the clearing when Aden pulled his sword.

Figures jumped down all around them, figures the shape of men but wrapped tightly with green leather skins. White, oval armor like bone covered their chests, shoulders, arms, and legs. Twelve now surrounded them, and they held long, curved weapons in their hands made of the same material as their armor. Their faces were hidden behind the green leather.

She stepped away from Aden and turned, shifting her position so they stood back to back. The magic called to her. *I could drown them all in snow.* She held her breath, pushing it down, and drew her own sword.

The eyes of the men were visible – although with their shapes, at least one was a woman – and the irises were red. The tight, thick skins that they wore allowed for movement. They waded through the snow towards them as one, the circle tightening, and Tamya's numb fingers gripped her sword tight. Unlike the creatures surrounding them, her clothes were not designed for battle. She felt like she wore another person. She would fight, however, as hard as she could.

"We are not here to hurt you," Aden said, his voice firm but clear. "We do not want to fight."

The creatures around them shared glances. One stepped forward and spoke to them in a language Tamya could not understand, but it seemed familiar somehow.

"Crit on a frog," Aden said. "I think that's the First Tongue."

Her head swiveled; her sword was up and ready. "How?"

"I don't know."

The person that seemed to be the leader held a hand to the others, signaling them to stay while he approached alone. He held two long, curved bone weapons, one in each hand. The handles connected perpendicular to the bone blades that had been sharpened.

When the leader came to within two mitres of Aden, he leapt in the air, snow erupting in an impressive display of strength. He lifted his bone weapons and bore down on Aden as he descended. Aden met the weapons with his unforged sword.

The unforged sword shattered both weapons.

Gasps among the people around them, more shared glances. The leader's eyes narrowed as he stood a pace away from Aden. Aden stared back at him, the sword in a low guard.

The leader removed the leather across his face, and he had the face of a man with pure white skin. It was stark with those red eyes.

The leader pointed to the blade in Aden's hand. "*Barabrend.*"

"Yes," Aden said. "*Barabrend*." The unforged. He pointed to himself and Tamya. "*Sohan-el*."

The leader stared at him then pointed at the two of them. He gestured forward to the pass beyond the clearing where they stood. Then he began walking.

The others waited for Aden and Tamya to go first.

"You really think we should go with him?" Tamya asked.

"You got a better idea?"

She shrugged. "Not really."

And so they followed them into the pass.

———

Carys entered the command tent in the center of the camp where the leadership had met that morning. Caleb now sat alone, a brown, leather-bound journal open in his lap and a pen in his hand.

The meeting had not been fruitful. Iletus claimed he had no new evidence. The elves continued to contend they were not responsible, that they had been set up. Tobiah ended the meeting by stating he and the Liorians would head back to the mountains to the south in the morning.

Carys walked up to Caleb. His eyes were closed. Was he asleep? Praying? He looked as tired as she'd ever seen him, as drained as those days before they fought the demics on the wall of Ketan.

She dragged a chair across the ground and set it close to him, facing him. She sat in the chair, leaning back. "What you gonna do, Cubby?"

He hated it when she called him that, the name she used when she was a child. She hoped to get a rise out of him.

It didn't work. He opened his eyes, bloodshot, and closed the journal in his lap. He stuck the pen back in the ink on the table next to him.

"It's all falling apart."

"Certainly seems like it," Carys answered. "But it seemed like that the night you disappeared. Seemed like that the night we found out Earon's mother died and then Earon left. Seemed that way when I ran away and joined the Ghosts." She leaned closer to him. "Seemed that way every day in Ketan before we faced those hordes of demics."

"You've made your point. There is always hope. I get it. But sometimes I'm tired of mustering hope in the face of so much darkness, so much division. Don't you get tired of it?"

"We all get tired of it. That's why people quit. If it were easy, everyone would have hope. But it's not. Changing the world isn't supposed to be easy."

The tent flap opened, and Carys heard the rustling of feet enter the tent. She glanced over her shoulder. Iletus. She faced Cal again.

"We have to do something different," Caleb said. "I'm talking to the leaders, to the people, trying to teach them the truth of El, the vision of the revolution. You, the other *Sohan-el*, Eshlyn, Macarus, we're all trying to get them to see. But it's not working. I'm not Reyan."

Carys squinted at him. "None of us are. Don't try to be. Maybe that's the problem. You're not him. The solution isn't what the Prophet would do, but what would El have you do? What would El have us ..."

She heard the ringing of a sword being drawn, and the only warning she had was a slight tightening of Caleb's eyes before he launched himself from a sitting position, drew his sword, and leapt over her. She ducked on instinct and the clanging of swords met centimitres over her head as she tucked and rolled on the ground.

There was a scuffle behind her as Carys rose to a crouch, her own sword out and before her.

Caleb stood over Iletus, his unforged sword at the elf's throat, the elf lying on his back. Iletus' sword had tumbled to the side. Caleb snarled at Iletus like an animal.

What the shog just happened? Iletus had tried to kill her.

Iletus bared his teeth at Caleb, but his eyes filled with tears. "Do it, Caleb. Do it. Kill me."

—+—

Caleb wanted to kill his friend. Everything in him said to run the sword through the elf's throat.

Being trained as a Bladeguard, it all made sense. It was Iletus the whole time. And he had tried to kill Carys, his sister.

The familiar image appeared in Caleb's mind – holding his sister in a cave to the south, hiding while his mother screamed. The scars on his back itched.

But the sword grew heavy.

He didn't know how much time transpired, but he felt Carys' hand on his arm. He looked down at her, and she caught his gaze.

Caleb breathed and blinked.

His sister turned to the elf on the ground.

"Iletus," she said. "What the shog?"

Iletus begged. "Please, Caleb. Kill me."

Caleb had acted so quickly, but now he was able to replay it in his mind. Iletus stalking Carys from behind, drawing his sword high over her head, all where Caleb could see, block and react.

Caleb lowered his sword. "You wanted this. You wanted me to kill you."

"It's the only way," Iletus said in a desperate voice.

"What are you breakin' talking about?" Carys said.

Caleb frowned at him. "The only way for what?"

But he knew; the answer hovered in the back of his mind.

"The only way to be free of him," Iletus said.

"Who?" Carys asked.

"Tanicus," Caleb said. "Galen didn't send you before he was captured. Tanicus sent you."

Iletus didn't answer. He looked away as tears broke from the corners of his eyes.

Caleb sighed. "You did this? You caused all this division?"

"No. Tanicus did send me, but he told me to wait for orders."

Orders. Caleb's jaw set. "You killed Shecayah?"

"No, no," Iletus said. "You don't understand. It's bigger than you think. He's here. He came back."

Carys leaned on her sword. "Who came back?"

"The first Bladeguard," Iletus said.

Caleb took a quick breath. *That makes even more sense.* "Get up." He pointed to a nearby chair. "Sit there."

Iletus groaned and obeyed.

Carys' brow furrowed at Caleb. "I thought you said you killed Galen."

"Not Galen," Caleb said. "Julius."

"Who?"

Caleb sighed. "The first Bladeguard, second only to the Emperor. He trained Galen and Iletus. You've never heard of him because he retired more than a century ago." Carys faced Iletus. "But Tanicus brought him back?"

"You woke something in Tanicus, Caleb." Iletus leaned over on his elbows. "This revolution, it has exposed the Emperor as a Worldbreaker, and he has brought every weapon he has ever forged to bear upon you."

"Including you," Caleb said.

Iletus nodded.

"So this ... Julius, he killed Shecayah?" Carys said.

"Yes," Iletus said.

"When did he come to you?" Caleb said.

"Two nights ago," Iletus said.

"And this is what he told you to do, kill Carys?"

"Julius told me to do the one thing that would end this revolution without killing the *Brendel*. And I knew what it was."

"Kill my sister." And he was right. It was the one thing that would send him over the edge, the one thing that could make him lose hope.

Carys glanced at Caleb with compassion in her eyes. "Why not kill Caleb?"

"Then I'd be a martyr," Caleb answered. "He wants this revolution to fail, and he wants it to look like my fault."

Carys squinted at Iletus. "You said, the only way to be free. You knew that killing me wouldn't stop Caleb, not really. You wanted to die. That was what you wanted."

"I thought …" Iletus took a deep breath. "I knew how you were trained. I knew there was one situation where your emotions would react and you would kill without thinking. But you didn't."

"Day is young, yet," Caleb said. Iletus had been helping him. Caleb ran through their discussions, their planning. Sure, he had argued with Caleb from time to time, but Caleb had never sensed it was out of betrayal or a wish to see the revolution fail. Iletus had, in fact, been legitimately shocked when he learned Tanicus was a Worldbreaker. All those years, Iletus had helped Galen. What would make him turn now? "What does Tanicus have on you?"

"Not what, but who," Iletus said. "He has my daughter."

"You have a daughter?" Caleb asked.

"I am a Bladeguard," Iletus said. "I am trained to keep secrets, especially the important ones."

"But Tanicus knew," Carys said.

"He found her. I thought she was safe. I don't know how, but he found her."

Carys crossed her arms. "And you think that if you're dead, he won't kill her?"

"I can't help him then, can I?"

"You could have come to us, told us," Caleb said. "Death was not the only answer."

"Yes, it is," Iletus said. "Julius murdered Shecayah, dressed as an elven militan. Tobiah looks for someone to blame. My daughter is probably dead, but I have to try to save her." Iletus reached under his tunic and brought out a parchment. "If I die, Tobiah can know justice. The people will realize who their real enemy is. You can have unity again."

"But you'd be dead," Caleb said.

"My daughter is in danger as long as I'm alive," Iletus said.

"Tanicus might kill her anyway," Carys said. "He's proven to be that ruthless, right?"

Iletus shrugged. "She is surely dead if I don't obey. That is all I know. And as much as I knew Tanicus was a tyrant, as much as I believed I should support Galen, being here and a part of his army, Caleb, I understand now what you're trying to do. I understand how El seeks to bring all races together in peace. I would rather die before causing that revolution further damage."

Caleb grunted and sat down. Carys pulled a chair and sat next to him.

"While I appreciate your willingness to sacrifice, there must be another solution," Caleb said.

"Trust me, Caleb," Iletus said. "There isn't."

Caleb pursed his lips and crossed his arms. He looked over at Carys and smirked.

"Maybe you both have to die."

CHAPTER 19

DRAGONMEN

The Dracolet under Aden's coat began to get warm.

At first, he ignored it, convinced it was a trick of his body or anxiety and anticipation. But it continued until his chest was slick with sweat in the brutal cold.

They stomped through the snow for hours. The men and women that escorted them didn't seem to have much trouble, their bodies lean but strong. Tamya grabbed Aden's hand, and he gripped it to give her reassurance.

Their escorts took them through a series of canyons and passages, some no wider than Aden. He had to remove his pack to navigate two of them. The mountains rose into the clouds above them and blocked out the sun, the air dead and frozen. The sun began to set, and while the light of the sky dimmed, they arrived at a cave. They entered a natural tunnel that descended into the mountain.

Within moments, it was dark, and the leader worked to light a torch. One now aflame, he lit others so four of them gave dim light to the passage.

The rock around them was black in the yellow light of the flames. The leader spoke to one of the others, one with a torch, and after he finished, the man raced down the tunnel.

They shuffled forward, and the air lost its chill.

"Is it getting warmer?" Tamya's voice echoed on the rock.

"I think so."

"How?"

Aden could only shrug.

Another hour of walking, and the tunnel widened to a cavern lit with torches. Three people waited for them there. Two were dressed in the green leather without the white pieces of armor, a man and a woman, both with stark red hair and red eyes. They rode enormous white insects like ants but longer, thinner heads, their mandibles closer to fangs or tusks. The exoskeleton was the same color and texture of the armor of the men and women who guarded them.

An older man dressed in a tunic and trousers stood with them. His nose was sharp and his head was bald. He did not ride an insect and appeared different from the others.

Something about him looked familiar.

The older man stepped forward. "Hello, and welcome to Dracoland."

Aden looked from the old man to Tamya. "Wait. You speak common?"

"I do," he said.

Aden felt relief. "And this is it? We're here? This is the Dracoland?"

"It is." The old man stared at him. "Is it true? You have an unforged sword?"

Aden pulled his sword from the sheath and held it horizontal in his hands.

The old man's eyes narrowed as he leaned down and inspected the blade. He rose and then bowed. "Then it is true. The *Sohan-el* have returned."

"To the sure. My name is Aden, and this is my wife, Tamya." He lowered the sword and gestured to the men and women in green leather. "Who are these people?"

"They are the Dragonmen." The old man pointed to the man riding an insect. "This is Abbott, the chief of the Dragonmen, and this is his wife, priestess Zemira."

Abbott and Zemira bowed from their greenleather saddles atop the insects.

"*These* are the Dragonmen?" Tamya said. "They are real?"

"They are," the old man said. "They protect the Dracoland from outsiders."

"You are an outsider," Tamya said.

"You speak true," the old man said. "I came long ago to learn the First Tongue, to properly translate the scriptures of El. My name is Redan Se'Matan."

Aden's brows furrowed. "Se'Matan ..."

Earon. Reyan.

"The Prophet," Tamya gasped.

Redan raised a brow at them.

"You are related to Reyan?" Aden asked.

Redan's face fell. "He is my son." He paused. "You ... know him?"

Aden and Tamya shared a glance. Aden faced Redan. "We did."

Redan's shoulders slumped. "Did?"

"I'm sorry to tell you that he was killed," Aden said. "Eight months ago."

Redan's face twisted in pain, his eyes brimming with tears. "How? How did he ...?"

Aden spoke with a soft voice. "A Bladeguard killed him."

Redan lowered his head. "I told him not to go ..."

"When was the last time you talked with him?" Tamya said.

"He and my daughter left long ago," Redan said. "They were raised here, learned the First Tongue as I did, but once they came of age, Reyan wanted to translate the scriptures and bring the truth of El to the world, to the humans. And my daughter wanted to go with him. I begged them not to go."

The Prophet had possessed such a zeal for truth, such passion. No way he could have lived his life in a cave.

"My daughter," Redan asked. "Did you know her?"

Caleb's mother. Aden stammered, awkward. "I didn't know her, but I know her children well. She ... I'm sorry; she died more than twenty years ago."

Redan's legs buckled, and he dropped to one knee. He groaned, and the sound broke Aden's heart. Aden stepped forward and knelt before him. Aden set a hand on the man's shoulder and let him weep.

Abbott and Zamira slid from their mounts, the insects chittering behind them as they approached and stood behind Redan, also laying hands upon his shoulder. Abbott spoke in a low voice in the First Tongue, and even though Aden could not understand the language, it was a prayer.

"I only knew your son for a few ninedays," Aden said. "But let me tell you, he finished the translation."

Redan sniffed and looked up.

Aden dropped his pack to the ground and dug inside. Within a separate leather pouch, he pulled out two books. He offered them to Redan. "He did it. It took him years. But he did it."

Redan took the books from Aden. He held them in his hands like great treasure.

"Your children and grandchildren," Aden said. "They brought back the *Sohan-el* and began a revolution. They're why we're here."

Aden stood and pulled the Dracolet from under his coat and tunic. It glowed and burned in his gloved hand.

Abbott and Zamira grunted and stepped back. The whole room gasped.

"We are here to speak to the dragons," Aden said. "We are here to see the fire reborn."

Redan's face was filled with the golden glow from the Dracolet. "No one has seen or heard from the dragons in a thousand years."

"But the *Sohan-el* have returned," Aden said.

Redan rose to join him. "The *Sohan-el* never disappeared."

"What?" Tamya said.

Redan stared at Tamya. "We have one here."

"You can't be serious," Macarus said. "You want us to lie to everyone?"

The leadership of the *Hamon-el* had been called back for a meeting that evening. The *Sohan-el*, Sergeant Gunnar, Andos, Eshlyn, Carys and Zalman, Jaff, Bweth, Caleb, and Iletus.

Eshlyn scanned the room, and her eyes rested on Tobiah, who sat to the side, his arms crossed, his brow pressing down on his eyes. He had remained quiet while Caleb told the group about Julius and Iletus. And then Caleb had explained his plan, which included pretending Carys and Iletus were both dead.

Eshlyn took a deep breath and crossed her arms. "I agree with Macarus. It won't work. I don't think everyone will believe it."

"It will work," Caleb said. "Remember, I trained with the elves. If we tell everyone that Julius killed Carys and Iletus and left once he was discovered."

Macarus shook his head. "But Caleb, Iletus targeted Carys for one purpose, he knew she was the one thing you would protect without thinking. And Zalman here, a notorious figure, is her husband. You would both have to play it unhinged. How would that unite us? The *Brendel* unhinged?"

"While true, that's not my problem with it," Eshlyn said. Caleb turned to her. "Let's say we convince everyone, and they unite under a lie. What happens when they discover the truth? They would have fought and died under a deception. The division would be worse."

"So what are you saying?" Carys asked.

"I'm suggesting we gather everyone and tell them the truth," Eshlyn said. "Tobiah needs this. The Liorians need this. Shecayah was beloved by them all. A lie, as well-intentioned as it may be, would only do more damage in the end."

"But if we tell the truth like that," Jaff said. "We place Iletus' daughter in danger, do we not?"

Caleb shrugged. "Possible she's already dead. Unless she's here with him, the Emperor will have to communicate across an ocean and give up his leverage."

"Can a revolution based on the assertion of truth survive the employment of a deception to continue?" Sergeant Gunnar pulled on his long beard.

"That's playing games with a person's life, however," Andos said. "We must go with what we know."

"Caleb's speakin' truth," Bweth said. "We can't trust Tanicus or what he says."

Eshlyn nodded. "I understand. We don't want to put the elf in greater danger if we don't have to." She turned to Macarus. "Can you get word to your mother? Does she have agents and resources to deal with this?"

Macarus shook his head. "And if I did, I would only expose her move before she made it."

Zalman gestured to Tobiah. "Ask him."

The room grew quiet and still. Eshlyn regarded the large man, changed in so many ways from months ago.

Tobiah lifted his eyes. He stood and lowered his hands to his sides. They clenched into fists.

"The naked truth is always preferred over the best-dressed lie," he said. "Knowing the truth of Shecayah's death comforts me, but I do not understand your strategy. Why are we not hunting Julius down like a rabid tiger? Why do we not discuss the betrayal of Iletus and bring him to justice?" He gazed at Caleb. "You are thinking like elves and not like men."

Caleb narrowed his eyes back at Tobiah. "Iletus has had difficult choices to make, and I do not believe he has betrayed us. He could have. He was willing to give his life so he wouldn't have to. He is to be commended, not brought to justice."

"How many more of these elves harbor other secrets dangerous to all of us?" Tobiah said. "And keep quiet as they justify the lies in their own mind? Commend the elf if you like, but it only confirms our suspicions were correct."

"Look," Macarus said. "I can only speak for myself, but I have no other agenda, personal or imperial, than to support this revolution. I snuck into this country for that very reason."

"With mercenaries," Tobiah noted. "Dwarves who are only here because they have been paid."

"He makes a valid point, Caleb," Jaff said. "While we appreciate the help, is the revolution really about who gets paid to get involved?"

"We were commissioned by King Ironsword," Gunnar said. "As we were informed, we are a repayment of a debt incurred."

"Yeah, a favor," Carys said with a pointed look. "And we still haven't heard *that* story."

Caleb took a breath and scratched his beard. "You're going to have to trust me. Some secrets are kept to protect others. Not lies, but information kept close because, if it was known, others would be hurt or placed in danger. As Iletus is an example. The Prophet traveled the land of humans, and his identity, his family, were kept secret for a reason. Once those connections were known, people died." Eshlyn breathed through her nose as Caleb's eyes grew cold. "That is why I have not told anyone about my connection with King Ironsword."

"I bet Iletus knows," Macarus said.

"I do not," Iletus said.

Eshlyn frowned as Bweth squirmed in her seat. Bweth had secrets, too, how the child could legitimately be in danger if it was known he or she was royalty in Valahal, Kryus, and Lior.

"My husband, Kenric, was a direct descendent of King Judai," Eshlyn said. "He kept that secret. Break it all, he had an unforged sword passed down to him over five generations. That secret protected his family. Protected me. Our son. Sometimes secrets are kept for a reason."

"We understand," Jaff argued. "But that was a different time. We were slaves under the Empire. The Prophet, your husband, they did what they had to for survival, waiting for the day when humanity would be free again. This is that time. We fight not to survive but to free our land. The same rules don't apply."

"And the trust between people here in the army is damaged," Carys added. "I lived through that time, too. Most of us did. Maybe telling secrets would help heal that damage, build some trust. If we promise, on our honor, to keep the secret with you, will you tell us, Cubby?"

Caleb cocked his head at her. He blinked and pursed his lips. "Tobiah, would that help you?"

"Your sister is wise," Tobiah said. "Perhaps. It is a beginning."

"Very well," Caleb said.

Resting a hand on his sword, he paced to the middle of the room with the Kingstaff in his right hand.

"There is much I haven't told you all," Caleb began. "Years of training and missions with Galen. Even those here that I've told much to, you've only heard a small amount. They were ... difficult years. And yes, there are some things even Iletus doesn't know. Just as I didn't know about his daughter. And if you must know, even Galen did not know what I'm about to tell you."

Iletus frowned while grunts sounded around the room.

"Six years ago," Caleb continued. "Galen started taking me on missions, as a part of my training meant to infiltrate human rebellion. Of course, Galen's purpose was to support the revolution, for me to do as I have done, to train and raise up an army. Galen was not allowed to take me on any missions in Kryus or against any elves of Kryus. But missions into Jibryl or other elven kingdoms were allowed. And the dwarves, as well."

"Six years ago," Iletus muttered. "That was when King Ironsword the first died and his son took the throne."

"You're saying you killed King Ironsword the first?" Eshlyn asked. "Doesn't seem like much of a favor."

Caleb held up a hand. "Do I get to tell the story?"

The room quieted.

Caleb shook his head. "As the elves in the room know, King Ironsword was actively competing with Kryus in trade, and to make matters worse for Tanicus, Valahal started an alliance with Faltiel and supported them in their conflicts with Kryus at the border. So Galen and I were sent to kill King Ironsword.

"The stronghold of Valahal is deep within Crutcher Mountain, and very few elves or humans get far within the stronghold. Even fewer into the King's quarters. Only slaves would get that far, and there wouldn't be any elven slaves, so I infiltrated the palace alone, as a slave. With some dirt, some ragged clothes, and a Faltiel slaver tattoo, it took me two ninedays to become a familiar face. I was Stewie, the slave."

"Stewie?" Eshlyn smirked at him.

"Would you think a *Stewie* was an assassin?" Caleb responded. "I made a lot of dumb jokes in my broken dwarven and smelled of ale, and it worked. I got close to the King.

"But over the course of those two ninedays, I noticed something.

"As a Bladeguard, I did things I'm not proud of, but I could justify it. Some enemies of Kryus were evil in their own right. Yes, it served evil, but I stopped it, as well.

"King Ironsword was different. I watched him, trying to get close to him. In the process, I saw how he led, how he treated those around him. He was humble and compassionate. Firm but not abusive.

"I realized I could not kill this king. Not and be the man I was training to be.

"That caused a problem, however. If I didn't kill Ironsword, then Tanicus would question my training, and Galen and the whole thing would unravel before it even began. And Tanicus would only send another assassin in my place. Ironsword would die anyway, even if not by my hand.

"So when I determined a time Ironsword would be alone, I stole weapons and cornered him. But I did not kill him. I offered him a choice.

"We could fake his death. The dwarves are notoriously isolated. If they put out the word Ironsword was dead and someone in the royal family stepped in, then the world would believe it. And if I told Galen I had killed him, he would report it to the Emperor as true."

Gunnar now frowned at Caleb. "Ironsword was a phenomenal warrior. Did he not attempt to overpower you?"

Caleb shrugged. "He did."

Gunnar raised a brow. "Impressive. And what did the King choose?"

"We spoke for hours, actually. I explained to him who I was and what I was training for, my purpose. In the end, he agreed."

"You told him the truth about you?" Iletus said.

"I did," Caleb said. "His closest advisors and the royal family helped with the deception. I left the stronghold before sunrise, and it was announced the King was found dead in his drawing room. Within a few days, Galen and I left the kingdom behind, and word came that his son, Behan Ironsword, took the throne. Ironsword II was crowned.

"Eklan Ironsword helps his son rule from the shadows, I would assume. And what Tanicus didn't understand was that the death of the king only further set Valahal against Kryus." Caleb turned to Gunnar. "Before I left him that night, though, Ironsword asked me what he could do for me, in return for not killing him. I told him that if he ever heard of a revolution rising in the land of humanity, I would appreciate any help he could give."

"Is that why Faltiel and Valahal are bringing more conflict to the east?" Macarus asked.

"Yes," Caleb said.

Bweth scowled at Gunnar. "And they sent mercenaries."

"They are mercenaries," Macarus agreed. "But the Steelsides are well known as near invincible warriors. He didn't just send anyone. He sent the best."

Gunnar bowed. "That he did."

Caleb gazed at Tobiah. "Now you know. While I do not expect it matters as much as it once did, we must respect the deception they continue to maintain. Does that help you trust? A little?"

"It explains much," Tobiah said. "Why you think like an elf. Why your solution is to bring deception to this situation instead of justice. But trust? All I hear is that more secrets exist."

Caleb's eyes hardened. "And you'll never hear them all. Let me explain something to you, Tobiah." He gripped the Kingstaff as it rested on his shoulder. "You lost your wife, and that is tragic. We all weep for you. But I have lost my wife as well. Carys and I both have lost most of our family, and our cousin, Earon, is as good as dead unless El performs a miracle. Eshlyn has lost her husband, as has Bweth. We've lost friends and loved ones to this revolution, either in battle or through betrayal and oppression. The list is too long to recite tonight, but believe me, I could. Every name.

"Shecayah's death hits us hard, and we grieve with you. But we also say, welcome to the revolution. I desire your input and perspective, but if you cannot trust me because of what you've lost, well, I will be sad to see you and the Liorians go. If you stay, then we will come to a decision together and stand in unity. That is the only way to move forward."

Tobiah' eyes glistened, his jaw muscles twitching. The room was silent for several seconds, and Eshlyn was sure Tobiah would turn and walk away.

But he didn't. He took a deep breath. "What, then do you suggest we do? Deception?"

Caleb relaxed. "No. I think you and others are right. For the army to get past this, we must tell everyone the truth about Julius." He sighed. "And I will go after the First Bladeguard."

The room, once quiet from the tension, erupted, and all Eshlyn could distinguish was her own voice. "No, Caleb."

Caleb held up a hand, and the room settled. "Galen may have been a better swordself, but Julius is a notorious warrior. While I respect everyone and their skills in this room, who better to track and face him?"

"That's not the point," Eshlyn said. "To unify the army, we need you here."

Jaff nodded. "She's right, Cal. There are other *Sohan-el*; there are other options."

Iletus gave a bitter chuckle. "None of you understand how dangerous Julius is. Even Caleb has only heard stories. Julius is cold, calculated, and zealous for the nine gods. I am the only one who knows him." Iletus scanned the room. "Which is why I must be the one that goes after him."

"A traitor? Going after him alone?" Tobiah said.

"It is the only way to ensure he does not report back to the Emperor. It gives my daughter a chance."

"If everyone here is united, you can work with the army until I get back," Caleb said.

"You can't do everything, Caleb," Macarus said. "I've only been here a few days, but they need you here."

"Then wait for me," Caleb said. "I keep telling you all, I'm no general. I'm no leader. I'm a weapon. Let me be that weapon."

"With respect, Caleb, you're wrong," Macarus said. "No one brings humans, elves, and dwarves together and brings them this far without competent leadership and vision. You may be the greatest weapon, but you are also the only one that could have done this."

"Not true," Caleb said. "It's been everyone else. Eshlyn, Chamren, and you unified Ketan as much as I ever did. And this army? Aden, Athelwulf, Bweth, and others, there have been dozens that have brought this *Hamon-el* together."

"All based on your vision," Eshlyn said. "Your passion for the revolution. Your training. How you've empowered others."

"It is an inspiring vision," Jaff said.

"So inspiring, we are fracturing," Caleb said.

Macarus chuckled. "Ask Andos or Bweth, if this had been a Kryan legion, the General would have executed half of the officers on principle and anyone who thought of disobeying. Instead, you're still gaining members of this army."

"We had ten more this morning," Jaff said.

"Ten?" Caleb said. "You're supposed to bring them to me."

"So you can learn their names and share with them the purpose of the revolution, personally," Eshlyn said. "Like a leader does."

Caleb lowered his head. "I'm a weapon," he said like a mantra.

"You're more than that, *Brendel*," Andos said. "You have to see that. We will need you here."

Macarus glanced over at Gunnar and the Steelsides. "We could go. Even in their armor, the dwarves track and hide well. He couldn't take us all."

"I've seen this elf battle," Gunnar said, pointing back at Macarus. "He could do it."

Caleb scratched his beard and opened his mouth to speak.

"There were three of us," Iletus began, his voice soft, and the room diverted attention to him. "Galen, Julius, and me. We confronted Elowen, the last elven *Sohan-el*. Before she began to follow El, she and Julius were ... close. We fought in the temple to El outside of Galya. It took all three of us to defeat her. She was mortally wounded, and I held her while he burned out her eyes, out of his need for revenge. She escaped, wounded all three of us, blind, and we left her to burn to death as the temple went down in flames." Iletus stared hard at Caleb. "I was there, Caleb. Me. I have to do this. No one else."

Caleb looked up at his friend. "Are you sure?"

"I am. As sure as I've ever been about anything."

Tobiah scoffed. "Very well. Then I am going with you."

Iletus shook his head. "That isn't wise."

"You're fighting for your daughter? She was my wife." And that was the end of Tobiah' argument.

Carys stood. "And I'm going, too."

Caleb squeaked. "What? No."

Carys sniffed at him. "Really, Cubby? We're going to do this again?" She addressed the crowd. "Out of everyone in this room, Jaff and I are the best trackers. To be honest, I'm probably better."

Jaff opened his mouth to protest but shrugged instead. "She probably is."

Zalman stood and towered over his wife. He looked down at her. "Going to track down the first Bladeguard? Suicide."

"Yep," Carys said, grinning. "Our specialty."

"This is a bad idea," Iletus said. "I should go after him alone."

"Doesn't look like that's an option," Eshlyn told him.

Caleb appeared pale, his face tight. Eshlyn turned to him and saw that invisible weight on him as she often did. He bore it with incredible will and strength, but her heart broke at the pain in his gaze.

"I just got you back," Caleb whispered.

Carys' face fell. She strode up to him. She touched his hand. "I know. But the end is coming soon, isn't it?"

Caleb didn't answer.

"This isn't a time to be safe. There is no such thing as safe, now. We've come too far."

Caleb raised his gaze and met hers. "And if I forbid it?"

"Didn't work last time."

After a few moments of silence, Caleb blinked. "Very well. We meet with everyone tomorrow, the whole camp, and tell them the truth. And the four of you will go after Julius."

Tobiah nodded. "Thank you. I will prepare for the journey." He left the room.

Everyone said their goodbyes, leaving the room in pairs. Eshlyn already noted a difference, a tenuous hope among the leadership.

Caleb, however, appeared more hopeless than ever.

Carys and Zalman were last to leave. Carys embraced her brother. She whispered in his ear, and he held her tight for a moment. He nodded as she pulled away and left with her husband.

Eshlyn and Caleb were alone.

Caleb leaned on the Kingstaff, despondent.

Eshlyn approached him, her boots padding on the stone floor. His eyes were bloodshot, and she swore there were more lines on his face than ever before. She remembered Mother Natali's words.

Remember to savor the sweet moments while you have them. Or create them if you have to. The fate of the world might depend upon it.

She reached out and touched his face, and when he looked at her, it was a desperate thing. She gave him a sad smile. He didn't return it.

So she leaned in and pressed her lips to his.

He grunted in surprise, and for one second, she felt his urgency in return.

Then he pushed and backed away, averting his gaze.

She gasped, her fingers touching her lips. "I – I'm sorry. I thought …"

"You're not wrong."

"Then … I don't understand," she said. "Why? Is it Danelle? Are you still …?"

"No," he said. "I mean, yes. Maybe. She's gone, but …"

Her heart felt like it was going to bust through her chest. "Don't you want …?"

"More than anything."

"Then why, Caleb? Tell me."

His sigh came from far away. "You've lost a husband. I can't do that to you again."

"I'm not some teenie girl at her first harvest dance. I know the risks."

"If it were just me and you, and there was no war, no revolution, then …" He shook his head. "But it's not just you and me. I did that before, and I put Danelle in danger."

She put her hands on her hips. "Losing Ken was the hardest thing I've ever had to do. But it doesn't make me regret the time we were able to spend together."

"How much time would we have?" he pleaded with her.

"What does it matter? We can't know. No one does. As safe as anyone thinks their life is, there are no guarantees. Not for anyone."

"You deserve a man who can stand by you, make time for you while you shine, Eshlyn. You deserve to grow old with someone. I'm not that man."

Her heart ached. "Who cares what I deserve? We could shine together, side by side." *As we've been doing. The very reason I've fallen in love with you.*

"I'm sorry, but I care what you deserve. Please. I have a destiny. I have to bear it. I can't ask you to take this on."

"Bosaur crit. Aren't we all in this together? Isn't that what we were talking about not two minutes ago?" She took a shallow, angry breath. "I get it. You're the *Brendel*. So much expectation from the Prophet and generations. But I never hear you say it. Can you say it? That you're the *Brendel*?"

He said nothing.

"You can't even say it. Destiny doesn't mean you have to be lonely, that you can't enjoy what's been given to you, to be happy for whatever time and opportunity El gives us. You can't bear this alone, Caleb. You weren't meant to. It will break you."

"I can bear it alone," Caleb said. "I must."

Eshlyn ran a hand over her face. "So that's it?"

"I'm sorry."

She couldn't look at him. "Break it all. Me too."

Eshlyn walked out of the room.

—†—

Aden pointed at the large insect Abbot rode while they traveled deeper into the mountain. "What are these?"

"They call them stalgest," Rodan answered. "When the Dragonmen came to this mountain, they tamed the stalgest and used the creatures to help them make these tunnels and rooms in the mountain. These caverns are heated by underground hot springs found and used by the Dragonmen."

"How long have they been here?" Tamya asked.

"Almost two thousand years," Redan said. "After the dragons disappeared due to the lack of faith in El, a group of humans and elves came looking for them. All they found were the remains of them."

"Remains?" Aden said.

"That's what they said," Reyan continued. "Dragons are difficult to kill. But as faith fades, so do they. They waste away until all that is left is their heart and bones."

Aden started to feel warmer as they descended. "Why heart and bones?"

"The Dragonmen say it is because their bones are near indestructible. The only weapon capable of breaking the bones of a dragon is an unforged sword."

"Which is what happened earlier today," Tamya said. "How they knew we were *Sohan-el*. Those weapons are made of dragon bone."

"Yes," Redan said. "When a dragon fades away, its bones remain. But also, its heart. The heart appears like a stone, but it is an egg, the essence of the dragon that is kept for a time until the faith of El returns to Eres."

"You came here when you were younger," Aden stated.

"I was twenty three," Redan said.

"How did you know about this place? About how to come here?" Aden said.

"The priests of El at the temple of Galya knew about this place," Redan said. "A few decades before Kryus invaded, the priests there began to migrate here. Only a few were left when the Temple burned to the ground. The knowledge passed to me, and I was the last to come. The faith of El had left the land, and I wanted to follow El in freedom and peace … and to further study the First Tongue in the only environment where it was still spoken."

Redan stopped before a round hole in the corridor to their right. A blanket hung over it, very ornate and embroidered with figures of dragons and flame.

"The *Sohan-el*," Tamya muttered.

"She lives here," Redan said. "Here they call her *Wealban*. It means Seer. She had another name. Come."

Abbot and Zamira waited outside while Redan entered, pushing the blanket aside. He brought a torch with him. He held it for Aden and Tamya as they followed him inside.

The room was carved in a spacious dome, the walls smooth rock. The torch in Redan's hand was the only light. Aden looked at the figure sitting crosslegged in the middle of the room, and he understood.

The female elf's long, black hair pooled on the floor. She wore only a gray robe. Her skin was dark, as dark as Athelwulf's had been. Was she from Jibryl? Or further south in Eviland? He heard those elves had darker skin.

A scarf covered her eyes, tied in the back. She was perfectly still.

An unforged sword lay across her lap, her hands resting upon it.

There was nothing else in the room.

Her head moved and turned to them. "Welcome, *Sohan-el*. The world has waited for your coming. You bring the Dracolet."

"They told you we were coming?" Tamya probed.

"No," she said.

Aden lifted a brow at Redan.

"No one here told me," the elf said. "El told me you would be here soon."

Tamya narrowed her eyes at the elf. "How long have you known?"

"I knew I would meet the *Arendel* when I first came here," she said. "But almost ten months ago, El told me the *Brendel* had come and the

Sohan-el reborn. You, the *Isael*, would follow as sure as water runs downhill."

"You know our names, too?" Tamya's tone carrying naked sarcasm.

"Tamya ..." Aden said.

But the elf did not seem offended or take notice. "El did not tell me your names. But I do know you. Young man, you have spent time with Reyan, have you not? And the *Brendel* has trained you."

"Not that hard to figure out," Tamya muttered.

"And you are a half elf, half human," the elf continued. "Part of two worlds. You have known great pain, and El has wept with you." The elf cocked her head. "A deep power seeks to overtake you, but with the sword of El, you will be strong enough to withstand it."

Tamya gasped. She grabbed his hand.

"Who are you?" Aden whispered.

"My name is Elowen," she said. "Here they call me *Wealban*."

"I didn't ask your name," Aden said. "I asked who you are."

Elowen smirked. "Yes, you have spent time with Reyan. I was the last elven *Sohan-el*, and I stood against the oppressive reign of Tanicus. I trained with the greatest masters of the sword in the world and learned the ways of El under King Sharan. His son, King Judai, was the last to climb Mount Elarus and get an unforged sword. At least, the last until now."

Aden took time to breathe for a moment. He did remember something about the last elven *Sohan-el*. But he thought she died. In a fire or something.

"What brought you here?" Aden asked.

Elowen lowered her head. "Three Bladeguard, all of them once friends of mine, came and attacked me at the Temple of El at Galya. I fought them, but they prevailed. They did this." She removed the scarf. There were only thick scars where her eyes should have been. "They left me to die as the temple burned down around me. But I survived."

"How?" Tamya asked.

"The secret room underneath," Aden said. "Reyan knew about it. It was where he had this hidden." He laid his hand upon the Dracolet. "Along with the translated scriptures and the Kingstaff."

"I was able to crawl my way to friends, priests of El in hiding, and they nursed me to health and brought me here," Elowen said. "Tanicus invaded Ereland not six months later."

"You knew Reyan well, didn't you?" Aden said. Tamya's hand gripped his tighter.

Elowen nodded. "Many here, including his father, forbade him to leave."

Aden frowned at her. "Forbade him to go and speak the message of El to others?"

Redan shifted on his feet.

"They did not understand," Elowen responded. "They believed this to be the only place where El was truly taught, where one could learn the ways of El. They thought it madness to leave such a place and branded Reyan and Sheron rebels. But the more they forbade them, the more they knew their destiny.

"Many here blamed me with my stories of the once great *Sohan-el*. I told them the young have their own path, even if it was out in the world. With you here, I assume Reyan fulfilled his destiny."

Aden's voice became a whisper. "At the cost of his life, yes."

"As it often is," Elowen said. "However, we find a greater life in return." She bowed her head silently. "And now you are here to bring the dragons into the fight."

"Yes." Aden stood straight.

"Then we must take you to the gate. If you get past, then we may know if they exist after all."

"If we get past?" Tamya repeated.

Redan stepped forward. "The elves that came with the first Dragonmen, they separated from the humans. The humans made a life here, and the elves went to protect the entrance to the dragon graveyard."

"Are the elves still there?" Tamya said.

"They are," Redan said. "But they've become ... perverted over time."

Aden narrowed his eyes. "Perverted how?"

"They are the *aelhund*," Elowen said.

"And what does that mean?" Aden asked.

"Loosely, a white ape," Redan said. "No one has been to the entrance to the Dracoland in over seven hundred years. The *aelhund* have killed many who have tried."

Aden peered down at Elowen.

"No," she said. "I have not tried."

"Why not?"

"Because I am not the *Isael*," she said. "However, here you are, together. When you are ready, we shall take the journey together."

"To fight big white apes that were once elves but now want to kill us?" Tamya spat.

Elowen faced her with absent eyes. "Come now. You didn't think this was going to be easy, did you? In many ways, your journey has just begun."

CHAPTER 20

AN EMPEROR'S STORY

Two Sunguard escorted Earon to meet with the Emperor.

He had waited alone in his luxurious room for two days. With plenty of elven books to read, they fed him with exquisite food at regular times. The trout dish with whipped potatoes might have been the best meal he ever ate.

He attempted to focus, pray, even recite passages from the *Fyrwrit* that he had memorized as a child. But the situation distracted him, and possible scenarios ran through his head.

A part of him had expected to be thrown in a dungeon and starved or beaten. The dignitary treatment threw him. Was that the intent? To convince him Tanicus was not a Trodall from the Underland? Earon had fallen for that tactic before, with Zarek. And his father had been killed as a result.

Earon recited the ancient scriptures, and they brought his father to mind. He had loved and respected the man, as any son would with a man who had done the things Reyan did. But every memory was tinged with regret, with wounds of an absent father and a lonely mother.

Earon, what have you done?

The look of disappointment in his eyes, the sorrow, the pain. All of that had been directed at Earon. Caleb's murderous visage and his father's disappointment had haunted him, driving him into Sorcos and ale, addiction and self-loathing. That would have only further disappointed and wounded his father. Had that been Earon's goal? He didn't know.

Now he had returned to what he had been taught, to what his father had spent time and energy trying to teach him. *Would he be proud of me?* He assumed his father was in the next world, the Everworld, and was too full of joy in the presence of El and Yosu to think much of Earon. Perhaps, though, the love of a son carried there.

Earon regarded the Sunguard as they escorted him further up the tower by way of a winding staircase. Odd elves. Full armor was rare, and elves possessed different body types or heights. The Sunguard seemed indistinguishable. Were these the same ones from before or different?

The mystery had to be by design.

They reached the top of the tower, and the stairs emerged onto a vast garden on the roof that looked over the whole city, far above the walls. The immaculate garden of exotic plants and trees shone with color, the grass soft under his feet. Clouds hovered close overhead.

The Emperor sat on a bench in the middle of the garden, dressed in his customary white robe trimmed in gold and silver. Tanicus nodded to the Sunguard, and they left Earon alone with the Worldbreaker.

"Welcome," Tanicus said. "Sit with me."

Earon walked up and sat on the end of the long bench.

"How is your room?" Tanicus asked. "Do you find it satisfactory?"

"It is more than enough, thank you."

"Of course. I apologize for the delay. We have been busy with preparations for the army that heads our way. You understand."

"I do." He sat straight and gazed out to the sky and the horizon that curved far in the distance. "Have you given thought to my message?"

"I have. While ludicrous, I am still fascinated by your bravery. It is based on either deception or manipulation, or both, but from your perspective, I assume it must be brave."

"I'm doing what I feel is right. I have learned it is better than fear."

Tanicus hesitated, pensive. "Exactly. Yes. We all do what we must." The Emperor stood, a graceful motion that seemed to take no effort, and he turned to face Earon. "You have expressed your position is one of compassion. For me and for the world, as you said."

"I implore you to meet with Caleb and make peace, yes. I don't believe you or I will like the result if you don't."

"Yes, exactly," Tanicus said. "Today, however, I will tell you my story. You may choose to believe it or you may not. But you must realize that I have no reason to lie."

Earon's brow furrowed. "Don't you? You could gain my trust and then get information from me."

"I have the ability to cause you agony that you cannot imagine. I could get you to say anything I desired. Why go through the trouble to gain your trust? You do not threaten me in any way. And how could I use you as a spy? As I have told you, I already possess an agent close to your *Brendel*."

"Very well. I admit, I am curious."

"Good." Tanicus took a deep breath and began.

"My mother was killed by raiders along the border to Faltiel when I was five years old.

"My father was a farmer, and as my mother bled to death, he wept over the burning grain. He had not fought the elves. My mother had, and she was dead because of it. As a child, I despised him for this. I did not care about the crops. My whole life ended with her death.

"I understood his sorrow the next year when we nearly starved to death. Without a crop, we had nothing to sell or trade. We did not have much to begin with. That winter was difficult. I still recall the hunger. Somehow we survived. I don't know all he had to do to keep us alive, but I suspect it broke him in a way I could not understand then. He had empty eyes the rest of his life.

"I vowed two things to myself after we survived that winter. I would get revenge on the people of Faltiel. And I would never be hungry again.

"The border to Kryus and Faltiel was a violent place then. It is a violent place now, but it was essentially lawless in those days. Bands and armies from Faltiel would raid into our lands. This would motivate the farmers and ranchers of Kryus to mobilize their own militias and retaliate. It was a cycle that had existed for a century or more.

"My father had served in the legions as a young elf, as many do. He was no better warrior than farmer, and he was not sufficiently skilled at either, but he still possessed the gladus from his service. At six years old, I forced my father to teach me what little he knew, and I practiced in the fields with dummies I constructed from branches and stalks of grain.

"Again, my father was not a skilled farmer, and he blamed the skies and the gods for our misfortune. Even though he blamed them, he believed in them, which I found odd. Why would you believe in gods that would not help you? Or perhaps couldn't? I grew older and began to understand he used his religion as an excuse for his weakness.

"I was twelve years old when the raiders came to our farm a second time. There were five of them. I don't know why there were only five.

"We were coming in from the fields when they attacked. My only thought was for the gladus. My father ran to hide in the fields. I ran for the sword.

"The gladus was in the barn, and I did reach it, but the raiders saw me and cornered me in the barn. I surprised them by going on the offensive, attacking them first. I killed one before they subdued me. I screamed for my father to come help me as they beat me. I knew they would beat me to death. They wanted me to feel the pain before I died. But my father did not come.

"I somehow knew he would not.

"As two of the raiders left to burn the crops, the anger and pain rose in me, and something happened that I did not expect. I imagined killing these elves, willing them to die, and suddenly, I felt power within me. And I used it.

"The raiders collapsed to the floor of the barn, screaming. I didn't know what I was doing, and I was frightened. We are often frightened of what we do not understand. I stopped, horrified, but I had enjoyed bringing these elves pain. While they writhed on the floor, I picked up my father's gladus and killed them both.

"I found the other two elves, and I was able to kill one from behind with the gladus. The other was surprised enough that he was not able to react in time. I killed him, as well.

"I remember the feeling of terror. Not at killing. No. They deserved it. But magic. I had used magic. And magic was illegal. Even at that young age, I thought, how could it be wrong? It had protected my father and my home, our farm as we put out the fires. And I had felt such ecstasy the moment I used it.

"The fear overwhelmed all other feelings, however, and I decided to never use the magic again. My father grew more paranoid, barely working and drowning his fears in homemade whiskey. I left home when I was fifteen to join the legions. I left my father drunk on the floor of our house.

"Lying about my age, I joined the legion. They assumed I had some private training since I was more advanced than the other recruits. I was driven and efficient, and they placed me in leadership. I was a sergeant within a year. My platoon turned the tide of an important battle with Jibryl in the south, a brutal and bloody affair. In fact, one Lieutenant died, and the General gave me a field commission.

"Within another fifty years and several battles, I was a General with my own legion. I requested to be sent to the east, and the request was granted. I won every battle.

"I never knew what happened to my father. I sought for him. I couldn't find him.

"The desire to use magic was constant. While the legions then were not what they became later, I still had access to resources as a General. I sent my most trusted officer, a Colonel Julius, to search for an elf that could teach me about *Tebelrivyn*. He and I often had long, drunken conversations.

"Julius' father was a Nican of Ashinar, and Julius believed that the faith of Kryus in the nine gods began to decline when we chose to make magic illegal. I sent him on this mission. I trusted no one else.

"He was gone for a year. He brought back an old female elf, the oldest I had ever seen. He said he found her in a monastery in the mountains. People in the village nearby called her a witch, and while no one would say she practiced magic outright, there were rumors. She would not admit it, either, which we understood for legal reasons, but I had to take a risk.

"I had become miserable in my success. My legion was feared above all others. But the passive nature of the Kryan bureaucracy maddened me. How could a nation with so much do so little for so few? I knew I was born for more than the military. I could create a great Empire with the power within me. *Tebelrivyn* could be used for good.

"The ancient elf's name was Keturah. I told her my story, much as I told it to you, and she was shocked that I would admit to such things. That admission placed my whole career in jeopardy, if not my life, and she understood that she had the power to destroy me, politically, in that moment. She was still skeptical, so I had to show her a demonstration of my powers.

"Over the years, I would find times and places to use my gifts. In those moments, I felt the greatest joy. And so I could do some basic manipulation of the physical world – move objects, create fire.

"Keturah was amazed. For almost every elf, the gift of *Tebelrivyn* is only to manipulate one aspect of the physical world. Keturah, for example, could only manipulate water, and she was deft at it. In rare cases, the gift was given for every aspect – air, water, stone, life, light. An elf either gets one or all. Keturah agreed to teach me what she could.

"Over the next few years, I learned from Keturah. She was more than five thousand years old, close to death for an elf, and she had memorized many of the *Tebelrivyn* texts. We spoke, and she taught me of what she knew about the manipulation of water, which was extensive and applicable in theory to all the others. The texts gave me details of what was possible, so I was able to explore those powers at great length.

"I had never believed in the gods, not really. Julius was the zealot. But when I tapped into those powers, it was like I could feel them, understand them. I felt connected to the planet, to the world around me. I realized the deception of those that believe in unseen gods, some other world beyond this one.

"There is no other world."

Tanicus gestured around him. "Observe the sky. It has always been there, and it will always exist. These trees and grass around us, while molded and tended by us, Eres will live on, and even if we destroy these plants around us, more will take their place. Only by connecting to this world are we immortal. That is what Keturah taught me.

"The more I learned the magic, the more I heard the cry of those gods to go farther, to do more. I knew the legends of how Worldbreakers went mad, so I limited myself.

"I also realized I was chosen for more. The gods had given me these powers for a reason, and it was to change the world. The Kryan Senate did nothing, dithering with each other over petty laws that only served their own interests and not those of the people. Their inactivity led to chaos, and the people required order. The King and the royal family were more concerned with their own lavish lifestyles than serving and extending control over a corrupt senate.

"We needed a powerful leader, one that would take control when the senate and other leaders required control and direction. That leader would require the power to take control and force direction.

"I was that leader.

"My plan formed when Keturah died. Her body was weak, and while I kept her alive for a time with my powers, she told me it was time for her to go. Keturah thanked me for showing me the possibility, the dream of a world where *Tebelrivyn* was not taboo but used altruistically.

"I mourned her for a ninedays. Then I met with Julius and my other officers to tell them my intent. I had handpicked my officers, weeding out those not loyal to me over the decades, and so they easily caught the vision.

"I marched our legion to the capital. I was a hero to the people. Our victories were praised in the streets. With music and cheers surrounding us, we laid siege to the palace. I took the royal family and the Senate captive. I gave the Senate a choice. Declare me Emperor. Or die.

"They did not believe me. They denied me. They threatened me. Julius and I took the King and the royal family ... and I slaughtered them with a sword before the Senate, one by one. The children, the females, the males, all that were in the palace at that time. They begged me to have mercy, but I did what I had to do for the good of Kryus. The Senate watched in horror as I killed them all."

"Great and mighty El," Earon whispered. He had heard, in the rare times he went to the Kryan schools for basic education, how Tanicus had deposed the corrupt and weak royal family, how he had liberated and strengthened Kryus through power and might.

Tanicus gazed at him. Earon caught a hint of sorrow in the elf's eyes. "As I said. We do what we must.

"They drafted a law and signed it, declaring me Emperor.

"In the following decades, I brought order to Kryus. And as I saw the corruption and fighting between the weak nations of humanity while the people starved, I brought order here. Over the centuries, I have protected that order, that control. I have brought freedom and provision to the humans. And how have you thanked me? By rebelling based on a mythical invisible god that you only use as an excuse for your own selfishness.

"Should I then meet with your cousin and treat with him? Should I compromise with madness and anarchy? Shall I make peace with chaos? For that is all your supposed freedom is. Chaos. Madness. Myth. No. I will not."

Earon took a deep breath. "Thousands addicted to a drug, barely surviving, their lands being raped of their resources. That is freedom to you?"

"I provide for the masses, and that takes resources. Your freedom to choose is the opposite of what provides for you. Look at the clouds, the mountains, the trees. None of them choose what they are, what they can do or cannot. All choices are made for them. And when the trees and the clouds rest in the choices made for them, they are free to be what they should be. All nature teaches us this. The freedom of order. The pain and suffering of your world is a result of rebelling against that order, which is chaos, which leads to destruction.

"Look at this garden, the beauty. It would not happen without control, intention, design."

Earon shook his head. "Those things may be true about a tree or a cloud, but we are not trees. We are creatures of thought and emotion and will. We were made in the image of he who created us, different and separate from this world in that respect. We were made to be like El, a person of intelligence and choice and love. Therefore, we can't look to the lifeless as an example. We cannot learn how to properly manage our thoughts, emotions, wills, not without knowing he who designed us, because we have no greater power here on Eres to teach us this. Within knowing El, and only there, are we able to find the order of life that rescues us from death."

"Your philosophy fails you," Tanicus said. "And your god has failed you. The nations of Ereland were corrupt and oppressed their own people, your fellow humans. That is the end of your freedom of choice."

"That is a risk, I agree," Earon said. "And yet there were times in our history, and in yours, when those that believed in El unified by choice and their own wills, and there was peace and provision."

The Emperor scoffed. "Those are lies in ancient books, manufactured to justify chaos and destruction."

"If you dismiss evidence contrary to your position, then all you will have is your position," Earon responded. "When given the freedom of choice, then evil is possible, of course. But so is good. Freedom is worth it, in the end. To force others is an evil. And when there is evil at the foundation, there will be an evil end."

"Justification. You do what you accuse, choose and select information that supports your position. You cannot know the end."

"And yet we have a history of your control leading to death and oppression, more than all the evils of any who ever claimed to believe in El combined. Every example of control, as you claim it to be freedom, has become evil."

"You claim this, but are you not part of a revolution responsible for thousands of deaths? This *Brendel*, he is a sword of El, correct? What does a sword do but kill?"

"It protects," Earon said. "That is why I am here. He is a sword, and he will break you. But he exists to protect the dignity of people created to make a choice, to not be forced into good, but to choose it. If you will meet with him and make peace, you both will save thousands of lives. Behind him is an army of people, dwarves, elves, and humans, united in that vision. You must create fear and control to do what is good, or what you feel is good, and give a semblance of unity, as illusory as it is. All Caleb does is speak truth and fight for others."

"I thought you worshipped El, and here you are speaking of the *Brendel* like a god."

Earon shook his head. "He is no god. He has his faults, as do we all. However, El is with him. That is enough."

"And the nine gods are with me," Tanicus said. "We each do what we must."

Earon narrowed his eyes at the Emperor. "I do not want you to believe that I have no choice, that Caleb does not make his own choices. We choose because we follow El."

"If you do not follow El, then what is the consequence?"

"About the things that matter? Slavery. Death."

"Does not sound like your god gives you much of a choice, either."

"He could leave us to our own devices, or the control of those who oppress us, and watch us destroy ourselves. Or he could care for us and lead us to life. He chose to do the latter. And that is why I follow him." Earon stood and placed his hands behind his back. "You, also, have a choice. You are not bound to do what you feel you must. There is no freedom in that thinking. I tell you that you do have a choice. And you do not have to meet Caleb on the battlefield and die. You can make peace with him and live."

Tanicus cocked his head, and his brow furrowed. "I must admit, you still fascinate me. You truly believe what you are saying, don't you?"

Earon paused. "I do."

"You are willing to stand before the most powerful person in Eres and argue with him," Tanicus said. "It is madness and folly."

"With all respect, Emperor," Earon said. "I disagree. If what I'm saying is true, and El is real, it is the sanest thing I can do."

"I'm sure," Tanicus said. "I will think on the things you have said, and we will speak again. Will you think on the things I have said?"

The slaughter of a whole family, one by one? For good? "Yes."

"Before you go, I will tell you that I would like to meet with the *Brendel*," Tanicus said.

Earon heard the shuffling of golden boots on the top of the stairs. The Sunguard stood ready. "You will?"

"Yes," Tanicus said. "At the very least, I should thank him."

"For what?"

"Without his rebellion, I would never have the opportunity to reveal who I really am, the powers that I possess. The world will see that it was foolish to outlaw the magic of this world, and you will see that your belief in your invisible god will disappoint you as I paint the field red with the blood of the *Brendel* and his army."

Earon shook his head.

"I will send for you again soon." Tanicus glanced at the Sunguard. "Take him back to his room."

—+—

Tamya didn't know how long they had slept when Elowen woke them, but it didn't feel long enough. After speaking with Elowen and Redan the night before, Tamya and Aden ate something and went right to sleep. She did have dreams where those serpents from the Geddai city chased her through the mountains and the caverns.

Tamya's sore muscles protested as she started to move.

Aden groaned and rolled over on the soft mat and away from the lamp in Elowen's hand. Elowen set the lamp on the floor.

Tamya sat up and looked at the elf, a tall, beautiful dark-skinned female. The light from the lamp glowed off of her skin. And the scarf over her eyes. "Do they hurt?"

Elowen stood like a statue. "Get dressed and ready. We will meet in the courtyard to the north."

Touchy subject, I guess.

"Where is that?" Aden said, standing, and Tamya grunted that he was only in his under trousers, but then she realized it probably didn't matter with Elowen. Probably.

"I will wait outside and take you there." Elowen laid green leather clothes on the floor. "Wear these underneath. To keep you warm." She ducked back out of the small cave and the thick drape over the door fell into place.

Aden and Tamya gathered the green leather trousers that covered the feet and a shirt that reached past the wrist. Their swords hung at their sides when they exited into the corridor. Redan stood there with Elowen, both waiting. Redan held the lamp now.

Elowen wore the leather underneath her robe, as well. A pack hung from her shoulder, and her sword was slung over her shoulder with the pack.

Elowen turned and walked through the corridor. Tamya blinked, startled. *How does she move like that? Blind?*

Redan followed, and then Aden and Tamya after them.

"You say the *Brendel* goes to meet the Worldbreaker?" Elowen asked.

I guess we skipped the good morn, too.

Elowen had many questions the night before, and the revelation that Tanicus was a Worldbreaker did not surprise her, although she did not know it. She claimed it explained much.

"The last we heard, Tanicus was at Asya, with several legions," Aden said. "And Caleb was taking the army from Taggart to Asya soon after we left. I assume they are almost there."

"There is much to do, then," Elowen said. "And little time to do it. El will help us, though."

They passed through an enormous cavern, its walls covered with the glowing moss, a mixture of colors – purple, red, blue, and orange.

"It will take us two days to reach the Dragongate," Elowen said. "The passes we take are high, and we go north. The cold is unforgiving. The leather wrappings will help, but be prepared. It will be difficult."

"You're a regular rosewater saleself," Tamya mumbled.

Aden shot her a glare, but he also smirked. Elowen didn't seem to care.

The corridor lost its warmth, and it felt colder and colder. A white light shone ahead, and soon they emerged from the corridor to a wide, open, flat plateau.

Just outside on the plateau, Abbott and Zamira and twenty Dragonmen on their stalgest waited for them.

Elowen stopped and held her hands behind her back.

Tamya glanced at Aden, both of them feeling the tension. Redan sighed next to them.

Abbott spoke in the old language, his tone firm.

"What did he say?" Tamya demanded.

Redan leaned down and whispered to them. "He tells Elowen goodbye. That she chases foolishness with these outsiders. It will mean her death."

Elowen spoke, which Redan translated. "Death means nothing to those truly alive. We go with El."

Abbott glared at her, and Redan continued to relay the conversation in the Common Tongue. "El lives here."

Elowen sighed. "El lives everywhere. Do you know nothing of those scriptures you say you believe? Story after story of people discovering El and moving forward to fight for the freedom of others."

Abbott hissed. "A different time. A lost time."

Elowen set her hand on her sword. "Nothing is lost with El. You were wrong to treat Reyan and Sheron as exiles, to forbid them to go then forbid them to return. But there is a way you can make it right again."

Abbott's eyes tightened.

"You have warriors in these caverns, thousands of them," Elowen continued. "And a man from El fights a great battle to the south. Leave here and join him. For if we survive the dragons, that is what we will do."

Abbott shook his head. "We built this great place for El. Why would we leave?"

Elowen smiled. "To build an even greater place for El in the hearts of humans, dwarves, and elves." She raised an open hand at the leaders of the Dragonmen. "I pray El's blessings and love on you and your people. Farewell."

She turned to her left to Redan. "You will stay."

His grin spoke sadness. "I will. You'll forgive me, but I'm too old to go climbing over ice and mountains." He nodded to Abbott and Zamira. "My place is here. I will tell them how wrong we were. How wrong I was. And how we should go south to be with my grandson."

"Nothing to forgive, brother." Elowen reached out, and he took her hand. "That is as it should be."

Redan's eyes glistened with tears, and he bent down and kissed Elowen on the cheek. "Until another time."

"Yes," Elowen said. "Until then."

Then she turned and walked past Abbott, Zamira, and the Dragonmen.

Tamya felt Aden take her hand, and they followed her.

North. To the dragons. To save the world.

Or die trying.

Chapter 21

The Heart of Faith

The sea of people stretched as far as Eshlyn could see. She stood on the top of a mountain. Lightning and thunder sounded all around her. She could not see grass or stone beneath her, not for all the people.

A few mitres above her, at the peak of the mountain, stood a figure. He appeared like a man with arms and legs, but he possessed the head of a male lion, the mane long and brown and flowing down his back and body. The face was fierce and feral.

The eyes were gray, and there was a long scar across his cheek. Other scars covered his body along his chest, his arms, legs, and a great number on his back. The lionman held a staff and a sword.

The lionman roared, and the sound drowned out the thunder. He lifted his sword, and the light that shone from his sword made the lightning seem dim and distant.

But she was afraid. She was afraid for the lionman because he perched precariously atop the highest point of the peak. One false step and he would fall to great injury or death. She was also afraid of him, for the roar spoke of anger and vengeance. The people, millions and millions of them, cheered and clamored for more.

That made her all the more afraid.

To the east, she saw a figure slither through the clouds towards them, a long serpent that flew without wings. It did not have arms or legs but an enormous mouth with fangs that were too long. There was a golden crown on the serpent. It was as large as the mountain they stood upon.

The lionman turned and faced the serpent. He stood large, but he appeared small compared to the serpent. But he would face the serpent.

The lionman roared at the serpent. Eshlyn watched as the scars on the lionman hardened to steel. The steel from the scars spread across his body until it covered him. She didn't know if his roars were now from pain or anger.

The serpent hissed back, a shattering wave of sound that shook the mountain under the lionman. The lionman teetered.

Then she awoke.

Eshlyn sat up, gasping, and reached out next to her on the cot as a reflex. Javyn was there. The light outside was dim, a predawn light.

Javyn grunted and whined. "Mama?"

She had gripped his arm too tight. "Sorry, Javy," she whispered, keeping her voice calm although her heart pounded within her.

Releasing his arm, she pulled her son tight to her in the dim light. She stroked his hair, that soft child's hair that seemed from another world, another life. He hummed a little tune in her arms, and then he reached and embraced her neck. She closed her eyes and smelled his sweet breath.

The tune the boy hummed was familiar. The words came unbidden to her mind.

In another age, the children lead
The sons are kings, and the daughters queens
The crowns will bow at dragon's feet
And thrones will fall to find the Key

———————

Caleb stood on the back of a wagon outside of Vicksburg, and more than forty thousand people surrounded him.

Most of the humans were citizens of Giannis and Vicksburg. More than seven thousand were humans of the *Hamon-el* from Manahem, Lior, and the Ghosts of Saten. Another fifteen hundred were militan and Cityguard elves. Twenty-one were dwarves of the Steelsides, a gift from King Ironsword II.

Here together, thousands before him, he could see the division, people standing with those like them. His heart ached. This was not the vision of El. It was closer than it had ever been … and yet still so far.

Caleb was not alone on the wagon. Eshlyn stood next to him.

He could feel her emotion, like energy, but he couldn't interpret her silence and tension. Was it anger? Disappointment? He had wounded her. Despite how he had wounded her and the distance now between them, he had done the right thing. Giving in to their desires now would only hurt her more later. He didn't want that.

He scanned the sea of people around him. *Julius may be out there, as well.*

Carys, Zalman, Iletus, and Tobiah waited behind him and Eshlyn.

The *Sohan-el*, Andos, Macarus, Bweth, Sergeant Gunnar, Jaff, and the two elven Stewards gathered on the ground in front of the wagon.

Beyond the crowd, the hundreds of tents of their camp rustled in the summer breeze.

The crowd buzzed with discussion. Caleb had called this meeting, and while the people knew it was about Shecayah's death and rumors of more, the leadership had not given any more information. This was Caleb's purpose, his role, something they said only he could do. And so he did it.

I am no leader. I am no general or king. I am a weapon. I should go alone to infiltrate Asya and assassinate the Emperor. But that was not the point of the revolution.

Caleb gripped the Kingstaff with one hand and raised the other. The crowd fell silent. He lowered his hand.

"A year ago, I landed in Asya and traveled west. I thought I would travel alone, but a handful traveled with me. Aden and I, the two of us, made it to Ketan and farther, to Mount Elarus, to the Living Stone. A year later, it is amazing what El has done. Now we have an army of elves, dwarves, and humans, almost two legions worth, all of us free. All of us with the desire to fight for freedom and against tyranny.

"We have lost loved ones and friends, but we have also seen the redemption of traitors and the hopeless. It has inspired many, and it causes fear in the hearts of those that would oppress."

Caleb shifted the Kingstaff to the other hand.

"Our greatest test, however, is before us. There has been distrust and violence in our camp. That has caused division. That division threatens the whole future of freedom, and for all peoples, for we have all peoples here with us now.

"We are in the same place, but we are not united. There is a difference. We must heal that division as we move forward.

"First, let me tell you we know who killed the elf militan and Shecayah. His name is Julius, and he was the first Bladeguard. He was with the tyrant Tanicus from the beginning, and he was here in our camp. He killed Shecayah to cause more division among us. He succeeded."

Caleb paused while the crowd spoke among themselves, muttering to each other like a distant storm threatening on the horizon. He wondered if Julius heard his words. A part of him hoped so.

He raised his hand for a moment, and they silenced.

"We can't allow him to further succeed. Second, I will tell you what the leadership has decided our response will be. Tobiah will lead a team to hunt Julius down and bring him to justice.

"For the rest of you, I give you a choice. You are free to leave and go home if you wish. If you move forward and remain among the *Hamon-el*, you do so under the following conditions.

"Lady Eshlyn is now in charge of the bosaur cavalry. Tobiah has approved this. She is the *Bashawyn* of Lior."

He waited while the crowd responded and settled.

"Lastly, we have reorganized the *Hamon-el* into ten divisions. Each division and platoon and squad will have an equal number of Ghosts, Liorians, those from Ketan, and elves. Tomorrow we leave for Asya. Over the next few days, you will train and live with your new divisions.

"One way or another, we will be a different army when we reach Asya."

Shouts. Fists raised. Anger. *I told Aden long ago. They would hate me before the end.*

"Let me make this clear," Caleb shouted over them. His voice echoed and they glared at him once silent. "If you choose to continue to be a part of the *Hamon-el*, you choose to fight alongside brothers and sisters and learn to trust them, train to fight with them, no matter where they come from or what they've done. Otherwise, you are free to go.

"None of us are without fault or sin. None are beyond the need for forgiveness and change. In this, we are all equal."

Looks of stony anger crumbled.

"We stood against a legion with less than three hundred. It does not matter the number we continue with. It does not matter the race. But it does matter the heart. El will fight for those who are united in his heart for all races. We can't preach the vision of a world united under El and be so divided ourselves."

The crowd, silent, stared back at him with wide eyes. He stared back at them and placed his hand on the hilt of his sword.

"The *Hamon-el* leaves in the morning."

—

Aden thought he had known cold on the tundra two days before. He had been wrong.

The cold made his bones ache. It hurt to move. But it hurt worse to stay still.

Elowen led them across the peaks of the mountains of the Dracoland. Some of the paths were barely wide enough to stand on, sheer cliffs on either side a thousand mitres or more. The wind whistling dread and death in his ear.

All three of them were wrapped from head to toe in several layers, only a slight sliver open for their eyes. Elowen did not need that sliver, so her whole face was wrapped in the leather under the hood of the thick coat.

They often ascended above the clouds, and the clear blue expanse made Aden feel so small. A different world awaited above the clouds, fields and hills of soft white cotton as far as they could see. One would think that hours of peering at that scene would grow tiring, no matter how beautiful, but it mesmerized him.

The sun hung to the east, morning still, when Aden questioned Elowen. "You think any of the Dragonmen will go help Caleb?"

"It will be difficult," Elowen said. "There have been years of hiding, of protecting what they have instead of engaging the world that so desperately needs the message of El. Many will not. But I trust that El is good. I believe a few will answer the call."

"It's so far," Tamya said. "It's taken us days to get here. Even if they do decide, they can't make Asya in time, can they?"

"We shall see," Elowen said. "The Dragonmen can reach the tundra quickly. They know better paths than the ones you took through the mountains. And who knows what El will do from there."

It amazed him that a blind Elowen could maneuver the narrow paths and steep hikes along the tops of the mountains without a cane or staff or anything, at least not that he could tell. He thought perhaps the unforged sword had much to do with it, but she didn't touch it, not often enough for that to be the explanation.

He asked her about it that afternoon.

Elowen didn't speak for a moment, and he thought perhaps she didn't hear him in the wind. "There are different ways to see other than your eyes."

He frowned underneath green leather and a hood pulled tight, the words muffled. "Like your other senses are better or something? I know Caleb talked about learning how to be aware of everything, even when you couldn't see or hear or smell someone. Is it like that?"

"I have been trained in those ways," Elowen said. "But I speak of something greater. The sword communicates with you, yes?"

Aden nodded. *Oh yeah. She can't see that.* "Yes."

"The revelation through the sword is much like your other senses – sight or smell or hearing. It must be used, learned, trusted," Elowen said. "However, with your physical senses, you are still limited. With the revelation of El, there is no limit, for he is infinite and the sense is not a sense of this world. It sees into the next, and yet that sight allows you to see this world more clearly."

Aden's legs ached as he bent to steady himself on a low rock to his right. "Are you saying that you can see everything around us?"

"Not as you think or imagine, but yes."

He and Tamya shared a glance. He was proud of her for containing her sarcasm.

They were about to face elf-animal *aelhund* with a blind female elf who claimed to see everything.

And then look for dragons.

Elowen claimed to have fought three Bladeguard, three of the best swordmasters in recent memory, and she had held her own. At least, according to her.

Maybe she was the perfect person to have when they faced the *aelhund.*

That night, they reached an outcropping of rock ten mitres or so in diameter down out of the wind. Like the path, this place had been prepared for a journey, a rest point. Dried branches and logs were gathered along the edge. They camped and made a fire, although Aden wasn't sure the fire made any difference. He sat as close to it as he could anyway.

After gnawing through some provisions from the Dragonmen, Tamya huddled next to him. She stared down at the unforged sword in her lap, Xander's unforged sword.

"You okay?" he asked her.

She shrugged. "I want one of my own."

"You will. One day. When this is over, we'll go together."

"It feels … so far away."

"Yeah, it does." *Impossibly far.*

Elowen said nothing.

The three of them huddled that night under a tent. They slept little.

———

Carys checked her pack one last time. She looked up at Zalman next to her. He smiled, but it was a sad smile. Carys, Zalman, Iletus, and Tobiah stood with their horses. Eshlyn and Caleb gathered with them a hundred mitres to the northeast of the camp. The sun set to the west.

Cays had picked up a trail earlier that afternoon as she circled the camp. No one had come to the camp at all in the last two days, much less from the northeast. It was a faint trail, and it took her two hours to track it well enough to confirm that she could continue to do so. But once she confirmed it, the rest of the team gathered.

They had left the camp in disarray and chaos, people moving their tents to new divisions and assignments, complaining, grumbling. A lot of threats and conversation, but no one had left. Not yet, at least. And more important to her quest, not to the northeast.

She watched her brother speak with Tobiah, instructing and encouraging the man.

Then Caleb turned to Iletus as Eshlyn talked to Tobiah.

"We pray for you, my friend, for all of you," Caleb told the elf.

"Thank you," Iletus said.

"You come back before the next battle," Caleb said. "We're going to need you. I need you."

"I will do my best," Iletus said.

Caleb turned to Zalman, his neck craning up. Watching the two men she loved more than anyone else in the world shaking hands and smiling at one another warmed her heart. She blushed as the tears brimmed in her eyes. Caleb didn't threaten Zalman this time. He didn't have to.

Carys' vision blurred when Eshlyn approached her. Carys tried to smile back at the woman, but it came out as a grimace.

Eshlyn reached out and gripped her hands. "My sister. Why is the time between us always so short?"

"The way it is, I guess. But I agree. Not fair at all." Her eyes darted to Caleb and back. "So much to say."

"Then you have to come back," Eshlyn said. "So we may say all that we should. But allow me a moment to tell you this. I have seen you grow into such a strong woman, such a fine leader. I am proud of you, Carys, more than you know."

Carys couldn't speak. So she pulled Eshlyn into an embrace. "Thank you."

Eshlyn smiled and moved to speak to Zalman.

Then Caleb stood before her. "I don't like this. You're making me say goodbye to you again."

"Not doing it on purpose, Cubby. But you started it, remember."

"That doesn't make it right."

"I'm doing what El would have me do. Does that make it right?"

"It does, but I still don't like it."

"Neither do I."

She leaned into him, and he engulfed her in his arms. "What did you do to Eshlyn?" she whispered into his ear.

He hesitated before he responded, like a weak breath. "I refused her. But it was the right thing."

With tears streaming down her face, Carys pulled back and looked him in the eye. She touched his beard, the scar on his cheek. Eshlyn had already begun to walk back towards camp. "Oh, Caleb. When will you learn? I know you want to do what is right and noble. And I love you for it. But when are you not the *Brendel*?"

He didn't answer her.

"When are you simply a man? You have a destiny. We all see it. But in the end, you're also a man. In the end, she's not a Lady or a prophecy or a mother. She's just a woman, too. That's all she wants, Caleb. That's it."

"I don't know if I have that to give."

"Then what the shog is this all for?" She wiped her eyes with the back of her sleeve. "I pray you do. Because you're both worth it."

Caleb pulled her into another embrace, and he held her so tight she had trouble breathing. She didn't mind. She squeezed him back just as hard.

His voice was a groan. "You come back. If you don't, I will kill them all. I don't care what it costs. I swear it."

She smiled. "I love you, too, Cubby."

Mid morning the next day, they heard the roar of thunder. It sounded distant. Tamya looked to the north, where she heard it, and she couldn't see any dark clouds.

"Sounds like a storm." Her lips scraped on the green leather over her mouth.

Elowen continued to walk. "That isn't thunder. That is a dragon."

Tamya shared a glance with Aden. She wanted to ask the elf, *And how do you know?* But she would only get some breaking mystical answer that didn't make any sense.

Tamya could see the structure the afternoon of the second day.

They climbed to the top of another mountain. They ascended through the mist of clouds; a round, stone tower waited in the distance. Tamya squeaked a gasp underneath the leather wrap on her face.

"Yes," Elowen said. "That is the Dragongate."

Tamya gazed over at Aden, and even though only his eyes were visible, she could see them grow intense.

They neared the Dragongate, and a bridge led to the tower. The mountain they traveled on ended at a sheer cliff. At the edge, a bridge constructed of thick steel chains had been built to span the chasm beneath. The chains were attached to tall, heavy steel spikes driven into the rock and ice of the mountain.

The chain bridge stretched all the way to the tower from the cliff, an impossible two hundred mitres or more. When Tamya reached the edge, she gripped a steel spike and looked down to see the white billowy clouds fifty or seventy five mitres below them.

She looked back at Aden. "You're not serious."

Elowen's only response was to walk past her, grab the handrails, and begin moving across the bridge.

"Remind me," Tamya said to Aden. "Why didn't more of those Dragonmen come with us?"

Aden moved to respond, but Elowen's voice carried on the wind like a whisper from ahead. "This is your destiny. Not theirs."

"Then what are you breakin' doing here?" Not that she was complaining, really. Another experienced warrior to fight whatever was in that tower would be welcome.

Elowen turned her head to face Tamya. "I am a *Sohan-el.*"

Then the elf continued to move forward.

Tamya scoffed. "What the shog is she talking about?"

Aden shrugged as he stepped on the bridge. "She's a *Sohan-el.*" And she was about to smack him upside the back of his head, but then he said, "And so are we."

Motionless for a moment, she watched Aden walk across the bridge. *Shog a goat.* She placed her foot on the thick chain. It was icy and slick. She grunted in frustration and gripped the chains that functioned as handrails. The wind blew and the bridge swayed. She crouched and hooked her elbows around the chains and cried out. Looking up, she was only thirty mitres across. So far to go.

Aden glanced at her over his shoulder. "You scared of heights or something?"

"Well, I don't breakin' like them, that's for sure!"

"You need any help?" he asked her.

That made her angry, and she cursed at him. "No." She gritted her teeth and stood straight, forcing her arms to uncurl so she could use her hands.

She walked forward. Crossing the bridge while it swayed made her dizzy. She tried closing her eyes while she crept along, but that made it worse.

About halfway across the bridge, she could feel the bile rising in her throat. Her body was sore, all of it, from being so tense. With thirty mitres to go, Tamya tore the green leather from her face, the freezing wind hitting her skin like little knives, and she vomited over the side of the bridge and down into the clouds.

Aden was looking back at her when she recovered and stood. Her legs barely held her.

"You all right?" Aden called. He and Elowen stood at other end already.

"Hey, Aden, you read all those stories about the *Sohan-el*, right?" she said over the wind in return.

"Yeah."

"Did any of them spew their lunch before doing all that heroic crit?"

"Don't know. Probably. They don't write that stuff down, you know."

When she gathered her strength and started moving, she heard an echo of his laughter in the breeze. Now she really was going to smack him upside his head.

The bridge ended at a flat stone landing that led to a large wooden door. Aden stuck out his hand and helped the final two steps, and he embraced her there, at the top of the world, above the clouds. "Got you."

She pulled away, smiled, and smacked the back of his head, a padded strike with glove and hood. "That's for laughing. Let's go."

He grinned. They turned to face the Dragongate, a tall and arched wooden door to the structure.

Elowen laid her hand against it. "Wood from a dragontree. Almost as old as the world."

Tamya grunted, annoyed. Aden and Tamya held hands behind Elowen.

Elowen drew her sword from over her shoulder and pushed open the door. She entered. Aden and Tamya drew their swords and followed.

Everything was shadow; they could only see a few paces before them from the light of the open door.

But Tamya could hear faint noises. Like breathing. "Dark. Great. First heights and the dark. Got any more major fears to conquer for us?"

Elowen lifted her sword, blade down. Then she spoke some words in that maddening First Tongue – like a prayer.

Her unforged sword began to glow, bathing the area around her – a couple mitres in diameter – in clean white light.

"Well shoggit," Tamya gulped.

Aden reached up and removed the leather wrap from his face. He lifted his sword like Elowen had, blade down. "What did you say?"

"An old prayer from the first *Sohan-el*," Elowen said. "Michal and others used it."

"I remember something like that. Does it have to be in the First Tongue?" Aden asked.

"Do you believe El only hears one language? The words only have meaning when they come from the heart of faith."

Aden nodded. He looked at the blade in his hand for a moment, and his face twisted in thought and effort. "*Agadan ricel beacan-el.*"

The unforged sword shone in his hand. Combined, the two swords seemed to have more light.

"I thought you said the language and words didn't matter," Tamya frowned.

"I – I don't know how that happened. I meant to ask El for the sword to light up, and it came out in a different language."

"You are both the *Isael*," Elowen said.

"Can I do it?" Tamya asked. "It's not my sword."

"You can," Elowen answerd. "Do not doubt. Have faith."

Sure. Sounds easy. Have faith. Will do.

Tamya's brow furrowed, and she stared at the blade. "Come on. Light up for me."

The sword did not become a light.

"Not working." She peered at the blade. "I don't know the right words."

"It is not magic," Elowen said. "It is faith."

"You can do it," Aden said. "It's okay. Ask El to help you."

Tamya relaxed and closed her eyes. *Please, El. Help me. I don't have faith like Elowen or Aden, but I need you. I don't want to fight in here without light.*

Nothing. No answer.

She sniffed and lifted her face. *I'll fight in the dark if I have to. Because, really, I know the sword can guide me, speak to me, help me even in the dark. It took me to that vision of the Living Stone. So of course it can …*

The words came to her mind. "*Agadan ricel beacan-el.*"

She opened her eyes to a shining blade. "Great and mighty El."

Aden smiled at her. He pushed the hood off of his head and walked forward into the tower.

The three swords together threw light across the bottom of the tower. The light didn't quite reach the far end of the room, but the glow of their combined light affected half, at least. Aden walked forward, step by step, his sword up and ready. Tamya followed with Elowen protecting from the rear.

The floor was bare except for some debris – a bone or piece of rotten wood. The walls had deep gouges and scratches in the stone.

It was a round room, the shape of the tower. Tamya looked up into pitch darkness. There was that breathing sound that could be the wind through or around the tower somehow, but it made the hair on her arms stand on end.

Once past the middle of the room, the other end came into view. It began as a shadow, but as they drew near, a figure sat on a makeshift throne. *Throne* was a loose term, but bricks had been gathered and arranged in such a way that it looked like a chair, an enormous one. The throne was piled against another large door, this one stone.

They got closer, and Aden lifted his sword even higher to light the figure on the throne of gray bricks.

At first, Tamya thought it was a skeleton in a long black robe. The nearer they drew, pure white skin stretched over bone and skull, the eyes bright and wet but sunken. The head was devoid of hair. With the pointed ears made it an elf – a male? It was difficult to tell.

A golden amulet hung from its neck.

"Who is it?" she gulped. The white light from the swords cast an eerie light upon the elf. "Why does it have a Dracolet like yours?"

Aden shrugged, but he didn't take his eyes off of the skeletal elf. "I don't know. Maybe ..."

The figure's bone thin right hand twitched, and all three froze. The hand lifted and pointed at Aden.

Growls and guttural cries from above them, from the dark.

They all looked up.

"Crit on a breakin' frog," Aden said through his teeth.

Shapes emerged from the dark, dropping from above them, mouths open with fangs and snarling.

"Yep." Tamya lifted her sword in a high guard. "Those are white apes."

CHAPTER 22

The Aelhund

Aden began slicing through the white shape coming at him before he got a full picture of it. He cut that one in half and severed a limb from another.

When the white apes surrounded them, he got the clear picture.

Long, round heads sat atop hairless, stark white muscular bodies with long arms and short legs. Their fingers ended in long white claws. The possessed pointed ears too large for their heads. They were naked and sexless.

The white apes came from everywhere – above and to the side. More than one ran on the wall, digging into the stones with their claws. Elowen, Tamya, and Aden formed a type of circle, their backs to each other. Aden swung his sword, but not wildly. He controlled each strike, the sword still glowing and flashing; he cut the wrist of one ape and ducked the swipe of another before stabbing it in the gut.

The ape fell back on his haunches, panting. Aden watched while the wound through the middle of it closed and healed. The ape snarled and attacked.

Aden cut through its arm, it screeched in pain, and then he struck along its chest, opening a large gash. It fell back, but another took its place.

"What the shog?" Tamya cried. "They're healing!"

If the apes could heal, then that made it difficult to keep track of the numbers. They were all around them. At the limits of the light from their swords, he could see one of the apes with a severed arm find that limb and hold it steady as it reattached.

Tamya screamed to his right, and he peeked over his shoulder. Her left arm was ripped and bloody. More *aelhund* came towards him, so he couldn't check the wound. *El help her …*

"Cut through them," Elowen said. "More serious injuries take longer to heal."

Aden's brow furrowed. He stepped aside to dodge the attack of an ape, and he moved back into the ape and cut through the torso of the creature with all his strength – the top half went spinning away. A second clawed through his thigh, and he decapitated that one while leaning back. The third missed him by centimitres.

Taking a breath, four more approached him. *How many are there?* He slid back, and Tamya and Elowen adjusted, Tamya with a curse.

Aden threw his shoulder into the chest of one ape, and he cut down into the forehead of another. The unforged sword sank into the neck. Pulling the sword from the falling *aelhund*, he stabbed into the face of the one at his shoulder, ducking a third at the same time. Aden swung back with his sword and sliced off the top of the head of the third. The fourth climbed over the fallen, and in the dim light beyond, three more approached.

In the chaos, Tamya cried out another time in pain, and he retreated from the onslaught before him.

"It doesn't seem to be slowing them down," Aden announced.

Two creatures roared and dropped from above him. Aden jumped back. His shoulder knocked Elowen; he cut the arms from one and through the chest of the other. But he felt claws tear his pack from his back. Tamya had already lost hers, as well. Blood had dripped on the stone floor, lit by their unforged swords. He wondered whose it was.

He thought maybe they should have put some of the Dragonmen armor in their packs.

"This is why I asked if any of those shoggers should have come with us!" Tamya shouted.

His body was cold and sore from the days of travel, from the lack of sleep, and he could feel the exhaustion creeping into his muscles – stiff and weak. It was like he was empty inside. And the air seemed thinner than before. He couldn't keep his breath.

"We can't keep this up," he panted. But what could they do? His mind raced as he cut to the right and left with his sword, severing one ape in two pieces diagonally. He took another step back.

A frail idea entered his mind, and he blinked as he tried to focus on it during the frenzy. Why was he the only one that needed to retreat? He glanced over both shoulders. Tamya fought one, then another, not three or four at a time. Elowen tore through the white apes, but not more than two at a time. In that brief glance, he saw her skill and grace, the violence a thing of beauty.

Aden looked up at the skeletal elf – a shadow in the dark beyond their glowing swords. Three apes came lumbering toward him, a fourth crawling to reach the other half of its body so it could heal.

Aden glanced over his shoulder.

"They are herding us towards the door," Tamya said.

He felt the weight and familiar warmth of the amulet under his clothes. "Maybe not. They're focusing more on me, the one with the Dracolet."

He severed another wrist to the left, then an arm to the right, but a strike raked across his chest. He grunted in pain. Even through his heavy coat, those claws found flesh.

"No." Elowen's voice echoed calm. "The elf. He is a wizard."

"You mean ..." Aden paused to think and remove the head from an ape and cut another on his right in two at the waist.

"He's keeping these shoggers alive," Tamya finished. "We have to kill him." Aden heard her grunts and the wet sounds of her sword cutting through flesh. "If we can."

"On my mark," Elowen instructed. "We will rotate right and I will attack the breaker."

Aden scowled and ducked one and then cut through the elbow of another. "I should do it."

"No," Elowen said. "This is why I am here."

"But ..." Aden started to argue ...

"Now!" Elowen commanded, and they all three rotated to the right so she faced towards the throne of bricks and the door beyond.

While Aden and Tamya protected her and stepped back, Elowen drove forward through the apes, taking the brunt of the attack. Aden was better able to watch Elowen in his periphery. He had been impressed with her abilities a moment ago, but now he saw the level of her skill. Leaping and spinning, she seemed to float in the air, the sword a blur of light. She cut through two at a time, her attacks perfectly timed and too quick for the apes.

The tower shuddered. Aden looked up, and more apes fell from the dark, five of them. Were there more up there?

They drew closer to the wizard, and Aden saw one *aelhund* bounce up the wall, twist, and launch itself at Elowen. She swatted him away with a flick of the sword, and he went tumbling. Within ten mitres of the elf, the wizard grew thinner, his mouth open and revealing an impossible darkness within. He spasmed, his bony fingers twitching, and the figure was thinner than before, the bones even more pronounced in his face.

Aden grew more exhausted. He gulped the thin and stale air around them, and his injuries stung and burned. He could feel blood flowing and freezing on his skin. He and Tamya had fewer *aelhund* to deal with, only one at a time; Elowen tore through a dozen as they were injured, healed, and returned to the battle. The strategy was clear, to keep Aden and Tamya busy but to protect the wizard.

They were three mitres away from the elf, now.

Elowen stumbled, and she cried out. Was she tired, as well? She had to be. She recovered, taking two down with her, but an ape ripped at her back and side with its claws. In her hesitation, three more rushed her.

Aden leapt to help her, but he moved too slow. His swipe gave one ape a superficial wound, and the other two were able to get their claws on Elowen. With an angry growl, she leapt and threw her unforged sword as they drug her down. The sword left her hand like a spear.

Aden watched the sword fly between and past three other apes and sink into the wizard's chest.

Then everything went white in a massive explosion.

The sound deafened him, the light blinded him, and without thinking, he found himself on his knees. He heard screaming. Was he the one screaming? Was it Tamya? Both?

He blinked away the spots in his vision, only his heartbeat stomping in his ears. Then Tamya's voice began like she was hundreds of mitres away, calling to him. His vision began to clear, the light of the glowing unforged swords dim compared to the blinding light from a moment before.

Tamya knelt next to him. "Aden? You okay?"

Her hand was on his shoulder. He shook his head. "Yeah, I think so." He stood and scanned the room.

The *aelhund* were scattered around the room, each one motionless. He counted twenty five of them, all burnt and smoldering. White stones from the wizard's throne were also strewn about.

Tamya's clothes, and his own, were burnt. But he didn't have any burns on his body.

"What happened?" Tamya whispered.

Aden turned his head back to where the wizard had sat, and the throne was gone. As was the wizard. Elowen's unforged sword was stuck into the white stone of the door. The second Dracolet hung from it.

"Elowen," he breathed. "Where is she?"

They both searched the room with the swords giving them light. Within a moment, they found her at the far side of the room next to the door they entered. She lay in a crumpled heap against the wall.

Aden and Tamya scrambled to her.

Her clothes were charred, smoking, and one side of her face was blackened flesh.

"Is she ...?" Tamya began.

Aden touched the unburnt side of her neck. A pulse. Elowen groaned.

"She's alive." He pointed to her twisted arm. "Her arm's broken, but she's alive."

"Why was she burned, but we weren't?" Tamya asked.

Aden looked down at the glowing blade in his hand. "The unforged swords. They're supposed to protect us from the magic, make us immune."

"She wasn't holding hers," Tamya said.

She had thrown her sword. "We need our packs," he said.

They grabbed their own charred packs, as well as Elowen's, and after a few minutes, they had gathered the few medical supplies they possessed. They removed the elf's tattered clothes and found a few more burns. That green leather worked well against flame, as well. After cleaning Elowen's wounds as much as they could with a little water in their canteens and a cloth, they applied ointment to the wounds and wrapped them in bandages. They pieced together a few blankets and the tent and covered her as best they could.

Then Aden and Tamya discarded their own burnt outerclothes and tended to their wounds before dressing again in layers they could reclaim from their own packs. Both had suffered deep gashes from the *aelhund* that needed attention. But they could continue.

Tamya retrieved Elowen's unforged sword and held the second Dracolet in her hand. Aden looked closer at it. It was identical to the one he wore.

He met Tamya's eyes. "Wear it."

"You think I …?"

Elowen's voice was raspy from a pace away. "Wear it."

Aden and Tamya started and knelt next to her. Elowen reached out a bandaged hand, and Tamya gave her the unforged sword.

"Wear it, young one." Elowen's lips barely moved. "You are the *Isael*."

Tamya glanced at Aden, and he urged her on. She placed it over her head and it hung from her neck.

"Now go," Elowen said. "The dragons await you."

"We can't leave you here," Aden said. "You're injured."

"I have done what I came to do," Elowen said.

"We – we can make a breakin' sling or something, take you with us," Tamya said.

"No," Elowen said. "I cannot go beyond the tower. That is your calling. Not mine. I was never meant to go further. El spoke to me of this."

Aden and Tamya shared an uncertain glance.

"You can do nothing more for me," Elowen said. "But return for me, if you can. You must get the dragons to the *Brendel*. The world needs them again."

Aden couldn't see the door on the other side of the round room in the dark, the gate to the Dracoland, but he knew it was there.

"Fine," he said. "But don't you die on us. We'll be back."

"I can make no promises," Elowen said. "Neither can you. Even if the dragons agree to return to the world, it may cost your life." The sorrow in her voice pierced his heart. "It will be as El desires. He will show his goodness."

"What the shog does that mean?" Tamya demanded.

Elowen didn't answer.

Aden lowered his head. Caleb said that the revolution would need the dragons. They couldn't win without them. Wasn't that worth any sacrifice? "I understand."

"I know you do, *Isael*," Elowen said. "You have a pure heart. Trust it. Now go."

Aden leaned down, and he cradled her head gently with his hand. He kissed her unburnt cheek. "Thank you."

"Thank you, *Isael*."

Tamya also bent down, laying her cheek on Elowen's forehead. Aden saw tears in her eyes. She stood, her lip quivering. Aden stood with her, and with a last look at Elowen, they walked across the bodies of *aelhund* and the white stones of the throne that once sat at the other end until they reached the gate.

The throne had covered the center of the stone door, and now Aden could see two circular indentations over four mitres away from each other, the same size as the Dracolet. It would take two people to place them in the indentations.

Aden and Tamya sheathed their unforged swords. With a shared look, they both removed the Dracolet from their necks and lifted them. "You ready?" Aden asked his wife.

"Are we ever shoggin' ready for anything?" Tamya responded.

"No. Not really. But El is with us."

"He better be." She placed her Dracolet within the stone.

Aden did the same.

The tower shook and groaned around them, like an old giant waking from a long sleep, and the enormous door split down the middle, an even vertical line. Had it been there before? The two parts of the gate swung away from them with a loud noise, dragging through pebbles and ice and snow to open wide and reveal the land beyond.

The light of the sun reflected off of the snow and ice, and Aden had to squint.

Aden walked to his left and removed his Dracolet from the stone. The gate remained open. Tamya grabbed hers, as well. They met together in the snow on the other side of the gate.

The wind whipped through him and tossled his hair. It stung his face and eyes.

There was a sound like thunder in the distance, straight ahead. But it wasn't thunder.

Even if the dragons agree to return to the world, it may cost your life.

He was afraid. He tried to deny it, but the fear filled his heart.

"Hey," Tamya said next to him. "I'm scared critless, too. But this is why we came, right? We need the dragons if we're going to beat the Kryan army." Tamya gestured back at Elowen. "And she needs our help. You heard her. She's gonna shoggin' die if we don't get her back to the Dragonmen or wherever soon, and those dragons can get her there. So let's go get them to help us."

He thought of the army moving to Asya. Those were his friends ... no, his family. His family. The Dragonmen might be traveling to join the fight, but would that be enough against the walls of Asya, an army of twenty thousand or more, and a Worldbreaker? And whatever else Tanicus might throw at them?

Aden frowned at her. "I thought I was the one that was supposed to give the speeches."

"I learn things. Plus, I don't want to cross that bridge again. I'd rather take a shortcut."

Aden's frown became a grin. "Okay. So let's go talk to some dragons."

"We leaving again in the morning?" Macarus asked Caleb.

They stood on the outskirts of the town of Giannis. It spread through a valley between the hills below them. The *Hamon-el* and elves and humans organized in the city for the night. The sun set, and torches and lamps were being lit and tents raised to surround the city.

"We'll see how tomorrow goes," Caleb answered. "Many of the former citizens of Giannis will stay here, and I'll leave a platoon or so to stay with them."

"You think you'll need to? I don't think Kryus will waste any more legions to attack you now. Tanicus will bolster the defenses and the walls of Asya and wait for you."

"I agree," Caleb said. "But we don't know all that will happen at Asya. We will leave what weapons we can for the citizens to defend themselves. The humans will need to see human leadership with the Stewards remaining."

"I understand," Macarus said.

Caleb leaned on the Kingstaff as he surveyed the activity below. After two days of travel, he thought the *Hamon-el* might survive. More training and learning went on between the different peoples – a Beorgai teaching the elves about the corran, the elves showing humans how to use a spear and link shields, the men from Manahem showing the Beorgai how to use the longbows. There had been meetings where different humans had taught from the scriptures to diverse groups. The night before, some Beorgai and Ghosts had shared songs of praise to El from their own culture.

Even now, he heard the faint echo of a song, a Ghost song that made him think of Reyan. He wondered if the Prophet had taught it to them.

His eyes stung with threatening tears.

Yes, they will survive. Well, until they get to Asya, at least.

They were another two days from Asya.

"Caleb." Macarus pointed to the gray sky. "What is that?"

A figure flew through the air. *Dragon?*

But it was not a dragon. It did have wings, and while difficult from the distance to gauge size, the figure could hold a rider. He could see someone there.

"That is the Mahakar," Caleb said.

"The what?"

Caleb grinned. "Come. You should meet him."

Macarus shook his head at the sky but followed when Caleb walked towards the center of the city where the Mahakar aimed to land.

Had Eshlyn felt him recently? She hadn't told him. He was surprised that it hurt his heart she hadn't shared it with him, but what did he expect? She could have known he was coming for the last few days, and he wouldn't know. He had to accept that things had changed. It was for the best.

Then what the shog is this all for?

He had the answer for his sister, now that she was gone. *For others. Not me.*

Giannis bustled with the view of the Mahakar, many speaking of it, others looking to the sky when told about him. They parted for Caleb, however. Some even bowed when he passed.

Caleb's jaw tightened in anger.

Caleb and Macarus traveled the main road through the town, and they reached the center within ten minutes.

Once there, Caleb stopped and became a spectator like everyone else.

Eshlyn held Javyn in one arm and embraced the Mahakar with the other. The child was delighted, his chubby hands in the white fur of the beast.

Caleb had never seen the creatue this close, and he was magnificent and imposing. Larger than a bosaur, his white fur was pure, and even sitting on his haunches, calm.

An old woman with long, gray hair sat atop the Mahakar. She wore a simple brown robe and leather sandals. Several of the Ghosts, seeing her, pointed and smiled.

"It's the Mother," they said. "Mother Natali."

No one would come close, however, everyone hovering mitres away from the winged tiger.

"Well, that's not something you see every day," Macarus mumbled.

Caleb stepped forward, all the way to the Mahakar. The animal eyed him and showed teeth, but Caleb approached anyway. He lifted a hand to the older woman, a half-elf. Her piercing eyes found him. She did not smile. But she did take his hand and allow him to help her down from the Mahakar.

"Mother Natali," Caleb said. "It is an honor."

Jaff approached now, and he took her hands and greeted her.

Eshlyn also greeted the woman. "Mother. So good to see you." They also embraced, and Eshlyn introduced her to Javyn.

"What brings you from the Saten?" Jaff asked.

"The Mahakar wanted to see his friend," Natali said. She turned to Eshlyn. "He missed you."

"And I missed him." Eshlyn beamed at the tiger.

"I have also come to speak to the Lady and the *Brendel*," Natali announced.

"Of course," Caleb said. "We can go to my command tent over at the …"

"No," Natali interrupted. "I will speak with the Lady alone, first."

Caleb nodded. "Very well."

Natali turned and met his eyes. "You, I will speak with in the morning. I am tired. After speaking with the Lady, I will rest."

"You'll stay with me," Eshlyn said. "And Javyn."

Eshlyn took Natali's hand, and they walked away.

"The beast is hungry, too," Natali called. "Feed him."

The Mahakar growled at them. Jaff raised a brow at Caleb.

Caleb watched the women go, and he realized Eshlyn had barely looked at him the whole time. Why did he feel naseous when he thought of that conversation?

While no one else drew near the Mahakar, Caleb could feel the hope rising within them, the energy.

Eshlyn disappeared into the crowd with Mother Natali.

The *Hamon-el* moved forward, unified. That was all that mattered.

If only his heart would believe that.

CHAPTER 23

DRAGONS

Tamya trudged with Aden through the snow, between large stones and hills of ice. While they wore a layer over the tight green leather, it wasn't enough for the frigid conditions. The air had improved from the Dragongate tower, but they wouldn't last long in these conditions.

They might not last long with a dragon, either.

The Dracolet burned under her coat. At least a part of her was warm.

How were they supposed to convince the dragons to join their revolution? Would the Dracolet work? Did dragons talk back? Did they have an "eat first and talk later" kind of an attitude? Her mind raced with questions about the unknown ahead of them, and she would have voiced them to Aden. But he didn't know any more than she did.

Even if the dragons agree to return to the world, it may cost your life.

Aden walked beside her, a man she loved more than she thought possible.

Not him, El. He has to survive. The revolution might need the dragons, but the people need Aden. I need him.

She would see to it, no matter what, that he lived.

She wasn't sure she would give her life for a cause or a revolution. But she would for him.

"Look." Aden pointed to their right.

A skeleton with a spine fifty mitres long lay on the top of a huge mound of snow. A fierce skull with a long snout and teeth faced faced them. A round, red stone huddled half covered in snow underneath the ribs.

"Is that the heart?" Tamya asked.

"I think so. Didn't they say something about the heart that turned to some type of stone when a dragon faded away or died?"

Over the next hour, they passed five more intact dragon skeletons. For two, the bones were scattered and there were no stone hearts that remained.

They also said something about the heart as an indestructible egg. Had they been born again? With a shared glance and a sniff, she knew Aden had the same thought.

They came close to the edge of the cliff. Different rock formations rose to their right and left as they followed the weaving path forward, some only a few mitres tall, others reaching like fingers dozens of mitres high.

A slight descent of their path led to the cliff, and they traveled with caution over the ice and smooth rock. When they reached the edge, Tamya's breath caught for a moment at the frightening beauty of the view – an endless sea of white clouds and hundreds of peaks that rose through the mists, like an immense and perfect painting.

A massive shadow in the distance flew between the peaks of mountains – a shadow with wings. Then it ducked and disappeared below the clouds.

She heard the roar that echoed around her, bouncing from rock and the sky in waves. She froze.

Aden took a step closer to within five paces of the edge of the cliff. He removed the Dracolet from his neck and the unforged sword from his side. He lifted them both together.

Tamya forced her body to move forward to join him. She pulled the Dracolet from her neck, as well, and lifted Xander's sword and the golden amulet.

The mountain they stood upon rumbled and shook. Tamya heard a deafening roar from the clouds beneath them. She cringed. Looking over the edge, her eyes bulged. The echoing roar diminished; she could hear the beating of a great heart, or something like it. But it was no heartbeat ... wings, wings that moved a great mass below. It grew closer.

A massive head parted the clouds below, part lizard and part lion with pointed ears, green-yellow eyes, large nostrils, and horns down the middle towards the snout. The mists swirled as leathery wings created temporary tornadoes, violently lifting the enormous body and serpent tail. Its skin and scales were blue and silver. Its four muscular arms ended in claws.

The dragon rose straight up, parallel to the sheer cliff. Tamya's mouth gaped at its size, as large as a battleship. It halted its flight upwards to hover over them. The wind around them from its beating wings pulled like a hurricane, but Aden held his ground, and she bared her teeth and stood next to him.

It all happened in slow motion, her mind unable to properly process the impossible enormity of the creature, the sheer horror of it as it hung in the air.

The dragon glared down at them. Its blue-silver head lowered, closer to them.

The mouth opened, revealing teeth larger than any spear she had ever seen, and a spark of flame it in the back of its throat.

Then she could move. She threw herself in front of Aden as they were both engulfed in flames.

———

Zalman stoked the fire as they settled in for the night.

Carys had tracked Julius – or who they thought was Julius – through the fields and the trees on a winding path. Tobiah was also a fine tracker on his own, and they worked well together. Apparently, every one of the Beorgai warriors, male or female, had to track some creature and kill it as a part of some maturity ceremony. He thought it a little crazy, but it interested him. As far as the tracking was concerned, Zalman knew his role was to follow, keep his eyes open, and stay as quiet as possible.

Carys and Tobiah did one last sweep of the area before the sunset, making sure that no one waited to throttle them in their sleep.

Iletus sat across the fire from him and gazed down at his lap.

The journey so far had been tense but without incident. Tobiah didn't fully trust Iletus, but their time together, all four of them, really, contributed to an ease that crept into the group.

Zalman didn't know how he felt about Iletus, either. He barely knew the elf, and he had experience with the machinations of the Kryan government, how they used people. Was Iletus the one being used? Or was he still a user? He had been one before, and while Zalman understood that people could change, he also knew how difficult it was to change who you were. So Zalman watched the elf closely, glad that Tobiah could track with Carys so Zalman could keep Iletus close.

Iletus was quite the swordmaster, however, from what others said. If Iletus did try something, what could Zalman do? Pray that Carys could put an arrow in his eye before Iletus cut him to shreds, maybe. He chose to pray that it wouldn't have to come to that.

Zalman rested on his knees and caught sight of what was in the elf's lap. It was a sword. His brow furrowed. "Not the sword you had before."

"No, it's not."

The elf had worn an elaborate sword with a gold-trimmed hilt before. This simple and elegant sword with solid black hilt had a double-edged blade. Most elven swords boasted a single edge.

It appeared different, but Zalman felt a familiarity with it. "An unforged sword?"

Iletus nodded, his straight and fine red hair falling down into his lap. "Caleb gave it to me before we left. It was Digby's. He fell at the Battle of Vicksburg, fighting trodall. Caleb said I would need it."

"How did he know?"

"I don't know." He looked up and met Zalman's eyes. "Do you?"

He asked the big man like Zalman was an expert or something, which he wasn't. He shifted in the grass. "Carys knows things sometimes. Says the sword tells her."

Iletus ran a hand across the blade, his fingers touching it. "Yes. I believe that. Do you?"

"Suppose. I had a dream. El spoke to me. Sounds stupid, but it happened."

"It would have sounded quite insane to me not long ago," Iletus said. "But not now. Not at all."

Zalman continued to stoke the fire.

Iletus scanned the darkening sky around them. "He's leading us into a trap, you know."

Julius. "How?"

"Not sure. He was the first, the most committed. He was with Tanicus from the beginning."

"So?"

"He's kept more secrets than we can imagine." Iletus ran his fingers along the sword. "I hope that Caleb's god will help us when we find him. I have a feeling we're going to need it."

Zalman narrowed his eyes at the elf. "I don't know much. But I know this. If you're here, and you're holding that sword, then it can't be Caleb's god alone. Has to be yours, too."

Iletus snorted. "You are correct. And wise. Do you think, if we survive this, that I could get my own?"

"Your own sword?"

"Yes. From the Stone."

"Sure."

"And you? Once this is all over, and there is time, will you go, as well?"

Zalman had to think about that one. A quiet life, somewhere far from everyone else, that all sounded good to him. Why would he need a sword for that?

Carys and Tobiah walked up. Zalman watched his wife and how she moved with so much energy and confidence. Could she live a quiet life? Was that even possible? Either way, he would do what it took to be alongside her.

"Maybe," he told Iletus. "I'll do what I need to do."

"No sign of anyone." She glanced at the two of them. "What were you boys talking about?"

Iletus shrugged. "That maybe, after this is all over, if there was time, we could go to the Stone and get our own swords."

Carys raised a brow at Zalman. "Really?" Her eyes sparked.

Zalman grinned. "Think the Stone makes axes?"

"Don't think so," Carys said. "You'll have to learn how to use a sword."

"Then I'll pass," Zalman said.

"Shoggers." She reached out her hand. "Take a walk with me?"

Zalman looked her in the eye. And stood.

She led him away from the camp and behind a copse of trees. Hooking her leg on the inside of his, she pushed him, trying to trip him. She didn't really have the strength, but he allowed himself to be pulled down to the leaves and grass with the darkening sky overhead.

Carys was on top of him in a moment, grinning.

"What are you doing?" Zalman grunted.

"They don't need to see us," Carys breathed back. "Especially Tobiah. He just lost his wife and everything."

She pressed close and kissed him. After a few moments, he parted from her and grinned. "Sensitive of you. But won't they still know …?"

"Who cares, you big gedder. We're married. Let them think what they want."

He kissed her this time, swallowing her in his arms.

Yes. She'll never stop long enough to live a quiet life. And no matter what, I'm in for the ride. I wonder how a sword will feel …

—+—

Mother Natali sat next to Javyn's cot and sang to him, a soft song that Eshlyn had never heard but fell in love with at once. The old woman ran her fingers through Javyn's mop of hair, and the boy calmed and smiled. Eshlyn stood in the doorway, a flap, really, to the separate room of the tent where Javyn stayed.

Eshlyn could have had a room in the administration building, and knowing Caleb, he would have insisted if they were talking. Well, to be honest, if she were talking to him.

No, I talk to him. When I have to. When we have to discuss important matters of the Hamon-el.

It was silly. She chided herself for allowing her emotions to be so affected. As she told Caleb, she wasn't a tween at her first breaking of a horse. She had been married and had a child. She had lost her husband and helped to run the city of Ketan before traveling the world with *Sohan-el* to help foster revolution. Surely a simple rejection from a man was nothing.

However, her heart didn't feel it was nothing, and she couldn't change that. She could pretend and reason with her heart but not change it.

So she hadn't attempted to get a room in the center of Giannis. She used the excuse that Javyn needed the continuity, the stability, of staying in the same tent as they traveled and set for battle. While true, it was a convenient excuse.

Javyn's eyes closed, and his breathing evened out. He fell into sleep, that place where she loved to watch him, a serene moment separate from the constant correcting and chasing and guiding, where she could feel the love for him overflow in waves.

Natali finished the song; the melody came to a natural resolution. Natali sighed and drew a blanket over the boy. She stood with a grunt and followed Eshlyn into the other area of the tent.

Eshlyn had made tea, and they sat at a small, round table on wooden folding chairs. The main area of the tent was big enough for Eshlyn's cot and a desk and a washing area.

They sat together and sipped the tea.

"Thank you, Lady, for allowing me time with your son. It has been quite some time since my own children were so young, and I do miss it. It is a precious time to be a mother, when they are young."

"Of course. You're amazing with him. He likes you. He doesn't like everyone."

"Children are wiser than we," Natali said. "We leave behind the awe and wonder and simple joy of being a child and call it maturity. It is instead a tragedy."

Eshlyn hummed an assent into her tea. Natali wrapped her wrinkled hands over hers.

"You have done well with him," Natali continued. "As you have with the *Hamon-el*. You are a mother to them, much as I was with the Ghosts."

"Aren't you now?"

Natali shook her head. "The time of the Ghosts is ended." When Eshlyn raised brow at her, she said, "Don't misunderstand. Many will stay in the forest and live there. But we are no longer Ghosts. We have rejoined the world, as have the humans from Lior. That is why I sent as many as would go to join the *Brendel*."

Hearing the term sent a slight pang through her. Eshlyn lowered her head.

Natali took a sip, her eyes staying on Eshlyn. "Something has happened with him. Between you and the *Brendel*."

Eshlyn licked her lips. "Caleb – the *Brendel* – and I have … grown close. Too close, I guess. I thought … well, doesn't matter what I thought. He did not want to pursue that between us."

Eshlyn watched Natali as she sipped her tea, the older woman pensive. Eshlyn waited for her to respond.

"Good," Natali said.

"What?"

"That is wise of him," Natali explained. "His way is only one of sorrow. It is for the good of all, but it is not a path of joy."

"But," Eshlyn began, but then she paused, sighing. "Weren't you the one that told me to remember sweet moments or create them? Something about the fate of the world might depend upon it?"

Mother Natali's brow furrowed. "I did say that, Lady, but I did not mean you must be with him in that way."

"You said he would need me before it is over."

"And he does. He needs you now. Just not like that."

"Then ..."

"He is a sword, Lady. You do not lie in bed with a sword. You remove it, set it aside, so you can rest. No." Natali pursed her lips. "What does a sword do? It protects or attacks, but in order to do both it kills. His way is one of blood and violence, and while it may be necessary for a time, the end of that way is only blood and violence. It must only be for a time, or none of us will survive."

Eshlyn shook her head, her eyes lowered. Mother Natali reached out and touched her hand.

"The world needs the sword to lead the fight now, but one day it will need a leader and a mother. And that is what you are. That is what we will need when the time of the *Brendel* has come to an end."

———

Aden rolled to his side and back with Tamya in his arms, trying to get clear of the flames. He couldn't breathe in the midst of the conflagration, but then it was over. He sat up, gasping for breath. He didn't feel any pain, however, and he thought he must be in shock or something.

Peering down at himself and Tamya, who sat next to him, they were both unburnt and unharmed, even their clothes untouched by the flame.

Tamya reflected his shock in her own face. "I – I don't understand."

The dragon rose higher over them, growling. A blue monstrosity with silver streaks. Aden stood, pulling Tamya up with him, and they backed away as the dragon landed at the edge of the cliff, its lizard stare bearing down upon them. It strode forward on all fours, and Aden was surprised to find that his unforged sword and the Dracolet were still in his hand.

He thought of how the gate responded to the two Dracolet, how it opened by some unseen force. Had the wizard constructed it? Had it protected them from the dragonflame? And if it had, how could magic accomplish something good? Had another power constructed it?

The questions ran through his mind, but he didn't have time for that now. A dragon crawled toward them. The dragon's face was paces away.

Setting his resolve, Aden lifted the Dracolet. "We are the *Isael, Sohan-el* with unforged sword. We possess both Dracolet."

The dragon cocked his head at them. "You," it began with a voice deeper and louder than anything Aden had ever heard, even the Demilord a year ago. The voice shook his heart. The dragon rose up and loomed over him. "Why are you here?"

Aden blinked while Tamya's face twisted. "What do you mean? Didn't you hear him? We've got the Dracolet. You have to come with us."

The dragon turned his attention to Tamya. "You do not control me."

"Look," Aden said in a loud voice, the sound echoing around them, so small in comparison. "There's a revolution to the south. The *Sohan-el* have returned. And the faith of El."

"There have been revolutions before, and there will again," the dragon said. "What does it matter to me?"

Tamya growled. "The revolution needs you! More people will die if you don't come."

"People will die whether I move from this place or not," the dragon responded. "Are you so young you don't know this?"

Aden held out a hand as Tamya gaped. He took a breath, blinking slowly to calm himself. Take a different approach. "My name is Aden. This is Tamya. What is your name?"

The dragon stared at them for a few moments, a fearful thing. Aden willed himself to stand, although he shook under the stare.

"I am Fryaco," the dragon said. "The First of Dragons."

Well, crit. "Then you should know." He lifted the golden amulet in his hand. "We have the Dracolet."

Tamya raised hers higher. "And we command you to take us to the revolution. And to fight with us."

Fryaco showed his sharp teeth, like a smirk. "You believe you have some magic object that can command me?" He filled his lungs with air, spread his wings, and blew fire into the air over their heads. Aden and Tamya cowered together. The dragon's jaw snapped shut as the flames ended. "I am the First of Dragons. I no obligation to a circle of gold."

Aden coughed. He stood straight. And he glared. "What about El? Do you hold any obligation to him?"

Fryaco roared in anger. "You dare?"

"I do," Aden said. "Have you been away from the world so long you can't see the signs? The *Arendel, Brendel,* and the *Isael.* We are here. El is bringing the redemption he promised. Who cares what we think? Won't you obey him?"

"You believe you're the first to believe you've seen a prophecy come true only to be proven a fool? Happens every generation."

Aden felt Tamya touch his arm. He leaned in to her. "Remember the remains from before," she said. She was right. There had been two missing the stone heart.

Aden stepped forward. "What gives dragons their power? Their life?"

Fryaco snorted flame from his nostrils.

Aden sneered and gripped the Dracolet tight. "Speak, dragon."

"Faith."

Aden nodded. "Faith in El. Have dragons returned recently? Have they been born anew?"

Fryaco's chest rumbled in threat, but he didn't speak.

Aden lifted his unforged sword and rammed the blade that had pierced his own heart into the snow and ice and stone at his feet.

The whole mountain shook.

"I call the dragons to the battle of El, the battle that will bring the final dawn to this world," Aden said.

He heard the distant roars, two of them, reverberate through the sky. Aden and Tamya raised their eyes and scanned the sky.

Two more enormous dragons descended through the clouds. They circled together and then separated, each to land on either side of Aden and Tamya. Both faced Fryaco.

The dragon on the right was thinner with green and black scales. Fryaco regarded him. "Malaki."

Fryaco turned to the one on Aden's left and said, "Bael." Bael, muscular with red and black scales, bowed back to the First Dragon.

"The dragons have returned. The fire is reborn," Aden said. "Come fight with us."

Fryaco shook his head at Aden. "We will not. Not with the *humans*."

"The human speaks true," the one with green and black scales, Malaki, said. "You've heard the voice same as we. The *Arendel*, the *Brendel*, and now the *Isael*. The final dawn of the *Dae'Grael* comes soon. We would not have emerged from our hearts had faith not returned to Eres again."

"And look, brother," Bael said like a hoarse whisper. "She is part elf, part human."

"We have elves and humans fighting together," Aden said. "And even a dwarf."

"Yes," Malaki said. "The races come to fight together. That is the mark of the coming Dawn."

Bael nodded his large head. "That is the mark."

"The prophecies." Awe filled Tamya's voice. "They're really coming true."

Fryaco faced Tamya. "What would you know of prophecies? You see or hear words, but I know the nature of this world. I was there at the beginning when lust, greed, and power split the First Race into three. I watched from the Everworld as a human killed the Master King."

"We were there, too," said Bael, the dragon with red and black scales. "Do you remember that, brother?"

"You abandoned the world once before," Tamya said. "Are you going to do it again?"

"The world abandoned us!" Fryaco shouted, and Aden winced at the deafening sound. "We came from the Everworld to help Yosu redeem this world once before. And after all the miracles and power you saw from El and Yosu, the world slipped into deception once more. What can redeem such a world?"

Aden lowered his head. He looked over at Tamya. He saw the tear in her eye, her sad smile.

Tamya faced Fryaco. "Love. Love can redeem that world. The love of El that would look at such weak and fragile humans, the same humanity that killed Yosu, and try to change them. How else could El show how much he loved the world but by using those humans to bring Yosu back for a final time, to finish the redemption we messed up?"

The noise that came from Aden was part laugh and part sob, so much joy his body didn't know how to react.

Aden looked up at Fryaco. "That's it. Without love, you're right. It doesn't make sense. It's not fair." He placed the Dracolet around his head and reached out his hand. Tamya's gloved fingers laced into his own. "That's why the *Isael* had to be two. Because love is the argument. Love is the call. Love is the reason."

Malaki turned his green scaled head from Aden and Tamya to Fryaco. "The *Isael* speaks true. That is the heart of El."

Bael swung snout covered in red and black to the First Dragon, as well. "That is the heart of the Everworld."

Aden looked from Bael to Malaki. "Will you come back with us and redeem the world?"

"We will," both booming voices from the two dragons said.

Aden addressed Fryaco. "Will you?"

"You know nothing," Fryaco said.

Aden faced him with the unforged sword in his hand. "I know the storm of the top of Mount Elarus and the words of El when he said he loved me."

"I am the First Dragon, the Prince of Dragons," Fryaco said. "You have no power here."

"I know the beauty of the pool at the Stone," Tamya said. "Yosu said that no power could overcome me if I clung to him." She held out her unforged sword in a low guard. "That includes you."

"I will not fight for a humanity that can only fail," Fryaco growled. "You are nothing."

The words came to his mind, and as he spoke them, Tamya spoke at the same time ... "*We are the Fire Reborn.*"

Bael bowed to them and then turned to Fryaco. "Brother. First of Dragons. When did you rise again?"

Fryaco snorted fire. "I have lived for thousands of years while you slept."

Malaki shared a glance with Bael. "All other dragons faded from the world, waiting. Why did you stay?"

"Faith waned." Bael showed his teeth. "Only one touched by the Sahat would stay."

Malaki's eyes burned. "Is this true, brother? Have you been touched by the lies of the Sahat?"

Fryaco snapped at the two dragons. "I am not your brother. I am your Prince."

"We serve only El," Bael said.

Malaki's stare narrowed. "Answer the question, brother."

The hesitation stretched, the whistling wind and Aden's hearbeat the only sounds.

Fryaco lifted his snout. "The Sahat spoke true, not lies. He knew of the corruption within human, elf, and dwarf. He knew they could never deserve this redemption."

Bael's jaw opened. "You defy El?"

"You stayed connected to this world because you believed the lies," Malaki said. "You are no longer one of us."

"I am the First and Greatest. And I will kill these humans before I help a corrupt redemption." Fryaco turned to Aden and Tamya. His wings extended, and he beat them. The wind pressed and chilled as he rose from the mountain, enraged. His neck arced and his mouth opened.

Malaki and Bael roared together, and before Fryaco could reach Aden and Tamya, two dragons attacked with teeth and claws. Three dragons collided thirty mitres above Aden and Tamya, grabbing and tearing with claws and teeth. The Prince of Dragons snapped and screamed; Bael and Malaki drug him off the mountain and into the air.

Chapter 24

The Isael

The Sunguard came to get Earon in the evening.

For the previous two days, Earon spent his time trying to figure out how to escape.

He had done what he came to do – plead with the Emperor for peace. And while a part of him wanted to hold out hope that the Emperor could change heart, he had no hope left.

The Emperor justified his own madness and violence at every turn, and no point of logic or faith could deter him. El could make a way where he did not see one; but that knowledge didn't penetrate his heart. His heart was full of sorrow.

Did he regret attempting to reason with the Emperor? No. He did what he felt El would have him do. He would die if he remained.

So he focused on escaping.

That didn't give him much hope, either.

Earon was not a warrior, so he couldn't fight his way out. Even if he had been trained in violence like Caleb, without an unforged sword, he couldn't get past the door and those Sunguard. But after his idealistic speech to Caleb, could he use violence to get away?

Could he talk his way out of it? The day before, he had tried to start some conversation with the Sunguard. Asked them innocuous questions at first. But they hadn't responded. He moved into crude and silly jokes, one he had heard about a dwarf circumcision that he thought was hilarious. Nothing. He had nothing to bribe or to gain their trust with. As a last resort, he tried talking to them about El and how breaking stupid their nine gods were. He didn't even make them angry, which probably wasn't a good idea anyway.

He thought about climbing out the window somehow, but that idea didn't go far when he observed the sheer glass and white stone of the tower.

One after another, he ran out of ideas. The only thing he considered might work would be to sneak into a lower part of the tower and pretend to be a slave of some sort. He was back to the first Tablet and getting past the Sunguard.

Earon kept his eyes open, though, watching for his shot.

The Sunguard walked him up to the garden like before, but this time they took him through a corridor that led to the throne room.

The massive throne room impressed with arched ceilings and weapons and tapestries hanging on the wall. The throne sat at the far side of the room. It was made of Jibrylan glass. Tanicus sat at the throne.

An old man dressed in tatters knelt on the floor in front of the Emperor. The man had tan, Veraden skin, and he was covered with cuts and bruises.

Earon gathered his wits, distracted by the old man, and he walked towards the Emperor.

"Earon," Tanicus began. "Welcome. I trust your stay has been well."

"It has been sufficient." He looked to his left and right, a high window on either side. He wondered what was beyond them if he jumped. He stood ten paces from the Emperor and nodded at the old man. "What is this?"

"I have thought much about our conversation," Tanicus said. "And I felt a demonstration was in order."

Earon narrowed his eyes at the Emperor. "That is not necessary."

"It does not matter what you believe. I decide it is."

"Who is this?"

"He was a prisoner in the Pyts, destined for suffering and death. Now I will give him a greater purpose. Truly, he is no one. He is nothing."

"Not true." Earon closed the gap to the old man. He walked slowly, but Tanicus didn't feel he was a threat. Earon knelt next to the old man. He touched the man's shoulder. "What is your name?"

"I told you, he is nothing."

"He has a name," Earon said. "Every life matters."

"Not to me."

Earon placed his hand under the man's chin and lifted it. The man's eyes were vacant, the pupils almost pinpoints. "What did you do to him?"

"Whatever I will," Tanicus said. "I told you. He is nothing but what I decide he is to be."

The man drooled through his toothless answer. "You are my light."

"I make him believe, Earon. Choice is an illusion."

Earon took a breath before he spoke. "You've abused him, manipulated him. You've proven nothing. Every life has value. Even you can't take that from him."

Tanicus smiled as he leaned forward, and Earon shivered. "Oh, but I can." Then Tanicus waved a hand to the Sunguard.

Unseen hands lifted Earon from the floor and threw him to the wall. Some force pressed him against the white stone of the wall. He grunted and struggled. The two Sunguard stood in front of him.

Earon watched as Tanicus hovered over the old man and stretched a hand to touch the man's head, like unto a child.

Then the man convulsed and groaned. He laid on the ground in spasms of pain. The old man screamed, "Master!"

Earon squinted, and tiny whisps of mist came from the old man's body into the Emperor's pores.

"Stop," Earon said, but his voice was weak. The Emperor wouldn't stop.

After another few seconds, the old man ceased moving, his skin stretched tight over bones.

"No," Earon whined.

"I took his life, his value," Tanicus said. "And now it is mine. It wasn't much, I admit, but I took it."

Tanicus stood and stepped over the dry husk that was once a man. He strode to Earon.

"You come to me with truth, and yet your truth has done nothing to harm me." Tanicus lurked behind the Sunguard. "Can it be true, then? I have weapons and powers you have yet to imagine."

The Sunguard on his right lifted a hand, and Earon's body was flattened more on the wall, his arms and legs splayed. He cried out.

The Sunguard on his left raised his hand, palm forward.

Earon coughed, the air suddenly stale and thin.

Fire blossomed from the Sunguard's palm, striking out like a snake toward Earon's right arm. The cylinder of flame reached his forearm just past the elbow and began to burn.

Earon panted, and his eyes bulged. The fire consumed his skin and then his muscle underneath. He smelled the scent of his own burnt flesh. For a long moment, he couldn't breathe from the anguish. Then he screamed.

The fire ate past flesh and into bone, a focused flame surgically removing half of his limb. It felt longer, but in only thirty seconds, Earon's arm fell to the white marble floor with a sickening thud. His arm ended at a blackened elbow.

Earon wept.

Tanicus nodded at the Sunguard, and they let him drop to the floor. Earon curled in a ball, holding what remained of his arm.

"I could take you, piece by piece, one small part of you at a time," Tanicus said. "I could take your life and give it to you, over and over. I could do so many things that you would beg me to end it. Like that nothing over there, I could have you believing that I was your light, that I was your god."

Footsteps on the marble, and now the Emperor stood over him. Earon could see his severed arm beyond the golden sandled feet.

"It is my choice. It is my will. Is that not what a god does? Now I will be a good god and tell you my will."

Tanicus paused as Earon sobbed.

"The army of the *Brendel* draws ever closer. They will be here within days. You will live and witness what I have in store for him. Now you know, Earon, that nothing can stop me. No one has the power to stand against me. My gift to you will be that you see that truth firsthand.

"Then you will truly believe."

—

The two dragons dragged Fryaco into the air. Tamya gaped and swayed under the force of wind created by three sets of wings rising and pulling into the sky above them.

Fryaco bit at Malaki and clawed at Bael; they snapped and tore at him in return.

Aden stood straight, clutching his sword in his right hand, staring at the battle. He walked to the egde of the cliff. Tamya followed him, wondering for a moment why Aden was silent. But what did one say in the presence of three supernatural creatures engaged in battle?

The dragons flew north and a hundred mitres high. Fryaco roared in pain as Bael's teeth sunk into his neck. Fryaco spun and knocked Bael with a leathery wing. In the same move, he kicked and clawed at Malaki, ripping a gash into the dragon. Malaki growled and retreated in pain.

Bael, falling, could only put his legs up in defense as Fryaco dove toward him. Fryaco caught Bael with his four claws, lifted, and threw the dragon. In her direction.

What did one say as dragons tried to kill each other?

"Run!" She grabbed Aden's coat at the shoulder and pulled.

They sprinted away from the edge of the clif when Bael struck the rock formation behind them to the right. There was an explosion of sound, and Tamya cringed as rocks scattered and flew. A stone clipped her shoulder, and she stumbled. She fell.

And Xander's unforged sword went spinning away into the snow.

Looking over her shoulder, Malaki grabbed Fryaco's wing from behind and yanked. Fryaco turned in the air, hissing, and belched fire into Malaki's face and eyes. Malaki could not see for a moment, and Fryaco used the opportunity to wrench free of Malaki's grip. Fryaco clutched the other dragon's neck, twisted in the air, and threw Malaki in their direction.

Malaki landed beyond them, and they both stumbled to a stop. The battle between Fryaco and Bael lowered toward them. Tamya scanned, spinning as she stood straight again. Dragon in front, two dragons coming at them, and cliffs on either side.

Stuck. Trapped.

Tamya screamed in anger and raised both her arms. Large swaths of snow and ice lifted from the ground.

Aden's voice came from so far away. "No! Tamya!"

She threw the snow into Fryaco's face, smothering him with it, stuffing snow into his open jaws. He released Bael and flailed. Bael fell to the mountain in front of her. Her eyes focused on the First Dragon, and she pelted him with ice with all her strength.

So much power in her anger and fear.

The dragon spit fire from his mouth in an explosion of steam and water, and he protected himself with leather wings from her onslaught.

Hands grabbed her wrists. "Tamya. Stop. Look at me."

She gasped and dropped to her knees. The magic stopped. Tears fell from her eyes as she looked at him. "Aden."

He placed an object in her hands. A sword. Xander's sword. "Not like this, Tamya. Please."

She gripped the sword, felt the calm, the peace, the love. Panting, she fell into him. "I'm sorry. I'm sorry …"

"Don't give into the fear. You're stronger than that."

Another roar from Fryaco, who had recovered. She held the sword with both hands, tight.

After a glance over his shoulder, Aden kissed her. "I love you."

Aden stood and ran toward Bael and Fryaco's battle.

Tamya scrambled to her feet. "What the shog are you doing?"

"We have to help them."

Tamya chased him. "What can we do?"

"Whatever we can." He sprinted forward, faster than she imagined he could run.

Fryaco saw them, and he roared, hovering for a moment and then advanced.

"Shog a goat, Aden." *Don't give into fear. You're stronger than that.* She tried to catch up.

Fryaco seemed to grin at the sight of two humans standing up to a dragon. Tamya had to agree with the dragon's assessment. It was ridiculous. But as usual, going with Aden meant doing ridiculous things.

Fryaco drew near, stretching his neck and opening his mouth wide. The spark formed at the back of the throat; it ignited and a fountain of flame poured over Aden. He covered his face by instinct.

Tamya cried out and stepped to the side. She lifted the unforged sword in her hand, leapt forward and sliced at the dragon's head.

Her blade opened a gash in the dragon's cheek. Fryaco bellowed and reared back.

Then he was attacked by Bael and Malaki, both back in the battle at once. Bael dug into his shoulder. Malaki landed on his back and bit into a wing.

No longer covered by flame and unhurt, Aden rolled his shoulders and stood. He stared at Fryaco.

Tamya's heart skipped. She knew that look. He had an idea.

Aden raised his unforged sword, and it glowed more than it had before. It shone bright in the light of day. The Dracolet burned with a golden light around his neck. And then he ran forward.

She tried to grab his coat, to stop him, but her fingers brushed the cloth. And she failed.

How did he breakin' get so fast?

Fryaco knocked Bael away with his right muscular leg and kicked Malaki away with his back claws. Malaki scrambled on the stone and fell over the cliff as Bael rolled through rocks. The mountain shuddered with the impacts.

Aden aimed his approach at Fryaco's exposed torso.

Tamya sprinted. She had to get there first. Get there in front of Aden, protect him. But he was too fast. "No."

Time seemed to slow as Aden jumped up on a fallen stone, a mitre high, and he launched himself at Fryaco's heart. Fryaco noticed him and reached forward with his forelegs. Aden yelled and flew like one of Carys' arrows, like the sword pulled him, and the unforged blade sunk all the way into the dragon's heart.

While Aden was extended, Fryaco's claw clasped onto his body, talons digging deep into Aden's chest. He grunted and released the unforged sword.

Frayco collapsed backwards, shuddering in pain and shock, flame and smoke billowing from his mouth and the wound in his chest. He fell on his back with a deafening crash. The claw that held Aden splayed, and Aden's limp body rolled to the icy, rocky ground.

"No!" But she didn't know who she was saying it to. She didn't know who was listening.

Fryaco spasmed and gave a deep squeal before falling motionless.

Tamya collapsed next to Aden. He lay on his back, blood pouring from an open wound on his chest, another at his side, and a third through his right leg. She lifted his head and cradled it in her lap.

"Tamya." He stared up at the sky. He said it again, a desperate call. "Tamya?"

"I'm here." She removed her coat, freezing but she didn't care, and she laid it over the wounds on his chest and side. *Apply pressure.*

"I'm sorry," he said. "I had to ..."

"Stupid shogging idiot, don't talk."

The ground shook behind her and stones crumbed before her. Malaki hovered over her shoulder. Bael crouched on the other side of the dead dragon.

"The Prince of Dragons has fallen," Bael said.

"The Fire Reborn slayed the First Dragon," Malaki added.

Aden just killed a shoggin' dragon. And he was dying in her arms.

"Listen," Aden said. "You have to ... the dragons ..."

"Shut up. I told you to shut up."

"No, listen. The dragons … you have to go with them to help Caleb."

"Stop it," she said. "I'm not going anywhere! I'm staying with you."

Aden's eyes scanned the sky, like he was looking for her. "Tamya, we did it. We found the dragons. They will go with you."

Both dragons lowered their heads.

Tamya closed her eyes, and in her mind she saw Berran burning at the stake. She saw her child's head dashed against a stone. She saw herself killing her own soldier, her friend, and she saw Hema bloody and dead on the black field. Athelwulf, Esai, Xander, the grief of all of them together in one second, and it coalesced into one thought.

Not again. Please, not again.

"Don't leave me," she said. "I can't do this alone. I can't. The *Isael* is two, remember? Can't just be one. Has to be *two*. So you have to stay with me."

He coughed and blood spurted from his mouth. "Don't worry. It'll be okay."

Aden gasped once more, and he fell still.

At that moment, there was no revolution, no cause, no love left, nothing left to fight for. There on the roof of Eres, she wept above the clouds, for the world had ended.

"So many have died," Johann said. "So many that will not see the redemption."

"Why do you believe they that pass from this world do not see the redemption?" Yosu asked. "They see it with better eyes, and they will see it more clearly.

"Do not fear death. Death has no meaning apart from the understanding of life. El values every life and its passing from this world, but not every death is the same."

"What do you mean?" Johann asked.

Yosu fixed him with brown eyes. "Those who do not understand life are already dead.

"You've been given a gift, to live and die for the greatest story ever told, to be remembered in the eternal Everworld as one of the heroes of that story, even though you may be forgotten here.

"Death cannot stand against life, just as dark cannot stand against light. Death makes way so that only life remains."

Johann sighed. "I do not understand."

"I know," Yosu said. "That is why I must show you."

- From the Ydu, the 4th Scroll, translated from the First Tongue to the Common by the Prophet

CHAPTER 25

THE FIRST BLADEGUARD

Carys put her fists on her hips and frowned. She looked down at the ground between the trees and then up at the city of Asya a kilomitre away. The sun hung overhead.

Tobiah stood next too her. "You're right. He is going to Asya."

Zalman grunted behind her, a sound of annoyance and impatience. They had tracked Julius for days, and now they reached Asya.

"We'll lose him in the city," Zalman said.

"But he's not going for the gate." She pointed to her right. "He's headed to the north."

"Why isn't he going to the gate?" Tobiah wondered.

"He's leading us into a trap." Iletus had said this many times, and as the first Bladeguard always seemed a step ahead of her, Carys was beginning to believe him.

"Not the gate?" Zalman asked.

Iletus shook his head. "He knows we won't follow him there, not during the day." Iletus paused and gazed at the beautiful walls of Asya. "There is another way in."

Carys spun and squinted at him. "What?"

The whole group stared at Iletus.

"After Tanicus and the legions conquered Asya, Kryus rebuilt much of the city," Iletus explained. "And when they rebuilt the walls, Julius had them construct a secret way in and out of the city for Bladeguard agents."

"Caleb knew about this?" Carys said.

Iletus shrugged. "Perhaps. I don't know if Galen told him."

"More secrets," Tobiah spat.

"Caleb thought we would find him by now," Zalman said.

"And if he did know," Iletus added. "He probably didn't think we'd follow him into Asya."

"'Cause it's breakin' stupid," Carys said.

"Julius knows that I can find the passage," Iletus said.

"And how does he know you're with us?" Tobiah said.

Iletus stared at the man from Lior intently. "He knows. He knows we are all here. He has led us to this point. He wants to lead us to a place where he has the advantage. That is the first rule of combat. We can follow him there without being seen. And we will be right where he wants us."

Tobiah looked from Carys to Iletus, distrust and skepticism coloring his face. He crossed his arms. "I will follow him."

Carys blinked and scoffed. "Didn't you hear Iletus? This is a trap."

"I don't care," Tobiah said. "He killed Shecayah."

Iletus sighed. "You go to your death."

"If that is the will of El, so be it," Tobiah said. "I will go alone, if I must. You will tell me how to find this passage. I will face this elf."

Carys ran a hand over her face. "Don't do this, Tobiah." She had gotten to know the man over the last few days, tracking with him. She hadn't liked him at first, when she first arrived with Zalman at Taggart. He and Shecayah seemed divisive. But she realized over time the honor in the man and the love he possessed for his wife. She didn't want to see him go to his death. "Not like this. Feels like a waste."

"I will go with him," Iletus said.

Carys' brow shot up. "B-but ... you're the one saying it's a shoggin' trap!"

"Remember he threatens my daughter," Iletus said. "If she's still alive. There may not be another opportunity. If he reaches Tanicus, my daughter is dead. The trap is my last chance to stop him."

Iletus drew the unforged sword from its sheath. He held it in his hands and looked at it. "Perhaps this is my destiny, after all. We set a trap for her. She was once our friend, a fellow warrior that stood by our side before Tanicus rose to power."

Carys took a deep breath. *Elowen.*

"She died that night, burning to death," Iletus continued. "And here I am, with an unforged sword, walking into another one of Julius' traps. With an unforged sword, she almost beat the three of us. I wonder if it will be the difference again. The cycle will be complete."

"Cycle?" Carys said. "What breakin' cycle? Different city, for one, and you won't be going alone. And I doubt she chose to spring his trap. You'll be going with a man who simply wants revenge."

Tobiah bared his teeth. "It is justice, Carys."

Carys bit her lip. "Not a clear line between them, seems to me."

Iletus lowered the sword and faced her. "Go home, Carys. You and Zalman. Go home. This is not your fight."

"Home?" Carys balked. "Where is that? I've never had a home, not like you mean. I've spent my life traveling across this world, one place after another, running to or from something." Tears rose in her eyes. She reached out, knowing Zalman's hand would meet hers. It did. "We didn't come this far together to let you go the rest of the way without us. That's not how this works."

Iletus' eyes softened. "Go back to Caleb, then."

"You think it's safer there with him?" She chuckled. "You know better by now. Besides, this elf trap might underestimate the four of us. We'll have a better chance together."

Carys peered up at Zalman.

He frowned down at her. "Guess we're walking into a trap together."

"Maddy plan if I've ever heard of one," Carys said.

Zalman grinned at her. "What else is new?"

———

Caleb was on his horse at the front of the moving column. The *Hamon-el* traveled from Giannis when Mother Natali came to speak with him.

A large portion of the former citizens of Giannis stayed in the town with a division of the *Hamon-el*. One of the *Sohan-el*, Kenneth, who had been at the Battle of Ketan, stayed with Andos and the Stewards and a force of 653 trained soldiers to lead and protect the people. Andos knew he was not a strategist and was better used in the town. Now that Macarus was a part of the *Hamon-el*, no elf would garner more respect from the other elves – a military hero and son of a prominent senator that opposed Tanicus.

The organization of Giannis came together quick enough to allow the rest of the army to leave that next day. Macarus rode next to him on his own horse. Caleb could look up and see the flying tiger circling their column, a figure he knew to be Eshlyn riding upon him. The sight gave him hope; and he knew he was not the only one. The humans and elves, all in a tense unity with new divisions, walked and worked with new purpose.

Mother Natali rode up on Eshlyn's horse. "Leave us."

It took Macarus a moment and a glance to Caleb to confirm.

"Yes, Mother," Macarus said, and he slowed his horse to join others five mitres behind.

Mother Natali simply stared ahead. Normally, the silence wouldn't bother Caleb, but her presence intimidated him. She was small and old but not weak. She exuded strength.

"We are honored to have you, Mother Natali," Caleb said. "May I ask why you have left the Saten to visit us?"

He saw her suppress a grin. "You are a sword, after all. Strike first to control the battle. Does that always work?"

"No," Caleb said. "But it is better than the wait."

"You believe that? I wonder if you will still believe that in the coming days."

Caleb didn't respond.

"You misunderstand, however," she continued. "I am not here to do battle."

"Then why have you come?"

"And he presses the attack," she mumbled. "You are the one, aren't you?"

Caleb sighed. "I did not choose this."

"That is not what you intend to say."

"Really? What did I intend?"

"What you intended to say is, you did not want this," she answered. "If you tell me that you did not desire to lead an army, or a revolution, that I will believe. But we often choose that which we do not desire to achieve what we desire above all else."

"Choice? My whole life has been chosen for me. A prophecy written thousands of years ago is determining my destiny."

"You were chosen, that is true. But that does not mean you did not choose. Both are true." Natali nodded over her shoulder. "This is an army of elves, dwarves, and humans, united and trained. That does not happen by happy accident. Every step of the way, you made a choice that led you here. You chose to protect the weak, fight the oppressor and free the oppressed. I suspect it happened in your earliest memory."

Caleb thought of a cave in the foothills to the south near Anneton, a dark place where he held his sister while he heard his mother scream in horror and pain. The scars on his back itched and he shifted in his saddle.

"At every turn, you've chosen to place yourself at great risk to protect and save others. That has drawn the revolution to you."

He thought of Reyan in the Pyts, of Tamya in Anneton, of exposing his identity at Ketan. Choice after choice.

"But not always," he said. "I just let Carys go to fight the First Bladeguard without me. I can't protect her where she is."

"I believe that, for you, letting your sister go is the greatest risk of all, the greatest sacrifice. Or perhaps denying the love of a woman. I'm not sure which."

To be honest, he didn't know either.

"Which leads me to why I am here," Mother Natali said. "I wanted to thank you."

Caleb frowned at her.

"Does that surprise you? I am old, and my time on this temporary land draws to an end. But I was a young woman when the Kryan Emperor attempted to lay the final nail in the coffin of faith in this land, in the world. I wept until I could not weep anymore. To witness the rebirth of faith and the emergence of the *Hamon-el*, it has been the greatest gift of my life. When the Mahakar desired to return to the *Bashawyn*, I took the opportunity to come and see the sword with my own eyes."

Mother Natali turned to him, and he saw her eyes glisten.

"I wanted to say thank you. Thank you for making those choices, from your youngest days to today. The whole world is in your debt. I wonder if you know what you have begun."

The air was still and the sun warm on his shoulders.

Mother Natali sniffed. "And that I am sorry."

"Excuse me?"

"You wear an unforged sword, a supernatural weapon from beyond this world. But you were forged to hold it, Caleb. Every choice, every sorrow, every wound became a scar and hardened you, strengthened you, made you the sword. El is forging you for what you must do so the world can be reborn. And I am sorry for the heat and the scars. But they were necessary.

"Take heart, however. Great sorrow leads to great joy. Many believe joy is the path to greater joy, but that is not the way of it. Sorrow digs furrows in our heart, deep chasms where joy can fill what was once empty. Many attempt to avoid the sorrow, but they are shortsighted and only rob themselves of the later joy. The greater the sorrow, the greater the joy in the end. I believe that the path you've chosen will lead to more joy than any has ever known before today, except perhaps Yosu himself."

Caleb's jaw tightened. "You said *forging*, as if El isn't done."

Mother Natali blinked, and tears fell down her cheeks. "I did. What do you believe we are marching towards? It will be a battle like the world has not seen in thousands of years. You are not yet the sword you need to be. There is great sorrow ahead, *Brendel*. And for that I am truly sorry. More than you know."

Caleb lowered his head and closed his eyes. "Break me."

"Yes." Natali's voice cracked. "I believe he will."

Who will break me? El or Tanicus? But he was too afraid to ask it. It probably didn't matter.

——

Zalman was almost too large for the passage through the wall. His body ached from bending over and crouching forward. The secret passageway had been made for elven Bladeguard, not a man bigger in both directions.

Zalman wished they had left their packs outside the wall.

Iletus had led them to the northern side of the city, although they took the long way to do it. There would be spotters on the top of the wall, so they kept to the brush and trees. The sun set by the time they made it to the wall. They took advantage of the shadows. Dark clouds gathered as they reached the wall, the air thick with the promise of rain. Rumbles in the sky confirmed the coming storm.

Zalman was glad that he didn't have to be as quiet. They were walking into a trap, after all.

Zalman didn't know if the dim light had anything to do with it, but he couldn't see the crack in the stone of the wall that Iletus pressed to open the passageway. A small door slid in and down with a hiss. They all stood there for a moment, peering into the blackness within. No one said a word as Iletus drew his sword and entered. Tobiah followed. Carys made him go next so she could bring up the rear of the group, her bow set with an arrow.

They walked forward in the dark, the passage narrow and short enough to feel their way forward.

Even though the passage seemed to be straight and uniform, Zalman hit his head on the ceiling more times than he could count. Every time, he would grunt or curse, and he could hear the sighs of annoyance from Iletus in front of him and Carys behind.

The axes hung at his belt, and he used his hands to follow the grooves in the brick to his right and left. The muscles in his thighs groaned at him.

They had been walking for less than a half hour when he heard a scratching sound in front of him.

"Another door," Iletus whispered. "Get ready."

Zalman didn't know what was on the other side of that door, but he felt relief that the trapped, claustrophobic feeling would soon end. Only, unless it was a smaller passage beyond.

He unhooked the axes at his belt, holding them in his hand, and he heard the others jostle in the small space to get their weapons.

The passage fell silent except the breathing, then the sound of Iletus searching for the way to open the other door. With a crunch, a crack of light appeared, a white and dim light, and the door slid down like the other one had. Zalman heard the patter of water on the stone ahead. The rain came while they maneuvered the tunnel.

Zalman saw Iletus as a shadow. The elf bent down and stepped out of the passage and into the dark and rain. Tobiah followed, and then Zalman lurched through, the drops falling upon his bald head and the shoulders of his tunic. Zalman ducked to his right side to give Carys room.

The four of them stood in a wide alleyway or street, perhaps five mitres wide or more, with tall brick buildings on either side.

Three figures stood at the end of the alleyway, ten mitres away. Lightning flashed, and the light gleamed off of golden armor on two of them – helmets and full armor made of gold. They held golden swords in their hand. In between them was an elf in a long black robe. One side of his face was scarred with burns. He was bald with a single braid down the back of his head. He held a sword, as well.

"Julius," Iletus said.

The elf in the center moved forward. "Iletus."

"Those others are Sunguard?" Carys asked.

The Sunguard. The Emperor's personal guard.

Iletus nodded. He spoke low enough so that only they could hear. "Carys and Zalman, you take the Sunguard, if you can. Tobiah and I will face the Bladeguard."

Zalman bristled at the *if you can*, but then he realized that the Emperor's personal guard might be better than he could imagine. He grunted.

"Come this far," Carys said. "Let's do it."

Zalman looked down at her, and he leaned down. She met his mouth with a kiss. They separated, and their foreheads touched.

So much he wanted to say, things that didn't matter like *be careful* and *do your best* and *kill the shogger* and other things she already knew.

"I love you," he said.

"You too, big gedder."

He grinned.

Iletus and Tobiah walked forward, their weapons ready. Carys moved to the right to face one Sunguard. Zalman rolled his large shoulders and stomped forward through a puddle to the one on the left.

He blew out a breath in the rain, spitting water. The clouds rumbled overhead. He held the axes in a loose grip.

The Sunguard separated a few paces from Julius, facing Zalman. The Sunguard raised his left hand, the one not holding the golden sword.

Over the hum of the rain, he heard Carys cry out, "Shoggers!" He didn't turn in her direction, however. He said a little prayer to El, trusting she could handle whatever it was.

His Sunguard's empty hand shook, and Zalman frowned, now within ten paces of the guard. The sound of scraping and cracking reached his ears, and it came from the ground before him. Three bricks lifted from the ground and hovered in the air before him. Zalman froze.

The bricks shot towards him, and the Sunguard rushed him.

Zalman moved.

—┼—

Carys approached the Sunguard at an angle, sliding to her right while the guard lifted his sword in both hands. She raised her bow, aimed for his neck, and fired.

She watched while the rainwater stopped falling, hovered in the air, and then coalesced into a ball of water a half mitre in diameter. This all happened in a split second – if she had blinked, she would have missed it – and her arrow pierced the ball of water and stopped.

"Shoggers!" She wove back to the left. She fired one arrow after another with varying targets like his knee or his head or his arm. The sphere of water grew bigger and flattened, like a shield over his body, more rainwater being drawn into the form.

The Sunguard moved his sword, and tentacles of water shot towards her. She ducked one but the second struck her shouder like a hard punch. She cried out and dodged a third.

Carys dropped the bow and drew the unforged sword.

She maintained her battle stance while she moved toward the Sunguard. More tentacles of water reached out for her, and she was able to block or cut through them. She was within two paces of him now, and with a wide swing, she cut through the water shield the Sunguard had made for himself. It shattered, throwing water in every direction, and her sword met his with a spark.

"Let's see what kind of swordsman you are," she said.

———+———

Julius watched the two men walk up the alley to him.

"Your daughter is dead," Julius said. "Because of your betrayal. You know that, don't you?"

He saw Iletus hesitate. The elf blinked slow. "I have no reason to believe you, one way or another. She may have been dead from the beginning. Neither you nor Tanicus have been people of your word."

Julius gripped his sword. "Have we not? It doesn't matter. You've betrayed your own country for these *humans*." Julius sneered at the dark skinned man.

Julius didn't honestly know the fate of Iletus' daughter. The Emperor had not told him whether she was alive or dead, only that he could use the threat as leverage. Iletus was experienced enough in the manipulations of a Bladeguard to realize that it didn't matter. Julius didn't see a moral problem. Who cared what a traitor believed?

"It is not for them," Iletus said. "It is for my own sanity, my own conscience."

"Your conscience dictates you betray your Emperor, your gods?"

Iletus' face fell. "They were not worthy gods to serve."

"We shall see," Julius said.

The dark skinned man moved to flank him.

"And who is this?" Julius asked, narrowing his eyes at him.

"I am Tobiah," the man said.

"Ah, the husband of the woman I killed."

They were within a few paces of him now, the man on his left, Iletus on his right.

Tobiah bared his teeth at him. "Justice will find you tonight. One way or another."

Julius shook his head. "I doubt it."

And then Tobiah struck to his left first, wanting to draw him in, but the elf was good enough not to take the bait. The man parried easily with those curved blades perpendicular to his fists. The weapons didn't seem practical; one would need to get close to the opponent.

The man blocked with his right and then attempted to spin within Julius' reach and punched toward his midsection. Julius leapt back and away, Tobiah's fist blade missing him, but only barely.

Julius frowned. He knew Iletus wasn't skilled enough for this battle. They both were aware of that from years of experience. But this man was an unknown. Julius had lived long enough to understand that to underestimate an opponent was as good as death. You would pay the gods eventually.

Iletus darted in and struck at Julius. Julius deflected the strike and ensured he kept his position away from the man. That was Iletus' design, to distract while the man could get close enough.

They danced like this for a few seconds, both Tobiah and Iletus attacking from one side or the other, each attempting to find an angle that could get through his defenses. The man was faster than Julius would have thought, and Iletus had improved somehow. The man and Iletus attacked simultaneously, and with a desperate slice from Tobiah, Julius felt a slight cut along his upper arm. Not serious, but the man had been able to get through.

This may be more difficult than I thought.

———

Zalman knocked two of the bricks aside, but he had to duck the next one. He moved directly into the Sunguard's golden sword. Zalman was able to deflect it with an axe, and the golden blade sliced along his calf, stinging.

Something hard hit his shoulder from behind, and it knocked him forward into another attack from the Sunguard. He had no time to react, other than to throw his large body forward into the guard, surprising and knocking him off balance. Zalman swung an axe at the elf's head, but the guard dodged the swing.

Another brick flew at him and struck the back of his knee. Zalman stumbled and blocked the golden blade coming towards his chest. He struck out with the other axe, and it glanced off of the shoulder armor. He hadn't the leverage while stumbling to put force behind it.

In his periphery, Carys dealt with water coming at her like long fingers.

The Sunguard were magicians, like the Moonguard had been. He thought it was illegal. How many breakin' magicians were there in the

Empire? And how many was he going to have to fight? He wished he had an unforged sword. Perhaps it would have protected him.

Zalman pressed forward, knowing that he should try to stay close to take away the Sunguard's advantage, but the Sunguard retreated. Zalman tripped over holes in the ground where bricks used to be, and a brick slammed into his back. He kept his feet but almost dropped an axe.

Zalman growled and came forward swinging the axes in a figure eight pattern. The Sunguard's defense was efficient as he blocked. Two more bricks rose above Zalman's head and lowered. He stepped to the side, swatting one to the ground with a wet crunch and avoiding the other.

Shaking his head of rainwater, he barreled towards the guard. A brick came at his head, but he knocked it away. He attacked with his axes, as fast as he could and still maintain control, fueling with his anger. The Sunguard retreated. He parried with his sword, and while Zalman overwhelmed him with his attacks, he put the wall of the building to his back so he could see the bricks as they came at him. Bricks joined the Sunguard offensive, but Zalman focused and either dodged or blocked them.

He was wearing the Sunguard down. Zalman controlled his breathing, kept the energy and control. The axes were blurs in his hands, shards of stone and concrete mixing with the rain on his face as he fought.

The wall behind him croaked and moaned, like the stone protested. The Sunguard lowered his sword and backed up.

Zalman dove away from the wall; it came down on top of him.

—+—

The Sunguard was pretty good, after all.

Carys held her own for a few moments, pressing, striking high and low. They circled one another, and he sliced back at her. He was fast, but not faster than he. The unforged sword sung in her hand.

In her periphery, Zalman was having trouble, as well, bricks pulled from the floor of the alley and hurled at him. The Sunguard were wizards, too? Who knew? But it made sense that the elves closest to the Worldbreaker were also illegal users of *Tebelrivyn*. She needed to help Zalman; he didn't have an unforged sword. But she had trouble enough on her own.

She ducked a strike and swung upwards, which he avoided. Carys spun and kicked. The guard blocked and stabbed straight towards her. She deflected the blade, pushing him back with her shoulder. He threw a backhand with his left golden gauntlet. She reeled and countered with a wide swing, more desperate and designed to create necessary space, which it did. The Sunguard hopped back easily, but it gave her the second she needed to strike.

Carys had the Sunguard on his heels when she heard the loud, deep creaking and cracking from Zalman's direction. Without taking her eye off her own Sunguard, she saw a piece of the wall behind her husband break free and fall on him as he jumped away.

Zalman ... In the distraction, her block wasn't quick enough, and the Sunguard's golden blade sliced at her left side below her ribs, opening a gash. She cried out, bending over from the pain.

The Sunguard advanced.

✦—

Julius centered and calmed himself. He continually moved, leaning forward or back, leaping over a strike. He kicked at the man while striking at Iletus with his sword.

He fell into the rhythm, the dance, of battle. It had been two centuries or more since he had fought for his life. When Tanicus first sent for him, Julius resented being extricated from his life of solitude and contemplation. But seeing the *Brendel,* his leadership, and the army he led to face Tanicus, he knew the Emperor was right to call.

Here was Iletus, once a great patriot and one of Julius' closest companions, trying to kill him. If this *Brendel* could turn Galen and Iletus against the Empire, what more could the man do? The man must be stopped at all costs.

On another level, Julius found he had missed the action, being a part of a larger purpose, the cause of the nine gods. He missed the battle, the adrenaline. The challenge. He wouldn't have known it if the Emperor had not sent for him.

He entered that place of nothing, where death and life did not matter, only the dance, the flow of battle. Once he found it in his mind, the patterns became clear, how Iletus favored his right, still, after all these years, and how the man's defense and guard was low. He recognized the patterns; he waited for a mistake.

Tobiah was good. In the nothing-place, he impressed Julius, an obejective and emotionless thing, a recognition of skill alone. As it happened with battles between experienced warriors, one had to simply wait for the mistake. And not be the one who made it.

The man spun and kicked as he ducked the counterattacks Julius threw at him. One blade struck high, then another at his waist. Julius' sword was a blur as he blocked the man's attacks. Iletus circled and sought a better angle.

The man punched forward with both blades at once, his teeth clenched, an angry grunt coming from his mouth, and that's when he made his mistake. The man overextended in his anger, and Julius stepped to the side.

He brought his sword down and across in a horizontal slice that the man did not have the time to avoid.

Julius cut through the man's stomach, a deep and killing gash. Intestines spilled, and the man coughed while he spit blood, falling to his knees.

Iletus yelled, "No!" from the other side, but it was done. Julius stepped through and pivoted to cut the man's head from his shoulders. It was a mercy.

Julius sighed as he faced Iletus. "I killed the wife and her husband. As the nine gods willed it."

Iletus glared at him.

The two Sunguard using their magic and martial skills to fight the big man and the woman. In that glance, Julius knew both Sunguard would kill their opponents.

"I suppose it is down to you and me," Julius said.

Iletus watched him, his face twisted in anger.

The rain fell straight down, a constant patter on the brick and stone as a background to the violence around and between them. They were both soaked. The man's blood mixed with the puddles of water at Julius' feet.

There was so much Julius wanted to say, to plead with his friend, but as he looked at the elf, his fellow patriot, there was no use. The only argument left would be settled with swords.

Julius lifted his blade.

Iletus, his long red hair plastered on his head from the rain, leapt and spun in his attack.

—+—

Zalman managed to avoid most of the bricks that erupted from the wall, but a few of them had struck him. Lying on the floor of the alley, he tried to roll over to get up, but several bigger stones and bricks pinned his leg. He shook his head; he had lost the axe from his right hand. Spitting rain from his face, his head spun around to look for it. There it was a pace or so away.

Stretching out his right hand, he couldn't get to it.

The Sunguard approached him and raised his left hand. Several smaller pieces of concrete and stone also rose in the air. They hovered over Zalman's head and dropped.

Zalman covered his face with his left forearm, reaching for the other axe with his right. He felt scrapes and cuts across his skin, bruises along his chest and shoulders. He squirmed, trying to free his leg from the debris.

The Sunguard raised more debris – not what pinned him down, unfortunately – higher this time, and more crushed down upon Zalman.

A third session rained down. He had trouble breathing. The brick and concrete on his leg shifted, and his fingers brushed the axe. Almost. He knew he couldn't take another round of falling debris, so he gathered his strength and held his breath. He waited for the Sungard to take a breath, pausing, and he flung the axe in his left hand as hard as he could at the elf's head.

Perhaps the Sunguard was too focused on his magic, or he was tired, but he wasn't expecting Zalman to throw the axe. He attempted to duck, but he couldn't get out of the way. The axe blade didn't strike straight enough to split the Sunguard's helmet, but it hit hard enough to dent it. The axe clattered against the wall beyond as the Sunguard staggered and swayed, knees buckling.

The guard bent over and shook his head. He reached up and removed his helmet, which took effort. The helmet dropped to the ground with a clank, revealing an elf with close cropped dark hair.

And eyes that were all white. Something had been written into the elf's skin, writing Zalman didn't recognize. Those eerie eyes turned to him. Zalman woke from the moment. He was pinned without a weapon and the Sunguard had a sword.

The Sunguard stumbled forward, lifting his sword. Zalman reached for the other axe, and in doing so, his gaze showed him Carys was injured and retreated from the other guard. He had to help her, but had to get free of this one, first.

The Sunguard stood over him, swaying, and lifted the sword. When the sword was over his head, Zalman punched the guard's knee as hard as he could. Armor dented and the knee snapped. The sword came down without much direction, and Zalman slid his torso out of the way. The golden blade stuck into the ground. Zalman rolled, trapping it under him, and he grabbed the Sunguard's right arm with both hands.

And he bent it a way it should not go.

The bone made an audible snap, and the Sunguard fell back over the debris that covered Zalman's leg. *Why didn't he make any noise?* The elf's face didn't change from a flat expression. Zal didn't care who you were, that had to hurt. A lot.

The Sunguard shot him another glance without emotion and then scanned the ground for Zalman's axe. He found it, picked it up with his left hand, and limped forward toward Zalman. What did it take to put this elf down?

Needing a weapon, Zalman pulled the golden sword from underneath him and risked a look at Carys fighting for her life.

—+—

Carys denied feeling the pain in her side; she didn't have time to feel it, to think about it. She batted away the Sunguard's golden sword and tendrils of water, side to side, as she retreated towards the secret passage through the wall.

The Sunguard continued to attack, and all she could do was back away, one pace at a time.

Zalman was stuck under some rubble on the other side of the alley, but somehow he was still alive and fighting. She was amazed once more at the warrior she married. Would she ever get used to it?

She needed to help him, but she had to deal with this elf, first.

The Sunguard backed her into a dead end. He knew he had the advantage; she was wounded and tired.

She went on the offensive, trying to keep from being cornered like a caged grider. She struck high and low, a feint to the side and then spinning into a kick followed by a cut that met his thigh. The unforged sword sliced through the armor easily, but it was barely a scratch. The Sunguard was able to cut her on the upper arm, however. She cursed and leapt away, right where she didn't want to be.

Carys stood in the corner, and her shoulder hit the wall. She leaned against it and sucked in a breath while the Sunguard advanced.

Suddenly, a dozen, perhaps twenty, tendrils of water came at her. She cut through three of them, but most of them struck her like fists all over her body. She gasped and staggered under the barrage, and then the Sunguard stabbed at her heart. She screamed in anger and knocked it aside.

Out of the corner of her eye, something golden flashed from the other side of the alley in the dim, rainy night. She frowned in the instant before a golden sword skewered the Sunguard from behind, the blade exiting at a diagonal through his stomach. The Sunguard went rigid in pain, and Carys didn't hesitate.

She leaned forward with all her strength and ran her unforged sword into the Sunguard's heart.

Then the air seemed to shake and everything went white.

—+—

Zalman covered his face with both hands in the explosion, like the Moonguard in the dungeons of Galya. There were spots in his eyes when he opened them, and after they adjusted, he saw the figure of the Sunguard moving to kill him with his own axe, a lumbering gait. And Zalman didn't have any weapons.

He tried to blink the spots away from his sight and shake his head free of them, but when he looked for the other axe near him, it was too dark now. He searched with his hand, his fingers scraping only the ground and bits of brick.

He peered over his shoulder at the Sunguard in time to see an arrow ping off the armor of his upper chest. Another smacked off of the golden metal on his shoulder. He stopped and turned, and they both saw her at once.

Carys walked toward them, firing her bow. And he smiled. How did he deserve her?

She found her aim, finally, and one arrow found the space between the Sunguard's white eyes. The Sunguard fell to his knees and his whole form seemed to shiver.

Well, shoggit, and he covered his face again as the guard exploded and everything went white.

———+———

Julius blocked low and countered with a strike high. Iletus slid off his blade, turned it, and forced Julius to reel back with a wide swing. Julius came forward with a kick and a backhand. Iletus stepped in to absorb the attack with a lifted leg and a shoulder so he could stab with his blade; Julius caught the stab with his own blade and attempted to twist the weapon out of Iletus' hand but was unsuccessful.

They both backed away with a flourish, panting.

Iletus had improved. It was difficult to discern at first, but Julius couldn't deny it now. He supposed that more time with Galen and a couple centuries of experience would explain it, but Julius also wondered if his own inactivity could account for his perception. Practicing forms alone kept one in shape, but it was nothing like extended battle with skilled opponents. Iletus had been a master before, one of the top swordelves in the world, but his forms had become more decisive and fluid, more graceful.

Iletus rushed in, a feint high and then a strike to the middle, which turned out to be a feint, also. Julius pivoted his body to get his blade around to deflect the low slash, and the blade cut the back of his thigh. Julius bared his teeth and hissed at the pain.

There was a flash and a deep sound of the air splitting. Julius cringed and leapt away from Iletus and the explosion. It took him a moment to realize that one of the Sunguard had been beaten and was now in pieces all over the alley. The woman had beaten the Sunguard. Scanning, the other guard still stood but staggered in a way that was not promising.

People had made attempts on the Emperor's life over the years. He had never known one of the Sunguard to be defeated, even when they had hidden their powers. Now these half-trained humans were about to beat two of them?

He didn't let these emotions overwhelm him, however. That would only ensure failure. Instead, Julius forced his breath into an even and consistent rhythm, finding strength and purpose within.

His nostrils flared. He pressed Iletus with a flurry of strikes that were both quick and brutal. Iletus met each attack with his own ferocity, but Julius was the better and forced Iletus to retreat a step as they darted back and forth. Julius scored a cut on Iletus' shoulder and then his forearm.

Within the place of nothing, the place where he didn't care whether he lived or died, the place where the game was the focus, Julius grinned. He could play it out from here. He saw the dance and how it would end.

Iletus leapt into a wide and desperate attack, putting all his effort into the two-handed swing. From his position, Julius' only choice was to raise his blade to take the full brunt of it, preparing to strike with his left hand into Iletus' throat since the elf came too close. Their blades met, and Iletus' sword sheared his in half, the top of the blade ringing and spinning away.

Julius could only watch as Iletus' sword continued unabated on its path and then sliced through Julius' left forearm.

In that split instant, Julius refused to feel pain or shock as his bloody appendage flopped to the ground. He was close enough to smell his opponent's breath, and he would not waste the opportunity. Julius took the remaining half of his sword and plunged it into Iletus' heart up to the hilt.

There was another flash and explosion, another Sunguard dying, but it was distant to the two elves, like brothers for so long, in a violent embrace.

Iletus spit blood, his eyes bulged, and he fell on his back, Julius' sword still stuck in his lifeless body.

Julius could not hold back the pain another second. He gasped and fell to his knees, holding his bloody stump with his right hand. He sucked in deep breaths.

Looking up, there were still two humans alive. Wounded, but alive.

Julius raised a knee and reached down with his right hand to tear a piece of black cloth from the bottom of his wet robe. The rain splattered on his head, shoulders, and back. He used the strip of cloth to tie a tourniquet at the end of his left arm, tying it as tight as he could, painfully tight, and he groaned as he finished.

The battle wasn't over yet.

+—

Carys lifted the bricks and debris off of Zalman's leg. He was able to help her with the last of it. Zalman hopped up. "You're hurt."

She raised a brow at how he had trouble putting weight on his left leg. "So are you."

He touched her bleeding side, and she winced.

"I'll take my shirt off and bind that," he said.

She smirked at him. "You would."

He shrugged. "You could take your shirt off and wrap my ankle."

Carys scoffed. "Shut up." She scanned the alley with pieces of golden armor and Sunguard around them, blood and gore mixing with the puddles of rain. "We made a mess."

"Better them than us." He nodded over to where Iletus and Tobiah lay on the ground, their bodies motionless, Tobiah's without a head. "They weren't so lucky."

Carys' heart dropped within her as Zalman limped to the entrance to the passage through the wall of Asya and knelt at their packs. She followed him, and they rummaged for the bandages. They didn't have time to sew her gash up, but washing it and wrapping her lower torso helped. Then she insisted they wrap his ankle.

When they finished, they looked to the figure at the end of the alley.

Julius, the first Bladeguard, stood there with a golden sword in his hand. The other ended in a stump with a torn black cloth as a tourniquet. He waited for them like a ghost.

The dark entry to the passage tempted her. She sighed as she gazed at it. They could go back to Caleb and the army, leave and fight another day. Then she looked up at Zalman. His brow was furrowed, but his eyes spoke of love and confirmed what was in her heart.

"He killed Shecayah," she said.

"And Iletus and Tobiah," he answered.

Carys nodded.

Zalman leaned in and kissed her. When he stood straight, he nodded back at her.

They faced Julius together and walked forward. She held her bow and nocked an arrow. Zalman lumbered to the left and picked up one of his axes. Then he veered to the middle and bent over to pick up Digby's unforged sword that lay next to Iletus' body. Zalman grunted in grief, anger, and pain as he stood and glared at Julius. Carys knew, from that glare, that one way or another, the First Bladeguard would die that night.

They stood ten paces from him.

"You could have left," Julius said. "I would have allowed it."

Carys shook her head. "Sorry. Not in the mood for banter. You ready, you big gedder?"

Zalman rolled his shoulders and lifted the unforged sword in his right and an axe in his left. He nodded.

Carys fired once then again from the right as Zalman approached from the left. Julius swatted the first arrow away and cut through the second. She fired twice more before Zalman reached the elf and engaged him with both weapons. She moved forward and aimed at his feet. While dodging the unforged sword and deflecting the axe, the elf managed to lift his feet at the last moment to avoid the arrows.

She was within five paces of Julius when she ran out of arrows. She didn't hit him once. Carys threw down the bow and drew her unforged sword.

Circling Julius, she attacked from behind. Julius pressed Zalman, engaging both weapons in a flurry, and then he spun to meet her attack. She noticed how he wouldn't meet her sword fully but redirected it instead. She tried to force his hand, but he was too good.

Zalman darted from the side, and Julius leapt into a back, one-handed cartwheel and kicked the axe from Zalman's hand. Carys sprinted forward and was on him by the time he finished the cartwheel. He slid to the side as she swung and then countered with a deft flick of his wrist and blade that she scrambled to block. Carys clashed blades with him for a few seconds until Zalman could recover his axe and stumble forward to flank the Bladeguard.

Her side ached and stung as she adjusted her position and attempted to create an opening for Zalman. Julius overcompensated, the unforged blade in Zalman's hand brushing the back of the black robe as he passed. Julius whirled around in a blistering attack that drove Zalman to a knee between her and the Bladeguard.

She ran forward and leapt, yelling, "Hold!" to her husband, hoping he understood. Planting her left hand on his right shoulder, she flipped over Zalman. While her feet were in the air, she sliced at Julius, who was engaged with Zalman. Her sword opened a cut on his chest. Carys completed the flip, surprisingly, but her right food landed on a piece of debris. Wet, it slipped out from under her, and she sprawled.

Julius kicked at Zalman's injured ankle, which Zalman was able to hop, but it allowed Julius to run towards her as she rolled on the wet and bloody ground. Carys completed her roll and came to her knees in time to intercept the golden blade on her unforged one. She grunted under the strain and leaned forward to punch Julius in the groin. His knees buckled, and a whine released from his lips. It gave her time to stand and strike back, which Julius had to retreat from as he blocked.

Zalman re-entered the fight, Digby's sword and his axe like blurs that Julius was able to defend somehow. Julius ducked a vicious and powerful swing of the axe, and Zalman's body bowed forward. When Julius rose up, Zalman was able to change direction and come back with an elbow to the Bladeguard's face. Carys heard a crunch and smack as the elf's head snapped.

Zalman turned with the axe, but Julius was already going with his body's momentum and turned it into another back flip, both legs kicking at

Zalman and catching him underneath the chin, teeth clattering. The large man reeled backwards, his eyes rolling back in his head, staggering.

Carys already sprinted forward and took swings at Julius as he finished his flip, which he deflected. He countered with strength and stabs so precise that Carys could only be impressed as she was driven backwards. Using the flat of his blade, Julius slapped her blade down and stabbed her in the upper chest, above her right breast, deep. Julius slammed the stump of his arm into her face, catching her in the eye. Spots exploded in her sight, and she was dazed while he lifted the golden sword over his head to finish her.

She was knocked flying to the side as a big figure caught the strike. With her vision clearing, she watched helpless while the golden blade stabbed straight through Zalman's lung. Zalman coughed but he did not hesitate to bring his axe weakly down onto Julius' back.

Julius cried out and knocked the axe from Zalman's hand with his stump and shoved on Zalman's chest with his shoulder. The axe fell from his back, trailing blood. Zalman fell, and Julius pulled the sword from Zalman's body and cut across his throat.

Zalman's eyes bulged and his face went pale white as blood gushed from the gash on his throat, soaking the front of his shirt.

"NO!!" A long, wailing sound from the depths of pain she could not truly understand.

Julius lumbered backwards, gasping and wheezing, taking several steps away from Zalman.

Carys barely saw him. She ran and dropped next to Zalman. His body was still.

She released her unforged sword into the water and blood, and she gripped his tunic. She shook him. "No, no, no, no, no …." He made no response. He was in a world beyond.

He was gone.

Carys buried her face in his crimson soaked tunic and emitted a wail.

Her uncle, the Prophet, had died from the sword of a Bladeguard far to the west. This was worse.

She didn't know how much passed when she looked up and glared at Julius.

He knelt three mitres away, bleeding from a gash on his chest and another wound on his back, his stump dripping blood through the makeshift bandages.

Carys picked up her unforged sword in her right hand. Then she grabbed Diby's from Zalman. Drops of water fell from the blades as she stood.

Julius sighed and lowered his head before joining her.

Bleeding from her side, her arm, and now her chest, she knew she didn't have enough time. It was more and more difficult to breathe.

El. I only ask one thing. Help me kill this elf. Whatever it takes. Help me.
The unforged swords hummed in her hand.

She bared her teeth, and she attacked. On the one hand, she didn't know how the Bladeguard was still moving, and on the other, she moved with more purpose and efficiency than she ever had. She thought of Caleb and his training, Esai and his, but it was more than that. The swords swung with her and led her at the same time.

Their swords clashed over and over. She felt no pain. It was odd. She felt peace.

She saw the opening. Julius overextended, and there was no resistance to both swords as they ran through his heart.

Julius' golden blade had been deflected; however, it drove under her left breast.

Carys held onto both unforged swords as Julius slid off of them, falling onto his back, open, glassy eyes that saw nothing. He took the Sunguard sword with him. It pulled from her chest, spraying blood.

Her head swam, her knees buckled, and she crumbled to the ground. She found herself lying on her side.

She could see her husband, laying not a few paces away. With her left hand, she reached out for him, but she couldn't touch him. He was too far.

She wished her brother was there, to hold her as he used to when she was a child. He used to make her feel so protected and safe. She didn't want to be alone. Not now. Not for this.

But she was.

She closed her eyes, her final tears mixing with the rain.

CHAPTER 26

THE BATTLE OF ASYA 1
THE BEAUTY OF GOOD

Caleb sat on his horse at the top of the hill, the morning sun forcing his eyes to narrow as he looked to the east. With him were Macarus and Jaff, also on horses. Bweth and Gunnar stood on the ground in front of the horses. Eshlyn loomed just behind him on the Mahakar.

The storm from the night before had blown over, and while the ground was still soaked, the sky had cleared. The dawn light was hazy and thick with humidity. Caleb gazed at the city; it looked surprisingly clean and peaceful in the silence. But within that city, great violence waited to be unleashed. He wondered if they were ready.

The *Hamon-el* arrayed behind him. Five major divisions faced the walls of Asya, each one led by a *Sohan-el* – Xak, Wes, Kenneth, Ewha and Jaff. Bweth was assigned to Xak's division, Eshlyn to Wes, Gunnar to Ewha, Caleb to Kenneth, the division in the center, and Jaff was responsible for his own. Each division had elves and humans, fighting together. Ewha was lucky enough to have Gunnar and Steelsides with her.

The cavalry waited in front of the divisions. One hundred Liorian bosaur at the front with five hundred horses behind them. The Liorians rode the bosaur, but the horses were a combination of elves and humans. Macarus led the cavalry.

Interspersed among the cavalry, 30 catapults and 20 ballista were pointed down the hill at the wall. Measured by Macarus and Bweth, they held a position seven hundred mitres from the main gate of Asya, far enough away to be out of range of any siege engines that sat on the top of the wall, and Caleb could see a hundred trebuchets. But they were close enough that their own catapults, adjusted by Bweth, could reach the base of the wall and the main gate.

"It's so quiet," Eshlyn said from behind him. She had left Javyn with Mother Natali in the camp half a kilomitre to the west. All the tents and supplies had been left there with the support staff and two more divisions to protect the camp or reinforce the lines.

"They're ready for us, to the sure," Bweth mumbled.

Caleb knew what Eshlyn meant. Before a battle, there were often these moments of quiet and calm, like the world was at peace, despite the death that waited just beyond the calm.

"They will make the first move," Macarus said. "The Emperor and the Lord General have been planning this for days."

"No, they won't," Caleb said. "I didn't come all the way for them to start this battle. We're going to let them see how Bweth improved their catapults. Bweth, let's knock on the door."

Bweth turned to him and grinned.

"All right, you shoggers!" she yelled back behind them. "Start your volleys!"

Caleb gripped the Kingstaff laying across his lap.

The catapults groaned and whistled as large stones flew through the air toward the wall of Asya.

So it begins.

Holding the stump where his arm used to be, Earon stood next to the Emperor at the top of a tower on the western side of the city that peeked over the wall. The battlefield lay out before them. Even without the peerglass, Earon could see the mass of troops to the west, the *Hamon-el.* On the wall of Asya, archers and trebuchets gathered with militan below them inside the wall. Thousands and thousands of elves, a sea of blue and gray steel.

Elves ran in and out of the spacious room to communicate with the Emperor.

Tanicus stood tall and imposing, his hands clasped behind him.

He had forced Earon to come and watch. Earon thought he might be able to fight and resist, get himself killed to end the wait and the pain, but he decided that might not work. The elf could take life and give it. Might make it worse. Instead, Earon decided to take advantage of the position and pray. And watch.

An echo of snapping wood and rope accompanied the dots in the distance that grew bigger as they approached from Caleb's catapults. The stones dropped and crashed against the wall and the gate, a noise that spread through the city.

Tanicus raised a brow. "Hmnn. Impressive." He nodded at Earon. "Another trick, however, will not save your *Brendel* this time. He stands to fight true power. You will see, Earon. You will see." Tanicus turned to an elven officer to his left. "Lietuenant, tell the General he may begin."

Earon lowered his head and prayed to El.

Three catapult volleys had reached the wall by the time there was movement from the Kryans. Caleb frowned. *Why aren't they firing back?* He raised the peerglass to his eye.

He heard the gasps all around him as bodies were thrown over the wall, dead bodies tied to the top of the wall that flopped like dolls as they came to the end of the ropes. They hung there, swinging in the wind. There was a body every mitre or two, hundreds of them, and as Caleb looked closer through the peer glass, he hissed as he noticed they were all drained of blood, simple husks that were once human.

"Great and mighty El," he heard Eshlyn from behind him.

"What happened to them?" Macarus asked.

"The shoggin' Worldbreaker." Bweth gazed up at Caleb. "He's trying to piff you off, get you angry and stupid."

"Well, the joke's on him," Caleb said. "They tried this before in Biram. Didn't do them any good. Besides, I brought an army to the walls of the strongest city in the land of men. I was already piffed and stupid."

"What do we do?" Jaff said.

The scars on his back itched. *Kill them all.* He rolled his shoulders. "We can't do anything for them now. We wait. We'll avenge them by bringing the whole Empire down. Wait for them to come to us. Keep firing the catapults."

Bweth shouted the order to continue, and a cloud rose from the city. Caleb brought the peerglass back to his eye. There were whistles coming from the top of the wall, coordinated.

"Smoke?" Eshlyn said. "Is he setting fire to the city?"

"No." Macarus used his own peerglass. "That's not a cloud. Those are grider."

Looking closer, Caleb saw the elf was right. They were grider. The scars from his battle with one itched on his body. He squirmed a bit in his saddle.

"There are a thousand of them," Bweth said. "Or more."

Caleb lowered his peerglass. "They are trained to attack humans, on scent of blood. Not elves. Macarus, send word to each division for the elves to get ready to protect the humans. Try to shoot them out of the sky. But be prepared with swords and spears, as well."

Macarus nodded and pulled the reins on his horse into a tight turn and rode off.

"I wonder if the grider have ever faced a Mahakar," Eshlyn wondered aloud.

Caleb glared at her over his shoulder. "Don't. There's too many of them."

Eshlyn rolled her eyes. "Has that ever stopped us before?"

The large tiger raised his head and roared. Eshlyn leaned down behind his head and grabbed ahold of his white fur as his enormous wings unfurled. The wind blew around them as the Mahakar shot in the air and flew toward the flock of grider.

Caleb could only watch her go.

Hunched over, Eshlyn drew her sword as they ascended, her heart beating hard in her chest. Her hair whipped at her face.

She could feel the tiger's anger, his anticipation and lust for battle. Was it due to the magic of the Worldbreaker or the grider? She remembered how he had attacked the trodall with such abandon and ferocity.

The grider had four wings and no eyes on their oval heads; their nostrils and ear-like structures were massive membranes. They navigated by smell and noise. They had six bony legs that ended in vicious claws.

The grider were within mitres, their screeching noises loud in her ears, and the Mahakar slowed to glide forward. He lifted his claws and opened his jaws wide and roared in return.

The grider shook with fear at the sound, their heads twitching. In their hesitation, the Mahakar attacked.

He swatted two down with his paws and grabbed another in his teeth, the screeching sound the grider made now one of pain. His front paws raised, and he tore the grider in half, blood everywhere.

They moved forward into the sea of creatures, and Eshlyn held onto the tiger's fur with her left hand and his shoulders with her thighs while she swung her sword at grider after grider. She sliced off wings and limbs and heads. The grider attacked from every side. She felt a scrape along her shoulder, a scratch, and a beak poked her back. These were minor injuries, but they seemed to further enrage the tiger.

She heard whistles from the wall of Asya, and more grider converged upon her and the tiger.

She gasped as a stone flew past them, taking out more grider, but it had been too close. *What the shog are they doing? That could have hit us.* But when she looked back at the *Hamon-el*, she could see they weren't firing.

Turning to the city wall in the distance, she saw more stones being shot at them from the trebuchets. Maybe they couldn't hit the front lines of the *Hamon-el*, but they could try to smack the Mahakar out of the sky.

Then arrows flew with a collective hiss toward them and their battle with the grider.

Down. Dive.

The Mahakar responded with a huff and drew his wings into his body. He dropped, head down. Wind ripped passed her as they dove at breakneck speed. Looking under her arm, she saw a hundred grider on their tail.

The tiger spread his wings and leveled out a mitre above the grass. Several grider could not change direction as well at that speed. Eshlyn heard crunching sounds as they hit the ground. With the rest still behind them, the Mahakar turned his wings vertical, catching as much air as possible, and he slowed. The tiger reached down and dug into the field with his claws. He dug furrows in the ground as he turned and spun to face the grider.

Dozens screeched in surprise as his fangs tore into them; his claws crushed them into the ground. One after another died from his attack. Eshlyn swung the sword with all her might, protecting the tigers back and hind quarters. She lost count of how many she cut through or dismembered.

We have to keep moving. A stone bounced off the ground a few mitres away. *We stay in one place and they can get our position and hit us.*

The Mahakar beat his wings with a growl and rose in the air again, spinning as he ascended, knocking several grider out of the sky with those powerful wings. Despite how many the tiger left dead behind him, more still flew after them.

Caleb rode across the line, guiding the horse with his knees. He swatted with the Kingstaff and sliced with the unforged sword, cutting many clean in two. Arrows from the humans and elves in the *Hamon-el* met grider in the sky, although many missed. Grider targeted the humans, so elves could also kill grider with spears when they got close.

Elves and humans paired up so elves could protect their comrades. Only a few humans died, but the grider had to get past their elven protectors first.

Eshlyn and the Mahakar had a few hundred grider engaged, but that wasn't even a third of the number. Driven on by the whistles from the wall, six or seven hundred grider fell into the *Hamon-el*.

Sprinting the horse back to his original position, Caleb could hear Bweth yelling at him. "Cal! They're usin' the distraction to put militan on the field!"

He knocked down a grider with the Kingstaff and cut the head off of another with his sword while he faced the city of Asya. He cursed. Militan poured out of the main gate of Asya.

It's a feint.

"We need to get the ballista and catapults firing!" he told Bweth.

Macarus rode closer to them. "Don't we need to wait for Eshlyn to get out of the way?"

Caleb stabbed a grider that flew at him through the torso and broke the neck of a second with the Kingstaff before he could answer.

He sighed and nodded at Macarus.

———

Arrows from the top of the wall arced toward them when they flew closer to the wall. The arrows fell short, but Eshlyn made sure to guide the Mahakar out of range of the elven archers.

And she kept him moving. They climbed high into the clouds, far above what the grider could accomplish, and then they would dive down into a concentration of grider. The ones that attacked them were growing less and less as the numbers dwindled.

Her right arm had several cuts, as did her left arm and shoulders, none of them deep. The tiger also sported a handful of injuries along his rear and legs, and a number of white feathers had been torn away in the fray.

The Mahakar could fly higher than the grider, so she flew the tiger up and out of range of arrow and catapult, as well. The hair on her arms and back of her neck shivered in the cold air, but those moments gave them some respite before the intense violence followed. She peeked down, and militan ran out of the Asyan gate. It was a gate large enough for wagons to enter twenty across and perhaps fifty mitres high. A whole legion was almost out of the gate, and another was right behind it.

She cursed under her breath. The grider were a distraction.

When they dove, she noticed a flurry of activity on the front line of the *Hamon-el*, like dots on the green grass. They seemed to be working around the catapults.

They need to get them working to start in on the legion. So we need to get the break out of the way.

She swung the sword Bweth had made her to the right and left, hacking into the creatures that remained. The Mahakar clamped down on two at once, tearing wings off with his front paws and kicking and clawing at three more with his back legs.

"Let's go, friend." The battle with the grider was ending. "We need to get back."

The tiger rumbled a low growl beneath her, and after killing a few more grider, they spun in the air to return to the *Hamon-el*.

They soared. Eshlyn sheathed her sword and looked back at the gathering legion. Something caught her eye coming from the city, and she squinted. Were those … humans? Tied to posts?

———

At a quick glance, Caleb noted two legions entering the field. His catapults and ballista would even the odds now that Eshlyn was out of the way.

Most of the grider were gone. Between the Mahakar and Eshlyn and the elves killing the creatures when they came close to a human, there were few deaths, although there were hundreds of injuries. They sent the more serious back to the camp, and the rest were bandaged. Caleb told them to send replacements for those seriously injured before the main battle began.

The Mahakar and Eshlyn returned, and he blew out a breath. He felt anger towards her for throwing herself into danger, although it was stupid of him to feel that way. He wasn't one to judge in that, to the sure. And what did he think would happen? There would be many casualties today.

"Bweth," he called with his gaze on Eshlyn and the tiger. "Are we about ready?"

"Hold!" Macarus called.

Caleb turned to face the elf as he approached on horse with a scowl.

Macarus pointed at the organizing legion. "Look."

Caleb put the peerglass to his eye and scanned the militan as they organized in their divisions. Several elves rode on horses and pulled a small wagon, each with a pole mounted upon it.

And humans were tied to those poles. Living men and women. He counted fifty of these interspersed throughout the two legions, and more were coming out of the city.

Caleb mumbled, "Cowards."

Macarus pulled up next to him. "What did you expect? Tanicus is in this to win, to crush you. He is an experienced general. He knows your weakness, and he's exploiting it."

Caleb sighed and lowered the peerglass. "Bweth! Hold until further notice."

Bweth walked up to join Macarus and Caleb as Eshlyn landed with the Mahakar in front of them.

Eshlyn met his gaze. He had to force himself not to get lost there. "You saw."

Caleb nodded.

Bweth cursed. "We can't shoggin' win today if we let him manipulate us."

"I won't fire and kill innocent humans," Caleb said.

"But that ain't our fault," Bweth argued. "He breakin' chose to put them in harm's way. The Emperor or General or whoever is responsible for them, not us."

"No." Eshlyn leaned over on the top of the Mahakar. "We are responsible. We can't fire and risk it."

Bweth scoffed. "Were we responsible for those dead bodies they got hangin' from the wall? They're only there 'cause we're here."

Macarus said. "That's true, but we can't kill ones that are alive. We have to find another solution."

"Then what're we gonna do?" Bweth's pregnant, armored belly stuck out with her hands on her hips.

Jaff rode up on his horse. "Cal. More humans." His face was conflicted. Gunnar ran up beside him, the thick armor clanking as he moved.

What now? He didn't want to look through the glass, but he did.

Humans came out of the gate, hundreds of them. They were not bound, however, walking in a loose formation past the militan. The humans wore tattered clothes and carried spears and gladi. *What's that on their face?*

"Are they attacking us?" Eshlyn asked in amazement.

Those clothes. Like the clothes the Prophet wore when they broke him from prison. Had the Emperor threatened them or their family? How had he …

Then Caleb saw their eyes. *White eyes. Like the ones in Ketan. Like Galen's when we fought. And the writing on their face and arms …*

"Wraith." He lowered the peerglass. "They are wraith. He made them wraith."

They all waited in silence and shock for a few moments.

"I know I'm the arse for sayin' it," Bweth began. "But ain't they dead already? I mean, there's no way back, right?"

"We don't know that," Eshlyn said through her teeth.

"I've never heard of a way back," Macarus said. "From what I've heard, they die when their mission is over. But that's rumor and legend."

"Galen changed back to himself when I stuck the unforged sword in his heart," Caleb said.

"But then they're still dead, right?" Jaff asked. "And we only have a handful of *Sohan-el* left."

Caleb hesitated then interrupted the litany of names of dead *Sohan-el* that began in his mind. "I don't know. But it means that there are ways, with El's help, to return from whatever it is that was done to them."

Eshlyn ran a hand through her tossled hair. "Like the healing of the Deadwater. With the water from the Stone."

"Or something like that," Caleb said. "But killing them now would be a hopeless act. They are alive, in a sense, and with El, there is hope."

Gunnar nodded. "The beauty of good, no matter the result."

"All fine as crit in a hole in the ground," Bweth said. "But *what are we going to do?*"

Jaff gestured to the east. "The legions are moving forward, using the humans as a shield."

He's right. The divisions advanced like a machine in divisions and platoons.

Eshlyn squinted. "Something else is coming out of the city."

Bweth leaned to the side to use her peerglass. "Trodall."

Caleb lifted his own peerglass. "Hundreds." The enormous, red and black creatures with four arms came barreling out of the main gate. He lowered the glass.

Macarus sniffed. "We need rope."

"Excuse me?" Eshlyn said.

"The cavalry," Macarus continued. "Bring up the supply wagons from the rear, and we can bind the wraith and gather them in the wagons."

Eshlyn's jaw dropped. "Like ranch boys?"

"There are a thousand of those wraith or more," Jaff said. "You think you can round them all up?"

"Not sure," Macarus said.

"Dangerous. They shall inundate you with arrows," Gunnar said.

Macarus' brow furrowed. "We have to try, right?"

"By El, we do," Caleb said. "Go get the rope and the cavalry. The rest of us, get the *Hamon-el* ready. Once we get past the wraith, our divisions have to engage theirs. Macarus, get word to the Liorians. We need the bosaur for the trodall. Jaff, spread word among our divisions. We do not kill the wraith. Injure, bind, incapacitate, whatever, but do not kill."

Gunnar placed his helmet on his head. "Allow the wraith within fifty mitres of the line."

"What are you going to do?" Caleb asked.

"I shall play the ancient part of bait," Gunnar said.

"What about those crittin' humans on stakes?" Bweth asked. "I might be able to hit one of their platoons or divisions once they clear."

"That's my job," Eshlyn said. "The Mahakar and I can rescue them."

"And go in among the legion?" Bweth said. "You maddy?"

Caleb hesitated before answering, wanting to come up with a better solution. He couldn't think of one. "Gonna get maddier by the minute. Let's move, everyone."

Eshlyn met Caleb's eyes one last time, a look of resolve. She patted the tiger's neck. He growled, spread his wings, and launched into the air.

He said another prayer to El. *Protect her, please. They will need her when I am gone.*

———

The Mahakar rose high above the wraith that wandered toward the *Hamon-el.*

There were maybe fifty of the humans on stakes, all positioned in front and middle of the militan. She pulled the peerglass from her belt and looked, worried that these were wraith like the others. But a glance told her they were not. They were bone thin, starved, and dressed in rags, but they did not have the white eyes or the writing on their bodies like the wraith – only the look of terror.

She guided the Mahakar to two that had been left in front of the lines, an old man and woman weeping and crying out in fear. Eshlyn drew her sword, and they landed between them. The militan paces away retreated and shouted, keeping spear and gladi pointed at them. Eshlyn hopped down, cut the bonds of the old woman, and helped her down.

While she worked on helping the prisoners, the Mahakar dove into the platoon of militan nearby, and he attacked. He swiped with his large paws and clamped down on elves with his fangs. Elves screamed and bodies flew mitres in the air.

Eshlyn hurried to the older man, cutting him loose. She gathered the old man and woman. "Come on!"

With a final smack with a paw, which sent three elves tumbling in the air, he leapt back to her. She threw the man and woman on the tiger and then climbed on in front of them. The Mahakar launched into the air.

Then the arrows began to fall. The tiger growled as an arrow hit his back. The woman squealed when one stuck in her leg, and the man coughed when another impaled his shoulder. An arrow barely missed Eshlyn's head as it passed. She needed to get a few shields next time.

They were out of range of the arrows in a few seconds. Safe, the Mahakar flew them back to the rear of the *Hamon-el* where physicians and others waited to bandage.

Eshlyn pulled the arrow from his back. He growled at her.

"Yeah," she said. "I know. You ready to go back?"

The Mahakar turned his head to the east.

Eshlyn jumped up and straddled his back. "Good boy."

The Mahakar snorted, and they were in the air again.

—✝—

Macarus gathered a loop of rope and joined the cavalry at the front of the line – 500 horses with humans and elves. Caleb and Jaff joined them.

The human wraith were sixty mitres away.

Gunnar and the Steelsides walked out thirty mitres from the front line.

"Gunnar," Macarus said. "How are you going to be bait?"

"We shall see if our machination is successful," Gunnar called back, his voice muffled under the helmet. "Please stand by."

"Until when?" Macarus asked.

"You shall understand when," Gunnar said.

When they were forty mitres from the front line, Gunnar, Ulf, and the rest of the Steelsides spread out. Then they crouched down into a little ball with their arms over their heads.

The human wraith reached the Steelsides, and they attacked.

The human wraith fell on the Steelsides with gladi and spear, hacking down upon them. The ringing of steel on steel echoed through the field. But as Macarus looked closer, he noticed that the armor protected the dwarves. Dented the armor, for the real, but the dwarves were protected inside.

Macarus was woken from his observation by Gunnar's voice. "Any time you are ready, Captain!"

Macarus grinned. *Dwarves.* He prepared a slipknot in his loop of rope, and he kicked his horse into action.

500 cavalry followed him.

They circled around the right side of the wraith, confusing them, and then Macarus gave the order to engage.

Macarus rode by a human wraith, a young man, and he threw the noose over head and shoulders, tightening once it reached the man's elbows. The human struggled, but he could not get free. Macarus tied the rope to his saddle and dragged the man back to the empty wagon.

Arrows arced in the sky, and they fell among the cavalry and the humans. Several of the humans were impaled with arrows and twenty of the cavalry suffered injuries, as well.

Macarus reached the wagon, and he finished securing the man, picked up another loop of rope, and returned to gather more.

"Drag them," Macarus ordered. "And keep moving."

The wraith seemed sightless, although that couldn't be true, and they continued to struggle against their bonds. It wasn't the perfect solution, Macarus knew, but this would keep them alive until they could figure something to do.

The *Hamon-el* ran past him towards the battle with a cry of passion and the *Sohan-el* at their lead, thousands of boots on the ground like thunder.

Bweth stood with two humans who worked the catapult at the center of the line. Well, it wasn't much of a line now with the *Hamon-el* advancing to engage the militan.

Her eyes scanned the battle with her peerglass. The Mahakar and Eshlyn lifted from one of the divisions with two tattered humans on the tiger with her. Arrows flew after her. Eshlyn had stolen a couple militan shields from somewhere to protect her and her charges.

Now that division was ready to target.

Bweth shook her head. "Smart girl. Maddy but smart." Then she spoke to the men with her. They had loaded the catapult. "Adjust two degrees right." She had to fire the stone ahead of the target so they would walk into it. "Shorten range, three hundred mitres. No, two fifty."

She held onto the wooden support as they adjusted and the catapult moved beneath her. "Stop." The men did. She waited. "Fire."

The catapult rocked as it fired, and she lowered the peerglass to watch the stone sail through the air and fall on the back part of the division. More than fifty militan scattered or crushed. Bweth sighed. She would have to do better next time.

From her position, she could see more activity at the gate. More trodall? No, they already had five hundred or so to deal with on the field. Behind the trodall were more militan.

"Holy crit of a crizzard," Bweth spat.

Legions of elves. They were already outnumbered two to one, not counting the trodall. But she didn't see any humans among them.

Bweth called down the line to the other ballista and catapult, "I need two catapult on the trodall and another ten on the gate!"

—+—

With the Kingstaff and the unforged sword, Caleb entered the fray. He left his horse behind with a runner so more of the humans could get to the supply stations to the rear.

Human wraith attacked him. He would cracked them on the head with the Kingstaff or smack them with the flat of his blade. They were difficult to knock unconscious, but he could incapacitate them enough for a cavalry member to grab them. Periodically, a volley of arrows would come his way, and he would use his weapons to clear the air of as many as he could, also protecting the human wraith.

The Mahakar soared overhead back to the line with two human prisoners on the tiger. Eshlyn used shields to catch arrows, although another had hit the tiger on its flank.

Caleb made his way through the center of the battle, along the main road to the Asyan gate. Platoons of *Hamon-el* fought on either side of him, elf and human together. They generally left the center to him alone, as they should. They would just get in the way. He and the cavalry needed to clear a path for the bosaur past the human wraith.

A stone whistled by and slammed into the middle of a platoon of militan ahead, where Eshlyn had just flown from. Bweth's aim was getting better. Two platoons of *Hamon-el* rushed in and engaged while the militan were vulnerable.

The battlefield was a roar of noise, of steel and crying and pounding of hooves and boots. He turned at the growling and snarling to the east. A column of trodall ran in his direction.

Caleb pushed three human wraith to the ground with his elbows and the Kingstaff. He crouched with his sword and staff and waited for them.

The whistling sound came again, and two large, jagged stones landed amid the trodall. He heard the screeching of pain but didn't have time to stop while he struck down the last two militan from a platoon.

A rumbling earthquake rose behind him, and one hundred bosaur tore up the dirt of the road as they galloped past him on either side to meet the trodall. Now he was the one in the way.

⊢—

Tamya held Aden's head in her lap. His eyes were closed, his face so peaceful. She stroked his hair but otherwise didn't move.

It was difficult for Tamya to know how much time passed. It seemed to be hours, but the sun never set.

Obasa, her mother. Berran. Her son Obasi, and his head bashed againt a rock. Dervan, a man she was supposed to protect. Hema, her protector. She thought of friends gone, people she tried not to love, but she had anyway – Athelwulf, Esai, Xander, others.

Now Aden.

Tamya felt her own failure deeply. She couldn't stop from using magic. Protecting him was her one job. Everyone she loved was bound to die.

She was freezing, but she didn't care.

"*Isael.*" Malaki's voice was like a tremor in the air behind her. "The battle of the *Brendel* begins. You have called us. We must go."

She shook her head. "I can't." She couldn't let him go.

"We must," Bael added from the opposite side, perched with his head hung low. "The *Brendel* will need us."

"I don't care," she said. "It doesn't matter. Nothing matters. Not anymore." She blinked, and a tear fell from her cheek. It turned to ice by the time it hit Aden's cheek.

"You do not mean that," Bael said.

"I do." *Everyone I love dies. Why go anywhere? Why do anything?*

Malaki snorted. "You believe death is the end of the story?"

Tamya didn't answer. She couldn't.

"Oh, beautiful, wonderful *Isael*. Death is not the end," Malaki continued. "All those you have loved and lost, they were born anew into a world more beautiful than you can imagine."

"Sure. Even I've heard that crit so much I could quote it. They're all resurrected into another place, and I'm sure they're all shoggin' happy." Tamya bared her teeth. "But I can't see that place. I'm the one left here."

The dragons lowered their heads even further.

Tamya wiped her eyes with the back of her sleeve, rough and cold on her face. "It doesn't matter. Not the battle, nothing."

Bael growled. "It matters, *Isael*."

"Maybe. But I'm the only one left. There were supposed to be two. And you saw what I did. I used magic. I got scared. How am I worthy to ride dragons? Supposed to be the righteous or whatever. Not … this. It was all about him. He was the one. I just … came along."

"We don't choose the worthy," Bael said. "El chose you as much as he chose your husband. He decides who is worthy. He has a reason, a purpose."

"What reason?" She clung to the bloody coat in her hand. "I can't leave him."

"I have not said that we would leave him," Malaki said. "You are both the *Isael*. It takes two, as you said. He must come with us."

Tamya scoffed. "Dead? You gonna fly around with a dead man? That's what El wants us to do?"

"*Isael*," Malaki whispered. "He is not dead yet."

Tamya sat up and spun on the dragon. She glared at him and wanted to throw all the ice and snow at him, bury him in her fury, which she barely held at bay. Her fists clenched. "What … what the shog … are you talking about?"

"Do you not know?" Malaki asked her. "You are the *Isael*, the one to bring us back. I thought you would know the power we hold. The power you called."

The dragon sighed, a monumental sad sound.

"The renewal is not something that happens in the next world alone," Malaki said. "It happens in this world, as well, when the Everworld touches it. Miracles happen."

The dragon lifted his foreleg and extended it to her, palm up.

When the Everworld touches this world … She closed her eyes. *Critters, where was Aden's mind when she needed it?*

Like the living water that touched the Deadwater. It was changed. Before her eyes.

Like Aden loved her so much that she learned to love and hope again. *Miracles happen.*

Then the memory spoke louder than the grief in her heart.

There had been a passage, words read to her on the flat grasslands near the lake … it said …

Tamya opened her eyes, and they bulged. "Your blood. It was in something Aden read to me about your blood. It can heal."

Malaki did not speak. He met her eyes.

Tamya moved and gently laid Aden down on the icy rock. She stood and approached the dragon's claw.

"But how?" The skin was supposed to be like armor. She frowned. She looked back at Aden ... and Xander's unforged sword.

She rushed back and grabbed it from the gound. She brushed Aden's face once with the back of her fingers. Then she hopped up and ran to the dragon. She raised the unforged sword. It hummed in her cold, numb hand. She looked up at the dragon.

The dragon nodded. "Hurry. There is not much time. He needs you."

Tamya lowered the sword and cut a deep gash in the muscle of the dragon's foreleg. Thick, golden blood flowed like honey from the wound. She caught as much as she could in her palm. Balancing the blood in her palm, she rushed back to Aden. Dropping the sword again, it clattered to the ground, and she opened Aden's jaw with her right hand and slid the blood into his mouth. Some spread on his lips and cheek, but most of it entered his mouth.

She closed his jaw and put both hands on his lips to hold it closed. She lowered her head and closed her eyes. How could she know the blood got into his body? It was liquid. She could manipulate it. Move it. Her hand shook. She couldn't. Could she?

She prayed. She begged El to forgive her, to help her. She would do anything, anything if only ...

Aden twitched. She opened her eyes and grabbed his shoulders. *Yes. Please. Please.*

His body went tense, and he groaned.

"Come on," she whispered, but her heart screamed.

The wounds on his body closed. She wiped the blood away from his torso and the rip in his coat and tunic, and it was just bare skin.

"Come on!"

Aden gasped, a loud and desperate sound, and his lungs filled with air. His eyes opened to bulging, and he sat up, coughing.

The coughs racked his body, and his face twisted into a wince. "What ..." He coughed and spat. "What the shog is that taste?" He frowned at her. "That is bitter as crit."

Tamya laughed and wept all at once and pulled him into an embrace. His arms gripped her tight.

Tamya sniffed as they separated.

Aden glanced from the dead dragon to Bael and then Malaki. When he saw Malaki, he narrowed his eyes at the wound on his leg. "Wait. Was I ...?"

"You're alive now." She kissed him. Aden was right. That dragon blood did taste like crit. "And Caleb needs us. How do you feel?"

Aden grunted as he stood, and she helped him up. He stretched. Tamya raised a brow at him, and he nodded.

Aden walked toward the dead dragon, Fryaco, and he climbed up the side until he stood on the chest. He reached down and pulled his unforged sword from the dragon. Smoke billowed from the wound.

Standing there, he appeared like a hero from one of the breakin' stories that couldn't be real. But he was real. Was he taller? Were his eyes brighter? It was like a dream.

Aden looked at Malaki. "Caleb needs us."

The dragon nodded.

Aden placed his unforged sword in the sheath. He grinned. "Time to see how fast a dragon can fly."

Tamya grinned back. "Don't forget Elowen."

CHAPTER 27

THE BATTLE OF ASYA 11
RED HANDS

One hundred bosaur barreled forward. With their flat feet and massive bodies, the charge shook the ground. Those beasts rammed into five hundred trodall, both running at full speed, and the impact carried a physical, explosive wave of sound that drove Caleb to his knees.

Trodall bodies flew in the air; others were impaled by the horns of the bosaur and dragged forward. Some trodall, even mortally wounded, leapt onto bosaur and used their claws to rip, tear, and gash animal and rider, killing Liorians. Eleven bosaur and riders brought down. Screams and shouts of pain and anger filled the air. Caleb could almost taste the wrath and violence.

It was the chaos of battle, and for a moment, he could feel the calm and the peace within, ironic for the level of violence. The brief glance up at the sky was interrupted by Eshlyn and the Mahakar passing overhead with two more human prisoners.

Caleb raced to his left to join Kenneth's division, three stones arcing by to strike cohorts of militan, destroying the temporary protection of their linked shields. Caleb joined a platoon that darted in to engage the confused and scattered militan.

More stones from the catapults and long spears from the ballista soared through the air, aimed hundreds of mitres past his position. To the wall? He couldn't see past the militan in front of him.

With his staff and blade, he crushed helmets and skulls and cut through armor and shields, flesh and bone. Men and elves died all around him, but with his weapons creating a storm of death and war, no one could touch him. He didn't know if the army was winning or not, and in the rage of death, it didn't matter to him. He reveled in adding more blood to his hands.

How much blood can there be on my hands? He would find out.

The bosaur to his right regrouped and widened their line to sweep over two cohorts of militan, crushing elves beneath their massive hooves, and the leader of the bosaur cavalry, a Liorian by the name of Nahom, did an excellent job pointing them back to the trodall.

The trodall had been scattered by the first bosaur attack, and now they slaughtered soldiers of the *Hamon-el* at random. The bosaur had to split into two formations to try and corral the rabid creatures. However, trodall stepped into platoons of the *Hamon-el,* ripping men in half. The men and women and elves of Caleb's army bravely attempted to wound the monsters as much as possible without much success.

"Kenneth," Caleb called. "I'm on the trodall!"

Kenneth paused to nod at Caleb and went back to slicing through militan with his own unforged sword.

Caleb finished the two militan he currently fought, and then he turned and sprinted across the field, blocking any elven strikes with the Kingstaff.

Red blood of elves and men mixed with the black blood of the trodall on the grass and covered his boots like mud.

A dying bosaur with half of its flesh ripped off lay on the ground before him with a trodall beyond. Caleb continued toward it; he planted the Kingstaff in the dirt next to the bosaur and used it to vault over the beast. He flew through the air feet first and slammed into the back of a trodall that had cornered two men. Falling together, Caleb cut the monster's skull in half. He jumped upon landing, rolling forward under the arms and claws of another trodall.

Caleb rose, still moving, and blocked one arm from the new trodall and cut another arm off at the elbow, black blood everywhere. The trodall reared back in pain, and Caleb used the opportunity to stab it in the heart.

Screaming louder, near him, and he turned. Five trodall surrounded him; three men of the *Hamon-el* stood with him. One of the men did not have a left arm and looked about to collapse.

"Behind me," Caleb said as he stepped forward. The man's name without the arm was ... "Put Chappy in the center. Fill the gaps as I fight."

If they didn't know what that meant, he couldn't teach them now.

He slid through the blood mud at his feet and ducked one trodall and stabbed at the knee of another. Two of the men crouched beneath another trodall attack, with two more trodall behind it.

Not bad. They would not last long with three trodall. But he couldn't worry about that. He cut through the leg of one trodall, and it fell forward. His only recourse was to spin to the left and into the claws of the second. He held the Kingstaff in front of him with both hands and took the full force of the trodall, which hurled him back two mitres. He landed on the back of the wounded trodall, which writhed around to try to grab him with its claws.

Caleb stabbed the one under him in the back of the skull. It twitched as it died, but he was beyond it, using it as cover while the second swung at him.

After the trodall swung, Caleb took the split second to jump on the dead trodall's body and swing his sword up and through the trodall's jaw and into its brain. Did they have brains? Black blood sprayed everywhere, and Caleb didn't wait for the trodall to die before he went to check on the men he had left behind.

Chappy was dead, and another was in the jaws of a trodall while the third ran for his life.

Caleb panted and was about to leap forward when he saw five figures completely covered in steel run past him. Two threw themselves on one trodall and three on another, hacking with maces and axes and wide bladed swords.

The Steelsides.

Thanking Ironsword in his head, Caleb leapt forward and decapitated the third trodall as it was distracted trying to kill the soldier.

The man – Jamm – fell to his knees in relief. Caleb grabbed the man's tunic and yanked him to his feet.

"Thank you, *Brendel*," Jamm began. "I ..."

Caleb spoke through his teeth. "Breaking battle isn't over. Stay on your feet! Go join a platoon and fight!"

Jamm gulped. "Yessir." He scampered off.

The trodall claws could only dent the armor of the Steelsides, and even though dwarves were shorter than men, they were stronger; their fine weapons cut deep into the trodall. The two trodall were dead in seconds.

Caleb scanned the field, and the Steelsides were focused on the single or small groups of trodall. Teams of two or three would take down a trodall. One dwarf picked up and hurled away, but the dwarf used the momentum to turn over and land like a steel ball, rolling to minimize the damage. The dwarf rose to his feet, running back to battle to support his teammate and fight the trodall.

The bosaur, of which he could only see fifty or so now, trampled militan and impaled trodall around the field in groups of ten or twelve.

One of the Steelsides approached him as the other four ran to more trodall. Caleb honestly didn't know which one it was.

The Steelside had a sword with a wide blade that was almost his own height. "*Brendel*."

Ulf. That sounded like Ulf, Gunnar's brother. Or was it Gunnar? He took a shot. "Ulf?"

The dwarf nodded. "We'll take care of these trodall. Been fought them before, y'know."

"I'm sure," Caleb said. "The human wraith?"

Ulf shrugged. "Saved as many as we could. Elves killed a critload of them."

Caleb nodded up the hill. The battle raged around him and stones and spears flew over him. "I need to get a better view of the battle."

"Go," Ulf said. "We'll end the trodall."

Caleb patted the steel armored shoulder and ran back to the west over bodies and limbs and blood.

——

It was the last of the living prisoners, and Eshlyn felt arrows hit the shield she had tied to her back, shattering or bouncing away.

Two women huddled on the Mahakar in front of her. They were bone thin and young, although to the real, not much younger than she was.

The Mahakar wavered and struggled to fly. He was tired and injured – several arrows protruded from his hide. Fifteen? Twenty? His breaths were ragged, and he no longer growled or made much noise. She grimaced at the bloody tear on his right wing.

These were the last of the humans that had been bound to stakes. Many had died as she saved them, and in the end, twenty-eight of the original fifty had survived, including these last two. She didn't know if the Mahakar could have made another run.

They glided over the battle. So much death below her. From the sky, she could see that more legions had exited the gate of Asya and circled to flank to the north and south.

Floating over the siege engines and the supplies, the Mahakar dropped too fast.

"Hold on," she told the two women, and they all leaned forward as one and gripped the tiger's fur with both hands.

The Mahakar landed, stumbled, and fell to the ground. His head dug into the dirt and grass, and the sudden stop threw all three from his back. Eshlyn had the presence of mind to turn over and land on her back, her arms crossed in front of her. Landing, she rolled, the hilt of her sword poking her in the stomach, knocking the breath out of her.

She rested on her back, holding her belly, and she forced herself not to panic until she could breathe. She panted once she could, sucking in the air.

A woman and a man from the supply line stood over her. "Lady Eshlyn? Are you okay?" the woman said. She didn't know her name. Caleb would know it, she bet.

Eshlyn sat up; others helped the two women she had rescued. One woman had a badly broken arm, and she wailed. But she was alive. They were taken to a wagon for the wounded headed to the camp.

Where Javyn was. She could see the dots of tents in the distance.

"I'm fine," she told the man and woman over her, and they helped her to her feet. She walked over to the Mahakar.

The massive tiger lay on his side, and she had to dart around him to get to his face. He breathed, a pained sound. His eyes closed.

Eshlyn buried her face in his fur, such soft fur. "You rest now." The man and woman stood a few paces away, watching her. She looked at them. "Have you been trained in field medicine?"

They shared a glance, and the man winced. "Basic, Lady. Not much."

"Get someone who knows what they are doing," Eshlyn told them. "Remove these arrows, stitch and bandage these wounds as well as they can."

They bowed. "Yes, Lady."

She didn't know why they were breaking bowing to her, but she didn't have time to care. She had to get back to the battle.

With a final embrace, she gave a kiss into the tiger's fur, adjusted her belt and sword, and jogged to the east to join the battle.

—┼—

All that remained of the original battle line were siege engines, and Bweth stood atop one of the catapults at the center. She watched the battle progress, trying to determine where best to send the spears and the stones from the machines around her.

What she wanted, however, was to be there amidst the blood and the action.

It wasn't a simple desire to kill. No, she had seen plenty of death and violence. While she knew that she accomplished a great deal with the catapults and ballista, she felt separate from the army.

The babe kicked within her belly, her skin bumping on the armor she had stretched out to accommodate her stomach. "I feel you."

The man on the ground behind her loading the stones said, "What did you say?"

"Nothing."

With the thirty catapults, she had done a great deal of damage to the new legions that entered the field, but even after she pummeled them, the militan reorganized into new cohorts and divisions. Bweth counted ten thousand more added to the field. The ballista were more difficult to use in the current situation; she could fire them in a type of arc over their forces, but the ballista were more designed for a frontal attack. In some ways, they had been more effective in getting past the militan's linked shields.

Caleb walked up to her. He was covered in mud and blood. His sword was bathed in black.

He stood on the other side of the catapult and surveyed the battle, those gray eyes taking it all in. "We can't make a stand here. They are moving around the north and south."

Bweth nodded. In the last hour of fighting, the *Hamon-el* had lost a third of their number. The militan had lost far more, but they had more to lose in the beginning. "Even with taking out half their number as they come through the gate, we'll be surrounded and outnumbered in the next hour."

"We could concentrate catapult fire on north or south and make a push with the bosaur and cavalry."

Bweth scanned the field, taking it in. Macarus and the cavalry did what damage they could on the right side. The remaining bosaur swept through the militan. "If we push through, we'll be clear for their breakin' trebuchet and arrows."

"So we have to retreat and regroup, change position." His voice was tired. She knew him well enough. He didn't like to retreat. Wasn't in his nature.

Bweth snorted. "Prolly the right thing to do. Or we could make a push through the center to the gate."

Caleb turned to her. "We'd be trapped on the wall."

"But with the cavalry and bosaur, we would have a single front to defend. And put the shields we have on the front."

"Better for a small number." Caleb grinned. "They don't have anything on the field that can deal with the bosaur."

"When we're on the wall, no way for them to get at us with the trebuchet."

"And the militan would be caught between our army and the catapult and ballista. They would be on two fronts."

"Unless they attack the line here," Bweth countered.

"We could bring up the reserves," Caleb said. "When we're at the wall, they'd have arrows. And maybe oil or tar from the top."

"Arrows, yes. But maybe not oil or tar. Do you think they'd expect us to get that close?"

"Tanicus might." Caleb rubbed the beard on his chin. "There would be reinforcements from the city, but we could hold the gate with a few platoons."

"If we can get there before they close the gate, then we'd have access to the city."

"That's a big *if*. If the gate closes before we get there, near impossible to break it down."

"We got bosaur," Bweth argued. "And unforged swords."

Caleb sniffed. "True"

"Anyway. We retreat now, we have the numbers to go full scale again?"

"No. We don't." Caleb's gaze darted back and forth, his gray eyes bright. "A bold move. An all or nothing move."

"You think they have more trodall or grider to throw at us?"

Caleb shook his head. "Doubtful. Emperor doesn't want this drawing out. He wants to crush us. The longer we last and the more damage we do, the more his image of power and strength is compromised. That fear is one of his greatest weapons."

"That, and he's a Worldbreaker."

Caleb was silent a moment. "Yes. There is that."

Eshlyn strode up from the rear and held her hand on the sword on her side. She stopped next to Bweth.

"How's the Mahakar?" Caleb asked.

Eshlyn continued to stare at the battle before them. "He'll live. I think."

Bweth felt the tenion between them and rolled her eyes. "Good. Brave tiger. We'll probably need him soon."

Eshlyn put her hands on her hips. "Looks like we need to do something. We're outnumbered and about to be surrounded."

"Funny," Bweth said. "We were just talkin' 'bout that."

Eshlyn finally turned to look at them. "So what's the plan?"

Bweth exchanged a glance with Caleb, the confirmation in the set of his jaw. "We're pushing for the gate."

Eshlyn chuckled. "Of course we are." She took a breath. "Since Nahom seems to have the bosaur in hand, I'll be with what is left of Wes' division."

Caleb tensed. He didn't want her putting herself in danger, but what could he say? He was smart enough to say nothing.

"I'll be at the center, leading the push," he said. "Spread the word to get in formation behind me."

"Just you?" Eshlyn asked.

"We'll see what I come up with between now and then."

"Fine. See you on the field." She walked off down the hill to the east and a slight left to Wes' division.

Caleb watched Eshlyn go.

Bweth looked at the man, a revolutionary, a warrior unlike any she had ever seen in centuries, the one person who might be able to fight and beat a Worldbreaker. But longing drowned his gaze as he watched Eshlyn.

When Eshlyn was out of earshot, Bweth said, "Forging a sword ain't no mountain love dance. Not at all."

Caleb frowned.

"First you gotta find the right breakin' steel, one that you can shape but will be strong enough not to break in the middle of a shogger. The right sword can take a long time. You heat it to the point it's so brittle it could almost crumble in your hands. Then you heat it so it's stronger than ever before. You do this over and over. Back and forth. So many decisions, such a crittin' process. It takes more patience than most can stand."

Caleb lowered his head.

"But that's just the blade," Bweth hissed. "Then you gotta find the right material for the pommel, the right weight to balance it, otherwise it's breakin' awkward and impossible to use in a fight. But if you do it right, and you take the time, it's ready for a master to use."

Bweth took a small leather bag from her belt. She took a step towards him and held it out. Pursing his lips, Caleb looked up. He took the bag and pulled the string to open it.

After he saw what was inside, he glared at her.

"I made it a while ago," Bweth said. "Waitin' for the right time to give it to you. Never a good time. Maybe there never is."

Caleb closed the bag and tied it to his own belt with the string.

"The best blade needs the balance or it's no good." Bweth said.

"Even if the balance causes pain?"

"Is there not pain one way or another?" She scoffed. She thought of Hunter and their brief time together. Too brief. And the babe in her belly. "Daft man, the greatest bravery is to love knowing the pain is worth it."

His steel gray eyes bore into her, then they softened, moving down to her belly. "I've been a fool."

"We've all been fools at one time or another. I know that as well as anyone."

He gazed out over the field of battle, a distant look. "And now it's too late."

"Maybe. Maybe not."

She hopped down and checked her mace and axe were secure on her belt.

He frowned. "Where do you think you're going?"

"I can't teach these shoggers anything more." She gestured at the line and ignored the confused looks from the men nearby. "I'm going with you."

It felt like the babe did a somersault in her belly.

———

Macarus rode into a small cohort of militan and slammed the horse into them. They scattered; he swung his sword to the left and the right, and his shield protected from behind him.

His sword was red with the blood of elves, his countrymen. Former countrymen? He no longer knew.

Binding and gathering the human wraith had felt better, useful. He and the calvary, half of them elves, had bound over six hundred of the original thousand. Kryan elves had attempted to kill as many as they could instead of allowing them to be taken. The cavalry took them to the wagons at the rear of the line, and of the six hundred they saved, more than two hundred had been injured but alive. But they had saved some, and Macarus took comfort in that.

Once that was done, however, he and the remaining riders turned their attention to the Kryan militan. To killing them.

When he left Kaltiel with the Steelsides, he knew he would come to the place where his countrymen were his enemy. That happened first at Vicksburg, but now he stood against his Emperor.

Macarus was a hero of a dozen battles in the War of Liberation, and the confusion and fear in the eyes of the Kyran military as he attacked struck him. He had the same question. How could a hero of the War of Liberation be fighting the Empire he once fought and killed for?

At Vicksburg, he fought in darkness, by surprise. Here, he was seen as a leader. If he hesitated, the elves in the *Hamon-el* would allow doubts to enter their hearts, for they were also under the same struggle, to the sure. These were their brothers in arms not long before, elves they would have fought and died with. Now they were enemies.

Macarus swallowed the guilt and had to remind his heart of the conviction he held back in Kaltiel, that this was a necessary recourse to end tyranny and an evil Worldbreaker. Even with that truth, his soul ached at the necessity.

The battle was chaos. The horses could do damage and disrupt the cohorts, but they had to do so on the fringe. The fighting was too close within to separate friend from foe. Attacking from the outskirts, however, opened them up to more volleys of arrows.

Macarus had started with 500 cavalry. After dealing with the human wraith and now engaging in the battle, his numbers were half that.

The legions attempted to surround the *Hamon-el*, and he did all he could to stop their movement. The bosaur were at the front of the army, tearing and trampling militan, so he had to focus on either the northern edge or the southern. He focused on the southern, forcing the Kyrans to fight on two fronts. He made headway, but he lost cavalry at an alarming rate, as well. He could only slow the legions down. They would have the *Hamon-el* surrounded in another hour or two.

They needed to retreat.

Macarus noticed Eshlyn, Bweth, and Caleb returning to the fight. He led the cavalry around at a gallop and met Caleb at the rear of the *Hamon-el*. He knew Caleb saw the same developments he did.

"You ready to lead the retreat?" Macarus asked. "The bosaur and I will keep the Kryans busy while ..."

Caleb didn't stop walking. None of them did.

"We're not retreating," Caleb said. "You'll need to bring your riders down the middle and support the bosaur. We're making a push for the gate."

Macarus' brow furrowed. "You're serious."

"It's now or never," Caleb said. "We won't get another shot at this."

"Understood." He signaled the cavalry around him. "Shields and spears up, brothers and sisters! We make our way to the gate of Asya."

———

Eshlyn jogged beside the bosaur as they made the push for the gate.

With the trodall all dead, there were now only forty two bosaur left of the original 100. Without the trodall, however, only militan cohorts remained to stop the bosaur charge. Nahom, in charge of the bosaur in Tobiah's absence, had the bosaur in the front twenty across with the other twenty-two behind. They charged ahead, crushing and scattering militan in their path.

Macarus and the cavalry rode behind the bosaur. He led the cavalry to clean up the scattered militan with their shields and spears.

The *Hamon-el* moved after the cavalry, three thousand soldiers still mobile, human and elf and dwarf. They came together in a shared moment of clarity.

Eshlyn felt the connection and assumed they all did, as if something beyond guided their steps. She had never felt anything like it.

Nothing could stand in their way.

Caleb was on the other side of the bosaur, pacing with the enormous beasts. Had the bosaur been going at full speed, only the horses could have kept up with them, but Nahom reined them in enough to stay with the rest of the army.

When they closed within 300 mitres of the gate, arrows came from the top of the wall, a thousand at a time. Eshlyn lifted her shield over her head at an angle and felt an arrow bounce off the steel. To her right and above her, she heard a gurgle over the pounding hooves, and when she glanced, the Liorian riding the bosaur next to her fell from the saddle with an arrow through a bloody neck.

Eshlyn had to leap over the body as it tumbled, and the riderless bosaur began to drift in her direction. Eshlyn grunted at the prospect of being trampled by the beast, and she sprung up and grabbed the saddle with her sword hand, dropping the shield in her left hand as she climbed up the strap to get to the top of the bosaur.

Lifting her leg over the top and straddling the saddle, she took a moment to sheathe her sword before scrambling for the reins. First her left and then her right hand found the leather straps, and she pulled them to the right, back to the formation.

Another volley of arrows dropped her way. She ducked behind the frills of the bosaur. Three of the bosaur down the line fell to the ground from the arrows, mostly to being struck in the eye – their hides were too tough for the arrows to do much damage. When those three bosaur went down, though, they took a few horses and soldiers with them.

Eshlyn sat up straight. They were now 150 mitres from the gate.

And it began to close.

"Break it all!" she shouted. Measuring the distance and the pace, they weren't going to make the gate in time. The doors were swinging closed. But something exited the city before the gate closed.

Two oxen dragged a steel, boxlike structure on wheels out of the city. The box was three mitres tall and fifteen mitres long. An elf in a black robe rode atop the structure.

They were past any militan; only grass and mud lay between them and the gate. Eshlyn kicked the bosaur under her and urged the bosaur on to top speed. They had to reach the gate before it closed behind the steel wagon. She separated from the other bosaur, and she could hear Nahom shouting orders for more speed of the rest of the line.

But even as fast as they were going, they were not going to reach the gate in time.

Fifty mitres from the gate, it closed.

She cursed behind the frills of the bosaur as more arrows rained down on them. Looking over her shoulder, she saw a sea of militan now between them and their original position at the top of the hill. Five thousand? More? The catapults fired, but would it be enough?

She faced the gate. Thirty mitres away, she decided to pass the structure and ram the gate. *We'll see how strong these bosaur really are.* Perhaps they wouldn't have the bars secure on the other side yet.

Since she was out in front, the elf in the black robe raised a hand in her direction. She frowned, confused at the smile on his face. Until the bosaur under her made a strange, strangled sound ... and toppled.

Eshlyn went flying forward, her arms and legs flailing. Fortunately, she recovered from her shock in time to tuck and roll as she landed. She tumbled for too long, until she rested on her side, panting. Her clothes were ripped and torn at elbows and knees, and her body throbbed from the impact. But she didn't think there was any serious injury. She sat up, her hair falling in her face.

The elf in the black robe continued grinning and extending his hand, and he strained. Eshlyn looked back at the boaur, and the creature's tongue lolled around and its legs kicked, squirming in pain.

Some kind of breaking wizard. What had Carys called it? A Moonguard?

Eshlyn stood and drew her sword. She limped toward the wizard.

The bosaur fell silent, motionless, and appeared to be sucked dry, skin wrinkled and stretched tight over bones.

Then the wizard raised his hand to her.

The pain was unreal. She collapsed to the ground.

—+—

A Moonguard.

Eshlyn crumpled under the power of the wizard, and Caleb couldn't get there fast enough. The bosaur had slowed to a walk under Nahom's orders, seeing that it was a wizard. Caleb set out at a full sprint, and he caught up to them.

"Go, go!" he called to Nahom. "Distract him!"

From his reading at the Citadel, there was little about *Tebelrivyn*. Even Reyan hadn't spoken much of it. But the topic had fascinated him when he first came to the Citadel, and he read all he could. That had been years ago, but he seemed to remember something about how one of the *Tebelrivyn* wizards would weaken their power to focus on more than one target at a time.

Carys had also told him about their confrontation with a Moonguard, and his theory seemed right based on her story. At least, he hoped he was.

Before Nahom and the bosaur could reach them, Macarus galloped up at full speed past them and held a spear in his hand. He reached Eshlyn's position and reared back and threw the spear the twenty mitres at the Moonguard.

It was an impressive throw, to the real, and the Moonguard's eyes bulged as he had to duck to avoid being impaled by the spear. Eshlyn gasped and rose to her hands and knees. The Moonguard straightened and extended both hands.

Eshlyn cried out again, and Macarus fell from the saddle to the ground next to her.

Neither one of them have an unforged sword.

The first line of bosaur closed in on the Moonguard. The elf noticed them, and he appeared to strain even more. The twenty bosaur at the front of the line slowed and staggered.

Caleb raced forward, now behind the line of bosaur as they passed him; he saw Eshlyn and Macarus begin to rise to their hands and knees. The Moonguard attempted to draw the life from twenty bosaur and two humans at the same time. Every vein in his neck and hands were pronounced, and his teeth were bared.

Caleb was within ten yards of Eshlyn and Macarus. Both in pain, but Macarus was up on his knees and reaching for his saddle. He had thrown his spear, so Caleb assumed he was going for the bow, which was a great idea.

Sliding in the mud, Caleb withdrew his sword and came to a stop in between the two of them. He stuck the unforged sword in the ground and yanked Macarus and Eshlyn's hands to touch it. They both grabbed the hilt and gasped at once, like they had been drowning and got the air they needed.

Caleb's hands deftly extracted the bow and quiver from the saddle in a flash, and he barely took time to aim, firing an arrow at the Moonguard.

The Moonguard cried out as he ducked the first shot – where was Carys when he needed her? The elf had been distracted by twenty large beasts barreling toward him. Taking Caleb into account, he frowned at him.

Caleb felt his body lose energy and strength. He had trouble breathing, and he fell to a knee.

But a hand lay upon his shoulder, and the pain was gone. Looking down, it was Eshlyn holding the hilt of the sword and touching the skin where his shoulder met his neck. Caleb snorted, remaining on his knee, and he fired three more times.

The first arrow went wide, but the second arrow stuck in the Moonguard's shoulder and the third in his thigh.

Now the Moonguard fell to his knees and jerked in pain. The bosaur line recovered, and Nahom urged them forward.

The Moonguard reached for the lever. *That seems bad ...* Caleb took more time to aim and fired an arrow that soared through the air and hit the elven wizard in the heart.

The Moonguard froze for a moment but then had strength enough to grip the lever on his way down. His weight pulled it all the way.

Air hissed through the steel structure, and mists puffed from the doors on the side.

With the Moonguard dead, Caleb took the unforged sword from the ground and his friends and stood tall. The steel doors of the box wagon slid upwards, slowly. His brow furrowed.

The second line of bosaur also passed him, all moving towards the large steel box with twenty open doors and the closed gate beyond.

Macarus and Eshlyn both stood with him. Macarus spoke to Eshlyn. "You all right?"

She nodded. "Nothing broken. I think." She gestured at the structure on wheels at the gate. "What is that thing?"

The rest of the cavalry reached them, and Bweth called out from behind one of the elven riders. Caleb turned to her.

An elven rider reined in to a stop next to Caleb, and Bweth slung herself down off of the horse and landed on the ground, her armor clattering. "Caleb. You shoggin' idiot, why did you kill him? We have to get everyone back."

His frown deepened.

"What are you talking about?" Eshlyn asked.

But Caleb had a suspicion.

Bweth pointed to the steel structure. "That was Eraeus the Moonguard. I worked with that crittin' elf. And the Deathguard's in that breakin' box!"

Caleb looked from the wagon to Bweth. "Fine. But we don't have anywhere to go but the gate. How do we get past the Deathguard?"

Bweth shook her head. "That's what I'm tryin' to tell you, big shogger. You can't. Eraeus is the only one that could ever stop them, and now I know why. He was a crittin' wizard. But you killed him."

"The legions are surrounding us as we speak," Macarus said. "And you want us to retreat?"

"I'm tellin' you unless we get far away, everyone on this field is dead," Bweth answered. "Without that Moonguard, they'll kill anyone. Anything."

Caleb grunted and gritted his teeth. "We'll see about that. There are ways we don't see now. Macarus. Spread the word. Get everyone in a perimeter around us and the *Sohan-el* to me. The *Hamon-el* will deal with the legions, as we said. Our only way is in that gate. I'll deal with the Deathguard."

Bweth unhooked the spiked mace from her belt. "Not without me, you're not."

Eshlyn said, "And me."

Macarus swung onto his horse. "I'll be back to help, as well."

Gunnar and the Steelsides walked up behind Bweth. Caleb counted only 18 of the dwarves now. Casualties of the trodall? Gunnar placed his hands on his hips. "Pray tell, where are we going?"

Caleb cursed and shook his head.

+

Eshlyn jogged forward behind Caleb.

He held his unforged sword in his right hand and the Kingstaff in his left. She held her own sword. On the other side of Caleb was Bweth with a spiked mace in her right hand and a triangular shield in her left. Behind them were the Steelsides, Gunnar and his brother and 16 other dwarves with wide blades, maces, axes, and shields. They sounded like an army alone with all the armor and weaponry.

Her eyes scanned ahead between the bosaur in front of them, and the doors – ten on each side – moved.

It took her mind a moment to register it, to see past the horror and see that it was not a nightmare come to life. Or perhaps it was.

It used to be an elf, but iron and steel had been fused and inserted into its skin. There were plates on its chest and back and groin and legs and arms, the edges of each plate secreted small drops of blood. The skull was exposed metal with holes where the ears once were. The skin of the face was mostly intact, but the eyelids were gone from the eyes, like permanent shock. The teeth constantly bared with no lips. Tears and drool came from the eyes and mouth in a steady stream.

Blades had been embedded into the forearms and wrists along with spikes along the shoulders and arms and knees.

It wore no clothes, but they were absent of genitals. The body shape seemed generally male, but with all the alterations, she couldn't be sure.

Eshlyn addressed Bweth. "Um, what did you do with the …?"

"Not now," Bweth growled.

Other Deathguard exited the doors, like they woke from sleep.

The first Deathguard stepped from the structure and faced Nahom and a bosaur approaching. Eshlyn could see Nahom's strategy – to trample the Deathguard. The Deathguard ran towards the bosaur.

The bosaur lowered its head and growled, aiming its horn at the Deathguard. The Deathguard leapt up high, three or four mitres in the air, and landed on the bosaur's snout, stabbing the long blades from its wrists into the creature's eyes. The bosaur reared and spasmed. The Deathguard stabbed several more times into the forehead before being thrown off when the bosaur tumbled. The earth shook, and the Deathguard was crushed underneath the bosaur.

Nahom was flung in the air and fell hard. Eshlyn winced when he landed. She heard the bones break and crunch.

The body of the Deathguard bounced from under the bosaur, and any normal being, even in armor, would have been destroyed by the weight. But the Deathguard rose from the mud, its limbs turning in awkward direction. Bones, or whatever its skeletal structure was made of, snapped back into place.

Caleb rolled his shoulders and dashed toward the Deathguard. The twisted being faced Caleb and attacked, swinging blades and rushing him. Caleb blocked the blades with his own and the Kingstaff, and he avoided the spikes. The Deathguard struck, and while he blocked it with the Kingstaff, he was nearly knocked off balance with the strength of the blow.

Bweth reached the Deathguard before Eshlyn did, and the half dwarf rammed the Deathguard from the side. She bounced off, tucking and rolling, but it gave Caleb enough time to slap aside a blade with his staff and then stab the Deathguard through the heart with the unforged sword. The supernatural blade slid through iron and steel and came out the other side.

The Deathguard gave a gurgle, blood flowing from the mouth, and tried to stab back at Caleb. But Eshlyn was there. She blocked the blade, and that gave Caleb time to yank the unforged sword out of the Deathguard and then decapitate it with a wide swing of the unforged sword.

The head popped up with sparks and blood, and the Deathguard finally fell and stayed still.

Caleb took a deep breath. "They can be killed after all."

Bweth stood and walked to him. "Didn't know about unforged swords when we made 'em."

Caleb looked at Nahom, frowned, and shouted to the other riders. "We will take care of the Deathguard. You have to help take out the legion on the other side!"

The Liorian rider, another leader, a woman by the name of Falati, nodded and led the bosaur away.

The Steelsides ran past, and Bweth darted to join them.

Eshlyn and Caleb shared a look. Caleb shook his head and ran after them.

✦

Nineteen of those abominations stood there in front of the gate of Asya, waiting for her.

Bweth ran toward them, keeping pace with the Steelsides.

Bweth had made them. Years ago in a different life. Before Hunter. Before Caleb and Carys and Eshlyn and the family she now had. But that didn't make her any less responsible. Knowing what was good and real, after so many years lost and alone, made her more responsible.

She had to kill these things.

Bweth didn't have an unforged sword. But if Caleb could find a way, she should be able to, for the real.

The babe within her was still. Usually, during a battle, the babe kicked her ribs to breaking.

Eighteen Steelsides and Bweth spread out to face nineteen Deathguard. The Deathguard also ran as one, and when the two sides met, it was deafening as steel met steel.

Bweth lifted her shield and took the blows her Deathguard rained down upon her. She almost fell backwards. How had they gotten so strong? Was that more of the magic? Instead of falling, she spun, ducking two swipes, and came around with her mace and smashed it into its face, blood spurting her helmet. The impact shuddered down her arm, but she didn't stop.

She batted its blades aside with her shield and hit the Deathguard in its groin and stomach, trying to remember this specific one. She had tried to make each one unique. Did it have any weak spots? She didn't build any into them – like an idiot, she had tried to make them invincible – but that had been centuries ago. She had improved as a smith and weaponsmaster since then.

It was difficult to think of such things while trying to stay alive. Her armor deflected a strike and her shield others as she struck with the spiked mace, without much affect.

Caleb and Eshlyn joined the battle, engaging a Deathguard that had killed a Steelside, and they worked as a team. Eshlyn distracted or blocked the attacks while Caleb used the Kingstaff to get beyond any defenses and cut the Deathguard off at the knees. Caleb stabbed down through the brain before he and Eshlyn moved on to another.

A few moments passed, and amidst the din of battle, Bweth remembered this one. The way the spikes set on the shoulder more across the muscle of the shoulder instead of around the shoulder joint. Was the shoulder and knee joint vulnerable? Vulnerable might not be the right word … not as strong as other parts?

And then she felt like a real idiot when she remembered … the eyes.

Bweth was knocked back two paces by the Deathguard, taking the brunt of his attack on her shield. Digging in her heels, she countered with two mace strikes, one at each eye, plunging the spikes in and around the eyes without lids. She decimated them. One eye hung on a nerve and vein while the other came of with her mace.

"The eyes!" she yelled out to whoever could hear her. "Go for the eyes!"

The Deathguard went rigid for a split second and twitched. It recovered enough to swing blades at her, but it was blind. She easily dodged them. Bweth jumped up and brought all her weight down on a mace strike at the knee. The joint bent and snapped.

But she didn't stop. She struck the knee three more times. Bweth had forged the steel that protected the knee, but the steel of her mace was more recent and pure, the work of a true weapons master. The joint snapped and deformed past the Deathguard's ability to fix or heal. It lay on its side, slicing at her from the ground.

She used the shield and her armor for protection, and then she struck at the base of its neck. With a few seconds of bashing at its neck, the Deathguard was still.

Panting, she scanned the field in a wide but quick glance. She couldn't see past the *Hamon-el* to see how they fared against the legions, but one Steelside stabbed through the gut with a Deathguard blade, even through the dwarven armor. As the Steelside fell on his back, crying out and cursing, the Deathguard lifted blades for the killing blow.

Bweth was there and took the blades on her mace, and it drove her to her knees. She stood, however, knocking aside the serrated blades of this one, and she struck it in the face, aiming for one of the eyes.

Halfway through her strike, she had her first contraction.

No, little one. Not now.

Her stomach tightened, and she hesitated. Her mace did not hit with full force, and the Deathguard was able to adjust its head. She struck the top of his skull instead, and the mace bounced off with a clang.

The Deathguard moved like a snake and stabbed at her head. She turned, and the blade scraped off of her armored shoulder. It almost took the plate off, and she hit the Deathguard again at its face, taking an eye this time. The Deathguard did not seem to care, and it stabbed at her with both blades. She caught one blade on her shield.

The other punctured her armor with a whining groan and slid into her chest.

Her eyes rolled up into her head, and the sky turned upside down.

—+—

"No!" Eshlyn screamed when Bweth went down. She left Caleb with the Deathguard behind her as she closed two mitres within a few leaping steps. The Deathguard stood over Bweth, who gasped for breath on her back, and Eshlyn engaged it with her sword.

She swung her sword hard at the Deathguard, on his arm and back, sparks flying. Her attack did little damage, but it did distract the thing from Bweth, which had been Eshlyn's plan.

But it was not a very good plan, considering now she dealt with a Deathguard by herself. She scored a hit on its chest as it turned, but she ducked away from it and Bweth as the blades sliced through the air, first high and then low. Eshlyn rose to her knees and countered with her sword on its thigh and stomach. It moved forward as if it never felt her blade at all. She stood and retreated while blocking one of its blades and the other just missing her head.

She needed to get back to Bweth and check on her.

Eshlyn noticed now that one of its eyes was missing, the right one. When she dodged the next vertical strike, she slid to her left, out of its vision. The Deathguard twitched and scanned with its left eye. She used the moment to circle out of its range, and she returned to Bweth.

Her friend struggled with her breathing. But alive.

The Deathguard was right behind her, and she desperately picked up Bweth's shield with her left arm and turned to the Deathguard. The twisted thing flailed with its blades on the shield, and it was strong enough to drive her back.

Blocking the Deathguard's blades with the shield, she bided her time. One of its blades stabbed straight and stuck in the steel of the shield. The Deathguard tugged to remove the blade, but it wouldn't come free. In that moment, Eshlyn struck with the point of her own blade and drove it into its remaining good eye. The Deathguard spasmed, and she screamed while she plunged her sword as deep as she could. The Deathguard went rigid and fell back.

Eshlyn breathed in through her nose as she stood over the dead Deathguard with her sword and Bweth's shield. Scanning the scene, ten Steelsides were on the ground with the remaining eight fighting for their lives. Caleb attacked one Deathguard while a Steelside distracted it.

She saw ten Deathguard still upright and fighting.

She heard the pounding of horses' hooves, and she looked over her shoulder, her dark hair falling to cover half her face.

Macarus and the five *Sohan-el* arrived. Macarus pulled to a stop and leapt from the horse in one move. The *Sohan-el* imitated his move.

Eshlyn hurried to Bweth while the five *Sohan-el* – Jaff, Xak, Ewha, Wes, and Kenneth – spread and sprinted to help the Steelsides with the Deathguard.

She knelt down next to Bweth with Macarus joining her on the opposite side.

The wound was above the breast on the right side. It looked to have avoided the heart, but there was a lot of blood. A lot.

Eshlyn removed the helmet, the half-dwarf's curly red hair falling free. "Bweth."

Bweth coughed and opened her eyes to a squint. "The Deathguard?"

"Caleb and the *Sohan-el* are taking care of them," Macarus said. "Don't you worry."

Bweth winced and her eyes fluttered closed. "Eshlyn …"

"Yes," Eshlyn said.

"The wee one," Bweth sobbed. "It's coming."

"What?" Eshlyn said. "Now?"

Eshlyn and Macarus exchanged a glance. Macarus gaped. She had never seen the elf so helpless.

"The babe's always been a fighter." Bweth opened her eyes and reached out a gauntleted hand. Eshlyn took it. "Will you be with me? This child needs to live." Tears streamed down her cheeks. "It be all I have left o' him."

Hunter. Eshlyn looked down at the blood and the armor and her friend's beautiful face. She leaned down and touched her forehead to Bweth's. "I will."

She raised her head and glared at Macarus. "We have to move her."

Macarus looked around to the battle at the gate with the Deathguard and then the rear of the *Hamon-el* fifteen mitres away holding back ten thousand militan. "Where? Even with the cavalry and the bosar, the *Hamon-el* is being overrun."

Eshlyn scoffed at him. "You're telling me that we're about to deliver a baby in the middle of a shogging war zone?"

The elf's eyes softened to one of pain and deep sorrow. He reached over Bweth and rubbed tears off of Eshlyn's face with his gloved fingers. She didn't realize she had been crying. "I wish it were not so, Lady. But yes."

He glanced over at the gate.

"Go," Eshlyn spat. *Are males of every race this useless?*

Macarus ran a hand through her red hair. "Apologies." And he leapt up and ran to join the battle.

Eshlyn made her heart as hard as steel. *El, help me.*

She let go of Bweth's hand and began to remove her armor.

"It'll be okay, Bweth." But she didn't believe it.

———

Earon stood next to the Emperor and watched as the *Hamon-el* was trapped against the wall.

The bosaur swept through the legions, but the militan had found a strategy that worked. As a cohort of anywhere between fifty to a hundred, they would attack the bosaur from the side with spears. Twenty to fifty spears at a time could take a bosaur down. There were thirty bosaur left.

The cavalry did what they could at the edges of the legions, but with arrows and spears, their numbers were down to seventy-five or so.

The *Hamon-el* would be crushed at the wall with nowhere to go. Well, there was one place to go. Looking at the fighting at the gate, that was Caleb's plan – to enter the city with thousands of elves at his back.

And twenty thousand militan waiting on the other side of the gate.

Earon didn't need Tanicus' peerglass to see the sea of militan in the streets and the smaller open square on the inside of the wall of Asya, their bows and spears and swords pointed at the gate, waiting for Caleb and the *Hamon-el.*

Caleb, what have you done?

It didn't surprise him that Caleb made the most aggressive move he could, to point his army at the heart of the city. *That is what a sword does.* Tanicus, however, had prepared for the sword. And everything else, it seemed.

No. Not everything. He hadn't prepared for El. Earon held onto that hope, as slim as it was.

He clutched the bandaged stump of his arm.

A legion captain rose into the top room of the tower. The elf bowed and waited.

Tanicus lowered his peerglass. "Do you see, Earon? The revolution was doomed before it began."

Earon didn't respond.

Tanicus took a breath and turned to the Captain. "Is the vualta ready? The battle is almost over."

The Captain opened his mouth and stammered. "I apologize, my Lord. I do not know. Last I heard, it would not be ready until the morning. But that is not the message I was sent to bring."

Tanicus frowned. "We must send General Felix to speed up the process, if he can. That will be the last strike to crush this rebellion."

"Y-yes, my Lord."

Earon thought the elf was scared critless.

"What is the message?" Tanicus asked.

"I was sent to tell you ..." The Captain bowed lower. "They found Julius."

Tanicus raised a brow. "Where is he?"

"Downstairs," the Captain said.

"And the Sunguard he requested?"

"I do not know, my Lord."

The Emperor's brow furrowed. "They are dead, aren't they?"

The Captain hesitated. "I believe so."

"I want to see," Tanicus said.

"The General thought you might. That is why he sent for you."

"Very well." The Emperor sniffed. "Come, Earon. This will only take a moment."

Earon hesitated, but he followed the Emperor through the door and down the stairs, two Sunguard behind him.

They descended three floors to another room that was wider than the one above but just as sparse.

Five gurneys had been spaced evenly along the far wall. Sheets covered forms on the gurneys. Bodies.

Earon's heart began to beat faster, fear filling his nostrils.

High General Felix hovered to the side near the last gurney at the left.

"Care to explain, General?" Tanicus approached.

"We found them on the north side of the city," Felix began. "Near the passage." Felix glared at Earon.

"I understand," Tanicus said.

The Emperor stopped next to the gurney where Felix stood. He removed the sheet. A bald elf with scars on his face. Earon remembered this one from his first day in Asya.

"Julius," Tanicus said, and his sadness sounded genuine.

"Our physicians and the Moonguard attempted to ... bring him back. But to no avail. He was too far gone." The General clasped hands in front of him.

"Julius," Tanicus repeated. He laid a hand on the elf's chest. "I learned so much from him. When his Emperor called, he came. He gave his life for the greater good. We must remember that."

"Yes, my Lord," the General bowed.

"And the Sunguard?"

"They were in pieces in the street," Felix said.

"Yes," Tanicus said. "They would be." Sighing, he turned to the next gurney. Lowering the sheet from the face, Earon forced himself not to react. "Iletus," Tanicus hissed. "The traitor."

"Yes," Felix spat. "Every one of them."

"Of course," the Emperor said. "But Iletus was a Bladeguard, one of the most trusted agents in the Empire. The *Brendel* shall pay for this betrayal. As shall Iletus' daughter. Send word that she dies."

"It will be on the next ship, my Lord."

Tanicus nodded and walked around the dead Iletus to the next gurney. He lowered the sheet, and Earon winced at seeing a dark skinned man without a head. "Who is this?"

"Unknown," Felix said. "His head was removed."

The clothes, the form, it could be anyone from Lior, but he thought it might be Tobiah. Iletus and Tobiah went on some mission to stop Julius? Iletus made sense. But why Tobiah?

"Earon," Tanicus said. "Do you know this man?"

Earon shook his head.

Earon's gaze, however, was drawn to the last gurney. He didn't know why.

Tanicus turned to the other figure, a large one, and drew it down. Earon could have said the name as soon as he saw the bald head. *Zalman.* He clenched his fist.

Tanicus twisted his face in disgust. The man had a gaping wound at his throat and his normally tan skin was pale.

But if that was Zalman, then the last one ...

"No," he moaned. His feet moved on their own toward the last gurney and the small figure under the sheet. The Sunguard reached for him, but he was too fast. Their magic could have stopped him, but Tanicus raised a hand for them to wait while Earon rushed to the figure.

With his good hand, he tore the sheet from her body. His knees were weak, and he leaned on the gurney. His good hand covered his eyes.

Carys.

"No, please, no," he wept over and over under his breath.

"General." Tanicus rounded Zalman's body and stood at the end of Carys' gurney. "It appears our friend here knows this woman."

"The physicians were able to keep her alive," the General responded. "But only barely."

Earon lifted his head and wiped his nose on the back of his sleeve as he laid his ear down on her chest.

A faint heartbeat. A distant, wheezing breath.

"The physicians say she may still die at any moment," Felix continued. "Her internal injuries were extensive, and she lost a lot of blood."

Earon dropped to his knees before the Emperor. "Please, do all you can to help her, to save her."

"Interesting," Tanicus said. "Are you asking me to use my powers to save this woman?"

Earon swallowed hard. "Yes."

"Do you not believe that this magic I wield is ... evil? Would those be your words?"

Earon looked down at the stump of an arm. "Yes. But it doesn't matter. I would do anything for her. Please."

Tanicus' brow furrowed. "Who is this woman to you that you would go against all you believe?"

Earon shook his head. "Please. I beg you."

"Who is she?" Tanicus demanded.

Earon continued to shake his head.

Earon's body was lifted by unseen hands. And then a pain deep in his chest, as if other hands or claws squeezed his lungs and heart.

"Tell me, Earon," Tanicus said.

He tried to yell at the Emperor, but it came out as a wheeze. The air went stale and thin. "Only if you promise ... to keep her alive!"

"I promise nothing." The agony, which Earon could not believe was real before, became more excruciating. His whole existence spun in the room in the tower. "Now. Tell me."

He couldn't tell this evil tyrant, this horrible being. He knew Caleb would take torture. But he also couldn't bear the pain anymore.

"My ... cousin!"

Earon's body collapsed to the floor in a heap, the pain an ache.

"Your family. Fascinating." Tanicus looked at Carys. His eyes narrowed. "Wait. Aren't you cousins with the *Brendel*, as well?"

Earon coughed. He sobbed.

"You are," Tanicus answered himself. "So that would make this woman ... the *Brendel*'s sister."

Tanicus glided over to the side of the gurney and gazed at Carys' still form. He lifted his hand over her with a grin.

"Don't," Earon grunted. "Please. Don't. Take my life. Do whatever you have to do. I'll tell you all you want to know. Just don't kill her."

"You love her that much?"

"I do," Earon said. "But that's not the only reason."

"What more of a reason could you possess?"

Earon cleared his throat and rose to his knees. "If you kill her, if he knows you killed her, he will not stop. He will kill every elf in this city to get to you. There is no way you could hold him back."

"Who?" Tanicus asked. "The *Brendel*?"

Earon nodded.

"You believe I cannot stop a simple human?" The Emperor's voice carried outrage.

"A simple human, yes," Earon said. "But not the Creator god, not El. You cannot stop him."

Tanicus' grin widened. "You believe I fear a god I do not believe in?"

"I don't know," Earon said. "But you should."

The Emperor scoffed. "You ask me to spare this woman's life … to save … me?"

"Yes, but more than that," Earon said. "To save him."

"To save the *Brendel*? What do you mean?"

"He is the sword of El, and you cannot stop him. No one can. But if you kill her, it will break him. There will be no compassion, no faith, only vengeance, and you would need to pray to El himself to stop him."

"You think him able to kill me, to bring down this Empire?"

"You haven't seen his eyes." Those eyes that haunted him since a night far to the west in an inn called *The Blue Eagle*. His father dying on the floor. Carys crying out in sorrow. And Caleb …

Tanicus chuckled. "After all you've seen. You know your army is about to be crushed, do you not? Here I am with you and his sister in my power. And you still believe there is power greater than mine? Even now?"

"I know there is."

The High Evilord of Kryus didn't speak or move for a long time, his face blank.

Tanicus turned to Earon and said, "I must thank you, Earon. I could crush the *Brendel* with my army or with the vualta or with the power within me, but you have given me a weapon I didn't know I possessed."

"No," Earon begged.

"The nine gods have brought you and her to me," Tanicus said. "And I shall use their blessing. Once more, Earon, I thank you."

Tanicus raised his hand over Carys.

Earon roared and leapt to his feet. He reached for Tanicus' throat with his one hand. Tanicus backhanded him, and Earon fell, his skull smacking the stone floor. Disoriented, Earon tried to get up, and he was helped by the two Sunguard. But they also held his shoulders with a grip stronger than iron.

"Let him watch this," Tanicus said.

With both hands extended over Carys' body, the Emperor closed his eyes.

Carys' body went rigid, and her mouth opened. It made no sound, but it formed a perfect circle of agony. Mists rose from her body, from her pores, rising even through her clothes and entering Tanicus' fingers and palms.

Earon struggled and shook his head and cried out. To no avail.

Please, El, stop him. Please. Don't do this to Caleb. Don't.

But El did not answer that prayer.

Carys' skin shrunk and shriveled and her muscles and flesh grew smaller and tight on her bones, leaving her a skeleton with a skin.

She was only a dry husk.

Earon went limp, lowering his head. "You shogger. You maddy breakin' idiot. You don't know what you've done."

"I assure you," Tanicus said. "I do. And now, so shall you."

Tanicus turned to Earon and took three soft steps toward him.

Earon's body was lifted by unseen hands again. He did not resist. He felt as empty as Carys' body looked.

"If you see the nine gods, then you shall understand," Tanicus said. "If not, then it has been a pleasure speaking with you, Earon. You've been very helpful."

Tanicus lifted his hands.

Earon experienced the pain of his life exiting his body. His only hope was that it would end soon.

It did not.

CHAPTER 28

THE BREAKING

Eshlyn didn't know how Bweth was still alive, let alone with the energy to push another person out of her body.

The armor had been removed and piled over to the side. Eshyn had also taken the tunic and trousers from her. Bweth was only in her sweat and blood-soaked undertunic. Eshlyn had ripped the cleaner parts of her clothes away and used them as binding for Bweth's wound. The water had broken a few minutes before and spilled on the ground. Eshlyn knelt in mud and blood and held Bweth's hand with her left and used her right to hover the water bag from Macarus' saddle over the half-dwarf's dry lips.

Bweth's eyes were closed, and she breathed shallow, her skin a deathly pale.

Arrows flew overhead. The battle around them was a din of noise, steel of spear and blade and shield clashing, men and elves screaming in pain or anger or both, the pounding of hooves and feet. The Deathguard made no noise; Caleb and Macarus and others shouted, fighting. She had to speak above the clamor, and it made her sound as desperate as she felt.

"Drink," she said to Bweth. "Please. Before the next contraction."

Bweth's air wheezed, but her lips parted enough for her tongue to seek the water. Eshlyn dropped a trickle on her tongue. Bweth winced, swallowing, panting for a moment.

Then her body tensed, half sitting up, and the half-dwarf was breaking the bones in her hand with that grip. Eshlyn dropped the water bag into the mud and wrapped her arm around her. She didn't know how much it really helped. She just remembered her own mother doing it when Javyn was born.

Eshlyn had been raised on a ranch, and while she focused her attention on the business side of things, she had seen her share of horse and cow births. No two were exactly the same. But this wasn't an animal. This was her friend, Bweth, as much a sister to her as anyone could be.

She wished her mother was with her here. Eshlyn had never done this part, and she felt inept with only one child. With people all around her and two people in her arms, she felt alone. It didn't matter, however. She was all Bweth had … she would do what must be done.

Bweth's stomach tightened, and her brow furrowed. Sweat covered her face and body. She grunted. When Eshlyn had Javyn, she had screamed like the world was ending. It seemed to be ending now, and Bweth barely made a noise.

After the contraction ended, Eshlyn lifted up the undertunic. She could not see a head yet. She sighed and prayed to El.

Bweth collapsed as if dead, and only a fluttering of a nostril told Eshlyn she still lived.

"You're doing great," Eshlyn encouraged. "I think you're close."

Stones sailed over them, and Eshlyn was so focused on the birth that it took her a second to recognize the direction and distance.

Eshlyn lifted up her head as she watched three stones fly high and far from the top of the wall. She wasn't an expert at trebuchets, either, but she had seen enough to know that those stones would fall hundreds of mitres beyond the current battle. Who were the Kryans firing at? Their own militan? She couldn't tell from the ground.

Bweth grunted and crushed Eshlyn's hand. Eshlyn gasped in pain, held her close, and encouraged her to push. She didn't know how many more Bweth had in her.

———+———

Macarus blocked one swipe and another as he moved out of range of the Deathguard. Ewha slid behind the Deathguard and attacked with her unforged sword. The Deathguard leapt to the right, spinning and cutting with the spikes on its legs, forcing Ewha to stop.

The Deathguard landed and lifted its arms in defense while Macarus advanced, his sword clanging on metal. Bweth and Eshlyn had found the eyes were a weakness – several Deathguard were down because of that insight, but the Deathguard had learned. They also had learned that the unforged swords were stronger than their flesh armor, which was why this one struck at Ewha's blade hand.

Ewha didn't bring her unforged sword around fast enough, and the Deathguard cut deep into her right arm. The blade fell to the ground.

Macarus attempted to overwhelm the Deathguard with speed and volume, but he could not get through the Deathguard's defense enough to do any real damage. The Deathguard kicked out, and Macarus twisted to the side but was still struck by the bottom of its foot in the torso. He cried out, at least one rib cracked, and he fell back, finding a way to block two blades with his one as he did.

Ewha lifted the unforged sword in her left hand, blood pouring down her arm to the muddy ground. She had the tan skin of Veradis, but her skin paled swinging her sword at the Deathguard's back. The Deathguard spun to dodge, but she scored with the unforged sword. Since she attacked left-handed, and weakly, the unforged sword didn't dig deep.

Macarus bounced from his backside to his knees and then jumped toward the Deathguard, ignoring the sharp pain in his side.

The Deathguard continued with its spin, slapping aside the unforged sword with one blade and stabbing through Ewha's chest with the other. The moment slowed for Macarus, a helpless thing, while the woman's eyes bulged, blood bubbled in her mouth, and she collapsed. A *Sohan-el*, dead.

Macarus gritted his teeth and stabbed into a space between two steel plates on the back. The Deathguard stiffened but kicked out. Macarus avoided the strike, pulled his blade from the Deathguard with blood trailing, and hit the Deathguard with his own kick.

The Deathguard absorbed the blow, and Macarus ducked and leaned as the blades came at his face. He regained his footing and then changed direction, diving to the ground. His shoulder hit the mud. He rolled over and came up in a crouch to block blades with his own. He gave a quick stab between plates at the abdomen, which didn't go deep, but it drove the Deathguard back. Now that he created some separation, he rolled to his right once more, circling the Deathguard. He tumbled and reached out with his left hand and gripped the hilt of Ewha's unforged sword.

The Deathguard rushed forward, and Macarus could not stand against the barrage of strikes from the blades of the Deathguard. He blocked with both blades, grunting at the pure strength of the Deathguard. Macarus waited until the Deathguard lifted blades to strike, committed, and instead of blocking, Macarus lunged forward and past the legs of his opponent to get a better angle. Once past, he lurched to his feet, swinging.

The unforged sword in his left hand cut through the elbow of the Deathguard's right arm. The limb fell to the ground. Macarus deflected the left blade with his right, and he reversed the unforged blade across the neck of the Deathguard, removing its head from its body.

Panting, he stood straight and looked down at Ewha while the Deathguard twitched a few times before hitting the ground. He took a step and saw her glassy, empty eyes. Sticking his forged sword in the ground, he knelt and reached down, closing her eyes.

"Go with El, warrior," he whispered. "You've earned the rest."

I hope Caleb is right.

Macarus looked up, and a Deathguard bore down on a Steelside alone, five mitres away.

He switched the unforged sword to his right hand and picked the other sword from the ground with his left. He stood. Striding toward the Deathguard, he bared his teeth.

He had a moment to feel the weight of the unforged sword, lighter in his hand than the other, but he knew it was stronger. A sense of purpose warmed his heart, gave him courage despite his sorrow and exhaustion and pain.

Stones flew in the sky, and he frowned as he noticed them. Too strong to be aimed at the *Hamon-el* ... unless the reserves were entering the field. But the stones traveled to the north from the wall. The reserves would come directly west.

He glanced over his shoulder, and in his periphery, his guess was proven true. Fifteen hundred reserves came down the hill from the west. Who had made that decision?

The Deathguard had recognized his approach, and he didn't have time to do any more investigation. The Steelside was missing an arm at the shoulder and lay on the ground, clutching the wound that spit blood. The Deathguard lifted blades for a killing blow.

Macarus reached his left arm across his body and sent his sword spinning towards the Deathguard's head. The Deathguard had to change its tactic, going for defense instead by lifting the blades to block the flying sword.

In that instant of hesitation, the Steelside rolled to a safer distance. And Macarus leapt with the unforged sword.

Macarus had been in a hundred battles, maybe more. He had used a sword for more than four hundred years. He was used to feeling the sword as a part of him, an extension of his own body and mind in a way that very few ever experienced except for the great blademasters.

Wielding the unforged sword was different. It was similar in theory but more personal, as if the sword was alive and worked with him, helped to make that flow more sure and committed.

The Deathguard set its feet and engaged, and Macarus entered the flow as if for the first time.

Everything he ever learned as a swords-elf was available, and suddenly in new combinations he had never considered. His moves were not flashy or overdone; he blocked the blades with efficiency and calm, a greater calm than he could have forced upon himself. He saw the Deathguard as it was, a dark and evil thing, a creature whose soul had been twisted far more than its body.

The Deathguard struck, and Macarus was not there. Macarus believed his eyes could have been closed as he moved his feet and countered. One swipe removed one Deathguard arm, another the second. He stabbed straight through the heart and chest, to the hilt, but it was not out of vengeance or anger. It was what needed done. Macarus slid the unforged blade from the chest and brought it down upon the Deathguard's forehead, splitting it in two.

The Deathguard fell dead.

Breathing in through his nose, Macarus scanned the rest of the battle. Two Deathguard still stood, and he watched as Kenneth and Xak dispatched one and Wes and Jaff the other.

While bodies of *Sohan-el* and Steelsides littered the field, the Deathguard were all dead.

Caleb jogged toward the steel wagon prison where the Deathguard had been kept. Macarus wondered what the man was doing, and as Caleb climbed up on top, he realized Caleb wanted a better perspective of the entire battle.

Macarus sprinted and climbed to stand next to Caleb. Following the man's gaze, he looked to the north with the peerglass he unclipped from his belt.

The force that now engaged the Kryan militan to the north was unlike anything Macarus had ever seen. A couple hundred rode some sort of insect, like a large white ant, and the rest of them, another thousand or more, attacked with white weapons and armor.

The *Hamon-el* reserves approached from the west. The remaining line of Caleb's army was thin but held while the Kryan militan were being pressed now from both sides. The trebuchets had ceased, but *Hamon-el* and those from the strange new force had suffered casualties.

Caleb nodded at the white insects and strange army north of them. "Who the shog are those?"

"I have no idea," Macarus answered. Continuing to scan, he only saw a handful of horses still upright and perhaps ten bosaur.

"Looks like they're on our side," Caleb said.

"Agreed." The militan were caught from both sides. Macarus gave the Kryan legion another fifteen minutes before they were completely slaughtered. "Just in time, as well. Might be able to buy our retreat."

Caleb lowered his own peerglass and looked at the gate behind them. "Retreat?"

Then they both turned their heads as they heard Eshlyn scream.

———+———

Bweth hadn't spoken in so long, that when she finally attempted it, Eshlyn clung to a hope that was then dashed like a wedding vase in a divorce.

"E-esh," Bweth breathed after a contraction.

Eshlyn leaned close.

"You ..." Bweth licked her lips. "You will have to ... cut her out."

Eshlyn froze. She shook her head. "No. I can't. You can't ask me to do that."

She was so pale. Her lips were blue. "I'm sorry."

A strange groan escaped from Eshlyn's throat. "You can do this, Bweth. Look, the battle is almost over. We'll get you to the physicians. Don't give up now!" Eshlyn gripped Bweth's hands. "Just a few more. You're almost there."

"It's … over, Lady." Bweth opened her eyes and looked at Eshlyn with such pain and love that Eshlyn grunted as if she'd been struck. "Her name … is Gretchen."

Eshlyn gaped and then snapped her mouth shut. "Listen, don't you do this to me. If you do … I'll call him Snooky or something. He'll need his mother, you hear me?" She pleaded with Bweth through sobs. "Please."

Bweth glared at Eshlyn, and she squeezed her hands so tight it hurt. "Care for her, Lady. She's all that's left of him …"

Then Bweth Ironhorn collapsed back and fell still. The hands that had been squeezing Eshlyn's wilted.

Eshlyn cried out. She took Bweth's shoulders and shook them. But the empty eyes were glassy, gazing at the sky but they saw nothing. Not anymore.

Eshlyn laid her head on Bweth's chest, exhausted, her hand on her belly. Even with the chaos and roar of battle around her, Eshlyn felt kilomitres away.

The belly moved beneath her hand.

A foot or a hand rolled like a wave across the bare, round stomach. Eshlyn spread her fingers and felt the babe move.

You will have to cut her out.

Eshlyn's face twisted in anger. She rose to her knees.

"Shog you, Bweth! You can't leave me to do this."

But it was an empty curse. The dagger on the saddle of Macarus' horse drew her gaze.

The babe kicked her hand.

Eshlyn's shoulders slumped. She stood and walked over to the saddle. Licking her lips, she tasted her own tears. Her hand reached up and grabbed the dagger from the saddle. Eshlyn turned and knelt at the side of the dead body while the life struggled within.

She had watched her father do this, once, with a horse that died in labor. The foal had been alive, and Eshlyn was nine years old and watched her father, her hero, the strongest man she knew, reach down with his knife and carefully cut the foal from the mare. It had been the first time she saw her father cry.

Pressing the dagger to the skin just above the pubic area, she hesitated. How deep should she cut? While she had seen her father perform the surgery, he hadn't taught her enough. She strained her brain to remember the details of how he had used the small knife to get to the foal inside. Her dagger was too big, she knew, but it was all she had to work with.

The stomach rolled once more, and Eshlyn took a full breath. Her hand trembled, and she held the breath to still her hand, however much her heart pounded. Wiping her running nose with the back of her sleeve, she placed both hands on the hilt of the dagger and pressed.

She cut into the skin, a long and curved cut around the bottom of the stomach. The skin separated, revealing another clear and white layer underneath. More skin and fat. Using her fingers, she widened the cut. She gently pressed into the next layer and cut, forcing her fingers into the fat and making room.

Nothing else existed. Only her and the task.

The womb was visible now, more movement underneath from the baby, and she gritted her teeth while she pulled on the placenta with her left hand, pinching with two fingers, and made small cuts into the womb. The placenta ripped away to show the head of the baby.

Eshlyn used the tip of the dagger to widen the wound to allow her hands to get in and the baby to get out. When it was enough, she dropped the dagger and plunged her hands into the womb. She felt around the body of the baby and grabbed under the shoulders. And with a sob and a grunt, she lifted the wet and slippery baby out of Bweth's dead body.

It was a girl, her skin a light brown, and her head with red hair. She smacked her on the bottom, and her mouth opened in a dramatic wail that carried across the battlefield. Eshlyn cradled her, and despite the tragedy all around, she barked a laugh of joy.

Then she looked from the baby to Bweth, her body ripped and torn. She wiped the slime and blood from the girl.

She looked up to an audience, a silent one, the *Sohan-el* and Steelsides that had been fighting the Deathguard. That part of the battle was over. Gunnar had removed his helmet, his eyes glistening in anger and sorrow. Kenneth, Wes, and Xak stood with their hands clasped in front of them, holding their unforged swords. Macarus sniffed at Bweth's remains, a sword in his hand.

Caleb stood across from Eshlyn. His sword was in its sheath, and his knuckles were white on the Kingstaff. He met her eyes, and she could read the love and pain and sorrow there like a book. He touched a small leather bag at his belt.

Eshlyn gazed down at the baby, and a tear fell from her cheek to her forehead.

"Hello, Gretchen," she said with death and war surrounding them. "Welcome to the world."

Caleb lowered his head.

The anger within him simmered, hotter than the fires in Bweth's forge. The scars on his back itched like maddy.

Ewha dead and her sword now in Macarus' hand.

Bweth gone and her baby girl wrapped in Eshlyn's arms.

He breathed in and out. He calmed the anger within. It cooled.

Caleb pulled the unforged sword from its sheath.

"Caleb?" he heard Macarus ask.

He glared up at Macarus, and the elf flinched.

Caleb marched toward the gate. Macarus and the *Sohan-el* shared glances and followed him, Gunnar and the remaining Steelsides not far behind.

He wanted to tell them he would do this alone, that he didn't need them, but his jaw was clenched shut.

Within a minute, he stood at the gate, an imposing structure of thick dragonwood and steel thirty mitres tall and wide.

Caleb lifted the unforged sword in his hand, and he struck the gate with it. The gate of Asya shuddered and cracked.

He hit it again.

Macarus stood behind him. "Caleb. We don't have the numbers to invade the city. We have to find another way."

The fissure in the gate widened and the wood and steel bowed when he struck the gate, the sound reverberating across the field.

Caleb sliced horizontal and then vertical. There was a rift in the wood now enough to see through. Caleb snarled and looked through the sliver.

The blue and steel of militan, waiting for him.

Caleb lifted the sword.

The air above split and the ground shook with an explosion. He lowered the sword and turned to see a flash of lightning from the sky impact the ground on the field and throw men, elves, and dirt and mud mitres into the air. Then a third.

Macarus jogged away from the gate and strained his gaze to the sky. His brow furrowed, and he put his peerglass to his eye.

"Tanicus," he sighed. "He's on the top of the wall."

Caleb stared through the fissure in the gate to see the militan beyond.

"We have to retreat," Macarus said. "We can't stay in the open like this."

More lightning, screaming of men and elves dying behind him. He glared at the militan in the city. He could see them. *If we can get beyond the gate and into the city ...*

"Caleb!" Macarus shouted.

Even if they got into the city, they'd be in the open and vulnerable to the Worldbreaker. And how long would it take him to get up to the top of the wall to defeat Tanicus? If he could? More would die. Maybe all of them. Even then ...

His army. If they kept fighting, he might win, but everyone would die. Or he could help save some now. He glanced at the baby in Eshlyn's arms near Bweth's dead body.

He gazed at the sky. *This would be a great time for dragons, Aden. That would make a great story.*

But the sky was empty. He took a deep breath and lowered his eyes.

Caleb gave the one order he never thought he would say. Not now. "Retreat." His heart sank. "Order a retreat."

—

Eshlyn hunched over Gretchen as death rained from the sky.

She thought the battle was chaos before. She had been wrong.

The horse had run off. She had been impressed by the warhorse's obedience as the battle raged, but she supposed an unnatural assult of lightning from the sky was too much.

Clumps of dirt pelted her back from an impact of lightning ten mitres away. The sky above filled with gray clouds; the blue sky beyond began to fade to gray.

Another bolt of electricity and an eruption to her left, people of the *Hamon-el* and militan all dying in broken and burning violence. Eshlyn looked up to her right and saw a distant figure at the top of the wall in a white robe. It had arms raised and moved in tandem with the lighting, like it responded to the figure.

The Worldbreaker.

The shouting and screaming deafened her, and she didn't hear Macarus until he gripped her arm. "We have to move. Now!"

Five Steelsides surrounded her now, their shields up as if they would protect her and the baby from the power. The air, already filled with the stench of blood and crit from the battle, became stale.

She saw a bird fall from the sky, dead.

Lighting flashed to her right, and it struck a Steelside, frying the dwarf within his armor.

The remaining Kryan militan scattered. Outnumbered and now on the field with wrath pouring down on them, they ran to the gate in terror.

Who could beat such a thing? So much power.

Macarus and Gunnar lifted her from the ground and began to pull her away from Asya's city wall.

"No!" she screamed and reached out for Bweth's body. "We can't leave her!"

Macarus shook his head. "Lady. There's nothing to save."

She didn't know how she had more sorrow left, but it poured out of her when they pulled her to the west. Caleb walked towards them, but he was not looking at her. His head was lowered as he strode, calm and confident in the midst of terror. Thirty five mitres from the gate, he stopped and lifted his head. Their gazes met.

She read his lips. *Go.*

Caleb turned around to face the Worldbreaker. He raised his unforged sword.

The next bolt of lightning that shot from a dark cloud changed direction mid-air. It snaked down toward Caleb. Eshlyn cried out his name, and then watched in awe as the blue bolt slammed into the unforged sword.

The blade absorbed it.

"Great and mightly El," Eshlyn whispered.

Humans and elves ran from the barrage of lightning, and Caleb crouched.

Macarus froze, his face blank for a moment before releasing Eshlyn and looking down at the sword in his own hand. She knew it was an unforged sword. Where had he gotten it? She didn't see Ewha standing among the *Sohan-el*; the young woman had died, as well.

The elf Captain's jaw tightened. He ran toward Caleb.

Another Steelside took her arm and ran with her and Gretchen to the west.

———

Macarus knew he should run back to the camp, but he couldn't. Not with a *Sohan-el's* sword in his hand.

Jaff, Kenneth, Wes, and Xak stood with Caleb as well when Macarus reached him. Caleb directed all of them to spread out in a line north to south, and they did, the six of them about five mitres between them. While they got in position, Caleb raised his sword and deflected another bolt of lightning.

Militan passed them, racing back toward Asya. They didn't bother with enemies or battle. They wanted to get off the field, to safety. Some militan ran to the south, since the strange army with insects held the northern line.

Macarus lifted Ewha's unforged sword. He didn't know how Caleb attracted the bolts. He saw Jaff withstand one to his left.

None of the bolts hit the *Hamon-el* or the militan as they raced back towards the camp. Macarus looked up at the dark clouds and the gray sky, and the unforged sword hummed in his hand. He cocked his head in confusion until a bolt of lightning changed direction and head right at him. He braced himself.

The bolt struck him like kilograhms of weight, but it didn't crush him. He felt the impact through his whole body, but he stood unharmed when it was over.

More lightning shot across the sky, but each bolt was pulled by an unseen hand toward the unforged swords. Xak then Kenneth then others.

There was no pattern, and Macarus bent under another bolt. But he could tell when one would head his way since the sword would hum, like a call or a challenge.

He had to get one of his own.

Minutes passed, and as Jaff absorbed another stroke, Macarus glanced over his shoulder. The humans and elves and dwarves that could walk or move with help were two hundred mitres away. Macarus and the *Sohan-el* were alone on the field, except for the dead.

"Back away," Caleb shouted. The other five of them obeyed, taking steps back, continuing to face the Worldbreaker and absorbing the bolts of electricity. Caleb waited until they were ten mitres behind him before he followed.

It was a crawl that took patience and focus, but after another few minutes that felt much longer, they were a couple hundred mitres away from the wall themselves.

The lightning ceased. Macarus and the others picked up their pace, however facing the east, but Caleb stopped. His legs were spread. The Kingstaff was extended in his left hand and the unforged sword in his right. He stared up at the Worldbreaker, a white dot on the top of the wall. Macarus could also see hundreds, possibly a thousand, archers as well.

The man appeared as if he would charge the city by himself. As maddy as that sounded, Macarus could see him doing it.

He wanted to call out to Caleb, to argue with him to return to the camp with the rest, that he could not win a fight with the Worldbreaker and the legions that awaited him. But he couldn't speak. When would they get another chance? A large portion of their army was dead or wounded, and they had spent most of their ammunition for the ballista and catapults. Macarus knew retreat was the only option, as difficult as that was to accept. Caleb was a trained strategist, despite his protestations to the contrary. He would see it. Wouldn't he?

Caleb lifted the sword and staff. A bolt sliced the air to him, and instead of absorbing it this time, he struck it. The lightning bounced off the unforged blade and arced back at the wall. The energy slammed into the wall.

Macarus could hear the elves and militan scream.

Another bolt from the Emperor, and Caleb swatted it back. The reflected lightning hit near the top of the wall and the Worldbreaker.

Macarus froze, watching, like two gods at war.

The Worldbreaker lifted his arms; the archers at the top of the wall fired. The arrows hissed through the air and came down toward Caleb.

"Arrows!" Macarus heard Wes say beside him. "Down!"

Caleb grabbed a passing militan, who cried out, and dragged the poor elf in front of him as a shield. The arrows landed around Caleb, killing several militan still running past. The elf used as a shield died with five arrows in him. Caleb threw him off as another bolt came from the sky. He knocked it toward the wall of Asya.

Then the catapults fired.

Large stones sailed toward Caleb. He now stood alone on the field. One landed near him, three mitres away, and Caleb was thrown back by the impact. He lay there on his back and started to get up.

"We have to help him!" Wes said. "He's going to die out there."

Macarus nodded. "Let's get him."

Macarus and Wes ran forward together across the remains of battle. They reached Caleb as he staggered to his feet. Macarus grabbed Caleb by the arm, and the man whirled on him, those steel eyes full of wrath.

Macarus met the stare. "Come, Caleb. Now."

Caleb growled at him.

"We'll find another way," Macarus said.

Caleb's shoulders slumped.

Wes grabbed the other arm, and they ran, dragging Caleb up the hill to the camp, leaving the battle of Asya behind them.

—✦—

Caleb trudged across the grass, Macarus and Wes behind him. The tents were a welcome sight to his heart, that there were some who were safe, but it was also a reminder of his failure.

Eshlyn stood at the edge of camp and directed people. Wounded to the left where the physicians waited. Militan prisoners to the right where a clearing waited for them as they gathered – several hundred had surrendered with their imminent defeat and the Worldbreaker had counted them among the enemy in his assault on the field. Others went to their tents.

Far to the right were the creatures and the people that appeared from the north. A quick approximation of the large insects came to fifty.

An older man and two people from the new group stood with Eshlyn. The man and woman were dressed in green leather and that white armor. They carried themselves like leaders or people in charge.

Eshlyn looked as tired as he felt. Other than some scrapes toward the end of the battle, he realized he had not been injured that day. He couldn't remember the last time he had left battle without a major wound.

He hadn't retreated from one, either. Not a fair trade, in his mind.

Reaching Eshlyn, she forced a smile at him.

"The baby?" he asked her.

"With Javyn and Mother Natali. She's getting them settled."

"The Mahakar?"

Nodding back to the left, she said, "Back with the wounded. Patched him up, but not sure if he'll live."

"And these people?"

The old man used the question as an opportunity to step forward. "These people are the Dragonmen." Even the voice sounded familiar. "These are the leaders, chiefs if you will, of the Dragonmen. This is Abbott and Zamira."

A horn sounded from behind Caleb, from the city.

"Dragonmen?" Caleb said. "I thought they were myth and legend, a firetale to scare children."

"They are real," the old man said. "The Dragonmen have protected Dracoland for centuries. And I have been with them since I was young." His eyes misted. "We met your friends, Aden and Tamya, and they went to find the dragons."

"Aden?" A spark of hope appeared in his heart. He drew closer to the old man. "You saw Aden?" *With the dragons, we could attack again ...*

"Yes," the old man said.

Macarus shouted from behind. "Caleb! The gates are opening!"

Caleb looked over his shoulder at Macarus, a hundred mitres away to the east, peerglass to his eye. Caleb held up a hand to the elf for him to wait a moment.

Caleb squinted at the old man. "Do I know you?"

Eshlyn moved back as the old man came closer and placed his hand on Caleb's shoulder. What did she know? "My name is Redan Be'Luthel."

He couldn't speak for a few seconds. "Be'Luthel ... like ...?"

"Reyan and Sheron were my children," Redan said. "They left the Dragonmen many years ago."

He heard Macarus' voice continue to try and get his attention, but he couldn't listen as his mind reeled.

The nose was different, but the shape of the head and the rest of the face were an older version of Reyan, his uncle. And the nose was his mother's nose. And Carys'.

"Then that means you're my ..."

Redan placed his other hand on Caleb's shoulder. "Yes, boy, I am your grandfather."

Caleb blinked and stared at the man.

"Well, I am your grandson, then. Caleb."

Redan grinned. "Yes. Well met."

Jaff stood behind Caleb now, waiting.

Time passed, and Caleb took another step closer to his ... grandfather. A man responsible for much of his legacy but whom he had never met. Here.

His grandfather had gray eyes.

Caleb had so many questions, so many things he wanted to talk about. There wasn't time.

"Aden," Caleb asked. "Did he find them? The dragons?" Perhaps this wasn't over, after all.

Redan shrugged. "I do not know. They left days ago, and I was able to convince some of the Dragonmen to come back to the world to battle with my grandson."

Caleb placed his own hand on Redan's – his grandfather's – shoulder. "And you're more than welcome. We'll pray they succeeded. We need those dragons now more than ever." He nodded over his shoulder. "They need me, I think. But we will talk soon."

"Yes, go," Redan said. "We shall speak soon."

With a lingering nod, Caleb turned to Jaff.

"I apologize, Cal," Jaff said, glancing from Caleb to Redan.

"None needed," Caleb said.

"The gate opened and let a wagon out," Jaff said. "Then closed behind it."

"More Deathguard?"

Jaff shook his head. "Not a wagon like that. Flat bed. Something in the back."

His brow furrowed. "Gather the *Sohan-el*. Let's see what this is."

Fear threatened his heart, and he didn't know why. It was an odd feeling.

Why just a wagon?

Caleb walked to the east to the top of the hill, a hundred mitres or so, and he stood with Macarus. Caleb used his own peerglass.

A man drove the two horses that pulled the wagon, and he wore tattered clothes. As they neared, Caleb could see the white of his eyes. A wraith. But not one that was violent, one tasked to drive this particular wagon. Caleb couldn't see what was in the wagon; a sheet covered the bed.

Militan gathered the dead on the field, close to the wall. They made piles, he could see. Human in one; elves in another.

Jaff, Wes, Kenneth, and Xak were there with them, now. The wagon drove along the road from the gate as much as it could. The wraith avoided holes from lightning or stones from catapults or trebuchets when needed. The air stirred with a slight breeze as the sky cleared now that the Worldbreaker was done with his manipulation of the created world.

Eshlyn joined them, silent.

The wagon was three fourths of the way up the hill, and Caleb's gaze was drawn to the top of the wall. The Emperor stood there, small even in the peerglass. It was like he waited for the wagon to reach its destination. Caleb lowered the peerglass. What kind of magic was this?

The wraith drove the wagon straight to Caleb, and when it was a few mitres away, the wraith pulled the wagon to a stop. Then his eyes closed, and he went limp in a heap on the bench.

Caleb's breath shuddered. He approached the wagon with the Kingstaff in his hand. The rest of them moved to follow, but he stopped them all with a glare. He walked to the side of the wagon. The Kingstaff in his left hand, he reached out with his right and removed the sheet.

Bodies lay in the back of the wagon. Five of them. Iletus. Tobiah. Zalman.

Two of them were shriveled husks. Earon and ...

His world ended. If time passed, he didn't know it.

Caleb dropped the Kingstaff.

He felt a hand on his shoulder and heard a soft voice, and he spun to see an elf. All he could see was an elf. He grabbed the elf by the neck and squeezed as hard as he could.

The elf beat against his hands and attempted to push him away but to no avail. Caleb was steel, cold and lifeless.

I will kill them all.

There were voices, and one broke through to his ears. "Caleb, stop!"

Eshlyn.

Something at his hip weighed him down. The sword. He fell to his knees, dragging the elf with him.

Another hand on his shoulder. Eshlyn's voice. "Caleb, please."

He released the elf. It was the hardest thing he had ever done.

The elf coughed and crawled away. Macarus.

Caleb covered his face with his hands, and the world was silent around him.

Caleb stood and leaned into the back of the wagon and lifted her body from the back of the wagon. She was so light, too light. He cradled her in his arms.

He heard sounds, not sure who made them or what they were. Could have been him. It didn't matter.

Caleb's knees buckled, and he sat on the ground with her in his lap and his arms. He held her close but not tight. He didn't want to break her.

He held her like he did all those years ago in a hidden cave in southern Erelon, weeping while they heard the horrifying sounds of his mother tortured by the militan. He had saved her. He couldn't save her anymore.

He stroked her hair like he did then, but now it was like straw, a dead thing like the world.

Nothing existed in that moment, not a revolution or dragons or a grandfather he never knew.

Carys was dead.

CHAPTER 29

THE FATE OF THE WORLD

High General Felix approached the Emperor on the top of the wall. Felix's eyes tightened at the setting sun in the distance.

The field looked like the gods had chewed through it, thousands of dead bodies littered among gaping holes and rips in the earth from the battle and the engines of destruction. After watching and giving orders through the day, the General was impressed with the human army, although he shouldn't be too surprised now that militan had joined the *Brendel*. There was even word that Macarus, the son of Senator Diona, was now among them.

Their strategy had been aggressive. He didn't know how they coordinated that separate force from the north. His scouts hadn't seen them over the past two days.

Between the new force with those strange insect creatures and the bosaur, the *Brendel's* army had defeated fifteen thousand militan on the field. Ten thousand with a force of five, perhaps six with the reinforcements. And they had killed the Deathguard, which the General had heard was impossible.

Without the Emperor, the Worldbreaker, the *Brendel* and his army would have entered the city of Asya. Felix believed with the thousands of militan waiting behind the gate, they wouldn't have gotten far, but he was learning not to underestimate the *Brendel*.

The wind whipped their robes, and Tanicus spoke while he gazed to the west. "You have word?"

"Yes, my Lord," Felix said. "Their camp is a kilomitre to the west, as it was last night. They have not moved."

"Are they preparing to further retreat?" Tanicus, who had once been the greatest general in Kryan history, knew as well as Felix the wise measure would be for the *Brendel's* army to withdraw even further, perhaps back to Giannis or Vicksburg. Felix would travel to Vicksburg – the River Moriel a natural barrier and easier to defend.

The *Brendel's* army was not a normal army, however. They didn't seem to operate by the same rules. "No, my Lord."

Tanicus turned to him, now, and his eyes narrowed. "They are preparing to attack again."

Felix shrugged. "Scouts could not say. They are gathering and organizing, but the scouts could not determine the purpose."

Tanicus returned to gazing at the sunset. "The *Brendel* is done, either way." The Emperor drew a deep breath. "What is the state of our forces?"

"Another fifteen thousand militan at the ready. We are clearing the field as best we can while they've drawn back. We could attack soon."

"And the vualta?" the Emperor asked.

Felix hesitated before answering. The vualta had been manufactured from the same Moonguard that designed the Deathguard. "The Moonguard say it is still recovering from the journey across the ocean. It can be ready at your command, but they suggest waiting until the morning."

Tanicus nodded, appearing pensive.

"We can attack now," Felix said. "With ten or fifteen thousand rested militan, there is no reason to wait. They are wounded and vulnerable with perhaps two or three thousand available for battle. Their bosaur and calvary are decimated. They have little to no ammunition left for their siege engines. There would be no contest. Now is our opportunity, my Lord, to end the *Brendel* and his army forever."

The Emperor did not respond for a moment. He laid his hands upon the parapet in front of him.

"The age of the *Brendel* is over. It is only a matter of time," the Emperor said. "Your advice is prudent, General, but it matters now the method by which we end him. We are at the crux. The revolution of the *Brendel* has won victories and inspired rebellion, even back in Kaltiel. We cannot simply beat him, which we have done, but we must do so in such a way that the name of Kryus causes such fear that no human or dwarf or elf would ever think to rebel."

General Felix clasped his hands before him. *A weapon in the hands of a commander is a dangerous thing. They always seek to use it. The bigger the weapon, the more the temptation to put it to the test.*

Tanicus filled his chest with air as the sun ducked beneath the horizon, the sky darkening but retaining a hint of light. "I have realized that this war was a gift from the gods."

"A gift, my Lord?"

"Yes, a gift," Tanicus affirmed. "We had grown complacent, General, and Julius was correct. We were unfaithful to the gods. This war has wounded us, but we will return stronger than before. And with that strength, we shall rebuild and place the world under our dominion so they can know the peace and provision of the gods."

Tanicus turned to Felix, and the light of the setting sun reflected in the Emperor's eyes.

"We shall wait until the morning," Tanicus said. "And unleash the vualta upon them. The world will know the power that we have hidden. We hide it no longer. All will see it in the light."

"Yes, my Lord. I understand. Forgive me, but we have never used the vualta before in battle. We don't know what will happen."

"The gods are with us. They brought his cousin and his sister to me. The *Brendel* is broken, as is his army, but I will leave nothing to chance. We will give the vualta time to recover and attack at dawn."

—✦—

Eshlyn sat in the chair as the waning light wafted through the open flap in the command tent. Others sat in a circle – Jaff, Macarus, Mother Natali, Gunnar, and Falati, all of them caked with dirt and blood from the battle. Also seated there was Redan, the Prophet's father, and the leaders of the Dragonmen, Abbott and Zamira with their odd pale white skin, red hair and eyes.

Jaff lit a lamp and set it in the middle of the circle.

The space was quiet. The spectre of death and sorrow hung over them like a thick mist, difficult to navigate. It was difficult to see past her grief, but she knew they each shared it with her, however alone she felt.

Jaff saw another *Sohan-el* die, along with hundreds of Ghosts, many his friends. Macarus had fought his own nation, his county, watching thousands of his people die on both sides of the conflict. The Steelsides had lost thirteen of their number, most from the battle with the Deathguard. The bodies of Carys and Earon proved that Tobiah was dead, along with Shecayah and most of the bosaur and hundreds of Liorians. Mother Natali was calm and confident, but silent.

For Redan, she could see the conflict on his face. From what she gathered, the Dragonmen had been isolated for centuries, and he had been with them most of his adult life. In his return to the world, he found two grandchildren dead. Abbott and Zamira spoke little of the Common Tongue, so he was there to translate.

For Eshlyn, Carys was like a sister, and she had been an intimate witness to Earon's redemption. Tobiah and Shecayah were leaders of the Beorgai that she convinced to join the revolution. Bweth had also been like family. That wasn't counting Zalman and Iletus and Ewha and the many other names that ran through her mind.

All she wanted was to crawl into a corner and curl up and weep. But Javyn waited in Mother Natali's tent, as well as a new little one, Gretchen. But decisions had to be made. There were responsibilities.

Eshlyn voiced the question that burned in everyone's mind. "Anyone seen Caleb?"

The group did not respond, all but Abbott and Zamira gazing at the ground.

Jaff finally spoke. "He's in his tent. He fights everyone off that comes to see him."

Caleb had led the wagon off to the north, a half kilomitre from the camp in a wooded area. He had dug graves there. Eshlyn and others tried to help him, but he wouldn't allow it. Once he was done, he sat between the graves. His only words were to leave him, so they did.

Eshlyn's jaw grew tight and shook her head.

Jaff sighed. "His sister ..."

"That's no excuse," she growled. "We've all lost people. I lost my husband, my brother. You think I loved them any less? I loved Carys, too, you know. We all did. She was ..." She grunted as she suppressed a sob. "It doesn't give him the right to disappear on us. We need him."

The tent was silent for another moment. Eshlyn took a deep breath.

"But even without him, we need to make some decisions," she said. "What are our options?"

Macarus sat up. Eshlyn tried not to see how red his neck was. "The only option I see is to retreat."

"Retreat?" Jaff said. "This army has never retreated."

"We did today," Macarus countered. "And it was the right thing to do. With the Worldbreaker and our numbers ... we wouldn't make the wall again. We could retreat, find a defensible position, build our numbers again. Even from Lior and Veraden."

"There's no option for attack?" Eshlyn asked.

Macarus shook his head. "We won't make it in the city, to the sure."

"Even with the Dragonmen?" Jaff asked.

Redan started as if waking from a dream. He cleared his throat. "The Dragonmen aren't really an army, as it were. Each are individually trained well, as warriors, but only in groups of twenty at the most."

"Sounds like they fit right in with this army," Macarus mumbled.

Gunnar frowned, thinking. "What of those creatures they ride?"

"The stalgest," Redan said.

Gunnar nodded. "They appear to be some relation to an ant, correct?"

"Yes," Redan said with caution.

"Can they dig?" Gunnar pressed. "Make tunnels, that sort of thing?"

Redan sat forward. "They can."

Falati straightened and stared at Gunnar. "Then perhaps we don't have to make it through the gate. We could come at the city in different directions."

"Their defenses are focused on the field to the east of the city, to protect the gate," Jaff added.

Macarus held up a hand. "Are you suggesting we use these stalgest to tunnel under the wall and enter the city?"

"We could take advantage of our training, individually and in smaller numbers," Jaff said.

Falati pursed her lips. "And avoid conflict with the major force."

"Or the Worldbreaker," Gunnar added. "He could not sufficiently focus on a hundred groups of twenty."

"We don't know that," Macarus said. "This is maddy. It sounds like one of Caleb's plans ..."

"Well," Jaff said. "He did train us."

Macarus snorted. "You're going to have to deal with the Emperor, one way or another."

Jaff lifted his chin. "We've got unforged swords, as do you. Caleb showed us how to protect ourselves from his attacks. While the militan are focused on small groups moving throughout the city, we slip through and get to Tanicus."

"You say that like we sneak out of the tavern at the end of the night," Macarus said. "He'll have Sunguard and who knows what else to protect him."

"If we retreat now," Jaff said. "Then we don't know if we'll ever get a shot at this. We'll have to go back to the Forest of Saten and hide, and that'll only give Kryus time to adjust."

Eshlyn nodded and turned to the old man. "Redan, will you ask them if they'll be willing to do this?"

Macarus' jaw dropped. "Eshlyn ..."

She gestured to the Dragonmen. "It's all crit if they say no anyway. Redan, will you ask them, please?"

Redan looked from her to Macarus. He turned to Abbott and Zamira and spoke to them in the First Tongue. It was an odd sounding language, both harsh and soft at different times. Abbott and Zamira shared a glance with those red eyes and spoke to one another while the group waited. Abbott and Zamira ceased their conversation, and Abbott looked at the group. He said a few words and nodded.

Redan took a deep breath. "He says they will, but on one condition."

Macarus raised a brow. "And what is that?"

"They will not attack the city without the *Brendel*," Redan said.

Different reactions around the room, most of them disappointed.

"Tell them we feel that is more than fair," Eshlyn said then addressed the group. "We will prepare to attack in the morning. We don't have time to incorporate the Dragonmen into the divisions, so they'll be put in groups of fifteen or twenty, as will the rest of the *Hamon-el*. Falati, can you reorganize accordingly?" She nodded. "Good. Coordinate with the Dragonmen. Macarus, we'll need you to choose the most strategic places to burrow and dig, as many as we can find."

Macarus glared at her. Then he appeared resigned.

"What about Caleb?" Falati asked. "He won't see anyone."

Eshlyn spoke through her teeth. "He'll see me." She scanned the tent. "We will meet an hour before dawn. If Caleb joins us, we will attack. If he's not there ..." she paused, "then we retreat into the Saten. Everyone needs rest. Go."

Gunnar rose first with a grunt and left the tent, a look of respect in his eyes when he passed her. Falati was next, then Abbott and Zamira.

Redan stood to follow but hesitated. "Tell me true, Lady Eshlyn. I'm a scholar. I'm no warrior. But this plan sounds like suicide. Am I wrong?"

Eshlyn placed her hands in her lap. "You're not wrong. But if Caleb and the *Hamon-el* had turned away when it seemed hopeless, we would never have come this far. Now is not the time for fear, but courage."

"And prayer," Redan said.

"Yes," Eshlyn said. "And prayer. They go hand in hand."

"Yes. They do." He left the tent.

Macarus stared at her for a long time. She narrowed her eyes at him. "What?"

He chuckled. "I was thinking about this young woman I met a year ago in Ketan, full of passion and gruts. And now ..."

"Now what?" she asked. "Have I changed so much?"

"In a way, no," Macarus said. "But also, very much. You realize what you did, right?"

Her brow furrowed. To be honest, she didn't.

Macarus grinned. He stood and walked to her. He set his hand on her shoulder. "You just led this army as well as Caleb ever did. You may not need him, after all."

Eshlyn looked up at him. Her eyes blurred.

He was kind, but she didn't believe him. *A lion-man on a mountain facing the large serpent.* They would need Caleb before it was over.

Macarus gave her a sad smile. "See you in the morning." And he left the command tent.

Eshlyn licked her lips and wiped her check with her thumb. Her eyes rested on Mother Natali.

"You were quiet," Eshlyn accused.

"There was nothing I needed to say," Natali said.

"Nothing?"

Natali stood and leaned on her cane. "The elf was right. This army, these people who were not a people but now are, they no longer need Caleb to lead them now that they have you. And I said nothing because you do not need me, either."

Eshlyn stood to face the old woman. "That's not true. We do need you."

"You misunderstand, Lady," Natali said. "That truth does not wound me. On the contrary, it means I have done something right."

Mother Natali began to walk out of the tent, and Eshlyn spoke to her. "I'll be by to get Javyn and Gretchen in a few minutes."

"Do not worry yourself," Natali said. "The children are welcome for the night. Take time and get cleaned up. You need to rest. Come and see them when you are ready."

Eshlyn glanced down at her clothes and skin covered and caked in mud and blood. She shook her head. "Sounds like I need you, after all."

Mother Natali shrugged her shoulders. "In a different way, perhaps. I shall see you in the morning."

Natali left the tent.

Eshlyn stood alone in the tent for a few minutes, awash in the encouragement but still deep in the sorrow. Leaning down, she grabbed the lamp and stepped into the night.

It was dark now, the air cooler now that the sun had set. She intended to go back to her tent to clean up, but she wanted to check on the Mahakar first.

She walked through the camp to her left, weaving between tents as she made her way to the physicians.

Most of the wounded lay on the grass, many missing limbs. Others possessed deep cuts that were being stitched. She recognized every person, speaking to many as they called out her name. One couple caught her eye, two of the newer members of the *Hamon-el*.

Robb sat on the ground next to his wife, Aimi. She lay on the ground, her eyes closed. Her right leg was missing but heavily bandaged. Robb held her hand.

Eshlyn paused and placed a hand on his shoulder. He looked up. "Lady."

"How is she?"

"Physician says she may make it, but she lost a lot of blood," he said.

"It will take time to heal," Eshlyn said. "Make sure to clean the wound so it doesn't get infected."

"That's what the physician said, Lady."

If they needed to retreat further, how would all the wounded travel? Many of the bosaur and horses dead ... a logistics nightmare. But they would figure it out if they needed to.

Eshlyn saw the marriage bracelet on Aimi's right wrist, the hand he was holding.

"Stay with her," she told Robb. "She knows you're there. You give her strength."

"Yes, Lady," he said.

Eshlyn patted his shoulder and left them. She walked past the larger physician's tent where the more serious injuries were. She did not go in there. She told herself she didn't want to be a distraction to the physicians, but she realized she wasn't brave enough to deal with those tragedies. Not tonight.

In the clearing beyond the physician's tent, the Mahakar waited for her.

He lay on his side. She had to get closer to see his injuries, and she used the lamp to inspect them. The arrows had been removed and the wounds stitched. The Mahakar slept with deep breaths. She spread her fingers and ran her hand through his fur, still soft even after the battle. She placed her cheek and head on his chest and felt it rise and listened to the low rumble of his breath. After a moment hoping and praying he would be okay, she stood and made her way back to her tent.

The camp began to quiet down and darken. Fires glowed, and she could see sentries set up within the camp and on the outskirts. She knew Macarus would have scouts and sentries roaming the open areas around the camp, Ghosts, on a rotation so everyone could get as much sleep as they could. Passing the command tent, dark and empty, the lamp in her hand lit the way to the north side of the camp where she stayed.

She walked out to the eastern edge of the camp, a platoon of soldiers there to watch. They bowed. Eshlyn gazed down at the dark field. Without a peerglass, she could still see burning mounds of bodies, the flames rising high.

So much death. And Caleb hides away.

Eshlyn turned on her heel and marched back through the camp to his tent.

She approached it with the surrounding night. The flap was down, uninviting, closed. Her steps brought her to the door. She paused and bit her lip. With a growl, she tore the flap away and entered the tent.

It was darker in the tent, only the light of the three moons through the open door. Her eyes needed a few moments to adjust. She crossed her arms, waiting and searching the dark.

Caleb knelt in the middle of the tent, his clothes covered in blood and mud. He stared down at the floor in front of him. His unforged sword lay there, flat on the ground. His long hair hung over and shrouded his face.

He didn't look up.

The blade before him reflected the light of the moons, throwing rays upon the walls of the tent. She took a step toward him, her jaw tight. One of the rays from the sword passed over his face, and she saw lines made by tears down his cheeks, paths through the dirt and dust.

The anger within her rose and threatened to explode.

She wanted to curse him, yell at him, tell him he was weak. *Who do you think you are? I lost my husband and brother. Did it hurt me any less? Not to mention the countless others in this revolution. Does our grief matter less than yours? Why do you get to hide and quit? You don't.*

She wanted to say all those things and more. Her mouth opened to begin …

And she couldn't.

Eshlyn kept looking at him. She remembered all that weight on his shoulders.

It had finally crushed him.

And it didn't matter why or how.

She realized she didn't know what to say. Should she tell him about their plan? How they needed him? How the revolution needed him?

But what would that mean to him now?

In the end, what she wanted to say was that she needed him. Not the revolution. Not the army. Not anyone else. Her.

And she already knew the answer to that.

So after another tragic moment watching him, she spun to the open door.

"Don't go." His voice a hoarse whisper. "Stay."

Eshlyn stopped. She turned. He hadn't moved. She took one step toward him, then another. With one last step, she lowered to kneel before him. The unforged sword lay between them.

Eshlyn reached out, grabbed the unforged sword by the hilt. She lifted it, slow, and then she set it to the side, to her right.

They were a pace apart. Caleb reached out his hands, palm up. Tears brimmed in her eyes as she took his hands, both of them rough and dirty. Caleb's chest heaved with a breath, and he rose up on his knees and pulled her to him with one motion. His hands released hers and slid around her waist and back into an embrace. She rose with him and threw her arms around his shoulders. He buried his face in her neck, and she did the same in his.

Her heart was a mix of sadness and joy. She ran her hands through his tangled and matted hair. He clung to her, crushing her to him. They held one another there in the moonlight.

Caleb pulled back only a little, and when she faced him, he pressed his lips to hers, and she gasped. She recovered and leaned into him and the kiss. Her hands went from his hair to his cheeks, keeping him there to make sure it was real.

The kiss extended. Every part of her leapt at the longing within her.

Caleb pulled back once more, sitting on his feet. She panted, catching her breath. He brought his hands from her waist to his. A small leather pouch hung at his belt. He stuck a hand inside it. Her brow furrowed as he removed a golden bracelet.

A golden marriage bracelet.

She cocked her head and frowned at him.

Where did he get this? Why now? *Why do men choose the wrong time to do things?*

His eyes pleaded with her. He wanted this. He needed this.

As did she.

Remember to savor the sweet moments while you have them. Or create them if you have to. The fate of the world might depend upon it.

Gulping, she nodded.

He sighed, relieved. Like he didn't know what she would do.

Eshlyn held out her arm, and he clasped the golden bracelet around her wrist. The metal felt cool on her skin. Familiar. New.

Caleb took her hands and stood, bringing her with him. He kissed her a second time. His hands went to her hips and pulled at her tunic, drawing her close. They continued their embrace, and she moved her arms inside of his, clutching at the bottom of his tattered and ripped shirt. She drew it over his head and threw it on the ground. She broke the kiss and backed away.

He watched her while she gazed at his bare chest. So many scars over his torso and arms. She traced each one with the tips of her fingers.

She remembered the dream, those scars becoming steel. Leaning down, she kissed the scar across his cheek as her hands wrapped around him and felt the tough skin of his back and the mass of scars there. So much pain.

Caleb placed his hands on her hips, and he led her to the door of the tent. When they got close enough, he reached over and closed the flap, plunging them into darkness.

Their lips found each other, and she groaned. Caleb's hands gripped her tunic and removed it. He moved from her lips to kiss the bare skin at her neck. His beard traced her shoulders as he undid the buttons that fastened her divided skirt. She moved her hips, helping him slide it to the ground.

More kissing, touching, and she stepped out of the puddle of clothes on the floor. Eshlyn untied the cord at his waist, and the leather trousers came down. He used his feet to remove his boots, and they separated while she attempted the same. Awkward hopping in the dark to get rid of their clothes.

They both chuckled. Once naked, they embraced, kissing. Their bare skin met, and she shivered though the night was warm. Bumps raised on her arms.

The grief didn't disappear. How could it? But for now the sorrow stepped aside as they clung to one another and the love that had waited for so long. The revolution, the war, the dead all waited for this.

Eshlyn was consumed by him; she welcomed it. He was strong and gentle, and it felt like she floated as he led her to the corner of the tent and his cot.

After it was done, they lay entwined in each other. Caleb's breath drew even and calm. He was still.

She held him and enjoyed the peace, the intimacy. She whispered to him that everything would be all right.

She said it more for herself than for him.

CHAPTER 30

The Choice

Eshlyn slept in his arms.

They lay naked together on the cot barely big enough for the both of them.

Caleb couldn't see her, but felt the rising and falling of her chest. He felt a peace he could not explain, like he was clean for the first time in a long time.

After burying Carys and Earon, the rage was so strong within him, that he didn't know what to do. The sword didn't speak to him – even the voice of El couldn't break through the wall of anger around his mind and heart. He wanted to kill and slaughter out of wrath and vengeance, nothing more. He had been lost. And Macarus …

When he got back to his tent, the sword had been so heavy. He couldn't lift it.

There had been nothing, no reason. Nothing to believe in. No faith.

Then Eshlyn came to him. And she was in his arms. The one thing he denied himself. Here.

While she fell asleep, Caleb did not. The hours passed, and he wanted to remember every moment of this peace, this contentment. He had been a fool to deny it, however valid his memory of Danelle or his desire not to hurt Eshlyn. He stayed awake because despite how amazing it was, it could not last.

And within the peace, the stillness, the voice of El returned to him. He could not see the sword, but it called to him. It spoke to him again.

Caleb knew what he had to do.

Eshlyn was in a deep sleep, her exhaustion and their intimacy allowing her to sink down to a comatose-like state. He had waited for this and dreaded it.

He rolled her over slightly, slowly, and slid out from underneath her, using every muscle in his body to ensure she moved as little as possible. H extricated his arm, the last bastion of their embrace; she sniffed but then settled.

Sitting up on the edge of the cot, he wanted to touch her, to stroke her hair or her smooth skin. One last time. But he didn't.

He stood, his movements efficient, and even though it was pitch dark in the tent, he grabbed fresh clothes from his trunk. He reached and gathered his sword. He could have been blind and found it, the call so strong.

The unforged sword felt light.

He leaned the Kingstaff on the wall of the tent. He set his boots and shirt to the side.

All of this happened without a sound. He left the tent.

What remained, he must do alone.

✦——

General Felix stood mitres away from the vualta. Three or four stories tall, t towered over him in the darkness, an imposing shadow.

The two Moonguard in charge of the creature stood on either side of him. They both wore long black robes.

"Is it ready?" Felix asked.

The Moonguard on his left – her name was Dyusa – turned to him. One of her eyes was yellow and the other blue. Most of her hair had been shaved, leaving only three tufts of hair, one at the front of her head and two more at the back, all three of them in long braids. Her skin was an unnatural pink color.

"The spikes have healed." When she spoke, it was like a wet hissing through her teeth. "It is ready."

Now that the General knew these were sorcerers of *Tebelrivyn*, he wondered how the Emperor and others had kept it a secret. The Moonguard had always been strange, but now he could sense how unnatural they were. It frightened him, as did this creature in shadow looming over him.

Indyana, the other Moonguard to his right, was also female, and her skin was darker like molasses, her kinky hair cut into rows of spikes on her head. She peered with red eyes.

"We must remove the mental block," Indyana said. "And then form instruction into the mind. At your command, of course."

General Felix could hear the thing breathe, like a rushing wind, a coming storm. He fought a wince.

A part of him considered this a mistake. But one didn't deny the Emperor.

"Another hour before dawn," the General said. "The Emperor wants it to crush the rebellion while he watches from his tower. Will it be ready by then?"

"Or soon after," Dyusa said.

"Very well," General Felix said. "The order is given."

High General Felix lowered his head, spun on his heel, and left to prepare the rest of the Kryan army to clean up whatever came after.

＋——

Caleb stood in the predawn light at the top of the hill where the siege engines had been entrenched the morning before. He tied his hair back with a leather cord.

He lifted his head to the sky. Empty. *Did you find them, Aden?* It didn't matter now.

He stared to the east at the city of Asya.

The eastern horizon began to glow like the ocean beyond burned with fire. The city was silhouetted before him, the towers and spires and the wall. He rested his hand on the hilt of the unforged sword.

It was all his responsibility. The *Hamon-el*, the *Sohan-el*, the gathering of different races and peoples into a motley army that had beaten Kryan legions and marched all the way to Asya … and retreated and failed. All the deaths, all the pain, all the grief, it had begun with Caleb De'Ador and his return to his homeland to start a revolution and overthrow the oppression of the most powerful Empire in the world. And it would end with him.

The elves would attack soon to crush what remained of the army and the revolution. The *Hamon-el* – his friends, his love – could not move and retreat soon enough. In a fight, they had lost too much. Even with the Dragonmen, they were vastly outnumbered by the sea of militan he glimpsed beyond the gate.

Mounds of dead bodies smoldered and smoked in the dawn. So many dead.

No more of his own. No more. He didn't know what he could do, alone, against a city and legions of militan and more, but he could buy them time. He could do that. And maybe fulfill his oath to Carys.

I'll kill them all.

But it was more than that. More than vengeance. He wanted to see if it was all true.

He had not forced anyone. He had allowed for freedom and choice each step of the way. Break it, he had even warned and begged people to stay away. But they had been inspired by the idea of the *Brendel* and revolution. To be fair, the concepts of faith and freedom were real, and to a degree, Kryus simply reaped the rebellion it had sown with its oppression and denial of dignity for all – human, elf, and dwarf.

It was the work of El to fight for a real peace and right born of freedom and faith instead of control and power over others. He would believe that until the end.

But was he the *Brendel*? Even though he remembered well the words of El at the top of Mount Elarus and the Living Stone, that he was the *Brendel*, there were moments he doubted. He doubted because he knew his own heart, a heart that wanted to kill out of wrath and revenge. When he held Carys' shriveled and tortured figure, he had only thought of killing and revenge. The sword at his waist had hung heavy. It had been a relief to be rid of it with Eshlyn. Even for that moment.

He wore it now, however. Like he was born with it.

In his right hand was a letter he had written for Carys two days ago, a letter in case he died before she returned.

He would never say those things to her now. Not on this side of the Everworld, at least. It crumpled in his fist. He shoved it under his belt.

The light behind the city brightened, spreading from the horizon through the whole eastern sky.

Lyam had questioned whether Caleb was the fulfilment of that prophecy, and it only spoke the fears and doubts in his heart. But didn't everything hinge on this truth? That he was the *Brendel*? El had found him worthy at the Stone and spoke the words, the *Brendel*. Would a man who struggled with such vengeance and wrath be the instrument of a righteous god?

Seeing Carys' dead body, he had felt such rage. He almost killed Macarus, an honorable person, his friend. What kind of person does that? A man with darkness in his soul.

With Eshlyn, though, it had been different. Maybe there was hope, after all.

So Caleb knew what he had to do. He would not allow any others to go into battle with him until he tested the prophecy, fulfilled it. Eshlyn, Aden if he still lived, and others could lead the *Hamon-el* and carry on without him. He knew that, trusted it. But there was one task for which he had been trained, forged as Mother Natali explained, and that was to end the Worldbreaker.

Just as Caleb was the beginning and end of the revolution, Tanicus was the source and end of the Kryan Empire. It had all come to this. He would face the Worldbreaker or die trying. He had to end it. No one else.

He had left his armor, shield, and any other weapons back at the camp. All he needed was the sword. El would be his shield, his armor, or he would fail.

His body ached, stiff from the battle the previous day and the lack of sleep. He ignored it.

The sun broke above the horizon and rose to frame the spires and towers of the city. Caleb had to squint at the light.

With a deep breath, he walked towards the city of Asya to kill the Emperor with the unforged sword from the Living Stone.

———

"Sir, there is something you should see," the Lieutenant said from behind him.

General Felix stood on the top of the wall with a Major in the third reserve legion as the sun rose. The Major had been showing him details of the militan position within the city and possible strategies if they had to follow the vualta on the field or meet another force from the north or south. The General had decided the vualta was too unpredictable and needed contingencies in case it all went to crit. So often, in battle, it all went to crit.

Felix straightened. "What is it, Lieutenant?"

"Someone is coming."

Felix looked down the wall walk and to the courtyard below before the gate.

"No, sir," the Lieutenant said. "I apologize. There's a man approaching the gate from the west."

Felix frowned. "Across the field?"

The Lieutenant nodded.

"Show me," Felix said.

The General followed the Lieutenant to the parapet and took the thick peerglass from him. The lieutenant pointed straight out from the gate, and General Felix put the glass to his eye.

In the dawn light, it was only a dark figure, but he could tell it was a man with a sword jogging toward the city. Alone.

Felix grunted as he scanned the rest of the field. He could see no other movement.

"Any more word from our scouts?" he asked the Lieutenant.

"Only the same, Sir. The camp hasn't moved. They're quiet." The Lieutenant shrugged. "But that was an hour ago."

Could the *Brendel*'s army be pulling some sort of trick? Like the Emperor with the wagon of the dead? What kind of strategy was this? He scanned to the north and the south. Nothing for a kilomitre or more that he could see.

The Major stood next to him now. "Is it someone coming for parley?"

Felix focused the peerglass on the figure. "He holds his sword like he's ready for battle. And I know the mind of Tanicus. He will not accept surrender, even if they were to offer it."

The dawn light shone across the man's face.

The man was not coming to sue for peace, of that the General was sure.

The top of the wall was silent for a few seconds, allowing the General time to think.

If it was some sort of trick or distraction, then allowing the man in the city as a prisoner might be the play. The same could be said for sending out a delegation of some sort. If he sent out a force, even a large one, they could be caught unawares. How, he didn't know, but he hadn't expected that strange people from the north yesterday.

"Ready the archers, Lieutenant," Felix said. "And two of the catapults."

"Yes, sir." The Lieutenant left.

Felix turned to the Major. "Ensure the legion at the gate is ready, as well. Just in case."

"Yes, sir," the Major said. "Do you know who it is, Sir?"

"He's just a man," the General said. "And obviously a great fool."

"Yes, sir." The Major bowed and left to obey the General.

The General watched the figure approach as hundreds of feet shuffled along the wall walk on either side of him.

"A great fool," Felix repeated to no one.

—<small>+</small>—

Eshlyn woke in Caleb's tent, and he was gone.

Her eyes opened, the tent dark, and initially she didn't know much of anything. It took her a few seconds to get her bearings after being in such a deep sleep.

Caleb. The memory of the night before came rushing to her mind and heart so quickly she gasped. Had it been a dream? The weight of the golden bracelet on her wrist told the truth. No dream.

The last she remembered, she had been in his arms, but she was alone on the cot. She sat up and narrowed her eyes to look through the dark tent. There was a hint of light through a sliver in the flap of the opening, but it wasn't enough to see much. Her eyes adjusted. She swiveled her head, looking for him, but he was gone.

Where did he go?

But she had an idea.

She was naked, so she stood and found her clothes, still stained and bloody from the day before. His trunk was open. The sword was gone.

Dressing in her divided skirt and a blue tunic and boots, she pulled her belt and sword on before she opened the flap to the light outside.

The new light illuminated an object leaning on the wall of the tent to her left. Her brow furrowed. She reached out and took it in her hand. The Kingstaff.

A piece of paper was tied around the staff with a leather cord. Her stomach tightened in fear as she untied the cord and lifted the paper to read it as she stepped out of the tent into the light of dawn.

You must carry this now. Know that I will always love you. Always.

ps – Tell Macarus I am sorry.

The shogger didn't even sign it.

The script on the Kingstaff was rough under her hand, a message in the First Tongue. She knew what it said since Caleb told her several times. *To lead with compassion, justice, and strength.*

She gripped the Kingstaff and crumpled the paper in the other hand.

It was a goodbye. There was only one place he would go, now. The Worldbreaker. She heard him say so many times that he was not a leader, not a general. He was a weapon, a warrior. She knew that's where he was going, and he went alone.

Eshlyn shook her head and cursed him. She flew out of the tent into the dawn and walked to her tent. She needed to talk to …

"Lady Eshlyn!" Jaff's voice called. Her head turned to the voice, approaching from the direction of the sun.

Eshlyn stood straight and faced Jaff as he drew near. He was out of breath.

"Lady Eshlyn," he panted.

"It's Caleb," she said. "He's gone off alone."

Jaff cocked his head at her like a confused mutt. "Yes. Our scouts saw him just now. He's jogging toward the city alone." He pursed his lips as he looked from the Kingstaff in her hand and then to her face. "You know what he's doing."

Did he notice she wore the same clothes as yesterday? It took a good amount of her will not to reach up and straighten her hair.

"He's trying to finish it alone," Eshlyn said. "The whole war, the whole revolution, all by himself."

Jaff gazed to the east, disappointment on his face.

"But shog him," Eshlyn said. "We're not going to let him do this alone."

His head turned slowly back to her with a grin.

Eshlyn met his eyes and put a hand on his shoulder, the hand with the paper crumpled in it. "We have a plan. Get Macarus and get everyone ready. Tell them the *Brendel* is back. We have to help him if we can."

—+—

The sky was a light gray when the first volley of hundreds of arrows hurtled toward him.

The unforged sword spun in his hand. He picked up his pace from a jog to a run.

His change of pace affected how many arrows reached him. He watched their flight and arc and timed it so he waved the sword in a blistering figure eight and knocked several arrows away. None touched him, although one came close to his right ear.

He never broke stride. 150 mitres from the gate.

The second volley threw a shadow on the sky, three hundred arrows or more in a spread ahead of him. Caleb lowered his head and barreled forward at a sprint, twirling the sword in front of him like a shield, the sword incredibly light. The arrows fell upon him, all around him, and his sword connected with a dozen or more.

No arrows connected. He continued to run.

Ropes snapped and wood creaked, and two large stones hurtled toward him. The first would land beyond him, but the second arced to crush him.

He leapt high in the air and lifted the sword. Just as the stone, almost as large as he was, came close, he struck forward with the sword. With an enormous, explosive crack, the stone split, shards of rock flying in all directions, and his jump carried him between the two halves.

When he landed in a crouch, another volley of arrows rained down on him. He spun his sword with all his might, smashing through several shafts.

One impaled his left shoulder.

Caleb cried out; the pain shot through his body. He almost fell on his face. He paused for a moment, taking a breath. Then he shot forward at a sprint, his shoulder in excruciating pain. He ignored it.

His feet pounded on the road between mounds of the dead – elves and human and militan and animals. Crows and vultures warred over the dead flesh, despite the abundance of it. The smell of decaying and bloated bodies assaulted his senses. His eyes watered, and his stomach tightened at the stench.

He did his best to stay focused on the gate, his goal, to get there beyond the arrows.

Am I the Brendel? *Am I the weapon? Is El with me?*

Another two stones flew at him, a difficult shot as he got closer to the gate, and both would hit him square at this pace. He had to change speeds … faster or slow?

He chose faster, and with a burst of speed, he ducked under the stones. They landed behind him, but he wasn't fast enough. The dirt and grass hit and knocked him forward. He would fall. He rolled with it – on his right shoulder, not the injured left – and came up on his feet.

Then the fourth volley hit him. The sword sliced through several and knocked others over his head or to the ground.

Two more arrows struck him, in the abdomen above his left hip and the right thigh.

He growled in frustration as he tumbled to the ground. Somehow, he held onto the sword. Caleb leapt back up, but his injured leg collapsed under him. Gritting his teeth, he bore the sharp agony, blood pouring down his leg and body, and he stood. With a breath, he hobbled forward.

More stones. One badly aimed to his left. He stumbled to the right and backhanded the other. The stone he struck exploded into smaller pieces. He dove to the right, landing on his side. His thigh barked in pain, the arrow snapping off. Struggling to his feet, he caught his breath and walked forward.

The fifth volley launched from the top of the wall. He couldn't run, so he paused to lean on his sword as the arrows hovered in the air before falling upon him. Roaring in pain and anger, soaked with blood and sweat, Caleb waved the sword in front of him and connected with three arrows before several hit his body – the right shoulder, the left leg, his foot and left arm. The impacts knocked him back; he lost his balance and fell. Two arrows slammed into his chest. One arrow plummeted and penetrated near his heart. He bounced on the ground. Blood sputtered from his mouth. He held onto the sword.

Caleb gaped up at the sky and said a prayer to El. His head rolled over so he could see the gate to Asya. 30 mitres away.

I thought you would help me.

The voice answered him.

BRENDEL.

His vision narrowed. He couldn't move. He felt so cold. He stopped breathing.

The sky went dark, and Caleb left the world of Eres.

—✝—

"NO!" Eshlyn screamed from the top of the hill. Caleb shuddered once with arrows stuck in his body. He stopped moving.

We're too late.

Three hastily manufactured divisions rushed to organize behind her. Twenty-five stalgest in front of them.

Macarus stood next to her, and his shoulders slumped at the sight of Caleb lying on the field with arrows piercing his body. His face stretched in sorrow and horror.

Others around her cried out in anger and grief. They all shared it. The one man they would follow into the Underland itself died before their eyes.

Eshlyn leaned over and touched the once crumpled paper she had folded and placed under her belt. Only the Kingstaff held her up.

Thunder boomed from the north. From a clear sky. She thought at first the Worldbreaker attacked as he did before, but the second time sounded like a roar, like something alive.

Eshlyn blinked slowly and turned her head. Two shadows flew toward them in the distance. Was it the Mahakar? Had he recovered that quick? But as the shadows neared, their size dwarfed the tiger. Long necks, long tails. Vast wings.

"Great and mightly El," she whispered.

"Wait," Macarus said next to her. "Are those …?"

Dragons.
Aden.

———+———

The wind ripped through Aden's hair, and Tamya's arms wrapped tight around his waist. They rode Malaki together, their packs tied around his neck, their unforged swords at their hips.

Fortunately, the dragons generated a great deal of body heat, so they stayed warm huddled at the bottom of Malaki's neck despite flying at great speeds through the far north and high altitudes.

Elowen rode Bael behind them. After the battle of the dragons, they had returned to the Dragongate and used a drop of dragon blood to heal Elowen, who had been close to death from bitter cold as well as her injuries fighting the white apes.

They had risen on the wings of dragons and raced south to join the battle Malaki said took place at Asya. To the *Brendel*. To Caleb.

Traveling south, the air warmed through dizzying heights and invigorating speed, the foliage and geography so far below them that it seemed a dream.

But he saw the city of Asya in the distance; it had been his home until a maddy man sought his help in breaking a prophet from prison. Aden's whole life had changed. To think it had only been a year ago, less than a year, amazed him. He had lived another life in Asya, a life of danger and starvation.

Now he was flying. On a breakin' dragon.

Aden stared at the field in front of the gate. Mounds of bodies littered the field pocked with holes from siege engines. To his right, to the west, the *Hamon-el* gathered, the Dragonmen among them.

"Abbott and Zamira came!" Aden shouted over his shoulder.

"They are about to attack again," Tamya shouted back into his ear.

The army didn't look big enough to do much, let alone break past the walls into Asya.

They drew closer, more coming into view, Eshlyn, Jaff, and others at the front of the army. And another elf he recognized.

Aden beamed and pointed. "Macarus! It's Macarus!"

Tamya nodded, but she had never met the elf who had helped them defend the city of Ketan from the demics.

But if they were gathering, where was Caleb? Eshlyn and the others gazed up at him, but many focused on the field in front of the gate. Aden followed their gaze and saw a man lying motionless and freshly wounded, the blood bright red from the wounds of many arrows.

Aden patted Malaki and gestured over at the man. His heart sank even as Malaki tipped to the left and turned toward the body, Bael and Elowen following.

Movement along the top of the wall as they approached, bustling and shouting faint from the distance. With a glance, Aden saw archers setting arrows and militan working at the siege engines.

"Elowen!" Aden called, and she nodded to him. She sat straight with one hand on the ridges in front of her on Bael's neck and the other on her unforged sword. Elowen's long, black hair, tied back in a braid, fluttered behind her like a tail. They peeled off to the east to the wall.

Malaki circled the body of the man in the field, and Aden's fears were confirmed.

It was Caleb.

Tamya cursed, and Aden groaned.

Malaki beat his leathery wings and slowed to land between the wall and Caleb, a few mitres away from the man. Aden and Tamya leapt from the back of the dragon as one, and they ran. The stench of decay and death filled his nostrils. The field had been stained with red and black blood. He coughed but ignored it.

Behind them, a volley of arrows flew from the top of the city wall. Malaki spread his wings, and the arrows bounced from his scales and thick wings, protecting them. Bael and Elowen sailed to the wall, and Bael opened his mouth. He belched flame over the parapet.

Flame crackled. Elves screamed.

Standing over Caleb, Tamya leaned into Aden, and he put an arm around her.

His blank eyes were open, and several arrows protruded from the wounds, one missle had entered his heart.

"No." Aden released Tamya – she staggered to stay on her feet – and he spun on a heel and pulled the unforged sword from his side. He walked toward Malaki and glared at the dragon. "Give me your leg."

Malaki lowered his head and raised his foreleg.

"Aden," Tamya moaned at him. But she didn't move. She crossed her arms.

"No," Aden said. "Can't be over yet."

Aden sliced through the scales on the dragon's foreleg, a small cut, enough for a puddle of golden blood to pool in his palm. He strode back over to Caleb and knelt next to the man.

"Help me," he begged her. "Please."

Tamya surveyed the body on the ground and then met his eyes. "What do you want me to do?"

"Take the arrows from his body," Aden said. "All of them. Maybe that will help."

Tamya nodded and walked to the other side of Caleb. While she pulled the arrow from Caleb's side, a sob escaped her throat. No blood poured. His heart no longer beat.

Aden poured the small amount of dragon blood into Caleb's gaping mouth. He closed the jaw and held it there with his hands, the gold of the dragon's blood mixing with Caleb's crimson.

Tamya removed the arrow from Caleb's shoulder, breaking it in two since it went through the muscle, and she pulled it free from the other end. Then she yanked the arrows from his chest.

Aden kept watching for any sign, any movment, but nothing happened.

Nothing.

"Crit on a frog." He leapt to his feet and ran back to Malaki.

"It's not working," Tamya whined.

Aden's pack hung from a rope around the dragon's neck, and he opened it. He dug inside with his hand. "Keep removing those arrows." He turned to the dragon. "Can you help? Any ideas? You knew about the battle."

"I am sorry," Malaki said. "I felt him before, but now ... I can no longer feel his presence."

Aden shook his head, his jaw tight. He grunted when his hand found the cooking pot, and he pulled it from the pack.

"What are you doing?" Tamya called.

Aden winced at the dragon. "Sorry."

The dragon frowned at him, which would have been a frightening experience if Aden wasn't so focused on saving Caleb. "Sorry?" the dragon said. "For wha ..."

Then the dragon growled as Aden cut deeper into his foreleg. He held the pot under the steady stream of blood. "For that," Aden said.

"It's not working," Tamya said again. "It only took a few drops for you." She sniffed, and her brow furrowed. "He's gone."

"Get all those arrows out of him," Aden demanded as he waited for the pot to fill with the golden dragonblood. "He might be farther gone, but I won't stop trying. Not yet. If a few drops worked, then maybe more will work better."

Tamya shook her head but removed the remaining arrows from Caleb's body, the one in his heart last.

"*Isael*," Malaki said. "One or two drops have always been sufficient. No one has ever done so much. We do not know what that will do."

The pot was full, and heavy. Breakin' heavy. Aden sheathed his sword and held the pot with both hands. "Are you going to stop me from trying?"

Aden stared down a dragon.

"No," Malaki said. "You are the *Isael*. Much has been done that has never been done before. But it might be dangerous. Only El can bring back the dead."

"We need the *Brendel*," Aden muttered and carried the pot normally used for soup over to Caleb. He leaned over his head. "Open his mouth." He nodded at Tamya. "Please."

She hesitated, but then she reached up and pulled Caleb's jaw down and open.

Aden took a deep breath and began pouring the golden blood down Caleb's throat. Most of it pooled and poured out again. He cursed. "How do we get it into him? Down his breakin' throat?"

Tamya bit her lip. "I ... I could help."

He cocked his head. "What do you mean?"

"When you were ... there, and dead, I didn't know if the blood got into you, either. So I was about to ..."

He raised a brow. "Use your magic?"

Tamya cringed. "Yes. I would have done anything to save you. I'm sorry. But you came to before I could. But now ..."

Aden closed his eyes and breathed. Could they do this? Could they use the magic from *Tebelrivyn* to heal the man about to fight a Worldbreaker? No. They couldn't. That's maddy.

He put his hand on the unforged sword.

"The Kingstaff," he said.

Her voice sounded small. "What?"

Opening his eyes, he pursed his lips. "The Kingstaff came from the elves, centuries ago. Given to a human king."

"Okay."

"It was made with magic, Tamya. The elves made it with magic. Caleb's been using it and fighting with it all this time. A weapon formed by elves that believed in El and used magic to do it."

"What are you saying?"

"I don't know. Just that ... maybe you were supposed to be here, and have this ability so we could help him. Not to use it out of fear or anger, not for it to control you, but to help. This once."

"You're saying you're okay with this?"

Aden looked at Caleb's dead body. "I'm not okay with any of this." He sighed. "Put your hand on the sword."

Tamya gripped the hilt of Xander's unforged sword. Her eyes bulged at him. "I can't feel the magic, Aden. It's gone. But I feel something else. Coming from the sword."

"What?"

Tamya pulled the sword from the sheath. She held it over Caleb. Then she began to speak words in the First Tongue, words he did not know. She uttered them slow, calm. He could sense the peace and power within them.

The golden blood rose from the ground. Droplets formed a column over Caleb's mouth. Aden opened the jaws. The dragon's blood entered Caleb's mouth. All of it.

Aden let Caleb's mouth close after it was done.

Tamya lowered the sword. She panted. "That wasn't me."

"Sure looked like you."

"It wasn't. That was something else."

—+—

BRENDEL.

Caleb stood on a bridge with a dark mist all around him. He wore his leather pants and a white shirt and boots. His hair was clean and hung to his shoulders.

The bridge was made of white, smooth stone, like marble. He could only see a few mitres in any direction. Turning back and forth, he could not see where the bridge came from or where it was going. He leaned on the railing of the bridge, looking down into a white abyss.

A voice from his left. "Why do you doubt me?"

Caleb raised his head to see a man emerge from the mist. Of average height, he wore a long gray tunic that hung over brown trousers. His feet shuffled in brown leather sandals. His thick, black, wavy hair rested on his shoulders. His face was gaunt and narrow with a full beard. His skin was a dark tan, like a strong ale, and he looked at Caleb with eyes clear and green.

For a split second, Caleb wondered who the man was, but deep within, he knew. He breathed the name.

"Yosu."

The man did not respond. He kept looking at Caleb with that unnerving stare. Calm and peaceful, but Caleb felt a passion simmering beneath the surface.

Caleb shook his head, trying to wake from the dream, but he remained where he stood. It was real. It felt real. But a moment ago, he had been on the field in front of the gate of Asya. He remembered running toward the gate ... and arrows ... and then ...

"Wh-where are we?" he asked Yosu. The son and champion of El.

"It does not have a name. It is nowhere. Nothing. The inbetween that does not exist."

"But ... we're here."

"For now."

Caleb surveyed his surroundings. "You say the *inbetween*. Between what?"

"The world where you were born and the world where you were born anew."

Eres and the Everworld. "I'm dead?" He felt the shame of failure. He had never faced the Worldbreaker. But he also felt relief. Was it over?

"If you mean your body on Eres, your current physical form, then that is yet to be determined."

Caleb grunted and waved at himself. "So what is this? Not my body?"

"You are in a form your mind can understand. Once you step beyond physical death, you will possess a mind and body to process what you see. For now, these are symbols of things you could not understand if you saw them as they were. As they are, the revelation would be such that we could not talk as equals; the revelation would draw you into the Everworld without your control. That time may come, but not yet."

"Why as equals?"

"Because love does not force or intimidate, even when it can. And I do love you, *Brendel.* I do."

Caleb's eyes misted, and he took a breath. "And why am I here? Why are we here?"

"For two reasons, the first of which I have already expressed. Why do you doubt me?"

"What? How do I doubt you?" Caleb countered. "I built a whole army based on your model, your example. How do I doubt you?"

"After all the training, all the signs, all the pain and victory, you still doubt what I say about you."

Caleb almost asked what he meant, but he knew.

BRENDEL.

"You're the El-son, one with him," Caleb said. "You know everything, right? Don't you know?"

"It is not for me that I ask the question."

Caleb turned and gazed out into mist, into nothing. But he was in nothing already. His head spun.

Caleb blinked and focused. He breathed through his teeth, making a hissing sound.

Yosu did not press. He did not prod. He waited.

Caleb raised his hands and looked at them. "I've killed out of wrath and anger and vengeance. I could justify it by saying it was the right thing or even to protect others, but there were moments it was selfish. I wasn't a hero, not the hero many seem to think I am. I cringe when they call me that name. How can I be the one to bring freedom to others when I am so weak?"

"And yet you have inspired people to faith and freedom and cooperation all at once. That is quite rare. Impossible, some would say."

"At the cost of many," Caleb said. "So many have died, all because of me."

"Not because of you. Everyone loves to dream, to envision the freedom and joy they so crave, but great dreams require great cost to become reality.

You know this. There is cost to allowing evil to continue, as well. Which cost did you choose?"

Caleb lowered his head.

"Were there not times you acted out of love and compassion with no regard for yourself?" Yosu asked. "And remember, as you said, I already know the answer."

"Yes. That is true."

"You were weak and selfish? That does not prove your unworthiness. Only proves you were learning, growing. Rather, your fidelity despite your failings proves your worth. The proof of the supernatural is when you were strong, when you acted as I would have, as El would have acted. No one does that unless touched by the love of El."

Caleb stood straight and rested his hands on the railing.

"I have made you, forged you, brought you to this place," Yosu said. "When you doubt who I say you are, you doubt who I am. It is not pride to speak the truth. It is pride to deny it. You are the *Brendel*. You see this, don't you?"

Caleb's jaw tightened. "It is difficult to believe."

"Belief is your weapon, *Brendel*. More than the sword or staff or your training or the army we gathered. Belief is what will see you to the end, if you choose."

A brow rose on Caleb's forehead. "If I choose?"

"Yes. It is always about choice." Yosu stared beyond Caleb and into the mist. Was that the Everworld or Eres? "Until it no longer is."

"Are you saying I chose my parents to die? Carys?"

"Those were not your choices. They were the choices of others, for evil and good. And I used those choices to bring redemption, despite the original intent. There is much you do not choose. But your responses to the choices of others are yours to own."

"Are you saying I chose to be the *Brendel*?"

"I chose to forge you. But that metaphor has a fundamental flaw. You are a person, not a piece of metal without thoughts or feelings or a will. Your participation was required, yes."

Yosu fixed him with a firm and intent look.

"As it is now."

Caleb's eyes narrowed. "What does that mean?"

"This is the second reason we are here," Yosu said. "You are as close to death as you could be back on Eres. The *Isael* believe you are dead. They will complete your forging."

Isael ... "Aden and Tamya are there?"

Yosu turned to his left, and the mist parted for another few mitres. A vision appeared within the mist of Aden and Tamya kneeling over him, downcast. And behind them, dragons.

Dragons! They came!

"You can send me back?" Caleb whispered.

"I can."

Caleb licked his lips. "You ... spoke of a choice. I have to choose to return or stay here?"

"There is no here, *Brendel*. But there is a choice."

Yosu gazed past Caleb in the other direction, and Caleb turned to see the mists parting and another image beyond.

It was faint, but he could see great plains and mountains and trees and rivers and waterfalls, all in colors too vibrant to be real. They were real, however. *The Everworld.*

Then the image shifted as people walked into his vision. His father and mother were first, beaming at him with pride. Then he saw Reyan and Aunt Kendra. Others came into view – Athelwulf, Esai, Xander, other *Sohan-el* that had given their life for the cause. Zalman, Iletus, Tobiah, Shecayah, and Galen.

Earon and Carys were last, and Caleb's heart ached. He bent over, the grief still fresh and real. He stared at all of them, and he reached out, wanting to hold them close, each of them, all of them.

"You are a step from either, *Brendel*," Yosu said. "Make your choice."

"You ... you're really saying I have to choose between them?"

"I am telling you that you must choose whether or not to return to Eres and finish you what were chosen to do."

"I don't understand," Caleb said. "Why are you asking me?"

"I am not asking," Yosu said. "You have to choose. As you say to others so often, and is true, it cannot be a revolution to freedom without freedom as its foundation. You must choose."

"But if I don't return, the Worldbreaker wins, right? Eres burns under his oppression. I have to go back."

"You believe deliverance is dependent upon you alone? It is not."

"You mean someone else will defeat him?"

"Eventually, yes, he will be defeated, or he will destroy himself, as often happens with evil. The goal of this revolution is more than the death of a tyrant. El seeks the freedom from the tyrants within the heart of all races. No tyrant can ever rule that people. That is the purpose. It may take a day or a generation, but another *Brendel* will rise."

"Another *Brendel*? There are others?"

"You believe you were the first to be chosen? Others were chosen but they did not endure. There will be others after you. There may be one now ..."

"But it could take time," Caleb clarified. "And more die in the process. And more pain."

Yosu nodded. "There is no shame if you do not choose to return. You have more than earned your place among the heroes in Everworld. You have suffered much and endured until this moment. Despite your self-criticism, your faith has been strong. Your entrance will be one of joy."

"But you'll have to find another *Brendel*."

"I forged one. I will forge another."

Caleb looked from one to the other, from Aden and Tamya and a dragon hovered over him, then to the Everworld and the faces of those he loved more than anything in existence.

"Don't make me do this," Caleb said. "Please."

"I am sorry, *Brendel*," Yosu said. "But I can't choose for you. What comes next is too important, and you must choose to fulfill it. That is the only way."

"If I face him, will I win? Will I beat him?"

"All who follow the way of El possess victory," Yosu said. "But it may not appear like you think."

"But it will be over."

Yosu gazed past Caleb to the Everworld. "It will be a beginning."

Caleb sucked in air through his nose, thinking, shaking his head. He couldn't decide.

"Take your time. I leave you to it."

Yosu walked past Caleb toward the Everworld.

"Wait," Caleb said. "You're leaving me?"

Yosu hesitated and peered over his shoulder. "My *Brendel*. I have never left you, and I never will. I have been with you since the moment you were conceived. I laughed with you. I wept with you. I felt each wound and bore each scar with you.

"Whichever you choose, you will spend forever with me and my Father in a place more beautiful than you could imagine. Even if you return to Eres, you will find that the rest of your life is but a breath.

"Remember I love you, *Brendel*. Either way, I will see you soon."

Yosu turned for the last time and faded into the mists.

Caleb gaped after him. How could he make this decision? He closed his eyes.

For another to be forged, that person would have to go through the tragedy and pain and grief and hardship that Caleb had endured, or something similar. How could he do that to another person?

But when he thought of the Everworld, the desire overwhelmed him. To be with those he loved, those he grieved, his heart soared simply thinking about it.

No more war. No more fighting. No more death or pain.

There would be peace, serenity, joy. Only joy. The faces of those he loved radiated with a pure ecstasy he wanted more than anything.

More than anything.

He looked at Carys, into her eyes. She mouthed a single word.

He made his decision. Caleb turned and took a step.

CHAPTER 31

GOLDEN BLOOD

Dragons. There were dragons on the field in front of the gate of Asya.

They were enormous and frightening with horns and long teeth and leathery wings. With the peerglass, they came into focus, and Eshlyn watched arrows bounce off of them as they landed between the gate and Caleb. Aden and Tamya rode one of them, and her heart leapt with hope. A female elf with long black hair and dark skin rode the other. A scarf covered her eyes.

The dragon with the elf spun and bathed the top of the wall with flame, like fire shooting from a fountain. The echoes of burning elves reached her ears, and the faintness made it even more horrifying.

Eshlyn lowered the peerglass. She looked over her shoulder, and the *Hamon-el* froze behind her, awestruck at the dragons.

She turned back to the field. Aden and Tamya had stepped down from the dragon. They reached Caleb and knelt beside him.

Caleb. Her right hand went to her heart, the one with the golden bracelet, and her other hand gripped the Kingstaff. She had to go to him. And she might as well bring an army with her.

Her eyes narrowed, and she rounded on the motionless army.

"Form up," Eshlyn called.

Macarus raised a brow at her.

Jaff cocked his head. "Lady?"

Others woke from their daze as she addressed them. "The dragons have returned to the world. Aden and Tamya have brought them to us. Get in your divisions, but there's a change of plans. We are going to attack the gate."

Jaff's brow furrowed.

"With the help of the dragons," Eshlyn declared. "We take the city of Asya."

Macarus looked from the dragons and back to her. "Yes, Lady."

—✛—

Minutes passed, and Tamya touched Caleb's shoulder with one hand and her sword with the other. He didn't move.

Aden fell to his knees next to her, and his shoulders slumped. "We were too late."

She leaned over and put her arms around him. He collapsed into her.

"It can't be over," he mumbled. "Not after all this. It can't."

She reached up and stroked his hair. She didn't know what to say. Her heart dropped in grief, as well. *I felt El touch him with ... whatever that was. He can't be dead.*

But he was. The *Brendel* was dead.

"It is not over," Malaki said. "There is still an army to lead and a revolution to win."

After a moment, Aden nodded on her shoulder. He straightened. "He's right."

"What are we going to do?" Tamya asked him.

Aden shrugged. "Go back to the army and talk to Eshlyn and Macarus, try to make a new plan now that ..."

In an instant, a roar came from Caleb's throat, and he jumped to his feet, knocking both of them aside and back two mitres. They rolled to a stop, and Tamya recovered from her shock enough to come to her hands and knees to see him.

Caleb stood there with the unforged sword in his hand, his eyes bulged and his teeth clenched, spittle spraying from his mouth as he forced breath. His arms and legs quivered. She could see the veins in his arms and face.

"WHAT THE SHOG DID YOU DO TO ME?"

Caleb turned to look at them, and his eyes ... they were no longer steel gray. They were golden.

Holy El.

Caleb grimaced down at his arms and legs. "WHAT DID YOU DO?"

Aden rose to his feet. "D-dragon's blood. We brought you back with dragon's blood."

Caleb drew a deep breath, as if he couldn't get enough oxygen. He peered past them with golden bloodshot eyes to the creature that cast a shadow over them all.

"Dragons." Caleb swallowed. "Those are dragons."

Malaki bowed his head. "*Brendel.*"

Bael, with Elowen on his shoulders, soared down and landed next to Malaki. He also bowed. "*Brendel.*"

Caleb gazed at Aden with those golden irises. "You did it. You found them and brought them here."

Tamya stood next to Aden as he grinned back. "This is Malaki and Bael," Aden said, pointing at each in turn.

Tamya took a step toward Caleb with Aden at her side. "Are you okay?" She still couldn't get past the fact that he had been dead a moment before and now looked like he could wreck the whole city of Asya.

Caleb looked confused for a moment, gazing down at his body and the sword in his hand. "I ... I don't know."

Tamya believed him.

Caleb grunted and touched his belt, a piece of paper there underneath it. He sighed in relief.

Caleb gestured at the elf on Bael. "And who is this?"

"My name is Elowen. It is good to meet you, *Brendel*."

"Elowen?" Caleb said. "The one that fought Galen and Julius and Iletus?"

Elowen nodded.

Caleb scoffed and placed a hand on Aden's shoulder, then Tamya's. He pulled them closer. "You have been busy. But time is short. You will tell me what you can on the way."

Tamya and Aden shared a glance. "On the way where?" Tamya asked.

Caleb didn't answer but released their shoulders. He walked past them to stand before Malaki. He stared the dragon in the eye, and Tamya swore the dragon was more afraid than the man.

"Will you take me to the Emperor?" Caleb asked.

"I am honored to serve," Malaki answered.

"Wait," Tamya said. "You know where he is?"

Caleb looked at the sword in his hand. "I do." He raised his head and met her stare. "You coming?"

—✝—

Eshlyn rode a horse and raced back and forth across the line while the *Hamon-el* formed up in their divisions. She commanded three in the front and four behind them. Each division consisted of twenty stalgest and two hundred warriors. Other warriors stayed behind to protect the camp.

"Lady Eshlyn!" she heard Jaff call her name from behind her. She spun the horse to see Jaff wide eyed and pointing toward the dragons.

Caleb was on his feet. He was alive!

She fumbled for her peerglass and put it to her eye. It was true. Caleb conferred with Aden and Tamya. The three of them climbed up on the dragon. And then the dragons flew away.

"What is he breaking doing?" Eshlyn cried out.

"He's going for the Worldbreaker," Jaff said. She marveled at the confidence in his voice, but when she turned to him, his hand was on his sword.

"Fine," she spat. "Let's hope those stalgest can eat through the gate. We're going."

Jaff nodded. "Yes, Lady."

Then the ground rumbled beneath them.

Was it the dragons? Eshlyn looked, but no. It came from the city.

—+—

Three of them sat on Malaki, but there was plenty of room at the base of his long neck. Caleb rode at the front, Tamya and Aden last.

Aden held Tamya around the waist, the air warm on his face. They flew towards the morning sun. Malaki's leathery wings shuddered in the wind, and he adjusted his path.

Elowen rode on Bael to his left, her face serene.

Caleb had directed them to go to the palace complex, to the high towers on the eastern side of the city. He claimed Tanicus, the Emperor, the Worldbreaker, waited there for him.

They passed over the burning walls first. There was little movement, hundreds of bodies smoking from Bael's flame. Thousands of militan waited in the courtyard behind the gate and spread through the western edge of Asya in the streets.

The bellow reached his ears, a faint noise, like a bosaur drowning. It came from ahead of them.

Their flight followed the main thoroughfare through Asya, a wide street. Aden looked below them, scanning. The city seemed deserted. He supposed he would hide if he was stuck in the city, as well. Something caught his attention ahead of them, a creature large enough that when it raised its head, it rose above the four and five level buildings on either side of it. When Aden looked at it and they got closer, the sun gleamed off of it.

It was the biggest creature Aden had ever seen.

The head and snout looked familiar, as did the body and prehensile tail. The six legs. He knew it well. Too well. It was a crizzard. One that barely fit in the street.

It had been altered in other ways – red scales instead of dark green and two black, curved horns reminiscent of the Demilord a year ago. Iron spikes had been fused to its spine somehow, reaching twenty mitres high. Metal plates protected the eyes, like iron blinders.

"Shog a goat," he heard Tamya say in front of him.

It walked slowly, struggling to move with all the weight of steel upon it, each step laborious.

"Crit on a frog," Aden said. "What is that?"

"Another abomination of the Moonguard," Caleb said. "Like the Deathguard, only bigger." Caleb shouted to their left. "Elowen, you need to warn Eshlyn and Macarus. It's coming for them."

Elowen faced forward but nodded. Bael and Elowen peeled away and circled back to the west.

Then Caleb turned his face toward the east, toward the tower that waited.

It was only another few seconds before they reached the two towers connected by a long covered bridge. A garden enclosed in glass stood atop the first tower. A long porch open to the air faced the west. Malaki slowed and landed, his front legs on the porch and his back talons gripping the white stone of the tower. The tower groaned at his weight.

Aden dropped to the porch first and took a few steps into the garden filled with exotic plants – trees, flowers, shrubs of different colors. There was a clearing in the middle, a few mitres ahead of them. The sun through the glass made the garden appear like paradise. And if Aden had not been to the top of Mount Elarus to see the Living Stone, it might have been the most beautiful thing he had seen. Instead, despite how well it had been made, it was manufactured and stale compared to the Garden of El.

Tamya stood with him, and Caleb walked beyond them. Lowering his head for a moment, he sighed. He turned to them both.

"Aden, Tamya," Caleb said. "This is goodbye."

"What?" Aden said. "We're going to help you beat the Worldbreaker."

"No. That is for me alone."

"Are you still trying to do this by yourself?" Tamya squealed at him. "You haven't learned by now?"

Caleb turned to her. "I have." There was no anger or wrath in his eyes. Only power. Peace. "You have a different destiny. You have to take the dragon and fight that creature before it kills everyone." Caleb reached out with both hands and pulled the two Dracolet from beneath their shirts. "The *Isael*. Together."

Aden gaped at him. "But ..." He couldn't finish it. He didn't want to leave Caleb again. But who else could tackle that enormous crizzard thing? Tears filled his eyes.

"Why you acting like this is goodbye?" Tamya growled. "You beat him and come back to us, you hear me?"

"That's not how this works," Caleb said. "I'm sorry, Tamya. I am."

"No," she said. "This can't be the end. Not after everything."

"With El, there is never truly an end," Caleb said. "Only another beginning."

There were tears in her eyes as Caleb let go of the Dracolet and pulled her to him in an embrace. She threw her arms around his neck, and a sob escaped her throat.

"I'm so proud of you," Caleb said into her ear. "Thank you for taking care of him. The world will need him after this. And he'll need you. Understand?"

They separated, and he kissed her cheek. Then he turned those golden eyes on Aden. There were tears there, as well.

A tear rolled down his face, and he swallowed hard. He couldn't speak.

Caleb reached out and embraced him. Aden groaned and threw his arms around Caleb, as well. They held each other for a long moment, and it ended too soon. Caleb drew back.

Meeting with him and Freyd, a fight with the crizzards under the Pyts and saving the Prophet. Journeys and battles and training, lifetimes lived over the past year. And it was all due to the *Brendel*.

"I – I don't know what to say," Aden muttered desperately. "Thank you. For everything." But that seemed trite, like the words weren't enough.

Caleb's brow furrowed. "No, Aden. Thank you." He leaned in and their foreheads touched. "I've traveled the world, and I've never known anyone like you. Reyan was right about you, as he was about so many things. You never gave up. You never surrendered. You kept pace with me every step and fought at my side.When Lyam argued that you were the prophecy back at the Acar, a part of me wondered if he was right."

Aden shook his head. "It's you. How could you doubt it? You're the *Brendel*."

"I know that now," Caleb whispered. "I do. I want you to know. I came back for you."

"Came back?" Aden asked.

Caleb stood straight and smiled at him with such warmth it broke Aden's heart. "When next we meet, you'll understand." Caleb took both of them in with a glance. "You have so much left to do, even after today, a long life full of joy. Know that I love you both. Now go."

He stood there, his face expressing a contentment Aden had never seen in him before. There was no weight on his shoulders. He stood free.

Aden took Tamya's hand, and they walked together back to the dragon. They climbed up on Malaki's back, and Aden looked back once more at Caleb.

Caleb put a hand on his sword. "There's something in my tent for you, Aden. A journal. It is for you and Eshlyn."

"A journal?"

"You'll know it when you see it. I wish I could give you more, but that is all I have."

"I'll get it," Aden said.

"And tell Eshlyn I love her, please," Caleb said.

"We will," Tamya said.

"Thank you." Caleb turned to walk into the garden. Aden lost him in the vines and the trees.

Malaki lifted his wings and leapt from the porch, twisting in the air. He caught the wind, and they rose, flying towards the west.

Aden held Tamya close to him and prayed. *El be with him.*

———+———

Caleb watched them fly away, and he prayed for them as they approached their next battle.

He walked and reached the center of the garden and the clearing there. A path led from the clearing to the door and the covered walkway ahead of him, bathed in shadows from the limbs over the path.

The double doors opened, and three figures in gold armor stepped through the doors, golden swords in their hands. They strode forward, one in front and the other two behind, their golden boots crunching on the fine gravel of the path. The light shone through the glass and limbs above them and flashed and gleamed off of the gold.

They came to the clearing and spread in a line across from him.

Sunguard.

Caleb pulled his unforged sword from its sheath and glared at them. With his left hand, he touched the crumpled letter to Carys under his belt.

"So be it. If this is what must come first."

And he attacked.

CHAPTER 32

THE VUALTA

Eshlyn trotted at the front of the *Hamon-el*. They raced down the hill towards the gate. She could hear the rumbling grow louder, the ground shaking underneath the horse. Were those the dragons? She didn't think so, but what else could it be?

A dragon soared over the wall the field before them, and the wings spread to catch air for a descent. Not Aden and Tamya but the elf. The dragon floated down and landed in their path, digging into the dirt with its claws and coming to a complete stop, rearing on its hind legs.

Eshlyn got the message and slowed her horse. She raised the Kingstaff over her head as a signal, and the army came to a panting stop behind her. They were quiet, in awe this close to a dragon.

Steeling her nerves, Eshlyn walked the horse, trembling, to the dragon.

The dragon fell to all fours and crouched so the female elf on its shoulders could slide down to the ground.

The elf was a head shorter than Eshlyn, but she stood tall in her trousers and long tunic. She wore a white scarf around her head to cover her eyes. A sword hung at her hip. Eshlyn had held and been in the presence of an unforged sword enough to recognize one.

The elf walked with authority and power but not arrogance. How was she doing that with the scarf over her eyes?

Eshlyn dismounted from the horse, and with the Kingstaff in her hand, she marched to meet the elf.

"Lady Eshlyn," the elf said.

That caused Eshlyn hesitation. "You know me?"

"Aden and Tamya spoke of you. Well met. My name is Elowen."

Eshlyn frowned. She recognized that name from somewhere. Macarus grunted behind her.

"The *Sohan-el*?" Macarus said.

Elowen bowed. "I have been among the Dragonmen for all these years and returned with the dragons."

The dragon also bowed its head. "I am Bael, Lady. Honored to meet you." The voice was deep and full, like a wave of sound over them.

Macarus blew air from his lungs and chuckled in amazement.

"This is Macarus," Eshlyn announced.

Elowen didn't turn to him, but she cocked her head. "Senator Diona's son?"

Macarus stood next to Eshlyn now, and he blinked. "You know her?"

"We were … friends once. Long ago. Well met, Macarus. It pleases me that you are here with the *Hamon-el*. Now there is not much time. I bring you a warning."

Eshlyn's frown deepened. "What type of warning?"

"A creature comes this way," Elowen said. "And with thousands of militan."

"What kind of creature?" Macarus asked.

Eshlyn shot Macarus a grimace. *Why are you asking a woman with a scarf over her eyes?*

"I do not know how to describe it to you," Elowen responded. "I only felt evil, pain, hopelessness. Death."

As if on cue, a loud wet sounding roar bellowed from behind the wall.

"It is a twisted, monstrous thing," Bael, the dragon, answered. "Its purpose is to crush the *Hamon-el.*"

Great. "Where is Caleb?" Eshlyn asked. "And Aden and Tamya?"

"The *Brendel* has gone to face the Worldbreaker," Elowen said. "The *Isael* will join us soon, I suspect."

Gone to face the Worldbreaker. Would he return? She shook her head to clear it.

Macarus sighed. "We don't have time to move the camp."

"Not with the prisoners we have, some still wraith," Eshlyn said. "Not if we retreat now. Can we slow them down and give them time?"

Macarus glanced up. "Who knows? We seem to have dragons, though."

"For the real," Eshlyn said. "Send a runner back to the camp and tell Mother Natali to pack up the camp for retreat. Organize one of the divisions to load and fire the catapults and ballista. We will buy them as much time as we can."

"We don't have much ammunition left for the siege engines," Macarus mentioned.

"Well, if those stalgest can dig and eat through stone, they should be able to help make stuff to throw."

"They can," Elowen said.

Macarus pursed his lips and nodded before turning to walk back to the army.

Eshlyn blinked. Unbidden, the fresh memory of Caleb and his touch from last night came to her mind. The towers of the city beckoned in the distance.

"Do not fear for the *Brendel*, Lady," Elowen said, her voice soft. "He is now the warrior he was meant to be."

Eshlyn's brow furrowed. How did she know? Could the elf read thoughts?

"I know," Eshlyn said. "And El have mercy on any that get in his way."

———+———

The giant, red crizzard creature was fifty mitres from the gate by the time they flew over it. Even if it hadn't been following the main street through the city, tracking the creature's progress would be easy. Buildings were half destroyed or worse along the path. The courtyard was empty by the time the creature arrived; militan had cleared the area, waiting on side streets as it passed.

Aden patted the scales on the neck of the dragon. "Let's see how tough that skin is."

They circled around for a pass at the creature, and Aden glanced to the west, his hair stinging his cheek. The *Hamon-el* was two hundred mitres from the gate; Bael and Elowen stood with them.

Malaki angled and came at the creature from the south, from the side. The dragon's skin became hot to the touch as the neck straightened and his mouth opened wide. Malaki belched yellow and red fire in a powerful stream at the creature, the roar of flame deafening.

Fire covered the front fourth of the creature, and it lowered its head in defense, sensing the attack. For a few seconds, all Aden could see and hear was flame. Then they rose on powerful wings, his stomach lurching, and he looked over his shoulder to see the damage done.

None. The tall iron spikes glowed with heat and red scales sparked with the remnants of flame, but the creature did not stop.

It raised its head again, higher than before. Within thirty mitres from the gate, the crizzard jaw opened wide. From within the maw, a snake-like tongue extended, wiggling with a smaller mouth at its end.

Well, that's new.

A stream of dark liquid spat from the center of the smaller mouth and sprayed the gate and the wall around the gate. The liquid met the surface and began to smoke, eating away at the wall.

A year ago, he had used a similar substance under the Pyts. "Acid. It spits acid."

"That eats through stone?"

Holes and cracks appeared in the stone, and the wall began to crumble. The serpentine tongue retracted, and the snout slammed shut. The crizzard creature lowered its head as it rammed the crumbling wall with the horns on its head. Stones fell all around the creature, but it shrugged them off, crawling forward.

———+———

A monstrous creature, bigger than all of her father's stable barns put together, tore down the wall and gate of Asya and lurched onto the field. Eshlyn cursed.

"Macarus," she cried from her horse. "What are our positions?"

He had found a horse, as well, to better move and organize the army. Macarus focused his own bulging eyes at the creature to answer her. "I've sent two divisions on either side, one to the north. With the one loading and firing the catapults, there are three total between us and the camp."

Eshlyn thought of Javyn, how she had raced to the battle before saying goodbye. *Too much undone, unsaid. We must survive this day.* "Get them to fire on it as soon as they can. It's big enough. Should be easy to hit." Even without Bweth.

Iron spikes stuck from the spine of the creature, like the Deathguard. Whatever they threw at the thing would only annoy it. Could you kill something by annoying it? Probably piff it off, for the true.

Eshlyn led one of the divisions in the center; Jaff commanded the other one. As she scanned the troop movement, Kenneth and Wes commanded the two divisions to the south of the creature. Xak and Sergeant Gunnar commanded the two to the north.

Elowen and Bael flew past the creature and covered its head with fire. The creature bowed its head, taking the flame on the metal plates on the top of its head. The monster didn't seem fazed at all, its legs heaving forward steadily.

Eshlyn and Jaff made sure their divisions were ready, and they moved forward. Large pieces of debris arced over their heads. Stones and logs slammed into the creature, bouncing off harmlessly.

Aden and Tamya soared in the sky and dove at the creature from behind. The dragon's mouth opened wide and a fountain of flame covered the back half of the beast, to no avail. The creature opened its mouth, and a long snake tongue flew out. Eshyn groaned and her stomach churned as the end of the tongue split and sprayed liquid at Aden and Tamya. Tamya screamed.

The dragon twisted and dove, the spray narrowly missing.

Bael and Elowen flew in from the side; Bael shot fire at the open mouth and the serpent tongue. The giant creature turned its head away, roaring in pain.

Debris and arrows bounced off its hide. Flames barely affected it. *What can we do?*

Eshlyn and Jaff's divsions were within thirty mitres of the creature. She was about to command a stop, to keep their distance, when the creature turned its angry head their way, the open maw spread wide with reaching tentacles, and it spat a dark liquid over Jaff and his division.

Her first thought was for her own survival, and she pulled her horse to the right and away from the liquid attack. She heard the screams of men and elves behind her.

"Get back!" she screamed. "Get more distance!"

She looked over her shoulder. The liquid ate through shields and skin and bone, stalgest and soldiers howling in horror as they died with pieces of them burning away. The stench was acrid and strong. Most of the division was dead or dying. Smoke billowed from the carnage.

At the front of the division, Jaff clawed at his clothes, raking his flesh from bone until he fell, twitching. The unforged sword fell to the ground.

"Jaff! No!"

What the shog?

"Retreat! Fall back!" she called out to the north and the south.

How could they beat a creature like that?

What would Caleb do? *He would find a way to kill it.*

Those few that survived the acid spray and the rest of the *Hamon-el* obeyed. Jaff's unforged sword drew her eye.

"Break it all," she said and kicked her horse toward the sword.

The horse shot off at a sprint. She stuck the Kingstaff into the strap of the saddle next to her and grabbed a cloth from the saddlebag behind her. Her face winced at the bodies half eaten by the acid around her. Reaching the sword, she pulled hard on the reins. The horse snorted and slid, turning sharp, hooves digging furrows in the dirt.

In one move, she leapt from the saddle, keeping the reins in one hand and guiding the horse around to face the opposite way. With her other hand, covered in a cloth, she reached down and grabbed the hilt of the sword. When the horse had completed the turn, she stepped into the stirrup and launched herself back in the saddle and urged the horse back into a sprint.

Eshlyn rode the horse back up the hill to meet Macarus and the rest of the leadership. The *Hamon-el* continued to back away from the beast, out of range of the acid. Macarus raised a brow at her and shook his head.

Kenneth, Xak, and Wes hung their heads at the loss of another *Sohan-el*, Jaff, their brother and friend.

They were more than a hundred mitres from the creature, the dragons making useless passes with tongues of fire. She untied the Kingstaff from the pommel and dismounted.

"We cannot stop it," Gunnar, the Steelside Sergeant said. "The rest of the army would be better put to use to pack up the camp and get out before that monstrosity arrives."

"I agree," Eshlyn said. "Except for the five of us."

Glances were exchanged. "Who?" Macarus said.

Eshlyn raised the unforged sword in her hand. "The fire of dragons may not be able to get through the hide of that thing, but we can."

Macarus scoffed. "You want the five of us to attack it with swords?"

"These blades can cut through anything," Eshlyn said. "It can't reach the camp without legs."

No one spoke, but she could feel their fear, their hesitation.

"*Before the light of El*," Eshlyn began. "*The hand of Yosu, and the witness of the Living …*"

"*I dedicate my soul, my heart, and my life to defend the innocent,*" Wes said, raising his head.

Kenneth's back straightened. "*Free the oppressed …*"

Xak sniffed. "*And spread light in dark places.*"

Macarus gripped Ewha's sword in his hand. "Crit and piff. Let's go, then."

Chapter 33

The Sunguard

Caleb spun the unforged sword and rushed forward to attack the Sunguard in front of him. All three of the Sunguard raised their left hands.

The stone benches to his right and left lifted in the air and flew toward him to crush his body between them. At the moment of impact, he launched himself forward in the air, sailing vertically. The benches crunched and struck one another, shards of stone hitting his chest and legs. He tucked and rolled, or attempted to, as something grabbed his right arm and pulled.

He fell, his body twisted, and he looked to see a vine from the canopy of the garden snaking around his upper arm. It squeezed the arm that held the sword, so he used the momentum created by the pulling vine to lash out with his right leg. His ankle connected with the vine with force, and it snapped. He landed on his side, his teeth snapping from the impact.

Flames spread along the grass behind him. He came to his feet in a crouch, changing direction, leaping to his left as a ball of fire struck a tree instead of his chest.

A tearing sound from above, and the dome above him ripped apart, pieces of glass raining down. He covered his face with his left forearm and moved to the side, cutting through a branch that had bent down to impede him. With tiny cuts appearing through his clothes and on his arms, there was a groaning of metal and steel bars of the frame of the dome bending and breaking away to fall toward him like missles.

He missed the Kingstaff. And that made him think of Eshlyn ... and Aden and Carys and ... he pushed those thoughts from his mind.

Caleb cursed and dodged the steel bars, his feet constantly moving, the bars sticking into the ground. He stopped and spun to his right, a bar slamming into the ground where he just stood, and ducked another ball of fire while slicing through two vines coming at him from behind.

The Worldbreaker possessed every power, but other wizards of *Tebelrivyn* could use only one. As with the Moonguard, the Sunguard wielded the power over the natural, and it appeared one dealt with vegetation, another with air – like balls of fire – the third with things of the mind, telekinesis with inanimate objects. But they could not affect him directly, not while he held the unforged sword, for the natural can't hold power over the supernatural; they could attack indirectly, however.

They kept him at distance, seeking to destroy him and kill him without having to engage the unforged sword. It was a sound strategy. So Caleb decided to use it, as well.

He swatted aside a falling steel bar aimed at him, reached down and pulled another thin beam from the dirt with his left hand. Grunting from the effort, he spun away from a ball of fire and cut through a branch. He finished his spin and hurled the beam at the Sunguard in the center. The steel flew at his head, and the Sunguard had to duck to avoid it.

The vines shooting toward him from his left collapsed. That one had power over vegetation.

Caleb kept moving, however, snagging another beam from the ground while hopping to his right to avoid a flaming orb that singed his shoulder on the way past. The next ball of fire was right behind and impossible to dodge, so he slapped at it with the flat side of the unforged sword. The ball of fire dissipated into nothing.

He crouched under a thick vine; it stretched over his head, and he brought the steel beam in his hand across his body and threw it to the Sunguard on his right. The beam flew in a horizontal twirl toward the Sunguard's knees. The Sunguard took a step back and swiped the beam away with his sword.

No more fire but a steel beam lifted from the ground and shot at him as a burning branch – on fire from the orbs of flame – lowered on him.

The one on the right controlled fire. Process of elimination, the third was the mind.

Baring his teeth, Caleb made his way toward the three Sunguard. The one in the middle retreated a couple steps, but the other two moved further apart. Caleb took another steel bar and now used it as another weapon, swatting aside vines or other debris with it. He used the unforged sword with the flames.

He advanced on the Sunguard in the middle, and the other two adjusted their position to surround him. He made his move on his target, throwing the steel in his left hand at the face of the Sunguard and darting forward at a sprint, closing the distance. The Sunguard spread his stance and took his golden sword in both hands to knock the steel down.

Within three mitres, Caleb stumbled. How am I running so fast? But he didn't have more time for his curiosity, for a steel beam drove through his left side, the point coming through with a splatter of blood. His blood was orange somehow. He ignored the pain, blocked it out of his mind, and he lifted his unforged sword to engage the Sunguard.

The Sunguard met his sword, and Caleb struck high and then low. He circled the Sunguard, placing the guard between him and the other two, forcing them to adjust their attacks, another beam falling to the side and a ball of fire going wide. The pain in his side was sharp and intense, and he grunted at a wave of nausea. It didn't slow him down. He wouldn't let it.

The unforged sword sliced across, met by a golden blade, but the Sunguard wasn't fast enough to stop the next stroke at his neck. Caleb pushed the blade through the armor and the neck and out the other side. He slid the guard off of his supernatural blade.

The Sunguard went stiff, arms bending and twitching, and he was consumed by an explosion of white light. Caleb winced as the wave of power rushed over him, but it didn't hurt him.

The wound at his side would no longer be ignored, however. He cried out and dropped to his knees.

—

Tamya joined Aden's cry of grief with her own when the creature sprayed acid and killed a hundred men and elves, Jaff among them. Her heart broke with the weight of it. Jaff was a great man, a great leader, one of the Ghosts of Saten

She and Aden soared through the air atop Malaki. Aden pulled her closer, or tried to, his arm around her waist tightening, and she appreciated the comfort. Her eyes drifted down, the *Hamon-el* retreating … and Eshlyn maneuvering like a master horsewoman to get Jaff's unforged sword. She cursed in awe under her breath.

Aden and Tamya guided Malaki to fly by the head of the creature to spit fire at it. It didn't do any damage, but it distracted the thing and kept it from focusing on the *Hamon-el*.

Bael and Elowen approached the creature from behind. The creature's prehensile tail with steel spikes at the end of it lashed out at them.

Elowen and Bael were caught in the unsuspecting attack. Bael dogded the tail, but not fast enough. The spikes ripped through one of the dragon's wings, almost tearing it in half.

The dragon bellowed in pain and tumbled over and to the side of the creature. Bael tucked his injured wing and used the other one to stop the tumble so he would fall on his belly, to protect Elowen, Tamya assumed. His momentum carried him dozens of mitres away, and he spread his four legs as he landed. His claws and talons dug deep into the ground. Elowen leapt from his shoulder to get clear. She rolled in one direction, and he another.

The dragon moved far enough away from the creature to be clear, but Elowen was within range of the creature's acid. And the creature began to turn its neck and maw in that direction.

"Get her!" Tamya screamed, and Malaki acted. He dove straight down, her stomach lurching, his wings folded in, the speed dizzying. Aden held her tighter, if possible, and within thirty mitres from the ground, the wings unfurled, straining and catching air. She and Aden were crushed on his shoulder, pausing for the moment as wings flapped, and they shot up as a spray of acid met the ground behind them.

Tamya looked down and saw that Elowen was gone.

"You have her?" she said. "Malaki!"

"I have her," Malaki said, the body rumbling beneath her as he spoke.

She sighed in relief and made sure that Bael was clear. He crawled to the north. Malaki glided over to Bael and lowered Elowen next to him, launching back in the air, strong wings taking them higher and higher.

Tamya glanced over her shoulder, and five groups of the stalgest, the ant creatures, moved toward the crizzard beast. Each group was led by someone on a horse, Eshlyn and Macarus among them.

"What are they doing?" she shouted.

Aden took a moment to respond. "Unforged swords. Keep it from getting to the camp."

Cut through the steel-covered legs. Smart. "We can't have the dragons shoot fire at the creature while they're down there. We could hit them."

"Yeah," Aden said, sounding resigned.

"We could go down and help with our own swords."

He was silent for a moment, and she let him think. Which was dangerous. He came up with maddy ideas when she let him think. Before she could correct her mistake, she felt him sigh in satisfaction. He was always smug when he had a breakin' idea.

"Aden?"

"I've got a plan."

Shog a goat. "Of course you do."

—+—

Eshlyn and Macarus rode to the right, fifty mitres wide to avoid the acid from the creature. Kenneth, Wes, and Xak were to the left, also far wide. Each of them led five of the large, white ants with Dragonmen upon them. Macarus was in the lead. Gunnar rode behind a Dragonman on one of the stalgest behind the elf Captain.

Five groups and six legs. She prayed it would be enough.

After seeing the tail swipe and take out a dragon, Eshlyn wasn't so sure about this plan. Her plan. A suicidal plan like Caleb's always were. Did stupid come with the Kingstaff?

She held the Kingstaff in her left hand and Jaff's unforged sword in her right. The Kingstaff wasn't heavy; it was awkward, however. She hadn't had any training with it, not at all, and holding it reminded her of Caleb, how he fought with the staff like poetry in death on the wall of Ketan.

He said once that he was the weapon, that Galen had trained him to be the sword, and even Iletus had marveled in her presence at his skill and passion in the midst of battle. She believed it. How could she not? She had seen him fight too many times to doubt his ability and will. He was the weapon.

But I'm not. I'm a follower of El, a mother, a leader, but not a weapon, not a killer. Her time in Lior had taught her that. She was something else. *I couldn't be a weapon. Could I?*

Macarus made a slight turn to his left, sprinting toward the right back leg, the unforged sword in his hand. As she turned to follow, she could see the other three *Sohan-el* on the opposite side of the creature. They split and spread to take one leg each.

Only Aden and Tamya were left in the air. They swept in front of the creature, within its vision, and the creature followed them with its black eyes. *They're distracting the thing for us. And it's working. So far.*

Across from her, Wes reached the first leg and made wide swings of his unforged sword. He hacked at the thick leg. Eshlyn reached the middle leg on her side, and the creature swung its head toward Wes and now Kenneth cutting at the legs. The Dragonmen led the stalgest to the legs, as well, one each on a leg. The big white ants could eat through stone. Why not the scales of this thing? Their pincers ate away.

The crizzard thing roared, and its mouth opened. The serpent tongue extended.

"Watch out!" Eshlyn yelled. "Move under it!"

Wes and Kenneth, and now Xak, caught the creature's movement and ran under the body of the beast. The Dragonmen took notice and followed, eating through red, scaly flesh on the inside of the legs.

I have to get its attention.

She hauled back with Jaff's sword as Macarus reached the back leg, and she hacked with both hands over her head at the leg, close to the first joint. The unforged sword cut deep into the meat of the leg. She heard what could have been an echo with Macarus hitting the leg to her right.

White stalgest leapt over her head and latched onto the beast's leg with pincers and their own limbs.

"Lady Eshlyn!" Kenneth called, and she looked up to what she expected, the head turning her way now, the odd swiveling neck making its way her direction. She hacked once more at the leg, and she prepared to duck under the belly of the monster. But Aden and Tamya's dragon bore down on the monster's head with fire from above, forcing it to bow its head for protection.

"Take it down!" Macarus ordered, but no one needed motivation or direction.

Eshlyn leapt up and brought her weight down on the leg, and the blade cut halfway into the thick limb and hit bone. The creature squealed, the maw opening wide to emit a pained, horrible sound, the serpent tongue twitching. The leg lifted in reaction, the end dangling now and green blood spraying from the wound. When the creature attempted to put the leg back down, it wouldn't hold its weight, and the whole beast pitched to the side.

It pulled its other front leg up from in front of Wes to catch itself, but that one also had a great gash in it. The beast stumbled, and Eshlyn began to back away. She glanced over to see Macarus with one slash after another, biting into the muscle and hide in a circle. The stalgest, hanging upside down with their powerful limbs, focused their gnawing on the cuts, deeping the wounds. With a curse, Macarus spun to slice straight through the bone of the back leg.

With only the front leg uninjured on their side, Eshlyn watched as the giant body shifted in her direction. It would crush her.

The Dragonmen said something in their language, and they launched from the beast and scattered.

She turned and sprinted to the south, straight away from the creature. She didn't look behind her, but she felt the impact of its body upon the ground, dirt flying around her and hitting her in the back and the back of the head. Leaping forward, the staff and sword extended in front of her, she fell and landed on her chest and abdomen. It knocked the breath out of her for a moment, and she heaved twice before getting some air.

Rolling over to her elbows, Eshlyn saw the body of the creature shift the other way and fall to the north, on its right side. The air around her filled with an acrid stench, something similar to the smell at the Acar before Aden healed it. Hands grabbed her arms and helped her to her feet. Macarus, she saw with a glance. She hoped the *Sohan-el* on the other side were able to get clear.

She sighed. It couldn't get to the camp. They were safe. Javyn was safe.

The creature, stuck now on its belly, continued to make its horrible, gurgling squeal. It closed its maw as it swiveled its head and neck around, slow, to point to the sky, trying to track the dragon above. Its legs moved up and down, green blood flowing onto the ground. The maw opened again, and it sprayed acid through the serpent tongue and up at the dragon. It missed, but the dragon had to rise into the air on expansive wings to get out of range.

The ground shook with new footsteps, and Eshlyn turned to look behind her. Bael with his injured wing galloped along the ground, growling, smoke trailing from his nostrils. Toward the beast.

⊢

Caleb growled at the pain, at the orange blood around the wound. A ball of fire spun his way, and he slapped at it with the unforged sword. He gazed down at the bar of steel through his body.

Pull it free.

The sword. Yes. El or Yosu … did it matter anymore? Telling him what to do.

He grabbed the end of the steel bar at the front and pulled. It was slick with blood, but it came free with excruciating pain. He dropped it and fell to his hands, trying to catch his breath.

His vision narrowed, but he could sense a bar of steel darting his way. He had the thought to catch it with his hand instead of dodging it this time, so he straightened, reached out and grabbed it from the air before it got to him.

The steel beam lost all momentum. He barely had to use any strength to stop it. Batting away another fireball with the blade, he stood to his feet.

With the power of the unforged sword, when he touched the beam, he gained control over it.

He cried out as the wound at his side burned, suddenly, and he looked down through the orange-bloody hole in his shirt. The open wound – three fingers wide – began to close on its own. The orange blood bubbled, and the flesh reattached and repaired itself. In the same instant, he noticed the small cuts from the glass along his arms and skin were gone. Healed.

The golden blood. The blood of dragons. How much did they give me? What did it do to me?

He didn't have time to fully entertain the thought; he grabbed another bar from the air, cut through a ball of flame, and hurled the beam at the Sunguard behind him.

The Sunguard ducked down, and Caleb bolted toward him to attack. With his speed, Caleb was halfway to the guard before he looked up. Caleb had pulled another beam from the ground and threw it.

The Sunguard knocked the beam down with his golden sword and raised his left hand higher. Pieces of glass and several beams shot at Caleb at once, and he also heard the hiss of flames behind him. Caleb spun his sword from side to side, focusing on the beams and cutting through two larger glass fragments. He lowered his head to avoid another shard, but smaller bits got through his defense to cut through his shirt and skin. One scrap of glass stuck into forearm.

Caleb was on the Sunguard now. Spinning to avoid the golden blade, Caleb struck the guard in the shoulder with the flat of his hand, the contact shuddering up his arm, knocking the Sunguard off balance. The crackle of flames hissed behind him, and Caleb crouched and changed direction all at once. The ball of fire struck the Sunguard in the chest and neck, spreading over the golden armor.

The Sunguard shuffled back, his arms flailing. Caleb swung the unforged sword twice, slicing off both arms, cutting through armor and flesh. The Sunguard did not make a sound, but crimson blood sprayed from both arms.

Caleb reached out and caught him by the neck, his fingers gripping the edge of a golden plate of armor, and he spun the guard around to take two more flaming orbs on the golden armor. Lifting, pushing, dragging the Sunguard forward, he rushed the remaining Sunguard.

The last Sunguard lifted both arms, one with the blade down. The air began to move and swirl, small tornadoes picking up debris and leaves and grass and moving in Caleb's direction. Caleb had moved five mitres, and the wind began to swirl around the whole garden, lances of flame within the hurricane of wind.

Caleb was forced to stop and get his footing, but with his strength and the unforged sword in his right hand, he found the ability to walk forward, one step at a time, continuing to use the Sunguard as a shield. Branches and sticks and glass still struck him hard, but he kept upright and advancing. Caleb gritted his teeth and began to use his sword for defense in the maelstrom. His vision blurred in the wind and dirt and debris, so he trusted the leading of the sword, one side then another. One step then another across the clearing.

The force of the wind uprooted a tree, then a second one, spinning around him and missing him by centimitres. The wind roared in his ear and tore at his shirt and trousers.

He sensed he was close to the remaining Sunguard, so he took the one in his hand, lifted, and impaled him through the heart with his sword.

The Sunguard blew apart with a white light, pieces of armor and flesh flying in every direction.

The torrential wind fell still within a moment, trees and limbs and glass crashing to the ground. Caleb, unaffected by the exploding Sunguard, stepped forward blindly, and when he could see, the last Sunguard had been blown back and bounced off of a tree but was still on his feet. The Sunguard attempted to recover, arms swinging, his golden sword far to the side.

Caleb leapt toward him, blocking a wild fist with his left hand, and he removed the Sunguard's head from his body.

A final flash of white light accompanied pieces of armor and limbs shooting and arcing to the ground.

Panting, Caleb stood alone and alive in the garden, broken and torn, his unforged sword in a low position.

His shirt was in shreds, and he pulled it with his left hand. It unraveled and fell to the ground. He noticed the scars on his chest and arms, the scars Eshlyn had touched and kissed only a few hours ago, were golden. All other wounds healed; the pieces of glass pushed from his skin and fell to the ground.

Caleb closed his eyes and lifted his head to feel the warm morning sun on his face. With a sigh, he stood, and he turned to the covered passage that led to the other tower, the throne room, the Worldbreaker.

He opened his eyes and walked.

———

"They did it," Tamya said to him. "They stopped it."

Eshlyn and the others with the stalgest scrambled away from the creature. It writhed on useless legs.

But it's not dead. Aden leaned into Malaki's turn.

Bael had recovered and bounded on short, lizard legs toward the crizzard from the north. Aden set his jaw. "It's time."

Tamya squinted. "Let's kill it."

Aden guided Malaki in a circle over the crizzard beast. They approached from behind it, out of range of that tail. The creature swung the tail, narrowly missing them. Aden pushed with his legs and arms on Malaki's neck, and they dropped straight onto the creatures back between two of the steel spikes.

Bael and Elowen arrived, leaping onto the crizzard's neck next to another spike and faced Aden and Tamya on Malaki.

Aden peered around Malaki's neck. "We're going to pull this shogger apart!"

Elowen raised a hand in salute while Bael gripped the front spike with his front claws. Malaki did the same with the back spike. Both spikes were fused to the creature's spine. So Malaki and Bael leaned back with all their might.

Malaki beat his wings for more leverage, and Bael's lone complete wing swung. Tamya held tight to Aden, like her grip on her husband could contribute to the bulging muscles in dragon forearms. The dragons snarled. The large crizzard beast flailed, its head moving back and forth, trying to get around to face the attackers on its back.

The bones of the beast's spine began to crack, to snap. The skin on its back ripped apart, a gaping wound that grew. Green, toxic blood erupted from the wound. The creature screamed.

The crizzard's mouth opened, and the serpent tongue shot out and sprayed acid into the air. Bael released the steel spike, twisted, and reached out to grab the tongue. With a few attempts, the dragon caught the wiggling tongue with his right claw. In one deft move, Bael ripped the tongue from its throat. Acid spilled onto Bael's leg, the scales there smoking, burning.

Malaki aimed his jaws at the gaping wound bleeding on the crizzard's back. He poured fire and flame into the wound, burning deep into the creature. Tamya hid her face behind her arm at the immense heat.

Bael jumped over the crizzard's head, growling. Landing on the field before the beast, he grabbed the front snout, two claws on the upper and his lower claws on the bottom. He pushed the jaws apart as far as he could, lowered his head, and sent fire down the throat of the beast. Flame consumed the head of the crizzard beast from the inside. The eyes popped and flame exploded from the skull.

The dragons ceased their flame attacks at the same moment. Tamya took deep breaths in the searing heat that remained.

A burning husk was all that remained of the beast.

Tamya panted, her eyes narrowed, and her head scanned the field. She stopped, facing east, to the city.

Climbing over the rubble toward them were legions of militan, all armed with swords and spears and shields. An elf with a longer robe and an official-looking sash and thick boots led them, a sword gleaming in his hand.

Aden shook his head. "Crit on a frog."

CHAPTER 34

THE UNFORGED SWORD

Caleb pushed through the double doors and strode down the walkway. The sunlight streamed into the covered path through windows along the side. The banging wooden doors echoed through the stone structure, like a tunnel, and the flattened floor was transparent glass. Caleb paused before continuing. He took a deep breath and focused, calming the dizzying nature of the view, adjusting his mind.

His steady steps echoed. Another set of doors waited at the other end. Figures had been carved into the stone beneath and around the windows, depictions of battles and wars and the supremacy of elves over the appearance of humans and dwarves like animals.

Other than his footsteps and his own pounding heartbeat, it was quiet. He did not hurry. He did not rush to the end.

He reached them soon enough. He half expected the doors to be locked or barred against him. But he knew they would not be when he set his palm on the door to the left and shoved.

The hinges did not creak; they made the sound of a slow breath as the door swung wide and open to reveal the Emperor's Throne Room.

The throne itself was unimpressive, made as it was for the Steward of Asya and not for the High Evilord of Kryus. The Emperor stood before it in the center of the room, a golden blade on his hip, its hilt gleaming silver with jewels in the pommel. The round room filled the top of the tower, and the ceiling ascended to a point high above his head. Tapestries hung on the walls, circling the Emperor with depictions of the might of Kryus, great generals and one of the Steward appearing like a hero with his hands on his hips and gazing to some future envisioned. Weapons – swords, axes, spears, maces – were set between tapestries. High, open, oval windows let in the light of the sun.

Human bodies lay around the edge of the room, husks of bodies that reminded him of Carys and Earon. That was the point. His nostrils flared as he counted fifty of them.

The Emperor appeared like a god. He wore a long white robe with a golden belt. His long, straight blond hair lay perfect on his shoulders. The golden crown on his head was adorned with jewels. His blue eyes shone in the sun and the magic power he held within him, taken from the lives of humans around the room.

Caleb took the few stairs down to the main marble floor.

Tanicus showed his teeth. "It is you. The one they claim is a god, a fulfillment of crazed madmen thousands of years ago. As if people thousands of years ago could know anything of today. But we can dispense with the pretense. You have founded a revolution on deception and betrayal. It ends today."

Caleb stood five mitres from the Emperor. He pulled his hair back with a leather cord. "I am no god, but I serve one. You speak of deception and betrayal? I didn't need to force anyone to follow. Your whole rule depends upon fear and lies. It was born in a lie and murder and has continued as such."

"I saved this Empire from itself, from its own stagnation. I brought it forward, to progress. All you can do is steal and destroy what others have built. You attack this city with Kryan militan, Kryan slaves, and Kryan weapons. What do you have that is your own?"

Caleb lifted the unforged sword in front of his face, the blade pointing down. "This sword born from a Living Stone, given by the one true god. None of those people belong to you. Neither do they belong to me. They were free and chose to fight for freedom."

"One god, one way. I wonder if you are able to acknowledge your own delusion?"

"You are correct about one thing. It ends today." Caleb lowered the sword into a horizontal guard. "If you surrender now, you may live."

Tanicus narrowed his eyes at Caleb. "Earon said much the same, and you know his end."

Caleb's stomach tightened.

"Are you afraid?" the Emperor asked.

Caleb snorted. "Not anymore."

Tanicus nodded. "Very well."

Caleb leapt at the Emperor, and the Worldbreaker raised both of his arms with a mad grin on his face.

The weapons all around the room pulled from the wall and shot toward Caleb.

Caleb lifted his blade and swatted aside an axe to his left, ducked a spinning sword from behind him. Moving forward, he twirled and cut through the shaft of a spear. He lifted his left leg, and another spear cracked into the marble floor beneath him. Shifting his weight to the side, an axe sliced into the back of his upper arm.

The air in the room became a swirl of wind, and it forced Caleb to stop. His boots slid on the floor, his feet shuffling. He spun to avoid a mace, and its spikes raked at his back.

A bolt of lighting stretched from the ceiling, and Caleb could not get his sword up in time. He raised his left arm and took the bolt on his forearm. It burned his skin, and his body went numb. But it didn't hurt as much as he had expected.

Caleb held onto the unforged sword with all his strength while he was pulled into the storm around him. The wind lifted and dropped him, a spear imbedding into his right thigh.

Blood sprayed. Caleb growled, and he descended. His body tingled but recovered. He pulled the spear from his thigh; he landed on the floor and slammed the spear into the marble, the point digging deep enough to give him purchase and stability.

It was a mistake to give a weapon to a weapon.

Another bolt of lighting flashed, and he caught it on the sword. He took a step, and the wooden spear broke with the force of his grip and the wind. Cursing, he slammed the unforged sword into the marble to keep him steady. A fine sword flipped toward him, end over end. He crouched lower, waited, timed his move, and lashed out with his left hand to grip the hilt from the air. As with the beams of steel in the garden, it lost force and momentum in his hand, and he used the sword to crawl forward to the Worldbreaker.

Tanicus was at the center of the hurricane, the eye of it, his brow furrowed and teeth gritted in the effort. The veins in his hands and forearms were visible as he strained.

Caleb took a step, moved the fine sword in his left hand, and he batted away the weapons as they flew toward him or ducked. He cut through the metal of one mace and withstood a bolt of blue electricity with the unforged sword.

While he walked, no pain in his thigh. It had healed.

The Worldbreaker flicked his right wrist.

The tempest around him ignited and waves of flame filled the air. It was getting difficult to breathe. Caleb was able to battle through the flames with the unforged sword. The flames dissipated and did not touch him. He had to hold his breath at the lack of air.

All the while, he took steps and kept advancing. He was within five paces of the Emperor and sucked in a breath of air. The force of the wind died down, and Caleb didn't need the stability of the sword anymore.

He attacked, throwing the fine sword at the Emperor and rushed forward.

Tanicus took one step back, withdrew his golden sword from his hip with his right hand, and he swatted the fine sword. He then reversed to meet Caleb's attack. The blades clashed, and Tanicus somehow knew to deflect the unforged sword instead of taking the full brunt of the attack on his own blade.

Caleb had trained fifteen years for this. His destiny. To meet the Worldbreaker with an unforged sword. He would not be stopped.

Caleb pressed. He struck hard and fast, forcing his heart and mind to calm, to accept, to flow with the unforged sword. He swung high and then low, changing his pace and the angles. One after another, Tanicus deflected and blocked the unforged blade with ease.

They separated. Only a great swordmaster could do that.

Tanicus reset. "Galen may have trained you, but you face someone greater than Galen, now."

The Emperor turned his wrist and moved to the offensive, his golden blade striking at Caleb's knee then his shoulder. Tanicus held the golden sword with two hands, each move efficient and intentional. Caleb blocked each strike, but he retreated under the assult.

That sword was not a decoration.

Tanicus moved his grip to one hand – his right hand – and he lifted his left with the palm up.

The wind had died down, but out of the corner of his eye, the weapons rose from the floor and hurtled forward. Other weapons followed.

Caleb moved around the room, backing away from the Emperor, trying to keep distance. He blocked two strikes from Tanicus and then ducked a mace and spun on a heel to bat a spear away from impaling his sternum.

Dodging another sword flying at him, Caleb turned the Emperor's blade and stabbed at his chest, forcing Tanicus to retreat a step, and Caleb snatched a spear with a serrated point from the air with his left hand.

Snorting, Caleb twirled the spear like the staff above his head and brought both weapons to bear on the Emperor. Tanicus circled away and blocked the spear and sword with his own blade.

The other steel in the air picked up their pace but didn't have the precision as it did earlier. Caleb twirled the spear around him, knocking maces and swords and axes aside while engaging the golden blade of the Worldbreaker. All his training came to bear. Every muscle burning with effort, pushing himself beyond the limits, faster and stronger than ever before.

An axe flipped at his head from his right and a sword from behind. Caleb leapt back, spinning to deflect both, but he couldn't get the spear around in time to get a good hit on the sword. The blade sliced through his lower back. He cried out, and the pain slowed him. He came around to face the Emperor, and Tanicus slashed through the wooden shaft of the spear, shattering it in two. Caleb barely got his unforged blade around in time to stop the next strike.

The Emperor smiled.

The bodies around the room lifted like rag dolls, strewn about from the maelstrom earlier, ten of them at first, and they hovered like ghosts, their mouths and eyes bulging like they endured constant pain, skin stretched dry and tight on skeletons. Tanicus took two steps back, and ten bodies surrounded Caleb and sailed toward him.

The horrors filled his vision, his mind fighting thoughts of Carys, Earon, and his parents, Reyan, all the dead in his family. Every face was a skull, but he saw faces of those he loved that had died in the cause of the revolution – Esai, Athelwulf, Xander, Iletus, more. He knew it was false, it wasn't real, they were humans but not his friends and family, but it shook him.

Caleb shouldered past them. His elbow connected with their fragile bodies with crunching sounds. But when he got past them, more bodies awaited, a dozen more, and they piled atop of him. He fought his way through them, no other way than with desperation and strength and ignoring the gruesome tearing of skin and hair from the dead.

Panting, he got clear, and Tanicus waited for him.

With a skillful and strong move, the Emperor met Caleb's blade, turned it with unbelievable speed; he twisted and pulled the unforged sword from Caleb's hand. He clutched at the hilt, but it slid off his fingers.

Caleb watched, helpless, as Tanicus spun on a heel and flicked the unforged sword from the Living Stone out of the window. It fell out of sight.

＋

Eshlyn groaned.

Everything hurt. Her whole body was sore, but especially her left leg and back.

Macarus shrugged. "Two, maybe three legions are coming from the city. They're in formation and headed this way."

Eshlyn hesitated. They didn't have the numbers, not for two legions, but if the camp was already packing to move, then they might be able to buy some time. "You guys wouldn't happen to have a few thousand bosaur hiding somewhere, would you?"

"No," Xak said. He jerked his head to the east. "But we do have dragons. Something tells me that's all we'll need."

"Well, at least signal for some horses," Eshlyn said. "Wes there looks like he'll need one."

Macarus gave her a wry look, but after a signal to the scouts halfway to the camp, Sergeant Gunnar and Nahom rode up, leading five saddled horses. Abbott, Zamira, and Redan rode stalgest behind them. Within five minutes, they were all on horses and riding up next to the enormous, fried creature.

Elowen and Bael had crawled to stand beyond the creature near Aden and Tamya.

Eshlyn looked up at Aden and Tamya. "Good to see you." For a moment, the joy at seeing them made her forget the pain.

Tamya bowed. "Lady Eshlyn."

Eshlyn chuckled. "You're riding a breakin' dragon. I think we're beyond that now. I met Bael, but I haven't met this one."

The dragon gave her a fierce look, but he bowed. "I am called Malaki, Lady Eshlyn. It is my great pleasure."

When Aden smiled at her, he appeared … not older … more mature? "Good to see you, Eshlyn." Aden and Tamya greeted the others, being introduced to Gunnar and finally beaming at the elf. Aden spoke with a soft voice. "Macarus. I'm so glad to see you've returned to us."

"It was the right thing to do." Macarus waved at the dragons. "I see you've been busy."

Aden shrugged.

Eshlyn gazed toward the city. "Caleb get to the Emperor?"

"I believe so," Aden said. "Yes."

She lowered her vision to see thousands of militan arrayed in front of the walls of Asya, or what was left of it.

"They've just been waiting there?"

"Yeah," Tamya said.

Eshlyn pointed at the elf standing out in the front. "Who is that?"

Macarus squinted. "A general. Felix, I assume."

"You know him?"

"Not well," Macarus answered. "He is the High General, the Commander of all Legions."

"Is he waiting to fight or talk?" Aden asked.

"Hard to say," Macarus said. "He's not afraid of a battle, but he isn't reckless." He glared at Eshlyn.

She raised a brow at him. "Well, there's only one way to find out what he wants. Let's go talk to him."

"What is your strategy if he does not seek conference but a conflict?" Gunnar asked.

"I'm bringing dragons with me, as Xak reminded me," Eshlyn said. "That's strategy enough."

The group nodded, and Kenneth chuckled. Eshlyn kicked her horse and turned it to ride toward the General. The rest of them fell in behind her. With his injured wing, Bael limped alongside. Malaki rose on wings and circled them as they rode.

The legions did not move. The General did not move.

Eshlyn pulled on the reins of her horse and halted five mitres from the General. He stood twenty mitres from the front line of the legions.

When she stopped, the air moved like a heartbeat around her, and Malaki landed to her right.

The General blinked.

Next to her, Macarus gave a slight bow. "General Felix. It has been a few years."

"Captain," General Felix said.

"This is Lady Eshlyn," Macarus said.

Eshlyn set the Kingstaff in her right stirrup and laid her left hand on Jaff's unforged sword. She moved her horse forward a length.

"Well met, Lady," the General said. "I assume the same Eshlyn from Captain Macarus' report."

He put me in a report that made it to the High General? It took everything in her not to ask Macarus a dozen questions.

"Yes," Macarus said.

"In the *Brendel's* absence, are you the one in command?" the General asked.

"I don't know if I would put it quite like that," Eshlyn said. "But ..."

"Yes," Macarus and Aden said at once.

The General surveyed the group, his eyes measuring like a man weighing the value of a prized cow at market. His gaze rested on Eshlyn.

"Very well," the General said. "I would speak with you, if you would listen."

It was an odd feeling, to the sure. She sensed the power of the moment, the authority of the High General. But even covered with green blood from the creature, and with her body exhausted and sore, she knew she belonged there.

"We are here to listen, General," Eshlyn said.

"The *Brendel* raised up this army, and you have fought your way to this city," the General began. "Many died yesterday and today. You have even brought dragons to fight us. What is it you seek?"

Eshlyn frowned. "What are you asking me?"

"We are two armies standing here with blood on our hands and more blood to come," the General responded. "Before more blood is shed, before I command these elves to fight – against *dragons* – I must hear from you, Lady, what would satisfy you to bring this battle to an end? What is your end goal? What do you *seek*?"

The wind blew ruffled her hair. She took her fingers and pulled a strand behind her ear. Everyone, elf, human, and dwarf, stood silent.

Aden spoke first. "To defend the innocent."

"To free the oppressed," Tamya continued.

Macarus grinned. "And spread light in dark places."

The General's brow furrowed.

Oh, Caleb. How I wish you were here to see this.

"We seek freedom for all, General," Eshlyn said. "For every living being. Even yours. We seek the end of oppression. If you stay in this city, there will be new leadership, a new government, and it will not be under the authority of a foreign Empire. If you can't abide that new opportunity, then you will leave this city and return to your own country. I imagine there is enough to occupy you there."

"We seek that freedom for every city," Aden added. "And every town of humans. The freedom for every people the freedom to work together for the good of all."

"And you believe you can achieve that?" The General's voice held a tinge of sarcasm.

"We achieved it in Ketan," Eshlyn said. "And we have achieved it in this army, something unseen in this world for thousands of years. We may fail. But we have the right to try."

"If you achieve what you seek, you will allow us freedom to stay or leave? Unharmed?" the General asked.

"It is not our goal to harm you," Eshlyn said. Her gaze went to the bodies hanging from what was left of the wall, human bodies, pointedly. "The fact that these dragons have not made elf steak of your legion should be evidence enough of that."

The General blinked and nodded. "I have seen much over the last few days that I never imagined I would see. So one more should not pain me, but it does." The General drew his sword. Eshlyn squeezed the hilt of her own in reaction, but Felix drove the sword into the ground and bowed before her. "The city of Asya is yours, Lady Eshlyn."

Eshlyn's jaw tightened to keep from whimpering. "Does the Emperor know you're here? Is this his idea?"

"My Emperor is a Worldbreaker and has gone mad," the General said. "I do this to save what remains of my elves."

"I can appreciate that," Eshlyn said. "Now I have a question for you."

"Yes, my Lady?"

"Do you know where the Emperor is?"

General Felix turned and pointed to the towers on the other side of the city.

Eshlyn gripped the Kingstaff and took a deep breath.

Caleb.

CHAPTER 35

THE BLADE OF EL

The pain was so great, Caleb couldn't even scream.

The Emperor held him immobile, legs and arms spread in the air like a sacrifice, and those invisible hands pulled at his limbs away from his body.

Tanicus sheathed his golden blade and raised his right hand at him, as well. The Emperor snarled, his eyes crazed, and flames erupted from his right hand. The spout of fire arced over and struck Caleb's right forearm. The flames began to consume his skin, first with blisters, then blackening and burning away. The scent of burning flesh, his own, filled his nostrils.

Caleb's mouth gaped but made no sound.

The Worldbreaker began to speak.

"It is over, Caleb. Galen's betrayal has failed. Your army has been crushed. I will burn parts of you away, piece by piece. But I will leave your head and show it to your army. Then I will make sure any survivors feel more pain than they ever imagined. Just as you feel now."

No. Not Aden. Not Eshlyn. No. He saw others in his mind – Macarus, Tamya, Mother Natali. Without the unforged sword, he was powerless.

I need the sword.

Tanicus ended the flame, and Caleb's right hand and forearm burned down to blackened bone.

"You have failed. Your god has failed you. The nine gods are your only hope, and they have sent me to destroy everything you've ever loved. Tell me, how does that make you feel?"

Caleb's heart dove into deep despair, an emptiness that consumed him more than the flames had his flesh. All of his pain, all of the training, all of the years of work and struggle, all the deaths of all the people he loved, all the battles, all of it … for nothing.

For nothing.

I have failed.

Could the Worldbreaker manipulate emotions? In the midst of the pain and evident failure, it didn't matter. He had failed. Everyone would die. Because of him.

"See what you are without your tricks and your deception? Do you see what is true? I will be your final truth, just as it was for your sister and your cousin, and Galen. I will be the god on your lips when you take your final breath."

Caleb had no way to fight. He saw no way to fight back.

"You have failed, and you are nothing," the Worldbreaker said. "You are nothing without your sword."

Caleb knew pain, emptiness, darkness. Nothing else. The Worldbreaker spoke true. *I am nothing. Nothing without the sword.*

The Worldbreaker licked his lips and showed his teeth. "Now, I will take all the life from your body. Despite your rebellion, you will serve me after all."

The Worldbreaker's right hand became a fist, and when Caleb thought the pain could not increase, it did. It felt like Tanicus sucked his heart from his chest, his blood through the pores in his skin.

The Emperor's smile transformed into a frown. His brow furrowed. "What is inside you?"

BRENDEL.

Yosu? El?

BRENDEL. YOU ARE MY BRENDEL.

I lost my sword! Help me!

YOU ARE THE BRENDEL. YOU ARE THE SWORD.

What? The prophecy?

MORE THAN A PROPHECY. MORE THAN A WORD. YOU ARE THE BRENDEL. IT HAS ALL COME TO THIS.

He remembered the words of Yosu on the bridge – *I HAVE MADE YOU, FORGED YOU, BROUGHT YOU TO THIS PLACE …*

I am the sword. I am the weapon.

BELIEF IS YOUR WEAPON … MORE THAN THE SWORD OR STAFF OR YOUR TRAINING OR THE ARMY … BELIEF IS WHAT WILL SEE YOU TO THE END, IF YOU CHOOSE.

If I choose?

DO YOU BELIEVE WHAT I SAY YOU ARE? WHAT I HAVE MADE YOU?

I am the Brendel. I believe.

THEN SPEAK IT. SAY IT.

I can't. The pain …

SPEAK.

It came out like a groan at first. "I am the *Brendel.*"

The *Brendel's* arm burned, but not like before. With a glance, the orange blood flowed and covered his forearm and hand. The flesh that had been burned off began to reform. Hope blossomed in his heart where it had been so empty before.

The Worldbreaker's eyes narrowed. "What?"

It was clearer the second time. "I … am … the *Brendel.*"

The pace of healing on his arm quickened. Veins and muscles formed, then skin. But the skin was golden.

"What are you?" Tanicus asked. "There is no end! It is too much!"

"I am the *Brendel*."

The *Brendel* felt the invisible power holding him weaken, and then he dropped to the ground, free. He crouched on the marble floor.

There was fear in the Worldbreaker's eyes. "What are you?!"

The *Brendel* could feel the life being drawn from him, but he did not lack. Where life was taken, more took its place. Exponentially more. He was the sword of El. And as the sword of El, the Worldbreaker's magic had no power over him.

"*I am the sword. I am the Brendel.*"

The *Brendel* stood straight, his shoulders square. And he took a step toward the Worldbreaker.

"No," Tanicus shouted.

The *Brendel* knew that denial did not change was was real. What was true. He took another step.

"I AM THE SWORD. I AM THE BRENDEL."

The *Brendel*'s skin toughened, hardened, and his forearm was coated in a liquid, golden substance. He felt no more pain.

The Worldbreaker strained, his eyes bulging, spittle coming from his gaping mouth, sweat pouring from him and soaking the white robe, veins popping, muscles taut. He pulled life from the *Brendel* in a torrent.

The *Brendel* took another step, a pace away now.

With a gasp, the Worldbreaker ceased his magic, full of life but exhausted. As a last attempt to stop the *Brendel,* he pulled his golden sword. He raised it over his head with two hands and lowered it on the *Brendel*'s head.

The *Brendel* met the blade with his golden forearm. The Worldbreaker's blade shattered into dust, and the Worldbreaker fell back. The jeweled hilt clattered to the ground.

Lighting quick, the *Brendel* caught the collar of his robe with his left hand.

"*I AM THE SWORD! I AM THE BRENDEL!*"

The *Brendel* flattened his right hand, and his limb from the elbow down extended into a long, thick, golden blade. With a swing, he severed the Worldbreaker's left arm at the shoulder. The Worldbreaker screamed, red blood spouting. The *Brendel* grabbed the Worldbreaker by the neck and squeezed. The Worldbreaker choked, unable to breathe.

The *Brendel* took his blade-arm and cut the Worldbreaker's right arm from his body. More blood like a fountain on the marble floor.

The Worldbreaker looked at him now like a child, pleading with tear-filled eyes.

The *Brendel* carried the Worldbreaker's body over to the throne at the edge of the room. He climbed the stairs up to the top of the dais and sat the Worldbreaker on the throne.

The Worldbreaker could not breathe but mouthed one word … *no.*

"I AM THE SWORD. I AM THE BRENDEL."

The *Brendel* thrust his golden blade arm through the Worldbreaker's chest and heart. It shattered the throne beyond.

Everything stopped and went white.

WELL DONE, BRENDEL. THANK YOU.

—————

It hadn't been five minutes since the High General surrendered the last of the Kryan legions to the *Hamon-el*, and they were already arguing. Redan translated between Abbot and Zamira and the rest.

Aden stood with the others, discussing what was to come next. They congregated on the field twenty mitres from the militan to the west of the city. The dragons hovered another ten paces to the west. Bael sat on his haunches, licking his burnt arm. The tear in the wing had almost healed.

Aden tried to keep up with the translation. *We're really going to have to learn the First Tongue. Or they'll have to better learn common. Or both.*

"We have to go into the city and force all the elves into one area of the city," Falati stated. "This General may have surrendered, but all it takes is one elf to get an idea and get violent."

"Wait," Macarus said. "Didn't we just give some speech about they could stay if they were willing to work together for something new?"

"This is them working with us," Falati argued. "You think the humans in the city are ready to welcome these elves into their homes? Militan? Or former militan?"

"But segregation? That's how we're going to start this Quadi-bol game?" Tamya shook her head. "Sounds like crit to me."

Aden shrugged. "We didn't segregate everyone in Ketan when we fought the demics. Why do it now?"

"These elves were shooting arrows at us just an hour ago!" Falati said. "And in Ketan, you came together to fight a common enemy. This is totally different."

"Hate and misunderstanding are our common enemies," Sergeant Gunnar said. "It will take unity once more to defeat them."

Falati rolled her eyes. "While that sounds good in theory, we're supposed to protect the innocent, right? Isn't that part of the creed? Taking time to question and make sure the elves are making their own decisions will protect humans that have been victims for their whole lives. How else do we protect those innocents?"

"We train them to protect themselves," Kenneth said. "Like Caleb did with us at Ketan and then in the army."

"How will you know?" Macarus asked. "If we question the elves, then at what point will we be satisfied?"

"Segregation, separation, it will not satisfy anyone," Xak said. "Didn't we just learn this with the *Hamon-el*?"

Redan translated for Zamira. "Will we segregate the Dragonmen, as well? As was done in the camp?"

Abbott and Zamira tensed, and Aden winced. The Dragonmen were used as a curse word or stories to frighten children for so long. Aden arrived late to the battle, so he didn't know if that had influenced anything. But maybe.

"That's not the same," Kenneth said. "We ... didn't know you then, and ..." He searched for words.

Xak put a hand on Kenneth's elbow and looked at Abbott and Zamira. "No. We won't. We won't be segregating anyone."

Redan translated, and the Dragonmen elders relaxed.

Aden looked over at Eshlyn, and she listened, pensive, leaning on the Kingstaff. Much like Caleb.

Eshlyn nodded. "Falati, I appreciate your concerns. I do. But Xak makes a point, I think. What if we did something similar with Asya that we did with the *Hamon-el*?"

Falati frowned at her. "What do you mean?"

Eshlyn shifted her weight. "What if we taught on the ways of El, to the whole city, the ways of forgiveness, change, redemption? Isn't that what El teaches us? I believe that El would have these elves redeemed, not simply punished. In order for them to stay, they must learn the experiences and the stories of the humans they oppressed. They would learn to ask for forgiveness. And possibly those humans could do the same, where they were wrong."

"Humans were wrong?" Falati said.

"Is that so hard to believe?" Eshlyn asked her. "Humans are as capable of wrong as anyone. Isn't that how we became weak enough for others to oppress us? Let us correct that first. See where that goes. El will help us."

Falati lifted a brow. "I suppose it is possible ..."

A flash of light interrupted the Liorian, blinding for a moment. A deafening explosion followed. Everyone in the field crouched and cringed at the sound that hit them like a wave.

Aden peered to the east. A sphere of white fire engulfed the top of the palace tower, an orb hundreds of mitres wide and tall. It consumed the top of the towers and cascaded downward, turning the towers into dust and then crushing the palace compex below. The whole sky was bright with the explosion.

After that moment, Aden caught his breath and could gasp.

Everyone stood with caution and hesitation, in awe of the sight.

"What ...?" Macarus said.

"Wait," Tamya said. "Was that ...?"

No one could say the words. It took a dragon.

"The Worldbreaker is dead," Malaki said. "It is over."

Aden turned to Malaki. There was something in his throat. "And Caleb? Do you know if he …?" *If he's dead.* He didn't have the strength to finish it.

"The time of the *Brendel* is done," Malaki said.

Eshlyn's legs folded, and he had to catch her. She dropped the Kingstaff and fell onto his shoulder. He held her close to him. Tamya embraced them both. Then Macarus joined them. He heard Redan sob, and Kenneth grabbed the old man and pulled him into the group embrace. Wes and Xak followed. Falati, Gunnar, Abbott and Zamira drew close and laid their hands on shoulders.

They held each other and wept as one.

But there was more to do.

CHAPTER 36

The Beginning

Malaki landed in a clearing in the middle of the camp. People had been striking tents and loading wagons, but when the dragon landed with a gust of wind, everyone froze and stared in awe.

Aden and Tamya both slid down the side of the dragon. Aden greeted a young man and woke him from his daze.

The man, Qin, blinked. "Oh, Aden. Hello."

Aden pointed to the only tent untouched. "Is that Caleb's?"

Qin frowned and gazed over at the tent, his countenance falling. "Um. Yeah."

Aden entered the tent.

Without the lamp, the tent was dark, even in the light of day. Aden squinted. A stack of books sat on the desk, off to the side. The leather notebook in the middle of the desk drew his gaze.

He walked up to the notebook and laid his hand on it, gently.

"That's it," Tamya whispered. "That's what he told you about."

Aden picked it up with both hands and stared down at it.

Tamya reached for a match and the lamp.

"No," Aden said. "We have other things to do. I ... I can't do this now."

Tamya sniffed and grabbed a leather satchel from next to the cot. It had other personal effects in it, and she emptied it on the cot.

Caleb wouldn't need them anymore.

She opened the satchel, and he placed the book into it.

"Come on," she breathed. "Let's go."

They exited the tent, and Aden spoke to Qin. "Leave the tent. Just leave it."

"I will," Qin said, like that had been his plan all along.

———

The sun showed mid day before Eshlyn made it back to the camp. She rode her horse with the Kingstaff lying across her lap. Her shoulders wanted to slump, but she forced her back straight as she rode. She was a Lady, after all, and they had won.

They had won.

Why do I feel like we lost?

Macarus stayed with the General and legions, helping to organize for the transition, offering those that desired the chance to get on a ship and go back to Kaltiel. Elowen and Bael stayed with him. The rest rode back with her.

Aden and Tamya flew with Malaki to the west side of the camp. To be honest, it was difficult to listen.

The camp bustled with activity. People had received news that they were moving into the city, and so they finished packing the camp, this time with excitement and joy instead of desperation and fear. She heard her name called, and she willed a smile.

The *Sohan-el* and the Dragonmen leaders excused themselves with awkward bows and rode of to the north of the camp, the stalgest crawling along with chittering noises. It was going to take time to get used to those things.

Eshlyn navigated through folded tents and loaded wagons, and she rounded a half-struck tent. Her breath caught.

Mother Natali sat with the children while others folded Eshlyn's tent. Gretchen slept in a basket on the ground while Javyn stacked blocks.

Javyn.

Her heart pounded in her chest, and she didn't move for a second. Then he looked up and saw her.

He beamed. "Mama!"

She didn't have to will the smile she gave him in return. Eshlyn dismounted from the horse and walked to him. He ran to her like toddlers do, reckless and bounding with experimental coordination, and she knelt to catch and hold him.

Eshlyn closed her eyes. With Javyn in her arms, it was the first time she felt like they had won.

"Hey, my big boy." She led him to arms' length. She could see Kenric and Xander and her father in him. It warmed her heart. "I missed you today."

He looked sad. "Miss you, Mama."

"I know. And I'm sorry. You forgive me?"

Javyn nodded without hesitation. Did he even understand? She had a feeling he did.

"Good. Thank you. Now have you been good for Mother Natali?"

Mother Natali stood behind Javyn. "I found a wetnurse for Gretchen. One of the women working the supplies, and she watched the boys most of last night and this morning. I was needed elsewhere. Her name is Susan. She did a fine job. When we got word ..." Natali didn't finish.

Eshlyn swallowed and stood, holding Javyn's hand. Wetnurse. Of course. She hadn't even thought of it. Why didn't she think of it? "Good."

Mother Natali's gaze fell on the golden bracelet on Eshlyn's right wrist.

Their eyes locked, and knowledge passed between them. Natali's stare hardened. Eshlyn prepared herself for a word whipping.

But Natali's eyes softened, and she looked pained. She extended her hand and gripped Eshlyn's. "The *Brendel*?"

Eshlyn nodded. Who else did she breakin' think it was? "He ... came to me last night."

Mother Natali's chest heaved with a heavy breath. "I am sorry, Lady. I am so sorry."

"Mama?" Javyn's voice carried concern.

Eshlyn grabbed his waist and lifted him in her arms. He would be too heavy for that soon. "Mama's okay. I'm okay. We fought some bad people, but we won. It's over now."

"Over?" Mother Natali said. "No, Lady. It's just the beginning."

———

"So they just ... changed from being wraith?" Aden asked him.

Tamya stood with Aden on the western side of the camp with the wagons and supplies; Malaki perched off to the side. Thirteen wagons waited before them with men and women of all ages tied in groups of five to seven, at least that Tamya could see. The humans gazed about, confused. Their eyes were no longer white but human.

Hoddie, the middle-aged man in charge of guarding the supplies, shrugged. "Yessir. They, uh, had them white eyes, creepy things, you know, and then there was that 'splosion, like to split the world, and when I looked over at 'em, they no more had them white eyes."

Tamya and Aden shared a glance. "It happened after that explosion?" Tamya asked.

"Yes'm, it did," Hoddie said.

"The Worldbreaker," Aden muttered. "He made them wraith, controlled them, gave them instructions. When he died ..."

"The control was broken," Tamya finished for him.

Hoddie winced and shrugged. "Dunno 'bout all that, but ..." He gestured over the humans.

Tamya frowned at him. "Why are they still tied up?"

"Lady Eshlyn and that elf, that Mac'rus feller, they told me to keep 'em here," Hoddie said. "Plus, I didn't know what t'do. I dunno how this works. Maybe they change back and kill me? Maybe it's a trick?"

Aden scoffed. "We don't know how this works, either, Hoddie, but I don't think it's a trick." He leaned over to Tamya. "Guess we won't need to use the dragon's blood on these people."

"Guess not." She addressed Hoddie and pulled Xander's unforged sword from her hip. "Come on. Let's cut these people free."

———

Eshlyn exited the camp to the east and saw the Mahakar sitting there on his haunches.

She stumbled and gripped the babe as she caught herself. Gretchen lay wrapped against her with a long cloth. She had changed her clothes once more to remove the stench of the green blood of the creature, wrapped Gretchen to her, and brought Javyn with her to see how the enormous tiger was doing.

Her heart leapt with joy at seeing him awake and sitting up.

"Mama, tiger!" Javyn said, pointing. Javyn had ridden the Mahakar several times, never showing fear or concern.

"Yeah, baby," she said. "Let's go say hello."

Hurrying, she led Javyn by the hand and put the other arm around the babe in front of her. The Mahakar waited, patient. She couldn't see any wounds, no blood, nothing. Unless his white fur covered some scar, he appeared completely healed.

He was some sort of immortal being, after all. But she was relieved.

Reaching him, he bowed his head, and she released Javyn's hand and pulled his giant head into a furry embrace. He purred, like a gentle earthquake.

"You're okay. I'm so glad."

"Tiger!" Javyn squealed.

Eshlyn grinned, the happiness breaking through so much sorrow. Pulling away, the Mahakar bent even lower and allowed the boy to press their faces together.

The boy giggled. "Ride! Ride!"

The Mahakar lifted his head and met Eshlyn's gaze.

A new sorrow touched her heart. Her eyes misted, and she cocked her head at the tiger.

"No, baby, not today." She addressed the tiger. "You're leaving now, aren't you."

As usual, he didn't speak to her in words. In her mind, she received a picture of him flying high over the Forest of Lior, the wind in his fur, diving and weaving through the canopy and between the trees.

"I understand. It's your home. You've been gone too long. Thank you for staying to say goodbye. Will I see you again?"

Another vision in her mind, this time of her riding him high over the mountains. She couldn't tell which mountains, but she was happy in the vision. And so was he.

"Thank you. I know Javyn will miss you. But not as much as me."

The Mahakar's gaze was soft. Then his brows furrowed, and he leaned in to sniff the baby.

"This is Gretchen," she said.

The tiger stared at her for a moment, and a tear formed in the corner of his eye.

The Mahakar lifted his head high. He bared his teeth and shook his head. He took a deep breath and roared. Javyn covered his ears until the tiger was done, but he smiled.

Eshlyn grabbed Javyn's hand and led him back and away from the tiger.

The white wings unfurled, and the Mahakar shot upwards into the air. He hovered thirty mitres in the air, twisted, and darted to the south over the field and trees.

"Tiger?" Javyn whimpered.

"He'll be back, baby. He'll be back one day."

—✝—

The afternoon sun warmed Aden's back as they flew back to the city after helping Eshlyn and Mother Natali and others organize and move the camp. People and wagons and horses made their way down the hill and to the city.

Bael perched on the wall to the north, watching over the whole operation, his right wing healed. He still favored his front leg, though.

Since the courtyard was full of people, Aden and Tamya guided the dragon as he descended to land outside the wall. They both slid from the dragon's shoulders and walked with the rest of the people into the city of Asya. Approaching, Aden saw that Macarus stood with a middle aged woman and ...

"Freyd!" Aden shouted, and he ran. The man smiled back.

Aden extended his hand, and Freyd Fa'Yador gripped it with both of his. "Aden! This elf said you were here. And on a breakin' dragon!"

Shaking his head, Aden chuckled. "Come a long way, I guess."

"Yes. A long way. We must talk."

Tamya joined them, and Aden introduced her to Freyd.

"And who is this?" came a voice from behind them. Aden and Tamya turned to see Eshlyn walk up with Javyn next to her and a baby in the front sling. Bweth's baby. Gretchen.

"His name is Freyd," Aden said.

"The one that introduced you to Caleb?" Eshlyn asked.

"Yes."

"Caleb," Freyd nodded back at where the Kryan towers used to stand. "That was him?"

Aden's smile slipped. "Yeah."

A somber mood hung over the group, and Macarus broke it. "Freyd said he knew you. He and this woman, Rose, have been working here in the city as a type of resistance. The humans of the city see them as leaders."

The woman was heavy set but not plump, handsome in her strength and bright eyes. She brushed beautiful gray hair out of her face. "Rose Re'Wyl. My husband and I knew Caleb and his family when he was young."

Aden perked. "And the Prophet?"

"We knew Reyan well," Rose said.

"Your husband?" Tamya asked. "Where is he?"

"He ..." Rose began.

"Her husband, Jyson, was caught and put to the stake a few months ago," Freyd finished for her. "He was my friend."

Eshlyn stepped forward and took Rose's hand. "I am sorry. So sorry." Aden saw their gazes meet, and that female connection happened that he would never seem to understand. But Eshlyn comforted the woman, and Aden was glad. "Thank you both. I would love to hear more of what happened here in Asya, but we need to get these people settled. You know the city better than we do. Will you help us?"

"We will," Rose said.

"Good," Eshlyn said. "We can have dinner together later and talk. Would you like to take Javyn's hand for me?"

Rose smiled.

"I'm sorry, Eshlyn," Macarus said. "If you could wait a moment."

The group looked at him. Elowen came from behind him with a sword wrapped in a large burlap cloth.

A sword.

"I've had the militan cleaning through things, cleaning rubble, that sort of thing," Macarus said. "General Felix gave this to me an hour ago."

Elowen stood with the group now and removed the cloth.

"Great and mighty El," Aden whispered. He would know it anywhere.

"Caleb's sword," Eshlyn said.

"Critters," Tamya said next to him.

"I thought it was," Macarus said. "We can put it with the rest of the swords of the fallen *Sohan-el* to take to the Father Tree."

Eshlyn stared at the sword and didn't respond.

Tamya stepped closer to Eshlyn. Aden moved with her.

"We don't have to take it to the Father Tree," Aden said. "You could keep it."

Eshlyn pursed her lips. "That would be okay with you?"

Aden nodded. "He'd want you to have it."

Aden watched Eshlyn reach out her hand and take a dead husband's sword by the hilt.

"Thank you," Eshlyn said.

—+—

The sun had set a few hours ago, but Javyn and Gretchen were finally asleep in a back bedroom. Susan, the wetnurse, had her own room, as well. Eshlyn took the main room in the larger apartment in a building near the Square on the eastern side of the city.

Eshlyn had fought with the others about where she should stay. They wanted her in one of the large penthouses in a taller building further north. If the Steward's palace with the shoggin' throne room hadn't been turned to dust, then she was sure they would have tried to put her in the palace. This larger apartment was a compromise.

Eshlyn sat on a large, plush chair in the middle of the room. The Kingstaff rested against the wall to her right.

It had been a long day. The Kryan Steward and most of the militan planned to leave on ships, adding to the administration duties – supplies for the journey and other preparations. Other elves of the city discussed leaving with them, but this had been their home for years, some of them decades or a century. Did they want to stay in their home with the mystery of what this new city would look like under Eshlyn and Aden's leadership? Or did they want to leave their home and return to Kryus for another transition there? Possibly a Civil War? She did not envy their choice.

General Felix decided to stay. She did not fully understand that, but he and Macarus worked well together. Macarus had those militan working non stop.

The Steward sent pigeons out to the other major cities in the land of humanity, informing of them of the Emperor's death. The generals were also told of Aden and Eshlyn's expectations that they turn over control of each city to whatever human leadership the locals chose and take their legions and Cityguard back to Kryus. She hoped they would follow those directions. She did not want to march an army down to Veradis or over to Lior. Not now. Not ever, really.

She would have to send people to check on those cities.

Eshlyn looked out the window and could see the golden face of the Emperor's statue in the middle of the Square. The absence of the palace complex beyond was staggering and gave her heart the familiar tinge of sorrow.

"You get to be the hero and leave me with all this crit. Just like a breakin' man."

Now she talked to the air, to a man who could no longer hear her. Or could he?

She was exhausted in every way – physically, emotionally, mentally. *Getting in the chair might have been a mistake. I don't know if I have enough energy to get to the bed. Might fall asleep right here.*

A knock came at the door.

Eshlyn emitted a groan that came from the depth of her. With a sniff, she stood and went to the door.

Aden stood in the hall when she opened it. His eyes and cheeks were red. He was dressed in a long tunic and pants, barefoot. He and Tamya had an apartment below her. He held a leather notebook in his hand.

Eshlyn frowned at him. "Aden?"

He forced a smile at her and extended the notebook to her. Eshlyn's frown deepened. She took it.

"Before he went to meet the Worldbreaker," Aden said. "He told us about this notebook. It's for you and me, he said."

Eshlyn grunted like she had been punched. Her eyes lowered to the notebook. "You ... you read it?"

Aden shrugged.

Breakit, the thing was thick. "The whole thing?"

"It's a book of notes and thoughts about how to set up a new government. Books to read. Ways to handle the Kryan senate. Resources we need first. Things like that."

A sob broke from her. "Oh, Caleb." *You didn't leave me to do this alone. You thought of me.*

"There's a ... letter to the both of us in the front. You should at least read that." A tear escaped his eye.

"Aden."

He bit his lip. "I loved him, you know. None of this would have happened without him, but that's not why. He was a brother I never had, a friend. He gave me everything he had."

"He loved you so much. You should have seen his face when he spoke of you. I never saw anyone prouder than he was of you."

Aden glanced at the golden bracelet on her wrist. "He loved you, too."

Her jaw tightened. She nodded.

He gestured at the bracelet. "Did he tell you? Before the end?"

"He did. In his own way, he did."

"Good. I'm glad for that. It's important. Well, goodnight."

"Aden."

He paused. "Yeah?"

"There was no end, you know. Not for him. And not for us."

He grinned. And he didn't have to force it. "I know."

"You're right, you know. He gave us everything." She brought the leather notebook to her chest. "He gave us a beginning."

He walked down the hall. She closed the door behind him and sat back in the plush chair. She opened the notebook and began to read. And weep.

———

It was two days from the Battle of Asya. Morning, a clear and warm day.

The Square was full of people, a sea of human, elf, and even a few dwarves. Aden grinned at the Steelsides staying around a few more days. People leaned out of windows and stood on the tops of buildings all around the Square.

But no one stood within twenty mitres of the golden statue in the middle of the Square. They had been warned.

Aden raised his face with the throng of people as two dragons appeared in the sky and circled overhead.

He, Eshlyn, and the other leaders stood on the top of the wall, the ledge where countless people had been sacrificed to the Kryan Empire and their oppression.

Malaki and Bael circled and descended together. They each landed on one of Tanicus' shoulders, their talons piercing the gold and into the stone beneath. With massive flaps of their wings, they pulled on the statue, shaking it back and forth. The marble and iron base cracked and bent and creaked. The crowd cowered.

The iron held fast, so Bael and Malaki breathed fire, focused streams of flame to protect the people around them. The iron melted, and the flame ceased.

Dragon wings beat the air, over and over, causing a great wind. Aden's hair blew back. Claws dug deeper, the gold groaning, and the dragons pulled as one. The statue ripped from the base. People shouted and cried out as the dragons carried the humongous and heavy statue up in the air, higher and higher until everyone craned their necks.

Malaki and Bael turned and dragged the golden statue of Tanicus to the east, over Aden's head and then the missing palace complex. The Emperor sailed over the eastern wall to the ocean. Half a kilomitre out to sea, the dragons dropped Tanicus, the High Evilord, the Emperor of Kryus, the Worldbreaker, into the ocean and it sank out of sight.

The dragons bounded into the air and flew back to the city. They perched on the wall to Aden's right.

Eshlyn turned to Aden. "Are you ready?"

Aden gazed down at the line of people. Mother Natali, Gunnar, Macarus, Kenneth, Wes, Xak, Falati, Rose, Freyd, Macarus, and Elowen. Tamya stood next to him on the other side.

"Crit on a frog, Esh," he said. "I have to be, right?"

Eshlyn smirked at him. She held the Kingstaff in her right hand, the golden marriage bracelet glistening in the sun. Caleb's unforged sword hung on her hip. "You read his letter, same as me. It's all you."

"Fine," Aden said. "Throw that at me."

Tamya grabbed his hand and pulled him down to her. She kissed him on the cheek and whispered into his ear. "Don't talk too much. You ramble when you're nervous."

Aden glared at her. "Thanks. Love you, too."

Tamya grinned at him. A Dracolet was draped around her neck.

Aden stepped forward. He wore simple clothes, a finer tunic and leather trousers over clean boots. The satchel over his shoulder contained the Ydu and the Fyrwrit written with the Prophet's hand. He wore his unforged sword at his hip, and the Dracolet rested on his chest.

In a few days, he would take Mother Natali and the unforged swords of the fallen *Sohan-el* to the Father Tree. Then he and Tamya and Macarus would travel to the Living Stone, along with others who wished to go. It would be faster on a dragon. When they returned, Aden, Macarus and Elowen would begin training a new group of *Sohan-el*. He didn't know how many or who as of yet, but he expected it to be a large group of elves and humans and maybe even a dwarf or two.

But he had to do this, first.

It felt like the whole world watched him. The people filled in the gap where the statue had once been, now a jagged iron and stone stump.

Aden took a deep breath.

"The Emperor is dead. The *Brendel* defeated him."

The humans cheered, a sudden roar that made him blink. Some of the elves nodded or clapped.

"But he did not do it alone," Aden continued. The crowd grew silent. "This revolution was about more than one man, as he said many times. In fact, this revolution didn't exist for humans alone. It was for all people. Human. Elf. Dwarf. Everyone. And we have them all here, now."

Aden scanned the crowd. They looked at him, transfixed.

You taught me how to fight and believe, Caleb. But you didn't teach me how to speak in front of people.

Caleb's words echoed in his brain. *You're the redemption, Aden.*

"Most of you know me, but my name is Aden. I was born here, on the streets of this city. I lived in alleys, stealing and scrounging for food, watching people around me do horrible things to just stay alive. All of this in the shadow of the great and wealthy Kryan towers of Asya.

"I didn't even know my own name. I had to come up with a name. All I have is a name I took from a stupid show. The Empire caught me and put me in the Pyts. But I escaped.

"Then a man came to this city. Caleb De'Ador. A man trained by the elves but with a belief in El and the rights of people, of all people. He was the *Brendel*. Because of Caleb, I joined a revolution. I fought a war.

"That was a year ago. The war is over. We have won.

"But now the greater battle begins. We have to decide how to live together without the threat of an Empire over us. We will have no one to blame for the evil in our world but ourselves. We will have to fight the fear and the hate and the bitterness in our own hearts, and they are tough enemies. It will be the most difficult thing we have ever done.

"But with El, we can win the greater battle. I've seen it in Ketan. I've seen it in my own life.

"Many of you may be like me, whether elf or human or dwarf, wondering if you're enough. Wondering if you can be better than you were, if you can change. Let me tell you the secret now. All I had was a willing heart. And I refused to give up. If you have those two things, El can bring you to a place you never imagined. I know. I never imagined this. Yet here we are."

Aden glanced over his shoulder at Tamya and put out his hand. Tamya took it and stood next to him. He faced the crowd again.

"I chose my first name, Aden, when I was a child and knew so little. I choose my family name now in the light of El after being made a new person. I keep them both. One to remind me of who I was. The other to remind me of who I am.

"I am Aden De'Ador. I am a *Sohan-el*. And we are the redemption."

Aden took a breath. Several joined him as he recited the vow. More would know it soon. Maybe everyone. Why not?

"*Before the Light of El, the hand of Yosu, and the witness of the Living, I dedicate my soul, my heart, and my life to defend the innocent, free the oppressed, and spread light in dark places.*"

Epilogue

The Letter

Eshlyn and Aden,

I write this letter to you in faith.

It might be foolish, but I've prayed, begged, El that you would both survive. I've prayed that you both live to carry this on. El may have a different plan, but I would like to think my sacrifice means I live on in you. As I write this, the battle of Asya looms tomorrow, and Aden, you haven't returned from chasing dragons. Carys is still gone, as well. My heart longs to see her and hold my sister one last time before the end. I wonder if I ask too much.

Time is short. I know it. I sense it.

There never seems to be time. Everything happened so fast. I thought Reyan and I would have years to meet and talk and train people for a revolution. It hasn't been a year since I landed at Asya, and yet I have returned to do the impossible once more. One last time.

Aden, I wanted time to teach you more. I had fifteen years with Galen and Iletus and other masters. Even though many hated me, I learned. I pray my time with you was enough. I pray El brings you the people you need to grow the Sohan-el ... if you return from the north. Perhaps if Macarus survives?

Eshlyn, I feel like this revolution has robbed us of our time. Battles, missions, journeys, have kept us at arm's length, but not more than my own stubborn nature. I knew my time was short. I wanted to share it with you but wanted to keep you from unnecessary grief. Forgive me if I was wrong. I hope you keep the Kingstaff despite any pain I've caused you. I know no one else who deserves this. You told me how King Judai tried to give you his crown. It was right of you to reject a crown to wear because there is one in your heart. And everyone sees it.

Once the battle is over and the Worldbreaker is dead, forgive me for being absent in the aftermath. I can't imagine anything more exciting and challenging. It will feel impossible at times, just as it did in Ketan. I know you will remember all that we learned together there.

I began this book after we moved into Taggart. I have left you notes and ideas on how to begin to rebuild a people. Not an institution, not an organization, but people.

Every person is useful. It is worth the time and effort to discover those gifts. You will be surprised at what people can do. I was.

Teach them to provide for themselves and give generously to others. No one will starve.

Give ownership and responsibility. Everyone must know they have a stake in the success of what is to come. They will work harder and be more creative when problems arise. And there will be problems. Ownership helps people endure and give their best.

Connect people to the land as much as you can. People see El and his design more clearly when connected to his creation.

If you make a mistake, err on the side of freedom. Administration and organization are well and good, but take care it never gives leadership power over people, even if you believe it is for their own benefit. It will corrupt you and them. That is what Kryus did.

Keep things simple and flexible. Life is complicated enough without burdensome leadership.

Protect the innocent and weak. Kryus killed the smallest, most innocent, and weakest among us. A nation is only as great as its care for the small, the weak, and the innocent.

Train and stay prepared for war. You will seek love and peace, but there remain enemies in this world.

Do not reject every idea simply because it came from the elves or Kryus. There is benefit in some of their ideas. Some of the books I suggest are elven in nature. Don't discriminate. Allow an idea to have merit on its own.

Filter every idea through prayer and the teachings of El.

Kryus will be wounded and need to rebuild. Give them grace and mercy. They will need it. Be the people they should have been in our hour of need. Friends, not conquerors or enemies.

Teach forgiveness. We have all done wrong and need redemption. El is a god of second chances, and more.

I believe both of you are the most capable people I have ever met, but you will try things and fail at times. Be humble and learn.

We have been at war or running toward it every moment since I met both of you. Learn to have fun. Laugh. With a few notable exceptions, I was a bad example of this. Forgive me and be better.

Finally, be diligent in your faith in El. He is an unseen god so the seen will always threaten to distract us from his truth. You must be intentional in your devotion to him. Nothing good has happened apart from his grace and power. Nothing ever will. If you stray for a time, return. He loves us beyond what we do.

If you teach these things, you will never need rule them.

The following pages contain more details for further study on each of these instructions.

Or find your own way. I may have written this more for me than you. I suspect even without me, you both would have done miraculous things.

Eshlyn. Aden. Bashawyn. Isael. Go forth into a new beginning with my blessing and know you possess all you need in El, one another, and the people around you. I will see you in the final beginning. I will be waiting for you there.

There is another letter enclosed for Carys. If I am gone before she returns, please give it to her.

Caleb De'Ador

Acknowledgements:

This book was the most difficult project to finish yet. Not only did I have to say goodbye to many characters and bring an epic story to a close, but I had to do it without my friend and artist, Jeremiah Briggs. He passed into the next life during the beginning stages of the rough draft process. His family, community, and many friends miss him greatly.

But I did finish.

A huge thanks to the Beta readers, my great sister, Gina Deaton, at the forefront. Also, two incredible friends and missionaries, Rob and Amy Ellis. Their initial feedback and encouragement was crucial.

My two proofreaders were once again amazing – Shane Ardell and Gregg Mooney.

The search for an artist to take over for Jeremiah was daunting, but Sutthiwat Dechakamphu did a phenomenal job.

To my online Page 13 Writers Group: you gave montly inspiration and permission to be the weird one with those weird stories.

To the Brew & Ink Writers group: thanks for putting up with me and listening and encouraging and simply being great friends. I hope every author has a group like you.

To my kids: thanks for reminding me what it means to dream. Big.

To my amazing wife: thanks for the support, the sacrifice, and the understanding. It isn't easy to live an adventure on the edge of the world, gazing with longing into the next, but you do it with me. And that is a gift I can never repay.

Last and most important: to my purpose, my Yosu, and the one that gives me the fire of dragons in my soul, I choose to fight your fight with you for the needy and oppressed. It is my joy.

About the Author:

M.B. Mooney has traveled extensively and writes novels, short stories, and songs. He lives in Lawrenceville, GA, with his wife, Rebecca, and three children – Micah, Elisha, and Hosanna.

If you would like to see more of his work, check out his website at www.mbmooney.com.

Also like him on Facebook – www.facebook.com/MooneyMB and Twitter @MBMooney1

Check out the Brew & Ink Podcast on iTunes, Google Play, YouTube, and other formats.

93310531R00243

Made in the USA
Columbia, SC
09 April 2018